Still the Song

Still the Song

Nicole Feller

HennyBean Publishing
www.nicolefeller.com

"UNEVEN ODDS"
Written by Ryan O'Neal
©2013 Wine and Song Music (BMI) on behalf of
Itself & Asteroid B 612
International Copyright Secured All Rights Reserved
Used By Permission

Cover photography and design by Nicole Feller

ISBN: 0-9903644-0-2
ISBN 13: 978-0-9903644-0-5

Printed in the United States of America

To Daniel, who was worth waiting for

"Darkness exists to make light truly count."

– Sleeping At Last

Still the Song

NICOLE FELLER

ONE

I t had been five years since Jonah Weston had been home. He sat silently in his old car outside the familiar gray house, not quite sure he was prepared to face what awaited him inside.

Jonah had left the small Pennsylvania town after high school to escape the incessant ridicule of his father. He'd sacrificed everything, even his future with Hannah, to be free from the abuse. But Jonah never got to prove to his father that he was worth something...Maybe he still wasn't after all.

With a long sigh, Jonah opened the car door and stepped out, the crisp November wind stinging his face. Wrapping his pea coat tighter around his thin frame, he trudged through the gravel to the faded red door. He forced himself to knock before his nerves got the best of him. In just seconds, the door creaked open and his mother stood before him.

Scarlett Weston gazed up at her younger son with the absence of tears and the presence of apathy. She looked exhausted, her light hair disheveled. Scarlett reached out a hand to brush Jonah's brown hair out of his eyes before she pulled him in for a hug. He bent to return the embrace, towering over her by nearly a foot.

"I'm so sorry, Mom," he managed in a small voice. He

didn't know what else to say.

"I'm sorry too." Scarlett straightened her posture as if to prove her strength. "Nathan's here," she added to change the subject.

Jonah felt that same sense of inferiority creeping in. "Yeah, that nice Lexus in the driveway was a good clue." He pointed behind him with his thumb, following his mother into the house.

Jonah hung up his coat and took a deep breath, willing his reluctant eyes to scan the living room. He saw exactly what he'd expected, but his stomach still dropped at the sight of his father's empty recliner in the corner. The television remote rested on the arm of the chair, probably where he'd last left it, and his reading glasses sat on top of a wrinkled newspaper on the end table.

Tearing himself from the scene, Jonah made his way into the kitchen where he found his brother at the table, his hands wrapped around a cup of coffee. Even in his grief, Nathan Weston looked so dignified and pulled together. His blue eyes were red from what Jonah guessed was crying...or maybe too many double shifts at the hospital.

Regardless, he was dressed to the nines, his Oxford shirt and khaki pants devoid of a single travel wrinkle, and his belt and shoes coordinating perfectly. His face showed not even a hint of stubble, and his hair was flawless, as if it had just been cut that morning. Jonah self-consciously ran a hand through his own grown-out hair as he approached his brother.

"Jonah." A smile spread over Nathan's face as he stood to hug him. "It's good to see you, little brother."

"Yeah, I wish it was for a better reason. How've you been?" Jonah jammed his hands into his pockets. It had been so long since they'd spoken.

"Well, besides the obvious, I'm pretty well. I've been

keeping busy at the hospital, and Kendall has been planning our wedding in January. We just bought a house. We close on it next week, actually."

"Wow, man, that sounds great. Good for you." Jonah could only imagine the excitement of getting married and buying a house.

"How's work going for you? You're still doing the computer thing, right? Are you dating anyone?" Nathan returned to his chair and motioned for his brother to join him.

"Jonah? Dating someone? Yeah right," Scarlett chimed in as she refilled her coffee cup.

Jonah narrowed his eyebrows. "What does that mean?"

Scarlett chuckled. "Oh, don't get mad, Jonah. You haven't dated anyone since Hannah."

"I've gone on a few dates since I left home. I'm not a complete loser, thank you."

Nathan put a hand on his brother's shoulder. "It's okay, you're still young. Sometimes it just takes a while...I mean, I thought I'd be married *before* thirty-five, but Kendall was worth the wait."

Jonah sighed. He did not want any dating advice or dredged-up memories concerning his ex. He thought about her enough without being reminded.

"Let's just not worry about that right now, okay?" he requested.

After an awkward moment of silence between the three of them, Scarlett cleared her throat.

"So the service is in the morning at Saint Andrews. We should be there early. You have a suit, right, Jonah?" she asked, eyeing his ensemble. He wore a black cardigan over a white V-neck T-shirt with well-worn jeans and Dr. Martens boots.

"Yes, Mom," he answered, rolling his blue eyes. Of course she would never ask Nathan if he had a suit. He was wearing most of one right then.

"I'm glad you boys are home." Scarlett gave a thin smile as she turned away to her room for the night. She was never much for expressing affection, so when she did, it meant a lot.

Jonah endured the memorial service without breaking down. He did not muster a single tear for his own father, wearing his guiltless apathy like a countenance of stone. His father had been extremely difficult to live with and was undeniably the root of Jonah's insecurities, the maker of his timid disposition. There wasn't much good, except that he had provided for their family. He'd taught his sons how to be men. He'd sent them both to college. But he'd made their every move a contest for his highest affections.

In the early days, there were baseball games and playing catch in the backyard. Jonah had taken those fleeting days for granted, before they'd transformed into endless years of damaging, drunken parenting. Jonah wished he could figure out what had changed to make his father the eternal thorn in his side, the resounding voice of disappointment in his head. He wondered if he'd ever find the answers to the plaguing unknowns that still hung in the air.

The sun was gleaming brilliantly over the cemetery, the rows of headstones glinting in the early afternoon light, as the group gathered around the casket to pay their last respects to Jacob Weston.

While the pastor recited the last prayer, Jonah lifted his

eyes to sneak a glance at the dismal scene. He had wondered how many people cared enough about his father to be present in these heaviest of moments. He scanned the bowed heads, recognizing a few aunts and uncles and a handful of his own cousins in the small sea of black and gray. Just as he was about to return his attention to the prayer, his eyes locked with someone else's across the way. Jonah's breath nearly caught in his throat when he saw her.

Hannah.

Her blue eyes did not blink, nor did they look away. But Jonah couldn't handle the unwavering visual contact and he hastily dropped his gaze, disappointed in his weakness for her.

When the funeral ended and the seemingly endless condolences began to dissipate, Jonah felt his brother's elbow nudge his side in warning. Diverting his attention from an old family friend, he found himself face to face with his past.

"Hannah," he managed, forcing a nervous smile.

Hannah Morgan's lovely face lit up with a genuine, sympathetic smile of her own. "Jonah, I'm so sorry about your dad." Her voice was tender and kind. She didn't hesitate to reach out for him, her feminine frame dwarfed in his embrace.

Jonah breathed in her familiar vanilla scent as her blond hair brushed across his cheek. It was oddly comforting to feel her in his arms. He pulled back, shaking away the fog that was settling in his head.

"It's really good to see you," he said. "You look great."

She smiled bashfully at the ground, smoothing out her charcoal dress. "Thank you. It's good to see you too. It's been...a long time."

He nodded in agreement, a sense of shame washing over him.

"Well, I'd better get going," Hannah added, tucking a

stray lock of hair behind her ear.

"Maybe I'll see you around before I head back home," Jonah stammered.

Hannah nodded, and Jonah could almost swear he saw her eyes well up as she turned to leave. He didn't say another word. Instead, he watched her walk away, so gracefully across the grass, leaving him in his confusion.

Jonah slouched silently in the backseat of Nathan's Lexus. As much as he didn't want to admit it, it was a great car, complete with flawless beige leather and that glorious new car smell. Staring out the window, chin in hand, Jonah didn't hear his mother and brother chatting superficially in the front seat about how "nice" the service was. He was occupied with new pestering thoughts, emotions he hadn't expected to feel. Memories he didn't have the strength to revisit.

He hadn't wanted to leave, but he just couldn't stay.

The August night was warm and a bit humid, the sky lit by the sprinkle of stars overhead. Hannah leaned against Jonah as they sat on the steps of his parents' back porch. He lifted his arm and wrapped it around her, drawing her even closer to him.

"I wish you didn't have to go," Hannah whispered in the stillness.

"I know...I'm so sorry. I just can't be here anymore."

A tear escaped down Hannah's cheek. "But you could leave me?"

Jonah pulled away to look at her, his forehead creased by his troubled demeanor. "Hannah. We've talked about this. I don't want to leave you. That's the last thing I want, but you know how much worse things have gotten since the accident. I can't handle it anymore. I need to get away from my dad...not you."

Hannah knew he was right. Jonah needed a chance to live without fear. Without worrying if he was good enough. Without comparing himself to his brother. Her heart broke over the berating he'd endured through the years.

"I don't know how long I can stand being away from you." Hannah sniffled, wrapping her arms around him.

Jonah kissed her on top of her head, then rested his cheek in her hair to linger in its softness. "It's going to be hard. But I know we can do this. We can visit each other."

"I know...I can't believe how fast the summer went. I've been dreading tomorrow so badly, and I can't believe it's actually here." She began to cry again.

Jonah took her face in his hands and leveled his eyes with hers. "Hannah, I love you. I've loved you since eighth grade. We've been through so much together these past four years. And I know we can make it through these next four. I'll always love you, and I will be back for you. I promise you that."

Jonah gritted his teeth as the guilt consumed him. He leaned his head against the car window and closed his eyes, trying to wash away the flow of memories that haunted him.

He promised her. He told her he'd come back. He didn't know his father would refuse to pay for flights home as punishment for the major he'd chosen. Even after Jonah had changed it, his father still found other excuses not to help him. Jonah didn't know Hannah would be able to visit him only once before her parents got divorced, and all her extra money went to helping her mother pay the bills. It all proved fatal for their relationship, and by Jonah's sophomore year, they barely kept in touch.

Back at the Weston residence, family and close friends gathered for support over an early dinner. Jonah's aunts brought food and made sure Scarlett was taking it easy. Jonah encountered many of their attempts to catch up with the newly returned lesser son, but he'd become a stranger to the aunts, uncles, and cousins he'd grown up with. They'd never been an exceptionally close family, but the last five years had distanced him even further from everyone he ever knew. Had he made a horrible mistake? Had his need for independence without constant ridicule cost him too much? He'd only wanted to be able to breathe. That was all.

Anxious and overwhelmed, Jonah briskly slipped out the back door. He plopped down on the back steps, burying his face in his hands. All the weight he'd been carrying on his shoulders finally crushed him, and he sobbed, no longer able to contain his emotions. He cried because he couldn't believe he'd gone five years without seeing his own mother. He couldn't believe how much she'd aged since he'd seen her last. He cried because he barely knew his brother anymore, and maybe never had. He constantly had to fight the urge to resent his brother for things that weren't even his fault. He cried because his father died...before Jonah could find out why he was so unworthy of his father's love. He cried because he had shattered the heart of the most beautiful person he'd ever known, and he would never know anyone like her again. And Jonah cried because he was so broken, he didn't know what else to do with himself.

When he began to regain his composure, sniffling and wiping his tear-stained cheeks, he sensed a motion beside him. Jonah glanced to his right, shocked to see Hannah sitting just a few feet across the steps from him. He jerked his body to straighten his posture and quickly struggled to erase any indication of his breakdown. He swallowed the lump in his throat and ran a shaking hand through his hair.

"Are you okay?" came her sweet tone.

Despite his embarrassment, Jonah fought back the urge to get upset again. He didn't deserve her concern.

"I don't think so."

He looked out over the yard as the sun was slipping behind the trees, bathing everything in a golden sheen. Five years and three months ago, he sat right there with her and watched that same sun set from those same steps right before he'd promised her forever. He turned to face her, his eyes filled with grief.

"I'm so sorry, Hannah," he said quietly.

Her gaze fell to the ground, and she pressed her lips together to keep them from quivering. "I'm sorry too," Hannah whispered, meeting his eyes once again.

Jonah took a deep breath and let it out slowly. "I never wanted this. I didn't know...I didn't think this would happen."

Hannah scooted closer and gingerly touched his shoulder. "Jonah. Let's not do this tonight, okay? It's been a very difficult day for you."

He nodded with a sarcastic chuckle. "Yeah, my dad's dead. Oh, God...That's the first time I've said that out loud."

The ugliness of reality grabbed a hold of him, shaking him from his haze. The tears returned, whether he liked it or not. Whether Hannah was watching him fall apart into a pitiful mess or not. But with her usual unwavering grace, she placed her hand on Jonah's cheek and gently guided his head to her chest. She held him, letting him cry against her. Jonah pushed his pride aside and clutched her tightly. He allowed her arms to console him, just as he had consoled her in that very spot five years before.

Two

The following afternoon, Jonah cautiously pulled up in front of the Morgans' house. He had tried asking Nathan and their mother if Hannah still lived there, but, of course, they didn't know. He was surprised how little they knew of Hannah, as if they hadn't seen her at all since he'd been gone. *She must have been that hurt*, Jonah thought. *She couldn't even bear to see my family.*

Forcing some confidence, he plodded to the front door and knocked. He almost hoped a stranger would answer so he could avoid another potential disaster. But he knew more than anything, he desired to see her face again. He thought of the countless times in the past when he stood waiting for her at this very door. They'd spent nearly every possible moment together. It was as if there had never been enough hours, and never enough days, to satiate their undeniable longing for each other's presence. Truth be told, they'd been perfect together.

The sound of the unlocking deadbolt snapped Jonah back to the present, filling his stomach with butterflies. Hannah's smile graced him, like it always had.

"Jonah, hi. I did not expect to see you here," she said nervously, stepping out and pulling the door closed behind her.

He shrugged, eyeing her clothing. Jeans and a stained T-shirt, with a name tag pinned to the chest. Her hair was swept into a messy ponytail at the back of her head, a few stray golden tendrils spilling down her neck and jawline. Jonah swallowed.

"Are you about to leave for work?" he asked.

"Ugh, no, I just got home. Six lovely long hours at Murphy's."

Jonah frowned. "Do you always go in at the crack of dawn?"

"Sometimes. The elegant life of a diner waitress," Hannah replied, suddenly aware of her appearance. She tried smoothing her loose hair back.

Jonah cleared his throat. "I, uh…I just wanted to stop by to apologize for last night. I wasn't myself. I was a huge mess."

"Don't apologize for that," she insisted with a wave of her hand.

"It's been so long. I put you through all that, and then *you* have to come to *my* rescue? I don't deserve you being so nice to me. I just wanted to tell you I'm sorry for that." He looked away, ashamed.

Hannah stood there, perplexed, staring up at him. "Jonah. You're not at all the disappointment you seem to think you are. I came to you last night because I wanted to help you. I knew you'd be hurting."

Disbelief shrouded his features. "How can you just do that? After all the pain I caused you…"

Hannah sighed. "Will you stop talking like that? I don't resent you. I don't blame you. I've just *missed* you. I've always understood why you had to leave. The rest was just…out of our control. I stopped calling too. You don't have to keep taking the fall."

Jonah felt like he couldn't breathe. He crossed the porch to sit on the bench swing, leaning over with his elbows on his knees and his forehead resting against his hands. How could she be so gracious? She hadn't changed a bit since he'd seen her last. She'd carried her childlike sweetness into adulthood.

Hannah sat beside Jonah. "Remember when I came to visit you at school? Your dad wouldn't fly you home for Christmas, so I made my parents fly me to see you as my Christmas present."

A smile spread across Jonah's face as he straightened up to rest his back against the bench beside her.

"Of course I remember. You unknowingly spent your parents' last Christmas together with *me*. Looking back now, do you regret that?"

Hannah's eyes lit up. "How could I? It was the best four days of my life. Sneaking that Christmas tree into your dorm, laughing so hard and trying to be quiet so your RA wouldn't catch us. Finding hideous ornaments and half-burned out lights at Goodwill to decorate it with. Hot chocolate and movies in your bed every night, even though I was *supposed* to be staying with your friend, Jami."

Jonah grinned, lost in the reverie. "Yeah, and the night we finally let one thing lead to another…"

Hannah blushed a deep shade of red. "Jonah…" she said bashfully, trying to keep her composure.

"I'm sorry." His voice was low. "I didn't mean to say that…But I just think you should know that our first time is still my last time. There's never been anyone else."

Hannah searched Jonah's shockingly blue eyes as they burned into her. How was it possible that he could still love her after all these years?

It would seem that Jonah's grief had lent him a sense

of transparency, causing Hannah's heart to race with so many unforeseen emotions. She truly hadn't known what to expect when she heard Mr. Weston had died of a sudden heart attack and Jonah would be returning home. She hadn't believed it was finally happening. And now, she couldn't believe he was *here*. She nearly expected that if she blinked, he'd disappear.

Hannah had hoped for, at least, a civil greeting at the gravesite the day before. She'd even toyed with the idea of skipping it all together, so afraid to see indifference in his eyes when he looked at her, or even worse, a ring on his left hand. But neither had been the case in the slightest. Unbeknownst to her, Hannah was still his one and only.

And since their initial reunion, they'd cried together, held each other, and now, here they were, swinging gently on her front porch, after he'd unintentionally brought up the first and only time they'd been intimate.

"I didn't mean to make you uncomfortable," Jonah said suddenly. "I seem to have misplaced my filter since I've come back here."

Hannah laughed, her same melodic laugh. "Oh, I see that."

He hesitated, nervously tracing the knots in the wood on the bench between them. "What does all of this mean…for us?" he asked, fearing her response.

"I guess we'll just have to see. When do you go back to Florida?"

Jonah chuckled. "I was supposed to leave this morning."

Hannah's pretty lips broke into a pleased smile. "Well, that's definitely a start."

Jonah sped all the way to his mother's house, cursing himself the entire ten-minute drive. How could he have been so forthright with Hannah? So inappropriate? It seemed he'd forgotten there were nearly five years of distance between them and he didn't have the right to be so familiar, no matter how familiar she felt to him.

He trudged into the house and slammed the door behind him, irate with his stupidity. Nathan appeared from the kitchen.

"Whoa, Jonah," he whispered. "Mom's finally getting some sleep. Please keep it down."

Jonah caught his breath, feeling like a scolded child. "I'm sorry."

Nathan narrowed his eyebrows with concern, noticing his little brother's obvious frustration. "What's wrong? Did something happen?"

Jonah rolled his eyes. "I'm an idiot."

"What? Why are you an idiot?"

"I don't really want to talk about it."

Nathan approached his brother and reached behind him to remove his coat from the hook on the wall. "C'mon, let's go," he said. "I'm taking you out. You need a drink. And we'll talk."

Jonah shrugged. "I don't think that's going to help me right now."

Nathan opened the front door, and Jonah decided not to resist any longer. He wasn't much of a drinker, but if he was being honest, like he'd already been too much that day, he did agree he could use a drink.

Jonah threw his head back, guzzling the last of his fifth beer. Or was it his sixth? He shrugged it off and decided it didn't matter. His father was dead. His girlfriend—ex-girlfriend—

14

probably thought he was ridiculous. It certainly justified letting go for a few hours.

Nathan returned to his seat beside Jonah at the bar, chuckling proudly. He set down four shots of whiskey.

"Those girls over there bought us these!" he exclaimed, throwing one back. "Don't worry, I told them I'm engaged but I let them know that you're single...You *are* single, right, Jonah?"

Jonah twisted his body to glance at the booth of girls across the room. They were attractive but obviously trying too hard, with their revealing clothing and heavy makeup. Definitely not Jonah's type. And nothing like Hannah. One of the girls waved flirtatiously at him.

"I don't know, Nathan." Jonah turned back to the bar, finally answering his brother's question.

"Are you ready to tell me what happened?" Nathan asked, sliding a shot toward him.

Jonah eyed it for a moment before downing it. He coughed as it burned his chest, but he grabbed another one and did it again.

"Hey, buddy, slow down." Nathan laughed, patting him on the back.

"I went to see Hannah," Jonah began, sinking deeper into his buzz. "Everything *was* going pretty well..."

"So what happened?" Nathan asked again, consuming the last shot.

"She started bringing up old memories and stuff, like when she came to visit me that one Christmas...and let's just say I mentioned some happenings of a very personal nature, and I could tell she was really embarrassed—"

Nathan cut him off. "Whoa, wait. So you finally slept with Hannah?"

Jonah sighed heavily, wishing he'd never said

anything. "Yeah, once, whatever. But it wasn't just that. I was talking about 'us' and where we stand. Ugh, I'm so stupid." He put his head down on the bar, suddenly feeling light-headed.

Nathan snickered. "Well, hey, everyone puts their foot in their mouth at least once in their lifetime, right?"

Jonah didn't seem to hear him and rambled on. "I guess I just felt so comfortable with her. I don't know why. It's been almost five years, so it shouldn't have felt so normal to be with her, but it did. It's almost like I forgot we weren't just *us* anymore. But now it's like I'm coming on too strong after all that's happened, and I probably freaked her out...Girls like a chase, right? Or is that guys?"

Nathan flagged down the bartender for another round. "You wouldn't know about all those high school games, would you? Because you dated *just* Hannah the *whole* time."

Jonah groaned. "I really don't know what to do. Maybe I should just go home."

"Florida isn't home, Jonah. It never was. Dad's gone now, so why don't you just stay?"

Jonah froze. He had no idea what Nathan knew or thought of the complicated dynamics of his relationship with their father.

"Nathan, I'm sorry. I don't know if you knew how much Dad compared us, but I never hated you for it."

Nathan shook his head. "No, man. I knew everything. I saw the way he talked to you. I saw how he pitted us against each other, and I hated it. I should've stood up for you, but I was afraid. I wasn't sure what would happen. That's a really pathetic reason, but it's the truth. I'm sorry, Jonah." He took a long swig of his beer.

Jonah ruminated on his brother's words. He'd always

wondered what Nathan thought. Why had it taken them so long to talk about things?

"Don't get me wrong," Nathan added. "Dad and I had a decent relationship. But I felt like I had to fight to keep from losing that...Did I ever tell you I didn't even *want* to be a doctor at first?"

"That's terrible, Nate. Seriously, man."

"Well, now I'm happy with it, but back then, I just wanted him to be proud of me. I always worked hard for that reason. But he's gone, so what now?" Nathan scoffed.

"You get to marry Kendall, that's what. I've never met her, but I'm sure she's great if *you* picked her," Jonah said, picking at the label on his beer bottle.

It was strange, but nice to be so personal with his brother. Being twelve years apart, their age difference hadn't lent much ability to be a part of each other's lives growing up.

Nathan smiled. "She *is* really great. She's coming down from Manhattan next week to visit if you'll still be here."

"Oh, I don't know about that. I really doubt I'll stick around that long. I only took five days off from work, so..."

Nathan looked at him through squinted, inquisitive eyes. "If Hannah asked you to stay, would you?"

Jonah bit his lower lip. "I don't think she would."

Leaning against the wall outside the bar to keep his balance, Jonah held his cell phone to his ear, waiting anxiously as it continued to ring. It was unlikely that Hannah had kept the same number all these years, but he'd never had the heart to delete it from his phone. Finally, someone answered.

"Hello?" It was her.

"Hannah! It's Jonah. Wow, you still have the same

number!"

She chuckled. "Uh, yeah, so do you."

"I never changed it...in case you ever tried to call me." He was, once again, too honest.

"Ah, I see," Hannah replied, realizing he wasn't of sound mind. "Where are you, Jonah?"

"Umm...My brother took me to a bar. He's pretty wasted. I think I may have also had a *little* too much to drink."

"Do you need a ride home?" she offered, figuring that was the point he was struggling toward.

"You'd do that?" he asked. "I feel bad asking you. It's kinda far...like, half an hour away."

"Are you at Gatsby's?" Hannah guessed, assuming Nathan would choose a nicer place.

Jonah laughed. "Wow. You're good. That's *exactly* where we are. Are you sure you don't mind? I mean, I can always call a cab."

"No, just give me forty minutes. And be good until I get there."

Hannah spent the drive in deep thought, mulling over Jonah's reappearance in her life until Gatsby's came into view. After parking her Accord, she called Jonah, and it went to voicemail. She had no choice but to go inside and find him.

Hannah could hear the music before she'd even stepped through the door. The bar was alive with dancing, billiards, and loud chatter. She scanned the large, dimly lit room until she spotted his familiar face.

Jonah was leaning against the bar, beer in hand, looking unintentionally gorgeous. Hannah couldn't help but notice the way his black sweater complimented his broad shoulders. She stifled her smile and headed toward him. As she got closer, she realized there was a girl sitting on the stool beside him, flirting indiscreetly. An unexpected pang of jealously surged through Hannah when the girl reached out and touched Jonah's chest. He immediately pushed her hand away and removed himself from the bar just as Hannah approached.

"Hannah!" Jonah's face lit up with relief. He threw his arms around her, pulling her in for an affectionate hug. "I'm so glad you're here. The girls in this place are crazy…Where the hell is Nathan?"

Hannah looked down at his hand to see "Taylor" scribbled on it, along with a phone number. Jonah followed her gaze to the messy ink and sheepishly scraped it against the side of his jeans.

After they'd located Nathan, who'd been spending an obscene amount of money on the jukebox, they made it to Hannah's car. Nathan instantly fell asleep in the backseat while Jonah sat up front. The silence in the car was deafening, the high volume of the bar still ringing in their ears.

Jonah's deep voice pierced the quiet. "I'm sorry you had to come all the way out here."

"You've been doing a lot of apologizing lately," Hannah replied, pulling onto the highway.

He rubbed his throbbing temples. "I'm sorry, Hannah. I don't know what I'm supposed to do. I don't know if I'm supposed to act like I don't care or if I'm supposed to make you wait or whatever else those lame-ass dating rules say. I'm sorry I made you uncomfortable today. I know I said too much. I shouldn't have brought up sex. That's just awkward…and I just did it *again*. Shit." He dropped his head back against the seat and let out a defeated sigh.

"Jonah, it's okay. Yes, I was surprised by your boldness this afternoon. But honestly, I had no idea what to expect from you. I've wondered for five years how you've felt, and I was worried that you wouldn't care at all. So, if you want to know the truth..." She paused.

"Please," he pleaded.

"I think I'd rather you be too much than nothing at all."

Jonah peered at her through the darkness, her delicate features illuminated every few moments by the occasional streetlight. Her jaw was tight, and she didn't tear her eyes away from the road. Jonah struggled for a proper reply, but his head was clouded by a heavy numbness.

"I missed you every day," he finally said, looking out the window. "I wanted to call you all the time. But I was afraid to find out you weren't the same. I was afraid you'd moved on. I thought maybe *not* knowing would hurt less."

Hannah had ached for this. "I felt that way too. I worried you'd find someone else... someone you could actually see face to face."

"I couldn't replace you," Jonah said. "I know because I tried."

"You tried?"

"Well, after a while, I just didn't want to hurt anymore. And I thought if I started seeing someone else, maybe I could stop missing you. I went on a few dates, got set up on a couple blind ones, and it all sucked. I *hated* it. I felt guilty, and I had no interest...Have you dated anyone?"

"Um, I haven't really had time. I work so much, ya know?" Hannah answered quickly.

Jonah was relieved. "Isn't it funny how we both felt the exact same way, and neither of us did anything about it? Maybe that's why I'm being so bold now. I guess I'm tired of not knowing. They say honesty is the best policy, right?"

Hannah nodded. "Right."

"Can I take you out on a date tomorrow?" gazing at her through heavy eyelids.

"Maybe. If you're not hungover."

He laughed. "You're right, I'm drunk."

"Yes, you are." She chuckled.

"Then I can't be held accountable for anything tonight," Jonah claimed.

Hannah immediately felt the disappointment, like ache in her chest.

Before she could really worry what Jonah meant, he cheekily added, "I love you, Hannah. I tried to stop, but I couldn't."

Hannah kept her eyes fixed on the road, refusing to let his statement affect her in case it was nothing more than inebriated facetiousness.

After they'd made it back to the Weston residence, and Nathan was already safely inside, Jonah walked Hannah out. He stumbled over the front stoop and grabbed the doorway to catch himself. He burst out laughing.

"Shh!" Hannah laughed with him, placing her hand on his side to keep him steady. "You're going to wake up your mom."

"I don't care," Jonah scoffed with a big grin. "She took a nap today." He took Hannah's hand from his side and held it in his.

"You'd better stay right here. I wouldn't want you to fall and bust your head open or anything," she suggested. She didn't pull away from him.

Jonah kept a hold of the doorway with his free arm and leaned his cheek against the door-frame. He just looked at her, his weary eyes lost in something deep. Hannah wondered what he was thinking.

"Thank you for coming to my rescue." He grinned,

He pulled her hand to his lips and
leased her.

Good night, Jonah." She began to

eagerly. "Yeah?"

nder. "Can you call me when you get
. re safe?"

_d at his sweetness. "Yes, Jonah."

d night, Hannah."

Three

Jonah was miserable, curled up on the cold tile of the bathroom floor. His head pounded violently as he prayed for the vomiting to cease.

Wondering what time it was, Jonah fished his nearly dead phone out of his pocket. Almost 7:00 a.m. He saw he had a missed call and a voicemail from Hannah. He eagerly played it, happy to hear her voice.

"Hey, Jonah, it's Hannah. It's about midnight. You wanted me to call you when I got home, so here I am. I guess you fell asleep already...Um, I enjoyed tonight, I'm glad we talked. So anyway, I hope you sleep well. I guess I'll give you a call tomorrow to check in on you and make sure you're doing all right. Okay...Bye."

Jonah groaned, rolling onto his back, and stared up at the bathroom ceiling. He was disappointed that he'd missed another chance to speak to Hannah.

Everything felt so fuzzy in his mind. With dread, he wondered about all the things he might have said to Hannah. He closed his eyes, playing through the night, willing himself to recall every detail.

He remembered talking with Nathan, the shots, and the annoying girls at the bar, including the one who wouldn't stop hitting on him. He remembered calling Hannah and asking her to pick them up. He remembered getting into

Hannah's car, and that was where the biggest holes in his memory were.

Jonah squeezed his eyes shut tighter, forcing his brain to cooperate with him. *I'm glad we talked*, she had said. Then his eyes flew open as he remembered something else. He was fairly certain he'd told Hannah he loved her. Jonah covered his face with his hands and groaned once again.

Scarlett popped her head into the bathroom, having heard the sound. She found her son lying flat in the middle of the floor.

"Jonah. What are you doing? Are you hungover?"

He tilted his head back to look at her, upside down. "Yes, Mom."

She merely snickered and walked away.

When Jonah was convinced that his body was no longer conspiring against him, he gingerly made his way downstairs to the kitchen. He was irate to find Nathan lounging casually at the table, reading the paper, while he worked on a bagel and a cup of coffee. He was showered and dressed, not a hair out of place.

"What the hell, Nathan?"

Nathan looked up from his paper, his face bearing no signs of fatigue. "Ooh, rough morning, brother?" he teased.

"Maybe I *should* hate you," Jonah muttered, grabbing himself a bottle of water from the fridge. He sat down across from his brother.

Nathan laughed. "The key is hydration."

"But you drank so much more than I did."

"Yeah, and I drank more water than you did, too. How much water did you drink?"

Jonah grimaced. "None."

"Exactly. You obviously don't drink very often," Nathan noted, returning to his newspaper.

"You're right. And I'm never drinking again." Jonah's stomach churned at the thought.

"Oh, by the way, I'm going to need you to take me back to the bar today to pick up my car," Nathan added.

Jonah sighed. "Yay. Can't wait."

Jonah spent the next hour showering and pulling himself back together. He let out another groan each time his mind gave him back a missing piece of the night. Once he'd finally recalled all the horrifically bold things he'd said, he wondered if he could face Hannah again. Maybe he should go back home before he really disgraced himself.

Around noon, after returning from picking up Nathan's Lexus, Jonah's cell phone rang. His stomach dropped when he saw Hannah's name on the screen. He took a couple of deep breaths before he answered it.

"Hello?"

"Hey, Jonah. How are you holding up?" she asked cheerfully.

"I'm finally starting to feel better. I ended up getting pretty sick, actually."

"Oh no! I was hoping that wouldn't happen. I'm sorry."

He chuckled. "Oh, don't be sorry. I earned it, *trust* me."

"Well, I'm just glad you're doing better."

The dreaded awkward silence started creeping in, so Jonah said the first thing he thought of. "So, I'm pretty sure I told you I loved you last night?"

"Well...kind of, I guess," Hannah replied casually, but he could practically hear her smiling. "I think you were just being silly. Do you remember...everything?"

He sighed. "To my dismay, I'm almost certain I do. So yet again, despite the fact that you think I apologize too much, I still just have to tell you I'm sorry. I never drink like that. I never will again, I promise."

"I forgive you," Hannah said to appease him. "But, for the record, I don't regret a thing either of us said."

"That's good." Jonah grinned, thankful she couldn't see the goofy face he was probably making. "So, I seem to recall a certain date I may have asked you on? Any chance of that being true?"

"Oh, I'd love to, but I have to work tonight. I have the dinner shift at Murphy's, but I get off at nine. How about I stop by for a bit on my way home?"

The day dragged as if time was going backward. Jonah made it to 8:30 before he couldn't take it anymore. He went out the back door and made his way into the yard, where he decided his father's old hammock was a very good idea.

Making himself comfortable, he pulled out his phone and checked his e-mail. Nothing exciting, just a couple of work memos. He quickly sent an email to his boss, stating that some complications had come up and he may have to stay longer than he had anticipated. Hannah was definitely not a complication, but Jonah's need to stay longer was absolutely accurate.

He closed his eyes and let the soft, cold breeze rock him slightly. He listened to the sounds of the night and the faint hum of the highway in the distance.

"Can I join you?" came the sweetest sound.

Jonah opened his eyes to see Hannah standing over him, silhouetted by the porch light behind her.

"Uh, yeah," Jonah replied clumsily, shifting his body to make room for her.

Hannah carefully slid onto the hammock beside him, self-conscious over their closeness. She pulled her cardigan tightly around her and crossed her arms.

"How was work?" Jonah asked once they were settled.

"Eh, it was okay. I got some decent tips, so that was good."

They both lay there, somewhat tense, touching as little as possible. Neither was sure what was appropriate to the other.

"So, do you still play the guitar?" Hannah asked, thankful to have come up with something to break the stillness.

"Of course I do." Jonah was touched that she remembered. "I'm having the worst withdrawals right now."

"You didn't bring it with you?"

He shook his head, his dark hair falling into his eyes. "I didn't think I'd be gone this long."

Jonah rested his hand on his chest, and Hannah noticed the faded remnants of the girl's phone number from the night before. It sparked a memory.

"Hey, do you remember that time when we found those fake letter tattoos at the flea market, and we made my mom think we tattooed each other's names on us?"

Jonah grinned from ear to ear. "Oh, wow, yeah. That was hilarious! And she didn't even notice that your name was missing the last 'H.'"

She laughed. "Right, because there were only two Hs in the package…She was so mad."

Jonah reflected on the memory, feeling like it had happened yesterday. "Do you remember how your parents had that rule where I wasn't allowed in your room past ten?"

"I sure do," Hannah replied, amused. "And how about that one time when they went out of town and I wasn't supposed to have you over, but of course you came anyway."

"Oh my gosh, we fell asleep watching a movie and didn't wake up till, like, four a.m.," he recalled.

"You were freaking out. I was so scared you were going to get in trouble when you got home."

Jonah snickered. "I did. That was the night my dad backed me against the wall and lectured me on teen pregnancy."

"Oh, yeah, I forgot about that." Hannah grimaced and looked away, prodding Jonah to change the subject.

"Remember that summer when you and your parents were leaving for Texas to visit your grandparents?"

Hannah rolled her eyes in embarrassment. "I couldn't stop crying! You came over to see me off, and I was a huge mess. You just kept telling me it would go by fast and that it wasn't forever. Gosh, I don't know why I was so upset. It was only for three weeks!"

He laughed. "That *is* forever to a sixteen-year-old. And you wrote me a letter for every day you were away...ya know what?"

"What?" Hannah asked.

"I still have them."

She smiled as a newfound confidence came over her. "Do you remember the first time we kissed?"

Jonah thought maybe his heart had stopped. He turned his head to look at Hannah, their faces just inches apart.

"Yes." His gaze fell to her lips.

Turning onto his side, Jonah timidly touched Hannah's cheek. She stared back at him, watching the light dance in his eyes. She couldn't remember when she'd last seen them so bright. They'd dulled over time in their years together, the toll of abuse stifling their luminance.

With his heart pounding, Jonah cradled her head in his hands and closed the space between them. Their breathing quickened with anticipation until they met in a passionate, overdue kiss.

Jonah pulled away several moments later and rested his forehead against hers.

"Is this really happening?" he whispered, a blissful smile playing across his lips.

Hannah shifted their bodies so she could lay her head on Jonah's chest. He wrapped his arms around her, nestling his cheek into her hair. She listened to his still-racing heartbeat, lulled by the rhythmic rise and fall of his slowing breaths. Right then and there, the world felt perfect.

Jonah closed his eyes as he breathed in that familiar scent of vanilla. It carried him back to another time and place, but all he wanted was to remain in this one. The euphoria he'd fallen into had him nearly paralyzed. He wasn't sure he could bear for her to ever leave his arms. How had he managed to be without her for so long?

After savoring each other's silent company for a short while, Hannah sighed. "I have to go," she said reluctantly.

Jonah tightened his arms around her. "Aw, why? Do you still have a curfew or something?"

Hannah unraveled herself from his embrace and propped herself up on her elbow. Even in the dark, she was amazed by how captivating Jonah was: his full lips, square jaw, piercing blue eyes...Even the scar across his right cheekbone couldn't rob him of his beauty. She had to look away.

"I know, I'm sorry," she said. "I have to be up early for work."

He frowned. "You work too much."

"Trust me, I know." Hannah carefully got up from the hammock, and Jonah followed behind her as she traipsed through the yard to the driveway. He leaned in close to plant a soft kiss on her cheek before opening her car door for her. With a smile and a wave, Hannah got into the car and disappeared. Already, Jonah's heart ached.

Exhausted, Jonah headed upstairs to retire for the night. Nathan had gone back to Philadelphia earlier that evening, leaving just Jonah and their mother in the house. Jonah stepped quietly as he came upon his mother's door. It stood slightly ajar, a dim light spilling into the hallway. He paused when he heard her crying, immediately concerned. Cautiously, he eased the door open and peeked inside.

"Are you okay, Mom?"

Jonah saw his mother sitting on her bed, several tattered photographs splayed out in front of her. Scarlett began to scramble in his presence, wiping at her wet cheeks and trying to pick up the photos.

"What are you doing?" he questioned, crossing the room.

"I'm fine, Jonah." Scarlett turned her back to him as she gathered the photos into a sloppy stack.

"It's okay to be upset, Mom…Why are you trying to hide the pictures?"

Jonah reached around his mother and snatched the photographs from her hands. She reached back for them, but he swung around, hastily looking through them. A couple were of his father, but most of them were of another man. A man he did not recognize. In a few of the photos, the man was with his mother.

"Who the hell is this, Mom?" Jonah interrogated, holding them up to her.

Scarlett threw her hand over her mouth, trying to choke back the sobs that threatened to escape. She shook her head.

"Mom. Tell me right now."

"Jonah…"

He flung the photos onto the bed. "Mom! Why won't you tell me?"

Scarlett took a deep breath and fought to compose herself. She knew it was time. She'd gone much too long already.

"Dad and I got married very young, Jonah. We had your brother right away. And then we grew up, and things changed a lot. I got really lonely…"

Jonah held his breath, already suspecting what his mother was about to confess. "You cheated on Dad with this guy, didn't you?"

Scarlett darted her eyes away. "He was an old friend from high school. It all just happened so suddenly. No one ever found out about it. But then…nine months later, you were born."

Jonah's stomach dropped. "Wait…What?"

Scarlett hesitated. *"He's* your father, Jonah."

Jonah felt like he was about to hyperventilate. "No…That can't be true," he muttered, fighting to steady his shaking knees.

"I wish I could say it wasn't. I tried to keep it a secret so no one would ever have to get hurt. We weren't planning to have any more children, so I just let Dad think we'd had an accident. That's why Nathan's a whole twelve years older—"

"Oh my God! Are you kidding me? An *accident*? Thank you. Seriously, thank you."

"Jonah, I'm sorry! You're an adult now. It's time you heard the truth."

He ran a trembling hand through his hair. "So, what happened? Did Dad—Jacob...whatever the hell I should call him now, ever find out? He did, didn't he? Is that why he was always such a dick to me?"

Scarlett tried to reach out to her son, but he recoiled at her touch.

"He did find out, Jonah. Everything was good for a few years, but as you got older, he got more skeptical. You were so different from him and from Nathan. Physically, emotionally...You had a completely different temperament. Dad came home one day and told me he knew, but he wouldn't tell me how. And things were never the same after that."

Jonah uneasily shifted his weight from one foot to the other, stress and pain distorting his features. "How old was I? How old was I when he found out I wasn't his?"

"Seven."

Jonah thought back to when things changed, to when the baseball games and playing catch had stopped. While he remembered enjoying those things with his dad, he could also remember feeling inferior to Nathan even then. In hindsight, Jonah couldn't believe how obvious it was. He hadn't been crazy.

A switch had been flipped one day, the day a man found out his youngest son didn't belong to him, just as he'd suspected all along. And after he attained the confirmation, he cut that boy off, despite the fact he'd been raising him as his own for seven whole years. His anger and resentment for what his wife had done to him was stronger than his capacity for grace.

His entire life, Jonah had unknowingly paid for a sin he had nothing to do with. He was an innocent child, and still, he received the brunt of the bitterness. Every question Jonah had had for the last sixteen years had finally been answered. He knew why his father favored Nathan, his *actual* son. All those years Jonah wasted trying to impress his father were in vain. There was no way to win over a man who, all that time, had seen him only as a bastard and nothing more. Why had it been so easy for Jacob to disown him?

Jonah was sick to his stomach. "Is that why he started drinking?" he asked in a low voice.

Scarlett let out a troubled breath. "Um...I think that may have been when it started becoming excessive, yes."

"Wow. So, all of that was because of *me*?"

She approached him once again. "No, Jonah. It was not because of you. All of that was *my* fault. And I swear he made me pay for it by not divorcing me."

"I paid for it too, Mom. My entire life has been defined by him and the way he raised me. I left because of him. I left *Hannah* because of him! All of that for *what*? For a man who wasn't even my father?"

Scarlett felt helpless. "All I can tell you is I'm sorry. I really am. I can't take back all the poor decisions I made. But I can tell you the truth and just hope one day you'll forgive me."

Jonah crossed his arms over his chest and avoided his mother's eyes. It was too painful to look at her.

"Do you want to know anything about your father? Your real father?" Scarlett asked.

Jonah cringed at the word "real." The entire idea was sickening.

"No. I don't have a father," he replied through clenched teeth.

He turned and stormed out of the room, slamming the door behind him. As the countless emotions ripped through him, all he knew for sure was that he needed Hannah.

Bitter tears stained Jonah's face as he sped toward

Hannah's house. He couldn't breathe, his chest tight with a raging agony. He felt betrayed and alone, like a stranger to himself.

When Jonah arrived at Hannah's, he realized he hadn't thought things through in his manic state. It was nearly midnight, and it seemed inappropriate to knock on someone's door at that hour.

For a moment, Jonah sat in his frigid car, getting lost in the memories that flickered through his troubled mind. He recalled a summer night when he and Hannah were sixteen, and he'd gotten into a terrible fight with his father. Since neither of them had owned cell phones, and it was much too late to call Hannah's house, Jonah had ended up outside her window. He remembered gently tapping on the glass, so afraid to frighten her. But she'd bravely peered through the curtains, as if she'd known she'd see him there. He'd climbed through her window and stayed with her all night, her arms healing him. And so many years and so many lifetimes later, Jonah needed her still.

He made the odd decision to round the house to her window. If he could see that her light was on, he would text her to meet him outside. When he got there, her drawn curtains were illuminated by the light of her bedroom. With a rush of urgency, Jonah swiftly pulled his phone from his pocket, but it slipped from his numb, shaking hands and tumbled into the bushes against the house. Letting out a frustrated sigh, he crouched down to retrieve it. On the way up, he smacked his head loudly on the wooden ledge beneath Hannah's window.

Uttering a few expletives, Jonah winced and rubbed the back of his throbbing head. Suddenly, a patch of light spilled across him and he squinted toward it, seeing Hannah's outline between the parted curtains. In seconds, she was scrambling to open the window.

"Jonah?" She was startled, but concerned.

Visibly embarrassed, Jonah looked up at her. She could see the desperate expression on his weary face as his red eyes began to well up again.

"Are you okay? What happened?"

Without invitation, Jonah hoisted himself up and climbed into her bedroom. "I'm so sorry to bother you. I know this is ridiculous. I just didn't know what to do."

Hannah seemed uneasy. "Jonah, I don't know if this is such a good idea right now."

He was insulted by her reaction. "What, will your mom get mad that it's past ten?" he retorted, sitting down on her bed.

"Shh...No, it's complicated, I—"

"Hannah, I just found out that my *dad*...isn't my dad. I'm just the product of my mother's affair. I'm the biggest mistake in the history of all mistakes. That's why that asshole tormented me my whole life."

Hannah's eyes went wide with shock as she hurried to his side. "Oh my gosh, Jonah. I'm so sorry." She tried to console him with a hug.

He clutched her against him. "I don't even know what to do with this."

Hannah pulled away, and behind him, she watched her bedroom door slowly creak open. She froze, mortified, as Jonah turned around to see a small child standing in the doorway. He gawked at the petite girl, alarmed by her presence. She looked Jonah over inquisitively, her blue eyes familiar.

"Mommy, I heard a noise," she finally spoke, toying with the hem of her frilly pink pajama shirt.

"*Mommy*?" Jonah questioned in a hushed voice. He

tilted his head toward Hannah, avoiding her eyes at first. When he did bring himself to meet her gaze, his eyes tearfully expressed his anguish and confusion.

Hannah had to look away. "Gracie, please go back to bed. I'll come see you in a few minutes. Okay, baby?"

Giving Jonah another bewildered once-over, Gracie spun around and left the room, her long, dark ringlets dancing behind her.

Unable to process it, Jonah jumped to his feet and hurried to the window. Hannah grabbed his arm, but he pulled away. He turned to face her.

"How could you do this to me?" He trembled, tears escaping. "How could you let me say all those things? How there's never been anyone else...and you didn't bother to stop me from humiliating myself? You let me think you felt the same...You let me kiss you, Hannah. And all this time, you've had a *child*, and you couldn't even tell me?"

"Jonah, I was afraid," she cried.

"Are you still involved with her father? Is he why you stopped calling me?"

Hannah felt overwhelmed. "I told you I wasn't seeing anyone. I wasn't lying about that. I didn't lie about anything."

"You just decided to leave out the most significant part of your life. I guess I'm not worth it, right? Maybe I'm *your* biggest mistake too." His anger melted into a sea of pain, and he felt like he was drowning. "It kills me, Hannah. Someone else got the best part of you, and I can't handle that."

"Jonah," she tried. "Please let me explain."

He put his hands up in surrender. "I can't take anymore right now. Please."

Jonah brushed past her to the window and quickly slipped out into the darkness. Hannah collapsed to the floor, sobbing as hard as she had the day she found out she was pregnant.

Hannah took a deep breath and made her way to the kitchen, where her mother was cooking dinner.

"Mom," she said quietly.

"Yes, honey?" Caroline Morgan wiped her hands with a dish towel, turning her attention to her daughter. She could tell instantly that something wasn't right. "Are you okay?"

Hannah swallowed the horrible lump in her throat and shook her head. The tears came immediately as she trembled with fear.

Caroline froze, filled with worry. "Hannah, what? Please talk to me."

"I'm pregnant..." Hannah finally managed in a small, strained voice.

Caroline's stomach dropped, her breath catching in her throat. She stared in disbelief at her eighteen-year-old child. "What! Hannah! How could you let this happen?"

Hannah began to sob. "It was just one time..."

Caroline sighed. "Honey, that's all it takes." Hannah hung her head in shame as her mother approached her. "Are you sure you're really pregnant?"

Hannah slowly opened her shaking hand, revealing a dollar-store pregnancy test with a dark-pink plus sign in the small plastic window. She had been so embarrassed to purchase the test, she'd driven to the next town so as not to run into anyone who knew her.

"Well, I'd say that's pretty good proof," Caroline remarked, her anger slowly replaced by mercy. "What did Jonah say?"

Hannah shook her head. "I didn't tell him. I can't."

"What? Hannah, you have to tell him he's going to be a father."

The unbelievable words made Hannah cry harder. "Mom, I

can't! It'll ruin everything!"

"Jonah's a good guy. He's not going to let you do this alone, Hannah."

"That's the problem!"

Caroline's eyebrows were furrowed with confusion. "Can you please help me understand this?"

Hannah wiped the tears from her face with the backs of her hands and struggled to compose herself. "You know Jonah's father is a nightmare. You know how hard he is on him. He's always telling Jonah what a disappointment he is and how he'll never measure up to his brother...and that's all before *Jonah got his girlfriend pregnant. He is trying so hard right now to do something successful with his life and finally prove his dad wrong. Can you imagine what his dad would do if he found out about this? It would make things so much worse. I can't do that to Jonah." Hannah paused to choke back her emotions. "And maybe...if he doesn't have to come back here for me, he can finally be free from his father."*

Miserable tears poured down Hannah's cheeks as she fell apart. She couldn't believe this was happening, and she couldn't fathom how she would survive it without Jonah.

Caroline pulled her daughter close and held her. "I know this is a bad situation. I'm not happy about it, but being angry with you or punishing you isn't going to change it. Don't say anything to your father. I'll talk to him tonight. And as much as I don't think it's fair to keep this from Jonah, I respect your reasons. But you do understand what that means, then." Hannah bit her lower lip, waiting for her mother to tell her what she already knew. "It means you can't see him again. You have to let him go. Do you think you can do that?"

Hannah could barely stand as the sobs shook her frame. She crumbled into a chair at the table, her chest aching so horribly she thought she might die. She pictured Jonah's beautiful face and painfully imagined never seeing it again. She thought about never feeling his touch, hearing his voice, kissing his lips, laughing with him, seeing his smile ever *again. It extinguished the light inside of her.*

"No...I can't do it," Hannah brokenly admitted. "But I have to."

FOUR

Jonah's life was unrecognizable, shattered in fragments around him. The shards pierced him deeply, creating new wounds among the old ones. Of all the pieces that had fallen, Jonah was most plagued by the discovery of Hannah's daughter. How could she have kept such a monumental secret from him? He pondered the possibilities, struggling to understand. Maybe she'd never had the heart to tell him she'd moved on in his absence, beginning the family they'd always vowed to build together with someone else. It tore a gaping hole inside of him, instilling the notion that he didn't know Hannah at all. He'd been so honest with her. He wished she'd done the same.

Exhausted and overwhelmed, Jonah decided it was time for him to return home. He packed his bags and left his mother's house without a good-bye. He couldn't bear to face her. The hurt was still too fresh.

The only person Jonah had left was Nathan, though recent developments had reduced them to *half*-brothers. The distinction bothered Jonah, as he already struggled to feel close to his brother in the first place.

The burden of all these surfacing secrets confirmed that Jonah's initial plans to get away from this place had been right all along.

"What happened last night, Hannah?" Caroline entered the kitchen, having just gotten home from her nursing job at the health and rehabilitation center. "Gracie just said there was a man in your room?"

Hannah sighed as she slouched at the table, her rough appearance indicating a lack of sleep. "Jonah was here."

Caroline's eyes went wide. "Did you tell him?"

She shook her head. "He just thinks I had a baby with someone."

"Hannah! Why didn't you tell him the truth? He *saw* her. Your cover was already blown!"

"He didn't give me a chance to explain. Besides, he went through enough last night. I don't think he could've handled *this* on top of it. His mom had just told him that Mr. Weston wasn't his real father…She had Jonah because of an affair," Hannah explained.

"Oh. Wow. That's gotta be really hard." Caroline placed her hand over her chest. "But honey, Mr. Weston was the reason for all of this secrecy in the first place. There is absolutely nothing to stop you from telling Jonah the truth now."

Hannah begged to differ. "He's going to hate me, Mom. What if he never forgives me? What if he doesn't understand that I did it for him?"

Caroline gave her daughter a comforting smile. "Honey, if Jonah is still the guy he always was, then he will understand. Maybe not at first, but he will."

Jonah's eyelids fluttered in the glaring sunlight as he awoke. He had driven for four hours before pulling over to sleep. He'd almost enjoyed the night drive, listening to music and clearing his head.

He was glad to leave the chaos behind him and return to his simple life.

Just as he was about to continue his trip south, Jonah received a text from Hannah: *Jonah, I know you're mad at me but I would really like to talk to you. Your mom told me you left last night. Can you please let me know you're okay?*

I'm fine. Driving home, he texted back.

So that's it? You're just going to leave again?

Jonah snickered as he typed. *Why should I stay?*

Because I want you to.

Jonah stared at his phone. He thought of the conversation he'd had with Nathan at the bar. He didn't think Hannah would ever ask him to stay. And he was *leaving*? Again? Leaving was exactly what had ruined them in the first place. It had given Hannah the chance to replace him. Jonah forced away the thought.

With a small shred of hope, Jonah decided to turn back. He owed it to himself, to Hannah, and to their history together to face the situation, even if only to find closure. If he kept running, he knew the "what ifs" would haunt him always.

Oak Lake Park was veiled by a golden glow as the sun slipped lower in the autumn sky. A cool breeze rustled the changing leaves, scattering them across the grass and sprinkling them into the lake. Hannah watched the ripples on the water from her seat at the picnic table, Jonah sitting across from her.

Quiet times like these made her thoughts wander. She sometimes found it difficult to keep her affectionate musings to herself, especially when she was alone with him.

"We should probably get going." The sudden sound of Jonah's voice gave Hannah butterflies.

She rolled her eyes at herself and turned back to the open textbook in front of her. "Okay."

They were a few weeks into their freshman year and usually spent their afternoons studying and tutoring each other after school. Hannah was skilled in science and history while Jonah excelled in math and English. Together, they made the perfect student.

"So, who's this guy you were talking about today?" Jonah asked, trying to sound casual. He slid his books into his backpack.

"What guy?" Hannah questioned, slipping her bag onto her shoulders.

He shrugged sheepishly. "I kinda overheard you talking to Stella at the pep rally."

She froze, recalling the conversation she'd had with her friend. She hadn't realized Jonah had been listening. How much had he heard? Hannah was sure she had never said his name. No one knew. No one. Hannah tried to remember exactly what she'd said when she'd vaguely answered Stella's questions about her crush. Except it wasn't a crush. It was profoundly more than that.

"Oh...yeah. Um...he's just..." Hannah trailed off, wishing she could run away. Or maybe disappear.

"Do I know him?" Jonah wondered, looking intently at her. He didn't know why he was pressing the topic. He preferred not to know who was stealing her heart away.

Hannah bit her lower lip, toying with her bag's straps on her shoulders. Could she actually tell him?

"Well...I'd say you know him pretty well."

Jonah's eyebrows knit together in deep thought as he mentally sorted through his closest friends. "Is it one of our friends from your party?" he said, referring to the birthday party she'd had over the summer.

Hannah looked away. "No...but he was there."

Jonah had to remind himself to keep breathing as her reveal sank in. She hadn't been awfully explicit, but he was smart.

"Really?" was all he could muster, his tone hushed.

Hannah quickly turned away from him, tears filling her eyes. "So now you can start acting all weird and stop talking to me..."

Jonah came after her. "No. I promise I won't. I could never stop talking to you. You're my best friend, Hannah...and things won't get weird. It'll only be weird if you make it weird."

Hannah slowly faced him, her eyes so full of fear while his were warm and kind. Best friend? Wasn't that usually a bad sign? She immediately regretted her boldness, deciding that the hope of Jonah feeling the same was far more comforting than the bitter truth of the friend zone. Best friends falling in love? That only happened in movies.

"I'm sorry," she finally whispered, blinking away her tears as she started toward the sidewalk.

Jonah gently grabbed her arm, filling her with hope for just a moment. "Can I please walk you home?"

Hannah nodded, and he fell into step behind her. All the while, they both wondered what the other was thinking, but neither of them spoke a word. Hannah couldn't wait to rush into the privacy of her home and cry her eyes out over the terrible mistake she'd made. But she wished Jonah would say something — anything — before she disappeared behind that door. They always talked about everything. Why couldn't they talk about this?

Hannah placed her hand on the doorknob as Jonah stood at the bottom of the porch steps. She wanted him to stop her. But he didn't. She caught a glimpse of him turning away as she stepped inside and closed the door. Hannah couldn't believe he'd let her leave him without so much as a wave. That wasn't how they usually treated each other. Things were already different.

Just as Hannah was about to fall apart, she heard a knock. Her breath caught in her throat. There was no way. She opened the door, and there he was, his features soft but laced with apprehension. He nervously chewed his lip, struggling to put his thoughts into words.

Hearing her mother in the kitchen, Hannah stepped out onto the porch, shutting the door behind her. Jonah held her gaze, his eyes staring so tenderly into hers. It was a look she'd never seen before.

"Hannah," he started, his voice trembling. "I'm sorry...I just...I like you so much, I didn't know what to do."

A smile slowly curved her lips. "You do?"

Jonah chuckled self-consciously and looked at the ground. He hesitantly reached for her hand and pulled her closer, gently kissing her cheek. Hannah felt like she couldn't breathe, her fear transforming into bliss. Never before in the two years they'd been friends had she ever been this close to him. She'd imagined it a million times, but for once, reality was better.

Jonah pounded his fists against the steering wheel as smoke rose from the hood. He was only an hour away, but, evidently, his car couldn't handle another mile. Feeling defeated, Jonah dug his cell phone out of his pocket and called the only person he could think of.

Over an hour later, Nathan pulled up to the mechanic's shop Jonah had specified. He saw his ragged little brother heading toward the Lexus.

"Hey, thanks for picking me up," Jonah said, climbing in and closing the door.

"It's not a problem." Nathan pulled back onto the highway. "You doing okay?"

Jonah sighed heavily, rubbing his cold hands together. "Oh, you don't even want to know."

"I'm thinking something pretty bad must've happened for you to leave like that...especially after how things have been going with Hannah," Nathan said.

Jonah dropped his head back against the headrest. "Where do I even start?"

He proceeded to explain to Nathan the events of the last day, dropping the bomb about their father, which Nathan had no inkling of. Jonah also expressed his pain over Hannah and the extravagant secret she'd kept from him.

"Hannah has a *kid*? How old?" Nathan asked.

Jonah shrugged. "I don't know, I'm bad at that. She's not a baby. But she seemed older than a toddler. She's really tiny, though. Like, maybe three?"

Nathan glanced at his brother. "So, there's no way she could be yours then?"

Jonah exhaled sharply, as if the question had knocked the wind out of him. "*Mine*?" The thought had never crossed his mind.

"Why is that so impossible?" Nathan questioned.

"Hannah would've told me. She would never keep something like that from me. Next month will be five years since I last saw Hannah, and there is no way that little girl is that old."

"Yeah...maybe not," Nathan replied. "I'm so sorry about all this, man. I can see why you left."

Jonah laughed at his misfortune. "And *that* didn't work out either, did it?"

Hannah glanced in the rear-view mirror, making eye contact with her little girl. She immediately grinned as Gracie giggled.

"I see you, Mommy."

"I see *you*, Gracie."

"Where are we going?"

Hannah bit her lower lip. "We're going to the park to see Mommy's friend."

"I hope your friend is nice."

Hannah nodded. "He is."

She sighed, Jonah's voicemail replaying in her head. *"Hannah, it's me. Meet me at Oak Lake at four o'clock. And please bring Gracie."* She'd played it close to a dozen times. Hearing Jonah say Gracie's name made her heart ache. She had longed for the day when he knew his daughter existed.

Somehow, Hannah had to let him in on the rest of the secret. If there was any way to make him understand, she had to be sure she chose the best possible time and manner. She could not lose him again.

With a few minutes to spare, Hannah pulled into the small lot, parking next to a black Mercedes SUV. Jonah's Ford was nowhere in sight. *Maybe he's running late,* Hannah thought, helping Gracie out of her car seat. She tried not to worry he wouldn't show at all.

"Let's take a walk," Hannah suggested, zipping her daughter's jacket.

She took Gracie by the hand and led her down the path toward the lake. As the lake came into view, so did Jonah. Hannah was relieved but fought the urge to smile. He was sitting on top of a picnic table, his feet resting on the bench. He quickly slid off when he saw them, taking a few nervous steps forward.

"Hey," Jonah greeted her, jamming his hands into his coat pockets. "Thanks for coming."

Hannah nodded, Gracie shyly clutching her leg. "So, where's your car?" Hannah asked, making small talk to break up the awkwardness.

Jonah rolled his eyes. "It broke down about an hour south of here. Nathan let me borrow one of his cars for now."

"Wow, that's a pain. Guess you're stuck here longer then, huh?" Hannah waited eagerly for his response.

"Yeah. I guess that's not so bad." Jonah knelt in front of their daughter and smiled warmly, holding his hand out to her. "Hi, Gracie. I'm Jonah."

The little girl placed her small hand in his, and he gently shook it. "Hi, Jonah," Gracie replied, her voice like a sweet song.

"I brought you a present," Jonah said, reaching into the pocket of his pea coat.

Gracie's eyes lit up as he handed her a small stuffed turtle with a colorful shell. "Oh, he's so cute!" she shrieked, immediately cradling it against her cheek. "I love him!"

Jonah grinned, standing up. "I was hoping you would. Turtles are my favorite."

Gracie's tiny jaw dropped. "Mine too!"

Hannah tousled Gracie's curls, choking back her emotions. "What do you say to Jonah for giving you such a nice present?"

"Thank you, Jonah!" Gracie threw her arms around his leg to hug him, and Hannah tried not to cry.

He patted her on the head. "Aw, you're welcome."

Though it was difficult, Jonah had resolved to approach the situation with a different attitude. Sure, it hurt that Hannah hadn't been honest with him, but he realized he deserved some of the blame for leaving all those years ago. Despite everything, he'd never wanted anything more than he wanted Hannah. He had to at least try.

After tossing stones into the lake and collecting leaves with Gracie, the two adults sat nearby while Gracie played on the playground.

"I've missed this park," Jonah said, resting his arm along the back of the wooden bench.

"Yeah, this place is beautiful." Hannah glanced around them before returning her attention to Gracie.

A sly smile crept across Jonah's lips as he pointed to the tables on the opposite side of the playground. "That's where you told me you liked me."

Hannah blushed. "Yeah, because you forced it out of me."

"But it worked out, right?"

"Not at first."

Jonah narrowed his eyebrows. "What do you mean?"

"You called me your best friend, and you walked me home without even saying a word. And then you just *left*."

"But I came back."

Hannah chuckled. "You're right. You did. And you told me you liked me, and I was so nervous because I thought you were going to kiss me."

Jonah smiled sheepishly, looking away. "I *wanted* to kiss you...but I was being a gentleman."

Hannah was amused. "Oh really?"

"Yes. You really caught me by surprise, you know. I didn't think you saw me that way. So, I know at first my reaction was really crappy. It's just that I had this picture in my mind of how I was going to ask you out. It was all cool and perfect, but it ended with you laughing and turning me down because you didn't want to ruin our friendship." Jonah laughed at himself.

"It's funny that we haven't talked about this before," Hannah said.

"We haven't talked about a *lot* of things before," he replied, looking over at Gracie.

Hannah sighed. "I'm sorry, Jonah. I should've told you about Gracie. But there's so much you don't know. I'm working toward that, I promise. It's all just...really hard."

Jonah nodded. "It *is* hard. And I know it's been so many years, but I'm the same person, Hannah. You can talk to me."

"I know." Her eyes welled up. "I wish it was that easy. But you're going to hate me...and I'm just so scared to hurt you."

Jonah turned to look at her, studying the distress on her face. "I can't imagine what could hurt more than feeling like I don't know you anymore...or just walking away and losing you again because I feel like I can't handle it. What could hurt me more than that? Tell me."

Hannah looked back at him, her cheeks stained with tears. She desperately wanted to tell Jonah everything, but she wasn't brave enough. She wasn't ready to see the pain of her betrayal in his eyes.

"All right," Jonah said, dejected. "I can't come back here and expect you to just open your life up to me. I guess I have to earn that. But I'll wait as long as I have to...because I still love you."

"I'm sorry, Jonah. I promise I'm trying."

Hannah was surprised when he slid closer to her and put his arm around her shoulders. She melted in his embrace, folding toward him and resting her head against his chest. Her uncontrollable tears flowed silently.

"I still love you too," she whispered.

Hannah felt Jonah let out a shaky breath as he planted a soft kiss in her hair.

A couple of hours into his restless sleep, Jonah's phone began to ring. Startled by the sudden noise, he scrambled for the device in the darkness of his hotel room.

"Hello?" he answered groggily.

"Jonah, I am so sorry to call you so late." It was Hannah.

He bolted up when he heard the panic in her voice. "It's fine. Is everything okay?"

She sighed. "It's just...Gracie has a fever, and my mom's at work. I get really paranoid when she's sick, and I don't want to be alone."

Jonah turned on the bedside light and jumped out of bed. "I'm coming over."

"You really don't have to do that. I mean, if you could just stay on the phone with me...?"

Cradling his phone between his ear and shoulder, he pulled on his jeans and grabbed a flannel shirt. "Hannah, it's okay. I will be there in fifteen minutes."

A surge of relief came over Hannah when she opened the door and saw Jonah. He breezed in, giving her a brief, comforting hug.

"How's Gracie?" he asked, his face tinged with concern.

"Her fever was almost one hundred and two the last I checked it. She was really upset, but I gave her Tylenol and she's in my bed," Hannah said, wringing her hands.

Jonah unzipped his hoodie and peeled it off, draping it over the back of a chair before heading down the hall to Hannah's room. Deeply touched by his interest, Hannah followed behind him.

"Jonah!" Gracie exclaimed. "What are you doing here?"

A huge grin spread across his face as he knelt beside her. "I heard there was a big party going on."

She giggled. "Nooooo. I have a fever." She reached for his hand and brought it to her forehead.

"Oh, you're right," Jonah replied, gently running his knuckles down her soft, flushed cheek. "I guess we'll just have to have that party another time."

He was delighted when he spotted the turtle he'd given Gracie earlier, tucked beneath her arm.

"We can have a slumber party," she suggested with a yawn.

Jonah smiled. "Oh yeah? And what do we do at a slumber party?"

Gracie pointed to the television on the dresser. "We watch movies until we fall asleep."

"Well, that's up to your mom. I don't know what the rules are." He looked up at Hannah.

"All right," Hannah agreed, crossing the room to the TV. "What are we watching?"

Gracie scrunched up her little face as she contemplated. "How 'bout *Toy Story*? 'Cause Jonah probably doesn't like princesses. He's a man."

Jonah raised his eyebrows at Hannah with a playful grin, and she laughed, turning back to the DVD player.

"*Toy Story* it is."

After setting up the movie, Hannah climbed into the queen bed beside her small daughter, feeling her cheeks and forehead before getting comfortable. Jonah sat on the floor next to Gracie's side of the bed.

"Jonah," Gracie scolded him.

He looked at her. "Yes, Gracie?"

"Why are you sitting way over there? You're not at the slumber party."

"I'm sorry," he said kindly, exchanging glances with Hannah. "What do you want me to do?"

She patted the spot beside her. "There's room right here." Jonah got up and slid onto the bed next to Gracie. "Now lay down and watch the movie," she said.

Jonah lay on his back, his arm tucked behind his head like a pillow. Gracie quickly got tired and turned to her side, snuggling against him.

Hannah didn't pay any attention to the movie. She was preoccupied by the scene alongside her: her little girl snuggled up against her daddy. Hannah had always dreamed of them together, and it far surpassed the sweetness she had imagined. She looked away before she started to cry.

"I think she's asleep," Jonah whispered.

"You're really good with her. It's impressive, actually."

He smiled. "I dunno, I just like kids. They're fun."

"You are definitely not the typical guy."

"I know, I'm so weird, right?"

They continued watching the movie for a few moments until Jonah broke their silence. "Why were you so nervous about Gracie? She seems fine."

Hannah sighed. "I know. It's because when she was one, she had a febrile seizure. That's when a child gets a sudden fever that spikes so quickly, it causes them to have a seizure. It was so scary. The ambulance came and everything. At first, I thought she was going to die." Hannah looked down at her tiny sleeping blessing and ran her fingers over her brown curls.

"Oh, wow," Jonah breathed. "That sounds awful. I can see why you'd worry. But I'm glad you called me so I can be here for you."

"Me too. Thanks, Jonah."

"Now lay down and watch the movie," he teased, mimicking Gracie's tone.

Hannah smiled contentedly and nestled against her pillow, realizing it was the very first time she felt like they were a family.

FIVE

annah's heart leaped in her chest when she opened her eyes, Jonah's beautiful face just inches from hers. He was still asleep, Gracie cradled in the crook of his arm. It was surreal to wake up to him, yet so comfortable. Hannah smiled to herself, admiring Jonah's peaceful countenance, his perfect jawline, those dark eyelashes for miles. She could see their daughter in his features. How hadn't he noticed that Gracie looked just like him?

Hannah's unhindered marveling came to an end when Jonah awoke, raising his sleepy blue eyes to meet hers.

"Hi," he whispered with a sheepish grin, rubbing his eye with his free hand.

"Good morning," she answered.

"I didn't mean to stay all night," Jonah said, peering fondly at Gracie.

"It's okay," Hannah assured him. "I'm glad you did."

Jonah softly brushed the backs of his fingers over Gracie's cheek, then gently pressed his own cheek against her forehead. "No more fever," he concluded, his attentiveness making Hannah melt.

"Oh, good," she replied as Gracie stirred.

"Did I miss the slumber party?" Gracie asked, sitting up.

Jonah glanced at Hannah and chuckled. "We all missed it."

They heard Caroline calling them for breakfast and got out of bed. Jonah followed Hannah and Gracie out into the hallway, where the smell of bacon wafted from the kitchen.

His stomach tightened at the thought of seeing Hannah's mother again. He wasn't sure where he stood with her, having left her daughter behind so many years before, promising to come back but never returning.

"Good morning, Mom." Hannah kissed her mother on the cheek before sitting down.

Gracie jumped up into her booster seat at the table. "Hi, Gramma! We had a slumber party!"

Caroline turned away from the stove. "Well, that sounds fun."

Hannah could sense Jonah's nervousness. "Mom, you remember Jonah."

Caroline smiled warmly. "Of course I do. How could I forget?"

"Hi, Mrs. Morgan," Jonah said timidly, slipping his hands into his pockets.

"It's good to see you again, Jonah."

"And you too, Mrs. Morgan."

"Please. Call me Caroline. You're an adult now, I'll allow it."

Jonah took a seat at the table beside Hannah, relieved over Caroline's positive attitude toward him.

"So, I got your text, honey," Caroline said to her daughter. "I'm so sorry Gracie got sick while I wasn't here. How did that go?"

"Well, that's why Jonah is here, actually," Hannah explained. "You know how I get all freaked out...He was a big help. And Gracie seems to be better now, thank God."

"Well, that's good. So, Gracie, how do you like Jonah?" Caroline asked, spooning some eggs onto her plate.

Hannah shot her mother a stern, scolding look.

"I like him a lot so far," Gracie replied nonchalantly. "He is *very* nice."

Jonah smiled. "I like you a lot too, Gracie."

After Jonah left, Hannah showered and got dressed for the day. She was in her room making her bed when her mother walked in, closing the door behind her.

"You need to tell him," Caroline insisted.

Hannah dropped the pillow she was holding, her shoulders slumping. "Mom. I know. I'm working on it."

"You're *working* on it? What does that mean?"

Hannah groaned. "This isn't easy for me, Mom. I can't just be like 'oh hey, by the way, Gracie is yours, I forgot to tell you.' I need to find the right time."

"The sooner the better is the right time. Especially before he figures it out on his own," Caroline said.

Hannah looked away, defeated, tears flooding her eyes. "I made the wrong decision, didn't I? I should've told him right away. He should've had a choice but I made him miss *everything*." She paced the floor, nearly hyperventilating.

Her mother gently grabbed her arm. "Honey, you did what you thought was right. And at the time, it was."

Hannah looked at her with pleading eyes. "Why did you let me do this?"

"Hannah. This is what *you* wanted, and I supported your decision. You were old enough to understand the consequences. But you couldn't know how it would turn out later on down the road. So don't blame yourself for trying to protect him."

Hannah flopped down at the foot of her bed and sighed heavily. "I'm sorry. You're right...and I'll tell him soon, I promise."

Hannah reached down beneath the sheet, touching her nearly flat stomach. Fresh tears stung her eyes, but she fought them back; it hurt too much to cry. She felt so alone without the dancing little one she'd carried beneath her heart for twenty-nine weeks. It had all happened so suddenly.

Hannah winced as the stabbing pain from the incision in her lower abdomen returned. She pressed the button on the handheld device she'd been given to release more pain medication into her IV.

The mental and physical pain grew profoundly overwhelming, and she could no longer suppress her tears. She thought about the scary moments that had transpired that day: a routine doctor visit gone bad, the high blood pressure, the stressful ultrasound, the extreme decision for an emergency cesarean. They had told her she had preeclampsia, but she had no idea what it meant. All she'd understood was that her little girl had to be born, or they were both in serious danger.

It all had led her to this lonely moment—her tiny two-pound, ten-ounce baby fighting for her life in the neonatal intensive care unit. Hannah hadn't even seen her yet. Despite her anguish and the unshakable feeling of loss, Hannah couldn't help but think of Jonah, desperately wishing he was there with her.

As a part of her considered picking up her phone to call him, a nurse came in with a wheelchair.

"How are you feeling tonight, Hannah?" she asked cheerfully.

Hannah sniffled and wiped her cheeks. "Um...okay, I guess."

The nurse smiled, bringing the chair up to the bed. "Are you ready to see your baby?"

"I can see her?" Hannah wanted to cry all over again.

The nurse chuckled. *"Of course you can. She's stable now, so it's safe for you to come visit."*

Hannah nodded, pulling the sheets off of herself. *"Yes. I want to see her."*

The nurse placed a caring hand on her shoulder. *"Now, I have to warn you, you may feel a lot of pain getting out of bed. Your stomach muscles aren't going to work the way you're used to, so just take your time."*

She was right. Hannah had never before felt such excruciating physical pain in her nineteen years. It took fifteen agonizing minutes to maneuver her body out of the bed, mostly using her arms to do all the work. It hurt so badly to put any weight on her legs, but somehow, fueled by her love for her daughter, she lowered herself into the wheelchair.

Hannah clutched the blanket over her lap, a steady flow of tears streaming down her face as the nurse wheeled her down the frigid, fluorescent-lit hall to the NICU. She had hoped her mother would be with her when she got to see her baby, but she'd gone home to get some rest after working a double and then spending the entire day at the hospital with Hannah. Again, Hannah wished Jonah was there, holding her hand as they were about to meet their daughter for the first time.

The nurse picked up the telephone on the wall outside the NICU to request access, telling the nurse on the other end, *"Mom is here to visit baby girl Weston."* Hannah had given her daughter Jonah's last name, and hearing the nurse say it caused fresh tears to fall. Her mother had told her it was a bad idea, but she couldn't bear to deny Jonah on the birth certificate form.

In seconds, another nurse opened the door to the NICU nursery, smiling brightly at Hannah. *"Hey, mama, are you ready to meet your little girl?"*

Hannah nodded, annoyed by the effervescence of everyone around her. For all she knew, her daughter could die. Her body had failed, forcing her child into the perils of premature birth. Hannah didn't feel this was the same happy occasion the nurses seemed to be celebrating.

The nurse instructed Hannah to wash her hands at the sink just inside the door, and after she did so, she was wheeled to the other end of the long, dim room. She held her breath as they passed station after station, wondering which plastic box held her baby.

When they reached the very last one, the nurse turned her toward it. "Here she is."

Hannah stared into the incubator at the tiny red-complexioned baby nestled inside. A nasal cannula rested across her tiny face, delivering oxygen through her nose to her underdeveloped lungs. A thin tube was down her throat, anchored by tape to her chin, draining any fluids from her belly. Several leads with wires were attached to her small, bony torso to monitor her heart and breathing rates. A pulse oximetry monitor was wrapped around her tiny foot, emitting a red glow, and just above that, on her calf, was the smallest blood pressure cuff that ever existed. An IV line nearly the size of her arm stuck out from her hand, delivering nutrients and fluids. Her miniature, heart-patterned diaper was still much too large on her.

Hannah cried at the sight of her tiny baby. All she could see were wires and a baby that looked much too small and fragile to come into the world. Hannah was certain her daughter would never be all right.

The nurse noticed Hannah getting upset. "Hannah, she's okay. I know this is overwhelming, but she's doing so well. She's very tiny, and yes, there are a lot of wires and tubes, but she's doing much better than anyone expected, especially for her gestational age. She's breathing on her own, and that is a very good sign."

"Okay" was all Hannah could manage to reply.

"You can touch her if you'd like," the nurse said, opening one of the small windows on the front of the incubator.

Hannah gingerly reached her hand into the warmth, slowly approaching her baby. She lightly brushed her fingertips over her small belly, then gently ran her index finger down her teeny arm. The baby's skin was so soft under her touch that Hannah could barely feel it, but the contact sent waves of emotion through her entire being. The love she felt for this tiny person was so intense she could hardly bear it. Hannah painfully willed her body to straighten into a better position in the wheelchair, and finally, she looked into her baby's face. In that tiny face, she saw Jonah. And despite it all, she smiled, even as the tears shook her.

Jonah pulled a shirt over his head of damp hair as he heard a knock on his hotel room door. He wondered who it could be, since Nathan was the only person who knew where he was staying. He opened the door and was surprised to see his mother standing there, shame covering her face. Jonah was immediately filled with anxiety. He turned away from her, and she let herself in, letting the door close behind her.

"Jonah," she said timidly. "I just wanted to come and tell you how sorry I am. I know that doesn't change anything, but I need you to know that."

"Okay," he remarked curtly, his hands on his hips. He refused to look at her.

"Were you really just going to leave and never speak to me again?"

Jonah finally met her eyes. "What do you expect me to do, Mom?"

Scarlett nodded, looking down at the floor. "I know. And I deserve that. But there are things I need to tell you."

Jonah rolled his eyes. "What now?"

"I contacted your father...your real father. I told him everything. And he wants to meet you."

Jonah stared at her blankly. "You're kidding me, right?"

"His name is Elliot Tyler. He owns a store downtown. He's divorced with no children...except you," Scarlett spilled.

Putting his hands up to silence her, Jonah swiftly shook his head. "Why are you telling me this? I didn't want to know his name. I don't want to know anything about him." He swallowed hard, processing the new information. "Wait, *Tyler*? You couldn't give me my *real* last name, so you made it my *middle* name? Nice, Mom. No wonder Jacob found you out."

"I'm sorry, Jonah. I guess I wanted you to have some part of Elliot with you."

Jonah ignored her explanation. "How did you even know I was here?"

"I forced it out of Nathan," she admitted. "I had to try to make things right, even if I'm twenty-three years late."

Scarlett offered her son a slip of paper with Elliot Tyler's store address and phone number scrawled across it. When Jonah refused it, she placed it on the table.

"Fine, Jonah. I understand how upset you must be, and I don't blame you. Just please, at least text me good-bye when you decide to leave again?"

Scarlett briefly put her hand on her son's tense shoulder before she turned to the door and silently let herself out.

"Jonah, I was just about to call you! That's so weird." Nathan chuckled as he answered his little brother's call.

"Why the hell did you tell Mom where I'm staying?"

Jonah asked him bluntly.

Nathan groaned. "I'm sorry, man. She wanted to know you were safe. Did she come see you? I told her not to."

"Yeah, she did. She started telling me about my...biological father. She said he wants to meet me."

Nathan was confused. "He knows about you? I thought you said she never told anyone."

"Well, she contacted him, and she told him everything. I can't believe she did that."

"So, you have absolutely no interest in ever seeing him? Not even for closure?" Nathan asked.

Jonah didn't hesitate. "No. I want nothing to do with him. As far as I'm concerned, my father is dead. I don't need another one micromanaging my life."

"Jonah, I don't think it would be like that. You're an adult. And he's just as new to the idea as you are."

"I can't do it," Jonah said. "Just thinking about it makes my stomach hurt."

"I'm sorry," Nathan replied. "Look, I seriously *was* going to call you. I wanted to invite you out to dinner tonight. Kendall's in town, remember? I'd really love for you to meet her. Hannah's welcome too, of course."

"Hannah has to work tonight, but I'll be there."

"Things are going okay with you two?" Nathan asked.

Jonah smiled at the thought of Hannah, his previous frustrations fading into the background. "I'd say so. We had the talk, and we both still care about each other."

"So she told you who Gracie's dad is?"

Jonah sighed. "No."

"What? How was *that* not part of the talk?"

"I think it might've been a bad situation," Jonah speculated. "It's like she can't even talk about it."

Nathan tried not to judge. "Just be careful, okay?"

"It's fine, Nate. It wouldn't change anything anyway."

Nathan snickered. "Really. So nothing could ever make you walk away again? I mean, if she can't even bring herself to tell you the truth, then it must be pretty upsetting."

Jonah paused. "You don't know that."

"And neither do you. Just saying."

"Nathan, I have to go. I'll see you tonight."

After giving Gracie a kiss and a tight squeeze, Hannah stepped out the door into the evening chill to leave for work. As she opened her car door, she looked up to see her mother scurrying toward her.

"Hannah, we have a problem. My supervisor just called. She said I'm scheduled to work tonight. I must have copied my schedule down wrong."

"Did you tell her you couldn't?" Hannah asked.

"I couldn't say no. They're already two nurses short tonight," Caroline said.

Hannah tilted her head back and groaned. "Well, what am I supposed to do? I have to work too. Should I call Dad?"

Caroline bit her lower lip. "No, he's away for a seminar. Do you think you could ask Jonah to help?"

"Jonah, thank you *so* much." Hannah quickly bent to give Gracie another kiss. "I'm leaving her car seat so you don't have to miss your dinner...well, that is, *if* you don't mind taking her with you."

Jonah grinned. "I don't mind. Now hurry up and get out of here. You're already late." He happily accepted her brief hug before she jogged across the parking lot to her car. Jonah and Gracie waved as Hannah drove away.

64

"Is this your house?" Gracie asked skeptically as they entered Jonah's hotel room.

He chuckled. "No, this is a hotel. It's where people stay when they're visiting somewhere."

"Ohhh. It's small in here, and it's very boring. I'm glad it's not your house."

Jonah bent to her level, his hands on his knees. "So, hey. Since it's so boring here, I was wondering if you wanted to go out to dinner with me. My brother will be there with his fiancée."

"What's that?" she asked.

"A fiancée? It's someone you're about to marry," he replied.

Gracie thought for a moment. "Is Mommy *your* fiancée?"

Jonah laughed, blushing. He was amazed by how smart she was.

"Umm, no. She isn't."

Gracie seemed disappointed. "Oh."

"So, do you want to go have dinner, then?"

She smiled. "Yes."

Nathan and Kendall were already seated at a booth in a quiet section of the restaurant when Jonah arrived. Nathan was surprised to see a little girl clutching his brother's hand when he stood to greet him.

Nathan's eyes widened when he saw her face. "Is this Gracie?"

"Yes. And Gracie, this is my big brother, Nathan. Remember we talked about fiancées? That's Nathan's fiancée, Kendall." Jonah reached over to shake Kendall's hand. "Hi. Nice to finally meet you."

"You too, Jonah." Kendall Woods grinned, running a hand through her long, dark hair.

After getting Gracie situated in the booth with a kids' menu and crayons, Jonah sat down beside her.

"So…" Nathan insinuated his question, motioning to the little girl.

"Hannah's mom was supposed to watch Gracie, but she ended up having to work too, so I'm helping them out."

Kendall smiled. "Oh, that's so sweet of you. How old is she?"

Jonah narrowed his eyebrows, realizing he still didn't know.

"I'm four!" Gracie chimed in, diligently coloring on her menu.

"Ah, she's four," Jonah repeated. He began to ponder, but was interrupted by the waitress.

"What can I get you to drink?" she asked, looking down at Jonah.

"I'll just have sweet tea…and Gracie, what do you want?"

She looked up, her chocolate curls framing her small face. "Lemonade, please."

The waitress smiled. "What a sweet little thing she is," she said to Jonah. "And she's got your eyes, you know."

Before Jonah could correct her, she ran off, leaving him in a haze. He kept glancing at Gracie, wondering why the waitress would say such a thing.

"So, Jonah," Nathan started, knowingly snapping him out of his confusion. "The reason we're here tonight is because I wanted to ask you to be my best man."

A smile slowly brightened Jonah's demeanor. "Really? Me?"

Nathan chuckled. "Yes, you."

"Of course I will. That's awesome. Thank you."

"Are you going to wear a pretty dress like a princess?" Gracie asked. Her eyes were filled with excitement as she gazed across the table at Kendall.

Kendall laughed. "Yes, I guess I am."

Jonah eyed his buzzing phone. "Hey, Nate, do you mind looking after Gracie for a minute? Hannah's checking in."

"Sure, go ahead, man."

"Thanks."

Once Jonah was out of earshot, Nathan took advantage of his absence. He knew he shouldn't pry, but it was nagging at him.

"Hey, Gracie, where's your dad?" he asked. Kendall shot him a scolding look.

Gracie didn't stop coloring, nor did she miss a beat. "He's not here."

"Well, where is he?" Nathan pressed further.

"Mommy said he moved away before I was born," she answered casually, sipping her lemonade.

"Do you know his name?"

"Nope." She shrugged, choosing a different crayon and returning to her masterpiece.

Kendall nudged Nathan. "Stop it," she whispered. "What are you doing?"

Nathan leaned in close to Kendall. "I think Jonah's her father."

"Well, that was nice," Kendall said, adjusting the heat in the Lexus. "I think your brother is really nice."

Nathan pulled onto the highway. "Yeah, Jonah's a good guy. Too bad he's going through so much right now.

More than he even knows yet."

"Do you really think Gracie is his daughter?" she asked. "I mean, how could he not know something like that?"

Nathan sighed. "He's been gone a long time. I don't know, maybe Hannah just never told him."

"And even now? How could she let him be around his own kid and not say anything?"

He shrugged. "How do you just come out and tell somebody something like that? Especially if you thought you'd never see them again."

"That's true," Kendall agreed. "That would be really hard."

The couple drove down the dark highway in silence for a few moments, reflecting on the night and pondering Jonah's potential predicament.

"Ooh, you know what we haven't had in a long time?" Kendall said suddenly.

"What's that?" Nathan smirked at her cuteness.

"Cheesecake from Murphy's."

He grinned. "You're right, we haven't. It's been a while since we've been up this way."

"Should we stop then? Please? Can we?" Kendall pleaded, flirtatiously running her hand over Nathan's shoulder.

"You know what's funny? Hannah works at Murphy's."

"How serendipitous," Kendall joked. "It's meant to be. Let's go."

Ten minutes later, Nathan and Kendall sauntered into Murphy's, the quaint but locally loved diner.

Hannah turned her attention to the door and was shocked to see Jonah's brother.

"Hi, Nathan," she said, grabbing two menus from the

hostess station. "How was your night with Jonah? I hope Gracie behaved herself. I'm so sorry I imposed on your plans."

"Oh, no, don't worry about it. She was perfect. It was a good night," Nathan assured her, noticing how nervous she seemed.

She seated them at a nearby booth.

"You must be Kendall." Hannah smiled, handing her a menu. "I'm Hannah. Jonah's...friend. Gracie's mom."

Kendall nodded with a friendly grin. "Jonah talked a lot about you tonight."

Hannah blushed. "Uh oh."

"Don't worry," Kendall added. "Everything he said was adorable."

Hannah stifled her giddiness. "Do you know what you'll be having, or do you need a minute?"

"We'll both have the cheesecake," Nathan replied, handing their menus over.

"Sure thing. I'll be right back."

"She's so pretty," Kendall said quietly once Hannah had hurried away. "No wonder Jonah is crazy about her."

"Well, yeah. But she's more than that. I've known her since she was, like, thirteen. She's always been a sweet girl," Nathan remarked. "My brother chose a good person to be involved with for the rest of his life."

Kendall swatted at his arm. "Hey, be nice. First of all, you don't even know if it's true, and secondly, it doesn't have to be a bad situation. Maybe it'll work out."

They fell silent when Hannah approached their table with two very appetizing, generous pieces of cheesecake.

"Can I get you anything else?" she asked.

Nathan smiled. "Coffee sounds good. Thank you, Hannah."

The couple shared in some small talk here and there,

avoiding the topic of Jonah, while they enjoyed their dessert. As Kendall shoveled the last bite into her mouth, her cell phone rang.

"Oh, it's the wedding coordinator," she said, sliding out of the booth.

"At nine at night?"

"I'm sorry, Nate. Meet you in the car?" Kendall excused herself, answering the call as she exited the diner.

Nathan sighed, picking up the check and leaving the table. He approached Hannah at the counter, unable to resist any longer.

"Hey, can I talk to you? It'll only take a minute."

"Sure, I'm off now. You were my last table," she replied, both anxious and curious as she rounded the counter to sit beside him.

Nathan cleared his throat, unsure of where to begin. He decided it would be easier to be straightforward with her.

"Listen, Hannah…I know Jonah is Gracie's father."

Hannah's face went white. "Does Jonah know?" she fretted in a quiet voice, her eyes brimming.

Nathan shook his head. "I can see him starting to question some things, but he's too confused and distracted to really figure it out right now."

Hannah let out a shaky breath as she rubbed her temples. "Okay…good."

"How long are you going to make him wait, Hannah?"

Her fearful eyes met his. "I don't know what he's going to do."

Nathan's expression turned sympathetic. "He's crazy about that little girl, Hannah. I can see it. I don't think it'll go as horribly as you think it will. But the longer you wait, the more damage you may cause."

Hannah hung her head, tears spilling down her

cheeks. "I know he deserves the truth. I'm just so scared. I finally have him back, and I can't lose him again. I really want us to be a family."

Nathan put a consoling hand on her shoulder. "I do too. It'll all work out, okay? Just talk to him."

He stood and handed her the check along with a few bills. Wiping her eyes, she thanked him. After he'd gone, Hannah leafed through the money, shocked to see that Nathan had left her a fifty-dollar tip.

Hannah cried harder as they reached the tram that would take her to the airport terminal. This was as far as Jonah could go. This was where they had to say good-bye.

"Hey, hey...shh." He tried to comfort her, holding her face in his hands. He gently wiped her cheeks with his thumbs. "Please don't cry."

"I can't leave you," Hannah said through her tears. "Four days just wasn't long enough."

Jonah drew her to him, wrapping his arms around her slender frame. "I know. Nothing could be long enough," he said, kissing the top of her head.

Hannah looked up at him with weary eyes, still clutching him tightly. "I don't want to go."

"Listen to me, Hannah. I don't know exactly when, but I will marry you someday. And then we'll have no more good-byes. Just good nights. I promise."

She tried to smile, but her heart ached so badly. Her visit with Jonah had stitched them together more tightly than ever before. She could hardly breathe at the thought of being without him.

"I love you," Jonah said, leaning down and pressing his lips against hers.

"*I love you too,*" Hannah answered back once he'd released her.

Glancing at his watch, he frowned. "*You better take this next tram before you miss your flight.*"

"*If I miss my flight, I can stay longer,*" she half-joked.

Jonah chuckled, despite his sadness. "*I wish you could. You have no idea.*"

He held her close to him once more, closing his eyes as he breathed her in. He didn't want to think about watching her walk away. He didn't want to think about the weeks, maybe even months, that would pass without her. Jonah swallowed the lump in his throat as the tram doors opened.

"*All right, Hannah...It's time.*"

She nodded, letting Jonah lead her by the hand toward the tram. Hannah pulled him in for one more desperate kiss before she forced herself to let go of his hand and board the tram.

A few moments later, the doors slid closed. Through the window, Hannah mouthed "*I love you*" and blew him a kiss. Jonah held up his hand as if to catch the kiss and placed his clenched fist against his heart. "*I love you too,*" he mouthed back, forcing a teary-eyed smile. Then the tram moved onward, taking them away from each other for much longer than either of them knew was possible.

SIX

Jonah set his laptop aside, knowing full well that Gracie had fallen asleep long before the movie ended. At her request, he'd purchased and downloaded *Tangled* for them to watch together. He would be lying if he said he didn't enjoy it.

Jonah sat up carefully so as not to wake Gracie. He pulled the blanket over her, smiling at her sweetness. Already, he adored her. She was smart, funny, and well-mannered, and she hadn't ceased to amaze him. Hannah was doing a remarkable job raising her alone.

Jealousy gnawed at Jonah as he forced away thoughts of Gracie's father. Instead, he entertained thoughts of a future with Hannah and Gracie. He ached for it.

A soft knock halted Jonah's musing. He eased the door open, immediately troubled when he saw Hannah. She was crying, almost hysterically.

"What's wrong? What happened?"

"I need to talk to you," she stammered, fear in her voice.

Jonah turned the deadbolt on the open door to keep it from closing completely as he stepped outside. "You're scaring the hell out of me, what happened?" he asked, drawing close to her.

Hannah shook her head. "Nothing happened. I need

to tell you what I've been keeping from you."

His stomach dropped with an unshakable dread. He'd been eager for her to let him in, but now, he was afraid.

"All right."

Hannah took a deep breath, her body shaking. "Can you just hold me for a minute first? Because after I tell you this, I'm afraid you'll never want to again. You're going to hate me."

Jonah pulled her in, holding her tightly against him. "Hannah," he began tenderly, stroking her hair. "It's just me. Whatever it is, you can tell me."

She ran her hands up and down his back, petrified it would be the last time she could touch him. As her tears stained his shirt, she prayed for the strength to open her mouth. This was it, the moment she'd played repeatedly in her mind for the past five years. With the sound of Jonah's heartbeat drumming beneath her ear, Hannah squeezed her eyes closed and braced herself.

"It's you, Jonah," Hannah whispered, still clinging to him.

"What's me?"

"Gracie is your daughter." She felt Jonah's breath catch in his throat, his entire body tensing.

"What...?" he said in a small voice, slowly backing away from her. His eyes were wide with disbelief as he searched her face for answers.

"I'm sorry, Jonah," Hannah cried, her knees weak.

He cast his eyes to the ground, fighting to process the information while a million questions screamed through his head. "Why didn't you tell me you were pregnant? I would've come back." His blue eyes welled up.

"Things were so bad with your dad. I didn't want to make it worse for you."

"That should have been *my* decision," Jonah said through tears and clenched teeth.

"I know. I'm so sorry." The misery was apparent on her face.

He paced back and forth, his quick, stressed breaths forming dissipating clouds of vapor in the cold air. He found himself at a crossroads of joy and devastation. Anger seared through him as profound loss consumed him.

Jonah realized it wasn't just her he was angry with but Jacob. He was the reason Jonah had been robbed of his baby girl and of the woman he loved, but that still didn't make it any easier to accept.

Despite his internal struggle, Jonah ached at the sight of Hannah's grief. Her beautiful eyes, so pleading and desperate, brimmed with pain and remorse. Part of him craved consoling her, but the need was far overshadowed by the deep-seated notion of betrayal.

Finally, Jonah came undone under the impossible heaviness of it all. Overwhelmed by confusion and unfathomable hurt, he turned his back to Hannah, sobbing into his hands. He had never faced anything so devastating...and yet, nothing more glorious.

"If it helps at all, I have suffered with this every single day. I don't know how to tell you how sorry I am," Hannah said, shivering in the night air.

After regaining his composure, Jonah slowly turned back and stared at her in the dim lighting. "And to think, I've felt so guilty for leaving you here...when you're the one who made sure we stayed apart."

"Jonah..." She grew even more upset.

"No, I get it. My dad was an asshole. He probably would've killed me. And you knew that, so you did this without me. But it must have *really* screwed up your plans when he went and died and I had to come back, right?"

Hannah wiped the tears from her face, feeling defensive. "I came to the funeral, didn't I? I could've hid from you, but I didn't! I *missed* you. And I wanted to fix this somehow. I was just trying to find the right time."

Jonah laughed sarcastically. "The right time would've been when you took the pregnancy test." His coldness stung her.

"You know what, Jonah? I'm sorry you don't like how I tried to protect you, but I am *still* making sacrifices for the decision I made as a scared teenager. I can't change any of that. All I can do now is pray you'll somehow forgive me. But more than that, I hope you'll be a part of Gracie's life. I've wanted that for so long."

Jonah looked away, regretting his harsh words, no matter how justified they were. Whatever wrong Hannah had done, she'd done for him, with the purest of intentions. Still, he hated her sacrifice and what it had done to him.

"What are you thinking?" Hannah asked cautiously.

Jonah put his hands on his hips and tilted his head back, staring into the vast darkness of the sky. "I feel so stupid," he muttered.

"Why do you feel stupid?"

"I spent so much time with her...You had me babysit my *own* child, and I couldn't even see she was mine. You allowed me to think she was someone else's. God, Hannah, do you know how much that kills me? I feel like a fool."

She chewed her lower lip, fighting fresh tears. "You're not a fool, Jonah, and I'm sorry I let you think there was someone else. It was wrong. I never wanted to hurt you."

Jonah slid his hands into his hair and clenched his fists. "Four years...I haven't been here for her. She doesn't even know who I am." He dropped his arms to his sides, his shoulders slumping. "I wish you had told me. You should've told me...I can't believe you waited so long."

"I was going to tell you sooner," Hannah said. "That night after Jacob's funeral, I didn't come to check up on you. I was coming to tell you *everything*. But when I got there, you were a mess. I couldn't do that to you. Not then."

Jonah's lip trembled as he tried to hold back his emotions. "You don't have to protect me so much, you know. You didn't have to let Jacob ruin us."

Hannah raised her eyebrows. "Have you forgotten what it was like before you left? Do you remember how unbearable he became after the accident? I watched you fall apart, Jonah. It's like you let him turn off the light inside you."

"Stop," he said, his breaths quickening with his escalating distress.

"I found a way to save you from him," she said. "Without me, you would never have to come back here and face him. And you could move on with your life and be happy."

Jonah gawked at her, his mouth hanging open. "How did you think I could ever be happy without you?" He wiped at his wet cheeks. "Hannah, I would've done *anything* for you...and for our baby."

"I know you would have. That's why I did what I did."

He sighed heavily, his chest aching. "Hannah. I'm sorry, but I need you to go. I just...need some time alone right now."

Hannah nodded, trying not to break down again. "I understand. I'll just get Gracie and go."

She brushed past him, quietly pushing open the door to his room. She stood next to the bed, gazing fondly at her daughter. Gracie was still peacefully asleep, curled up beneath the covers.

Jonah appeared behind Hannah, his tears flowing silently. He finally saw himself in Gracie's small face. How had he been so oblivious?

"Here, I got her," he offered, lifting his little girl in his arms.

Gracie cuddled against his chest as he carried her toward the door. He felt an undeniable twinge of joy flooding the cracks of his broken heart. Hannah picked up Gracie's seat and led the way to her car. She opened the door and anchored the car seat inside. When she turned back, she saw Jonah swaying gently, his eyes closed, cradling Gracie. Though still wounded from her immense lack of resolve, Hannah finally felt whole. She decided it didn't matter if he ever forgave her. All she wanted was what she saw before her at that moment...Jonah loving their little girl.

He opened his eyes to see Hannah watching him, and he reluctantly bent into the car to carefully place Gracie in her seat. She stirred, and her eyelids fluttered in the bright light of the car.

"Thank you for watching my favorite movie with me," she mumbled, closing her eyes again.

He smiled, buckling her in securely. "Oh, you're welcome, Gracie. I loved it."

She rested her head against the seat. "I love you, Jonah."

He choked back a sob. "I love you too, baby."

As soon as Jonah closed the car door, Hannah threw her arms around him. He stood there rigidly at first, motionless with shock, before reciprocating.

"I'm sorry. I'm sorry..." she whispered over and over.

"I know, Hannah."

She composed herself and pulled away. "I brought you something." Hannah opened the door and retrieved something from the passenger seat. "I ran home and grabbed it on my way here. In case it would help," she added, handing it to him.

Jonah looked down at the thick album she'd placed in his hands. "Okay," he said plainly, tucking it under his arm.

Hannah fought to sound casual. "All right, well...Thanks for watching her tonight. I'll...see you later, I guess."

She got into the car and closed the door. After she started the engine, Jonah motioned for her to roll her window down. He leaned over and rested his free arm on the door, his face close to hers.

"Listen," he began, looking intently into her eyes. "You said I would hate you, but I don't. I couldn't let you leave without knowing that."

Hannah let out a shaky breath. "Okay," she managed, grasping tightly to even the smallest shred of hope Jonah had to offer her.

Jonah barely made it into his room before he broke down again. He pushed the door closed and fell back against it, sliding down to the floor and pulling his knees in to his chest. Jonah wiped his eyes and looked over at the worn album that lay on the floor beside him. Taking it in his hands, he stood weakly to his feet and dragged himself to the bed to sit down.

The first thing he saw when he opened the scrapbook were some old photographs of Hannah and himself together. It saddened him to see the blissful, naïve smiles on their young faces.

A few pages in was a sonogram photo with "Baby at eight weeks, due September 17th" written neatly beneath it in Hannah's familiar handwriting. Jonah ran his finger over the fuzzy image, tracing the bean-shaped baby. Beneath that was a second ultrasound image, with the baby much bigger this time. Her visible precious profile and tiny fingers amazed him. That one read "Twenty weeks. It's a girl!" He imagined being there with Hannah during the ultrasound. He pictured holding her hand, excitedly watching the screen and shedding joyful tears together over the gender reveal. He turned the page.

Next was a series of photos of Hannah, chronicling the growth of her belly each week. Jonah was awe-stricken, knowing it was *his* child that swelled her stomach. She was so radiant and beautiful, he noted with tears in his eyes. He was curious why the photos stopped at twenty-nine weeks, but he continued on.

Affixed to the following page was the tiniest set of footprints Jonah had ever seen. He read the information written on the crib card: "Grace Avery Weston. July 3, 2009. 12:37 p.m. Two pounds, ten ounces. Fourteen inches long."

She gave her my name, he thought happily. Then Jonah furrowed his brow, noticing how unusually low the birth weight was. He looked again at her birthdate, then flipped back to the due date on the ultrasound page.

"Oh my gosh," Jonah said out loud, realizing Gracie had been eleven weeks premature. It made sense now why she was so petite.

What had Hannah gone through? He continued paging through the scrapbook, poring over countless photographs of a miniature baby covered in wires and tubes in an incubator. Photos of Hannah holding a shockingly small Gracie against her chest with a content smile on her face. Photos with captions like, "Phototherapy," "Kangaroo care," "Learning to eat by mouth," "Off of oxygen!," "Finally up to three pounds!," "Finally allowed to get dressed"…

How had Hannah endured that on her own? Tears

streamed down Jonah's face as he thought of Gracie so delicate and small, born much too soon. He imagined how scared Hannah must have been. It broke his heart that he hadn't been there to comfort her, that he hadn't been able to share in those early fragile days with both of them.

The next several pages were covered in pictures of Gracie getting bigger and healthier. Jonah gathered that Gracie had been in the NICU for seven weeks, weighing just five pounds when she was finally discharged. He imagined driving her home, Hannah sitting in the backseat with her. He would've driven so cautiously. It would have been amazing to bring her home.

Jonah sighed sadly, flipping the album closed. He couldn't look at it anymore. As he slid it away, he noticed something sticking out. Turning to the last page, he found a small stack of envelopes tucked into the back binding. All three were sealed and addressed to him. He carefully tore open the first one and pulled out the letter, which had been folded around a copy of the first ultrasound. He read it:

February 22, 2009

Dear Jonah,

I'm assuming you've already seen the enclosed photo. I wasn't going to tell you because I knew it would cause so many more issues between you and your dad, but I just couldn't keep it from you any longer. This is why I have been so awful at keeping in touch. I'm so sorry about that, and I'm sorry this is how you're finding out about our baby. I've wanted to call you a million times, but I was so scared. This just seemed a little bit easier. I hope you're not mad. I know neither of us were expecting this, but I would love more than anything for us to be a family. Either way, please know that I love you and I miss you and I'm sorry. Hope to

hear from you soon.
Hannah

The other two letters were relatively the same, but at later points in her pregnancy. He wished she had sent him that first letter. How different would things be now? He knew without a doubt he would have come straight back to this town and taken care of her. If he was being honest with himself, he would have married her.

Having experienced more emotions than he could bear, Jonah collapsed against the pillows and closed his eyes. He was so overwrought, he felt his heart might explode. This new reality was difficult to absorb, but he did it anyway. He accepted it.

Jonah had loved Gracie so easily, without knowing who she really was to him. There was no question that he desired to be in her life as her father. To him, there was no other option. He marveled at the thought of being someone's father.

As Jonah lay there in that hotel room, staring up at the ceiling, tears rolling across his throbbing temples, he vowed he would never be the father Jacob was to him. He would never allow Gracie to feel worthless like he had. He would always make sure she knew she was loved. He wanted to be everything he never had. He felt empowered by the idea, a new purpose surging through him.

Jonah practically jumped to his feet, suddenly consumed by an insatiable need to see Hannah and their daughter. It had only been an hour since Hannah had left, but something had changed inside him. He couldn't quite explain it. All he knew was that they'd wasted enough time already.

When her weeping had relented, Hannah managed to stifle her tormenting thoughts long enough to drift off. But her eyes shot open when she heard a knock at the front door. She nervously slipped out of her room and down the hall to the front window in the kitchen. Parting the curtains slightly, Hannah anxiously peered out at the driveway. Her breath nearly caught in her throat when she saw the Mercedes. Jonah was the very last person she'd expected. Both hopeful and petrified, Hannah opened the door.

Jonah stood on the stoop, his blue eyes alive with whatever was racing through his mind. "I'm sorry I didn't call first," he said. "Can I come in?"

Hannah wanted to bawl at the sight of him, but she stepped aside with a nod. "You okay?" she asked, leading him to the living room. She sat down at the end of the leather couch, tucking her legs beneath her.

"I think so." He half smiled, settling into the old armchair across from her. "Is Gracie asleep?"

"Yes. It's almost one in the morning," Hannah answered.

Jonah glanced at the clock on the wall and bit his lower lip. "I'm sorry, I just *had* to come here. I looked at the album. I read your letters, Hannah."

She held her breath. "And...?"

"I can't believe you went through all of that by yourself." His eyes welled up. "Hannah...You are amazing," he whispered.

A tear rolled down her cheek. She had not expected that.

"No, I'm not."

"Yes. You are," Jonah insisted as he came to sit beside her. "I wish I'd been there with you."

Hannah looked away. "I'm sorry I took that away from you."

He placed his hand on her face, gently pulling her to look at him. "I want you to know I *would've* been there…and I want to be here now."

She stared at him in disbelief, whimpering. "But you were so angry with me. How can you say this now?"

Jonah sighed. "At first, yeah, I was pretty upset. If you want me to be completely honest, just looking at you hurt. But I'm sorry for that and for all the terrible things I said. I *know* you, Hannah, and I know you were only doing what you thought was best for me. Being angry won't change anything; it'll only waste more time. I can't lose you again. And I can't lose Gracie."

Hannah pulled her long sleeves over hands and dried her cheeks. "I know we still have a lot to deal with, but I really want to make this work."

"I do too," he said.

She let out a relieved chuckle. "You know, I was actually worried that I might never see you again."

Jonah shook his head, his eyes softening. "That's not possible. I think I've loved you so long, I don't know how not to."

Jonah was awakened by the sound of the front door creaking open early the next morning. Hannah had insisted he sleep on the couch instead of driving back to the hotel in the middle of the night.

"Hello, Jonah. Why am I not surprised that you're here?" Caroline chuckled, setting her bag on the foyer table.

He sat up and shrugged sheepishly. "Good morning, Mrs. Morgan."

She took a seat across from him. "So you know now, huh? Hannah texted me last night."

Jonah nodded. "Yeah…"

"Everything okay? I know it's a lot to take in."

He ran a hand through his messy hair. "Well, it was pretty bad at first, but, long story short, we talked *a lot*…and I think we'll be okay."

Caroline smiled. "I'm happy to hear that. I always liked you, Jonah. I didn't want to help Hannah keep Gracie from you. I felt you should have known. But it was so important to her that she protect you. She changed her mind about a million times after that, but there never seemed to be a right time to come clean. I can't even tell you how many nights I spent sitting with her while she cried her eyes out over it. It was not easy for her in the slightest. I just thought you should know that…and I hope you'll be able to work past it. She really does love you. She always has. Sometimes I think a little *too* much."

Jonah blushed. "That's good to know."

"So, listen." Caroline brightened up. "This is the second time you've paid for a hotel room you didn't sleep in. How about you stop wasting your money and just stay here with us?"

After leaving Hannah a note, Jonah slipped quietly out of the Morgans' home and headed back to the hotel, where he took a quick shower and packed up his things. He found himself stuffing the slip of paper with Elliot's information on it into his pocket. He put his bags in the car, then made his way to the hotel office to check out.

"Good morning, sir. How can I help you?" the middle-aged man at the counter greeted him.

"I'm just checking out. Room 121," Jonah replied with a thin smile, setting his key card on the counter.

"Sure thing." The receptionist consulted his computer, typing away on the keyboard. "I'll just need a signature, and then you're all set." He printed off a page and placed it on the counter in front of Jonah.

Jonah glanced over the bill, his mother's name catching his eye. The last four digits of the credit card used to pay for the room did not belong to him.

The receptionist peered over. "Is something wrong, sir?"

Jonah sighed. "No, I'm fine. Thank you." He signed "S. Weston" on the line.

The receptionist handed him a receipt, smiling cordially. "Thank you for staying with us, Mr. Weston. Have a nice day."

Scarlett was shocked to see her son standing before her when she answered the front door. Though it wasn't like her, she threw her arms around him.

"Jonah, I'm so glad you're here."

He returned her embrace. "I wanted to thank you for paying my bill at the hotel. You didn't have to do that, Mom."

She pulled away and looked up at him. "I know. But I wanted to. Would you like to come in?"

"Sure." Jonah followed his mother inside to the kitchen where they sat down at the small, round table.

"I really am sorry, Jonah," Scarlett said after a few moments of quiet.

He repositioned himself in his chair. "I know, Mom. I'm not here to talk about that right now. There's something I need to tell you."

Scarlett perked up with curiosity. "What is it?"

Jonah ran a hand through his hair, unsure of where to begin. "Did you know that Hannah had a baby?"

Scarlett's eyes widened. "She did? When? I mean, I haven't really seen her around since you moved away, but I would think I would've heard about that."

He shook his head. "Hannah kept her a secret."

Scarlett narrowed her eyes. "Well, why?"

"Because she's mine."

Jonah's mother stared blankly at him. "*Your* baby?"

He smiled. "Well, she's four now, but yes."

Tears formed in Scarlett's eyes. "What's her name?"

"Gracie."

"I'm a grandma," she said with emotional realization.

"Yes, you are," Jonah replied. "You all right, Mom?"

She nodded, laughing at herself. "I just can't believe it. Some good news for once! How come you're just now telling me?"

Jonah chuckled. "Well, *I* just found out last night."

Scarlett was confused. "What?"

"Yeah, it's a long story."

She got lost in her thoughts for a moment. "You and your father have a lot in common now."

"How so?"

"Just yesterday, you both found out you had a child," Scarlett said.

A chill ran through Jonah's body. "I didn't even realize..."

"Maybe you should rethink your decision to contact him," she said encouragingly. "I know you're grateful for the chance to know Gracie. I'm sure Elliot would love to have the same with you."

Jonah couldn't believe he hadn't realized the parallels

before. Though under two different circumstances, Hannah and his mother had kept their secrets to protect the people they loved. Both Jonah and Elliot had gone about their lives unaware of the children who belonged to them. Jonah was Elliot's son, just as Gracie was Jonah's daughter. Jonah could now step back with grace and see this outrageous situation from Elliot's point of view. Jonah was dismayed to have missed four years of Gracie's life, but Elliot had missed twenty-three years of his. How must that feel? Elliot never chose to be absent, just as Jonah hadn't. Suddenly, meeting Elliot didn't seem so out of the question.

SEVEN

Hannah waited eagerly for Jonah's arrival following their brief phone conversation. She felt like a teenager again, peeking out the front window from time to time to see if he had pulled up in the driveway. She was aware of the myriad of emotions waiting to be sorted through, but she found herself optimistic. The worst was over. Jonah finally knew her secret, and it hadn't sent him running.

When Hannah swung the front door open, Jonah was standing before her with his bags. Her grin was difficult to stifle.

"Hey," she said, motioning him inside.

Jonah set his bags down. "It's not weird that I'm staying here, right? Not too much too soon?"

She shook her head. "No, not at all. I was more worried that *you* would think that."

Before Jonah could respond, his cell phone went off. He retrieved it from his pocket and frowned at the illuminated screen.

"I've got to take this." He reluctantly excused himself, stepping back out to the front porch. "Hello?" he answered his boss's call.

"Jonah, hey. It's David Tucker."

"Hey, David, how's it going?"

"It's been better. Listen, Jonah, I know you're dealing with a lot right now and I hate to bother you, but when are you planning to get back?"

Jonah sighed. "To be honest, David, I'm not so sure. You got my e-mail, right?"

"I did," David replied. "And I know it's not very long, but our bereavement policy is five days. I would allow you a longer unpaid leave if I could, but we just landed a huge account and we're on a serious deadline. On top of that, Mike quit yesterday, so we need you back as soon as you can get here."

Jonah paused for a moment. "David...I'm sorry, but I can't leave now. I don't know what to tell you."

David let out a long, heavy breath. "Please don't make me give you an ultimatum, Jonah."

"Fine. You don't have to. I quit."

Jonah pocketed his phone and walked back into the house, finding Hannah in the kitchen. A plethora of thoughts and future plans were running through his head as excitement rose up inside him.

"Everything okay?" Hannah asked, leaning against the counter.

Jonah chuckled. "I just quit my job."

"What? Why?"

"No, it's okay. I don't want to go back. I can't. I want to be here with Gracie...and with you."

Hannah's heart fluttered. "So you're really going to stay?"

Jonah took a couple of steps closer, his eyes fixed on hers. "Of course I am. I don't know exactly what happens next, I just know that I want this." He took her hand. "What do *you* want, Hannah?"

She felt like she might lose herself. "You," she

whispered, almost afraid to be so vulnerable to him.

Jonah's serious expression brightened with a smile and he tilted his forehead against hers. "That's what I was hoping you'd say."

Hannah skeptically bit her lower lip. "How can you be so quick to jump into this, Jonah? You said it yourself—just last night you could barely look at me."

He grimaced. "I know it didn't happen the way I wanted it to, but I have *always* wanted this with you. Nothing can change that."

"It's just hard to believe this is happening. I always wished for it, but I didn't think it was possible for us to be together...the three of us," Hannah said.

"All you had to do was talk to me. You don't have to be afraid of me, Hannah." Jonah tenderly brushed a stray lock of hair out of her face.

Hannah nodded. "I know that now." She slid her arms around him, reveling in their closeness. "We still have to tell Gracie."

Jonah wrapped Hannah in his embrace, loving the familiar yet exciting feel of her against him. "I guess *that's* what happens next."

After picking up three hot chocolates, Jonah drove into Oak Lake Park, accompanied by Hannah and Gracie. The three of them traipsed down the path to the lake and found a bench to sit down.

Gracie blew into the hole in the plastic lid of her hot chocolate. "It's going to be too hot forever," she concluded with a frown.

Jonah chuckled, taking the small cup from her. "Here, I'll help you," he said, removing the lid. The steam danced wildly in the cold breeze. "It'll cool down in a couple minutes."

Hannah smiled, watching Jonah interact with their daughter. He was so natural with her.

When Jonah handed the cup back to Gracie, she sipped it cautiously.

"Much better," she remarked, traces of chocolate on her heart-shaped lips.

"So, Gracie, tell me about last night with Jonah. Did you have a good time?" Hannah asked, handing her a napkin.

Gracie grinned and nodded. "Jonah took me out for dinner, and we saw his brother. His fiancée gets to be a princess at her wedding! Then we went to Jonah's hotel. It's not his house. Hotels are for people that visit. And Jonah watched a movie with me. He laughed, so I know he liked it. And then I fell asleep." Gracie took another sip of her hot chocolate.

"Wow, that sounds like a fun night," Hannah said, exchanging glances with Jonah. "You really like Jonah, don't you, Gracie?"

She nodded emphatically. "I *love* Jonah. Don't you love him, Mommy?"

"Yes, I do," Hannah replied, gazing fondly at him.

Jonah took Gracie's cup and set it down on the bench beside his. "Hey, Gracie, let's go for a walk."

"Okay." She eagerly slid to the ground and reached for his hand.

Hannah followed as they strolled along the water's edge. Gracie kicked rocks, stomped on crunchy leaves, tossed stones into the water, and jumped over sticks, but she never once let go of Jonah's hand. With an encouraging nod from Hannah, Jonah stopped and knelt before Gracie.

"Can I tell you something?" he asked, his eyes level

with hers.

"Uh huh." Gracie placed her cold little hands on Jonah's face, feeling the stubble on his cheeks, and she giggled.

"Gracie, listen." Jonah smiled, unsure of how to start. "You know how everyone has a mom *and* a dad?"

"I don't have a dad," Gracie chimed in. "He moved far away."

Jonah pressed his lips together as tears filled his eyes. "Gracie, you *do* have a dad. He didn't know about you. That's why he stayed away."

She narrowed her small eyebrows. "How do you know?"

Taking a deep breath, Jonah put a hand on her shoulder. He couldn't force the words out, fearing the floodgates would crumble and he'd come undone. Hannah sensed his struggle and knelt beside him.

"Honey," she began lovingly, smoothing her daughter's breeze-blown curls. "*Jonah* is your dad."

Gracie stared at him with wide eyes, her mouth dropping open to draw in a small gasp. She reached out her hand to wipe a tear from his cheek, and Jonah opened his arms to her, a genuine smile squinting his teary eyes. She immediately threw her arms around his neck, nearly knocking him backward. Jonah stood, wrapping his daughter in his embrace as he wept. She didn't loosen her grip.

"Can I call you Daddy?" she asked, pulling back to look at him.

Jonah nodded, his heart swelling with joy. "Yes. I would love that."

Gracie grinned at him. "I love you, Daddy."

Once again, she took his face in her little hands. Then she kissed him on the nose and laughed.

Jonah parked in Hannah's driveway, next to an unfamiliar black Volvo sedan. Before he could ask Hannah who it belonged to, she sighed.

"My dad is here," she said, getting out of the car.

Jonah grew nervous. "Why is that bad? I thought you and your dad were cool."

Hannah opened the back door and helped Gracie out of her car seat. Gracie ran around the back of the car to Jonah. He hoisted her up and carried her toward the house.

"We're fine. I'm just not sure if he's fond of *you*."

"Of *me*? Why not? He liked me before."

Hannah snickered. "Yeah. Before. He never agreed with my decision to keep you out of things. He always said I let you get away with it. He was angry with my mom for being too easy on me. I guess he thought I should've had some sort of punishment or something. And he and my mom fought so much after that. I swear I'm the reason they split up. They couldn't see eye to eye and my dad just couldn't handle not being able to control the situation."

Jonah swallowed. "And I'm supposed to just walk into your house right now?"

"It's going to be okay. He might be a little intimidating because he's got almost five years of unresolved feelings pent up inside him. But we'll just face it. I'm right here with you." Hannah unlocked the front door and pushed it open.

Jonah followed her into the house, his stomach twisting as he clutched Gracie. She was quiet, grasping onto him as if she could sense his tension.

It wasn't long before Jonah made eye contact with Stephen Morgan, who sat at the kitchen table across from Caroline. Jonah saw Stephen's body stiffen as he stood. He'd put on a little weight and his auburn hair had thinned a bit over the years since Jonah had been away.

"Jonah," Stephen said, as if he'd been expecting him. "It's about time."

"Stephen," Caroline scolded him.

"No," he said, putting his hand up to silence her. "I have some things I want to say to this boy." He crossed the kitchen and approached Jonah, glancing over him as if critiquing him. "So *now* you're going to be here? After all these years, you're ready to be her father?"

Jonah felt the anger coursing through him but willed himself to stay calm. "Sir, you know just as well as I do that I was not aware of any of this."

Stephen dismissed Jonah's statement with a wave of his hand. "How do I know you won't leave my daughter again? How do I know you can even take care of her? Can you take care of a child?"

Gracie snuggled against Jonah's chest, and he held her tighter.

"I am not going anywhere. And if I'd been given the choice back then, I would've been here through all of it. But I'm here *now*, and I'll do whatever I have to, to take care of my family."

Stephen put his hands on his hips and nodded. "Okay. *That* is exactly what I wanted from you." He patted Jonah roughly on the back.

Jonah drew in a deep breath and slowly exhaled, trying to shake his aggravation. He could feel Gracie softly rubbing his shoulder to console him, and the anger dissipated.

"Really, Stephen? You just want to give the poor guy a heart attack? Geez," Caroline said disapprovingly.

Stephen snickered. "Hey, he should understand that a father has to look out for his daughter. He has one."

Hannah crossed her arms. "You know, you could just *talk* to him, Dad. Like a normal person?"

She stalked out of the kitchen, Jonah eagerly following suit. He set Gracie down in her room to play and continued down the hall into Hannah's room, closing the door behind him.

"What the hell was that?" Jonah fumed in a hushed voice, pointing toward the kitchen.

"I told you he would be intimidating."

"Intimidating? He was a little ridiculous, don't you think? And you just let him talk to me like that?"

Hannah chuckled. "Jonah. He was just testing you. Like a 'what are your intentions with my daughter' kind of thing."

Jonah shook his head. "No. I felt like I was being blamed for what *you* did."

Hannah raised her eyebrows, gawking at him. *"Wow.* And I guess I just got pregnant all by myself."

Jonah rolled his eyes. "That's not even what I meant. You have to understand that the decision you made affects a lot of things *now*, and not in a good way."

Her eyes welled with emotion. "And *you* have to understand that everything I did was for you. I don't know how many times I can tell you that, but I thought I was saving you from things that were much worse. I was willing to sacrifice everything so you could make something of yourself. I dropped out of community college. I blew off all our friends so they wouldn't find out and go tell you. I've only had two days off in the last year, one of them being for your father's funeral. I have already paid for making the wrong decision. I don't need you to make me pay for it too."

Jonah looked away, guilt devouring him. "Hannah, I'm sorry. I guess I'm not as okay with everything as I thought. This isn't easy; I need you to be patient with me."

"I don't want to fight with you, Jonah." Hannah broke

down. "I'm so sorry. I never wanted to give you up."

Jonah hated seeing Hannah upset. He approached her and drew her close, letting her cry against him.

"We've both made decisions that turned out badly," Jonah said. "Maybe if I never left...maybe it would be different. But I'd never want anything other than what we have right now—you, me, and Gracie. Does it really matter how we got here? Dwelling on the past will only ruin *this*. And what good does that do when we can't change any of it?"

Hannah dried her eyes. "You're right. Can we just start over?"

Jonah gently ran the backs of his fingers down her cheek, any shred of resentment melting away. "That's exactly what I want," he said, taking her face in his hands. He leaned down and kissed her softly on the forehead.

Jonah stepped inside his brother's extravagant home, taking in his surroundings. Despite the moving boxes stacked in various areas, it was rather exquisite.

"Sorry about the mess," Nathan said. "I'm still in the middle of packing."

Jonah followed his brother into the kitchen.

"Want a beer?" Nathan asked, popping the cap off his own.

Jonah scrunched his face. "I better not, man."

"True." Nathan grinned, setting a can of soda on the counter in front of him.

They relocated to the leather couches in the living room.

"So, what have I missed of the drama that is your life since we last saw each other?" Nathan joked.

"You've missed a lot actually." Jonah chuckled

uneasily. "Hannah's daughter, Gracie? Yeah. She's mine."

Nathan took a swig of his beer. "Yup, I saw that one coming. Damn, Jonah, she looks just like you."

Jonah snickered. "And apparently, I'm also a moron."

"You just weren't expecting it, that's all. So are you relieved? Surprised? Mad?"

Jonah shrugged. "Yeah, I guess I am relieved. For a little while, I was afraid she was going to tell me that Oliver was the father."

Nathan winced. "Right, the whole 'best friend getting with your ex' thing. That would've been bad. Are you guys okay now?"

Jonah sighed. "I think so. Things are still kind of up and down though. One minute it feels perfect, and the next, I find myself feeling upset again."

"That's understandable," Nathan replied. "I mean, you *just* found out something incredibly life-changing. It's going to take some time to adjust. It doesn't mean you two can't get through it."

Jonah nodded. "I know...and Gracie was thrilled, so that's good. But in other news, I quit my job. And on the way here, the mechanic called to say my car costs more to fix than it's worth and I'm better off selling it for parts. So, that's *really* good."

Nathan laughed. "My God, Jonah! You have the worst luck of anyone I've ever met, I'm serious. Is this usually how things go for you?"

Jonah scratched his head. "I don't know...maybe?"

Nathan finished off his beer. "And you suddenly have a family, but no job and no car. What are you going to do?"

Jonah rebuked his looming anxiety. "Well, first, I have to go back to Tampa and move out of my apartment. I was hoping Hannah could come with me. I think it would be good for us to have some quality time together."

Nathan raised his eyebrows. "You're moving back here then?"

Jonah half smiled. "Yeah, I am. Weird, right?"

"Not really. I always knew you'd come back for Hannah. Well, I hoped so anyway," Nathan confessed as the doorbell rang. "Ooh, pizza."

Nathan excused himself to answer the door and returned with a large pizza and an order of chicken wings.

"I hope you're hungry," he said, grabbing two paper plates.

"Famished," Jonah replied, joining his brother on the barstools at the kitchen counter.

"For the record, I'm really glad you're moving back," Nathan said, taking a slice of pizza from the box.

Jonah grinned. "I am too."

The two brothers spent the evening hours talking like never before until it came time for Jonah to go.

"Nathan, this was really great, man. Thanks for dinner."

"Anytime. I think I needed that," Nathan said, walking his brother to the door. "Listen…I know you never had Dad's help with anything, but I want you to know that I'm here, all right?"

Jonah nodded, pulling his coat on. "Thanks, Nate. I appreciate that."

Nathan bit his lip, unable to ignore the nagging feeling inside him. "Hey, Jonah…this might seem crazy, but I want you to keep my car."

"What?" Jonah's eyes went wide. He was certain he hadn't heard his brother correctly.

"You need it more than I do."

Jonah shook his head. "No, Nathan, I can't do that.

That's just too much."

"How about this? You give me the money you get for your car," Nathan proposed.

"That's only going to be like five hundred bucks. Your car is worth *so* much more than that," Jonah said.

"I paid that car off four months ago. And in the three years I've had it, I think I've only put maybe five thousand miles on it. I'm always driving the Lexus and I still have my Jeep, and when Kendall and I get married, we'll also have her car. I literally had a spending problem before I met Kendall. So I really don't need it."

"Then sell it," Jonah suggested.

"It's not like I can get what I paid for it. I'd rather it get good use. Look at it this way—Dad never did you any favors. He was never the kind of father that would help you buy a car or even cosign on anything. He gave me more handouts than you even know about. My Jeep? *He* bought me that. What did he do for you? Sure, he sent you to college, but it was mostly paid for by *your* scholarships. You've done everything on your own, and you've done an amazing job. For once, Jonah, you deserve something good."

"Nathan…"

"No, let me finish. I've watched you get knocked down over and over again your whole life, and you always get right back up and keep going. I've always been proud of you. If I can make even one thing a little easier, I want to do that for you. You're my brother…and if I've never said it before, I love you."

Jonah's eyes stung. "I don't know what to say."

"Just say you'll take it." Nathan grinned, putting a hand on his brother's shoulder.

"Okay," Jonah caved, hugging his brother. "Seriously, thank you…and I love you too."

Jonah sat in the Mercedes outside Hannah's house. He couldn't believe what his brother had done for him. It was ridiculous and much too generous. Jonah ran his hand over the leather steering wheel, unable to fathom that something so exquisite could belong to him. He still wasn't sure he could accept such an extravagant gift.

Jonah's eyes flickered to the lights in the rearview mirror when Hannah pulled up. He smiled and stepped out of the car, surprised by the butterflies in his stomach.

"Hey." Hannah grinned at him as he approached her. "You look happy. Did you have fun with Nathan?"

Jonah let out a chuckle. "Yeah…He *gave* me his car."

"No. You're kidding."

He shook his head. "He would not let me turn it down. I guess it's ours now."

Hannah was pleased by his choice of words. "So, have you decided what your next step is?"

"I wanted to talk to you about that, actually," Jonah replied, nervously slipping his hands into his pockets. "I'm going to rent a truck and drive down to Tampa to pack up my apartment. I was hoping you could go with me, so we could spend some time together…just you and me."

She pressed her lips together. "I would love that, Jonah. I just don't know if it's possible to take time off work. And what about Gracie? I don't know if my mom would be able to watch her."

Jonah couldn't give up. "How about *my* mom? She can watch Gracie on the nights your mom is working. I mean, she's her grandmother. I know she's not always the warmest person, but she's more than capable of taking care of a four-year-old."

Hannah looked troubled. "I don't know, Jonah. It makes me so nervous. I've never left her with anyone but my parents…and you."

"I understand," he said, placing his hands on her shoulders. "But I would never suggest it if I didn't trust her. You should have seen my mom when I told her about Gracie. I think this is the perfect opportunity for them to get to know each other."

Hannah nodded, convinced by the confidence in Jonah's eyes. "Okay."

He cupped her face in his hands. "We need this, Hannah. If we want this to work."

Hannah could feel her heart racing as he held her gaze, unwavering. Slowly, he leaned closer, hesitating briefly before he pressed his lips gently against hers. It was as if electricity shot through them as they kissed, reviving every fiber of affection they'd ever felt for each other.

Hannah pulled away first, her knees weak. She stared up at Jonah, a plethora of emotions clouding her mind.

"I never stopped loving you." She spoke her thought out loud, unable to contain it.

Jonah's face brightened and he took her hand, leading her up the front steps to the porch. When they reached the door, Jonah turned to Hannah and drew her close once more, his hands on the small of her back. He studied her face for a moment, memorizing her features all over again.

"I can't believe how beautiful you are," he breathed, planting a kiss on her forehead.

Hannah blushed and looked away from the intensity in his eyes. She had feared he would never look at her that way again, but already she recognized it. It was the same loving way he'd looked at her five years ago. The same look on this same porch nine years ago when he first confessed his feelings for her. And it was still the same look, even at the cemetery on the day of Jacob's funeral. Jonah didn't say it out loud, but Hannah knew he hadn't stopped loving her either.

EIGHT

Jonah knocked on the familiar red door. He still had the key to his mother's house on his key ring, but somehow it felt inappropriate to let himself in. It didn't feel like home, nor had it ever.

Scarlett grew emotional when she opened the door and saw Gracie in her son's arms. "Come in, come in," she eagerly greeted them.

After they'd hung up their coats, they settled together in the living room. Jonah immediately noticed that Jacob's chair had been removed. He was glad it was gone, the evidence of Jacob's presence quickly fading. He pushed the lingering thoughts out of his mind.

"Gracie," Jonah began as she sat timidly on his lap, "there's someone I want you to meet." He motioned to Scarlett. "This is my mom. That means she's your other grandma."

Gracie studied Scarlett, her bright blue eyes curious. "Hi, Gramma. I'm your Gracie."

Scarlett let out a joyous laugh that Jonah had never heard before. "Well, it's very nice to meet you. You look just like your daddy," she noted, getting choked up.

"I must be *very* pretty then," Jonah said playfully.

Gracie giggled. "Daddy, you're not pretty. You're *handsome*."

Scarlett observed her son in awe. Seeing him with his daughter warmed her heart. Jonah was certainly cut out for parenthood, proving it right in front of her with the way he spoke to and gently handled his little girl. No one would ever guess it was a new role for him.

When Jonah had taken Gracie upstairs for a tour per her request, Hannah was left alone with Scarlett.

"I never got a chance to talk to you last week at the funeral," Hannah said. "I'm sorry about Mr. Weston."

Scarlett shrugged. "Don't be. He wasn't a very nice man. I know you know that."

Hannah bit her bottom lip. It was strange to hear Scarlett admit it.

"Well…I guess he was a bit rough on Jonah growing up," Hannah said.

Scarlett snickered without mirth. "Yeah, to put it lightly. He never missed an opportunity to crush Jonah's spirit, and I hate myself for allowing that. I think I was too afraid of Jacob to stand up to him. And I was afraid he'd leave me alone with two boys to raise, or even worse, take them away just to spite me…I'm sorry, I don't know why I'm telling you this."

"No, it's okay, really. Sometimes it helps to talk about it," Hannah assured her.

Scarlett nodded. "You're a sweet girl, Hannah. I was always glad Jonah had you. And for the record, I understand why you did what you did. It may be causing problems now, but I truly believe you spared Jonah a lot of wrath. I honestly can't imagine what Jacob would've done…or how he would've used it against Jonah."

Hannah wanted to cry. Scarlett's words gave her the

affirmation that she had done the right thing after all.

"Thank you, Mrs. Weston. This hasn't been easy for us, but it helps to hear that it wasn't all for nothing."

"I may know a thing or two about that. I kept Jonah from his father for twenty-three years. Do you think he was happy with me when I finally told him? Not at all," Scarlett said. "But he was still interested in Jonah, and that means a lot to me. Listen, Hannah, I'm not sure how Jonah has been feeling about this lately, but I really think it would be good for both of them if they finally got to meet. Do you think you could encourage him? Elliot really is a great man. And Jonah could use a positive father figure in his life."

Hannah's lips curved into a thin smile. "I'll definitely try. I think it's a good idea."

Scarlett looked past her as if in deep thought. "It should've been Elliot…I should've stayed with *him* after high school…" Scarlett snapped out of her daze. "But then that erases Nathan. And I would never want that. Not even to spare Jonah."

Hannah was surprised by Scarlett's transparency, but she appreciated it. "We can't change the choices we've made, but we can make the best of what we have now. That's what I've learned lately, anyway."

Scarlett smiled, grateful for her compassion. "I'm sorry, Hannah…for all the things Jacob ruined. I'm sorry I wasn't a better mother to Jonah. Please have some mercy on him. Any of the shortcomings he may have aren't his fault."

Hannah shook her head. "No, Mrs. Weston. Your son is an incredible person, I promise you that. Please don't worry about him. He's smart and creative and respectable, and he's such a great father. Yes, he carries a lot of pain, but none of that is your fault."

Scarlett sighed. "I hate how I feel like I don't even

know my son. With Nathan, it's different. He's much more outspoken, and he has a much thicker hide. Jonah is more reserved, and he feels everything so deeply."

"Just talk to him," Hannah encouraged her. "I know he loves you. I know he wants to be close to you."

A tear slid down Scarlett's cheek and she wiped it away. "Thank you, Hannah. I really needed this. I feel like I've been trapped for thirty-six years. It hasn't mattered what I felt or thought. I'm sorry if I've carried on too much, but it's nice to just talk to someone again."

Hannah smiled warmly. "You're welcome, Mrs. Weston. Anytime. You'll be seeing a lot of us now."

Then Gracie came bounding noisily down the stairs, running to Hannah.

She beamed excitedly. "Daddy let me jump on his bed in his old room!"

"Oh, he did?" Hannah playfully smirked at Jonah.

"I would never." He winked.

Gracie laughed. "You're a fibber, Dad."

"Hey, Gracie, how about you and me go play outside for a little bit while Daddy talks to Grandma? I want to push you on the hammock." Hannah took her daughter by the hand and led her out the French doors off the back of the living room.

Jonah watched them walk away, then sat down across from his mother. "She's so awesome, isn't she?"

"Which one? They're both wonderful."

Jonah's face lit up. "Yeah, they are...Hey, thanks for agreeing to watch Gracie while Hannah's mom is at work. That is such a huge help to us."

"Oh, you're welcome. I'm happy to do it. Thank you for asking me. You leave in the morning?"

Jonah nodded. "Yeah. Caroline will drop Gracie off

here tomorrow afternoon."

"Okay."

The inevitable silence settled between them like it always had.

"I had a very nice chat with Hannah," Scarlett finally said, taking Hannah's advice to just talk to her son.

"Oh yeah? What'd you talk about?"

"You…Jacob…and your father."

"And?" Jonah prodded with interest.

"I always thought I failed you as a mother, allowing you to grow up under such brutality. I worry that I've raised you to be a damaged adult, but Hannah assured me that you are quite the opposite. And I realized how little I know about you these days."

Jonah looked at her with a pained expression. "Mom…"

"Now that…Jacob is gone, I want to start over. I want to be the mother he never allowed me to be. Affection was a sign of weakness to him. If I ever tried to stand up for you, I was undermining him. I wish I hadn't been so afraid. I wish I hadn't allowed him to hurt you all those years."

Jonah couldn't speak. He just sat there and cried. He had always wondered what his mother thought of everything. He'd always wondered how she could turn away as he was berated time and time again. He'd always been afraid that she hadn't cared. But now he knew it was because it broke her heart to stand by and watch when she was powerless against it.

"I love you so much, Jonah," Scarlett continued through her tears. "I know I've done a horrible job of showing it, but after a while I kind of shut down just so I could survive each day. I'm so sorry…for everything."

Jonah got up and crossed the room to sit beside her.

He crumbled against her as if he was a little boy again, desperately seeking the comfort of his mother. She held him, rubbing his back as she wept.

"I love you, Mom," he whispered, working to compose himself.

When he pulled away, Scarlett took his face in her hands and looked intently into his eyes. "I am so proud of you, Jonah. You need to know that. I've *always* been proud of you."

Jonah's chest ached so badly, he could barely handle it. Hearing the words he'd longed for his entire life rattled his entire being.

"Thank you," he managed.

"I'm sorry it took me so long to tell you. But I can start over now. I have a clean slate with my granddaughter. I'd like to have a fresh start with you as well. What do you think?"

Jonah nodded. "I think it's great." He could feel some of the broken pieces of his heart mending back together.

Gracie jumped into her bed, clutching the turtle Jonah had given to her. She lay down against her pillow.

"Ready for your story?" Hannah asked, picking up a tattered copy of her favorite book.

Gracie shook her head. "I want Daddy to read it to me."

Jonah melted, a smile forming on his lips. "Okay, I'll read it."

When he'd made it through the short story and closed the book, Gracie smiled at him.

"Guess what, Dad—I love you to the moon and back," she said.

Jonah grinned. "I love you to the moon and back...twice!"

Gracie laughed. "Well, then I love you to the *sun* and back!"

"Okay, you win," Jonah said with an exaggerated sigh.

Hannah smiled contentedly. "All right, Gracie, time to say your prayers."

"Okay!" She grabbed one of her parents' hands in each of hers and closed her eyes. "Dear Jesus, thank you for the sunny day and my new grandma. Thank you for my daddy and for making him not moved away anymore. Sweet dreams, amen!"

Jonah and Hannah laughed fondly at Gracie's wit as they kissed her good night and left the room. They separately prepared for bed and met back in Hannah's room.

"Tonight was really great, huh?" Jonah said, leaning his shoulder against the doorway. He was still amazed by the moment he had shared with his mother.

Hannah removed her earrings, placing them on her dresser. "Yeah. And Gracie loved your mom. It was just perfect."

Jonah thought to himself for a moment. "Well, we better get to sleep. I'd like to be on the road by five a.m."

"Hey, Jonah? Do you want to...stay with me tonight?" Hannah asked shyly.

He suppressed a smile and nodded, easing the door closed behind him. Hannah pulled the blankets down and climbed into her bed, watching Jonah cross the room and sit beside her.

"What is that?" She grabbed his arm and lifted the sleeve of his T-shirt, realizing it was the first time he hadn't been wearing long sleeves. Hannah gawked at the beautiful tree tattooed on his upper right arm and ran her fingers over the perfect detail of the trunk. The leaves were done in vivid autumn shades of red, yellow, and orange, bleeding together in a unique watercolor style, spanning just past his shoulder cap.

"When did you get a tattoo?" she asked.

"I got this one about…four years ago?"

"*This* one? Like there's more?"

He shrugged. "Yeah, I have a few."

Jonah adjusted his body and reclined, putting his hands behind his head. When he did so, he revealed another piece, a black-and-gray sparrow on his left inner bicep.

"That one too? Who are you?" Hannah asked playfully.

Jonah laughed. "What, do you see me differently now?"

"Of course not. I guess I'm just surprised. I had no idea you had them. What else are you hiding from me?"

Jonah turned to his side and propped himself up on his elbow, resting his head against his fist. "More tattoos," he answered plainly.

"Really?"

"Ah, maybe you'll find out someday," he teased her with a sly grin.

Hannah flirtatiously shoved him, but he grabbed her arm. He drew her in and kissed her.

Before they got lost in passionate oblivion, Jonah pulled away. "We should get some sleep," he said, lying on his back.

He reached for Hannah and gently guided her head to his chest. Lying on her side, she slipped her arm around him, soothed by the lullaby of his heartbeat.

"So, why the tree?" she asked after a few moments of quiet.

"Do you remember our tree in the park? The one we carved our initials into?" Jonah answered.

Hannah smiled. "Of course I remember. We were standing under that tree the first time you kissed me."

Jonah blushed. "Well, it's based on *that* tree. It reminds me of those happy, carefree times together…and how everything else seemed to disappear when I was there with you."

"What made you get the tattoo?" she asked, running her fingers over his chest.

He sighed. "I felt you slipping away, and I thought it would make me feel closer to you. I wanted to make us permanent somehow…if that even makes sense."

"No, it does. It totally does," Hannah agreed.

"Good."

"Okay, and why the bird?" she asked.

"I *really* like birds."

Hannah chuckled. "Nuh uh. Seriously."

Jonah's straight-faced expression cracked and he laughed. "Well…birds symbolize freedom. So when I graduated from college, got my own place, and was no longer supported at all by my father—uh, Jacob—I got that one."

"I like that," Hannah said.

"So, you approve?" he asked.

"I do. So, do you have more than that or not?"

"Yes. But that's for another time. We *have* to get some sleep," Jonah insisted, kissing her head.

Hannah sighed, turning to her bedside table to shut off the light before snuggling against Jonah. She was intrigued by the new mysteries of him, and she craved to solve each one. She felt like she had at their beginning, thrilled by his every word and touch. Hannah was falling in love with Jonah all over again.

Hannah nervously climbed the steps of the school bus, the rows of rambunctious middle school kids coming into view. She prayed she could find a seat to herself, or at least one far away from Aiden Buckley. It was the third day of school, and Hannah was the new kid in the seventh grade. She was also Aiden's latest target. Thankfully, seven rows back, she found an empty seat. She quickly slid in, slinking low and leaning against the window.

"Hey, Banana," came the dreaded mocking voice above her.

Hannah reluctantly looked up to see Aiden peering over the seat behind her, a mischievous grin on his freckled face. She rolled her eyes as he plopped down beside her. He leaned in close, and she cringed.

"Is that a new shirt?" he asked, pinching her side.

"Ow! Knock it off!" Hannah shouted at him. She fought not to cry as he laughed.

"Well, it's an ugly shirt," Aiden said.

"Can you just leave me alone?" she pleaded.

"Why? Are you gonna cry?"

"No...I just want you to stop bothering me," she replied in a small voice, praying she could keep the tears at bay. She'd failed to do so the day before.

"I'm sorry, I can't do that," Aiden sneered, grabbing her backpack from her lap.

"Hey, give me that!" Hannah struggled to reach it.

Aiden evaded her attempts and unzipped the front pocket of her bag. His eyes went wide and he laughed loudly as he discovered some feminine necessities inside. Just as he was about to stand up and publicly humiliate Hannah, a hand reached down from the seat behind them, snatching Hannah's backpack from Aiden's unsuspecting hands.

"Oh, you didn't just do that," Aiden fumed. He jumped to his feet and arrogantly took a swing at the boy who stood up against him.

113

When the boy dodged Aiden's blow, he delivered a punch of his own, his fist making perfect contact with Aiden's face. With a loud thud, Aiden fell into the aisle.

The bus driver finally looked up into her mirror. "Aiden, get back in your seat!" she scolded.

Stunned and embarrassed, Aiden scrambled toward the back of the bus, rubbing his aching cheekbone. The boy who had come to Hannah's rescue rounded the seat and sat down beside her, returning her backpack to her.

"You all right?" he asked, his lovely blue eyes piercing hers with kindness.

Hannah nodded. "Thank you," she said shyly, zipping the pocket closed.

"Oh, he's had it coming. I won't let him bother you anymore, okay?"

Hannah glanced at his trembling, swelling hand. "Is your hand okay?"

He flexed his fingers, opening and closing his fist. "I can't believe how much that hurt," he confessed with a laugh. "I've never punched anyone before."

She smiled. "Well, that's probably a good thing. I'm Hannah, by the way...Not banana."

The boy smiled back. "I'm Jonah."

From then on, he sat with her, to and from school, every single day, and Aiden never once bothered her again.

After Gracie's countless hugs and kisses good-bye, Jonah and Hannah climbed into the moving truck and set off on their long trip.

Hannah already missed Gracie. It was the first time she would ever be away from her daughter for more than a work shift. But as she thought about the next few days ahead of her, filled with nothing but Jonah, her sadness faded away.

"Okay, here's the deal," Jonah began, his eyes intent on the road. "This is our chance to catch up. No secrets. Nothing is off-limits. Complete openness."

"Deal," Hannah agreed. "But we can't hold anything against each other if something difficult should come up."

Jonah glanced at her for a second. "What, do you have deep, dark secrets to confess?"

"No. I don't know. I'm just saying."

"So you're preparing yourself for *my* deep dark secrets, then," Jonah joked.

Hannah laughed. "After last night, who knows?"

He chuckled. "I'm just so full of surprises."

Hannah leaned her head back against the headrest, looking at Jonah fondly. She smiled to herself. "I forgot how funny you were."

"Why, 'cause I've been such a basket case since I got here?" He mocked himself, shooting her a silly face.

"Oh, stop. You've had every right to have a mental breakdown. It's just really nice to see the real you coming out again...I missed it."

Without looking away from the road, Jonah reached over and took her hand, entwining his fingers in hers.

"Can I ask you something?" Hannah asked tenderly.

"Nothing's off-limits, go for it," Jonah replied.

"Have you thought any more about meeting Elliot?"

Jonah bit his lower lip. "Yeah...I keep thinking about how he and I are kind of in the same situation. But if I never knew Gracie...If she grew up and refused to see me, it would kill me. So, I *do* want to meet him, but..."

Hannah studied his perplexed expression. "But what? What's stopping you?"

He sighed. "I'm just...scared. What if I'm not what

he's expecting? I mean, I don't even have a job right now."

"So what?" Hannah said. "That's the last thing that defines you. You really need to stop underestimating yourself all the time. You are *not* who Jacob made you believe you are."

Jonah stared straight ahead, his jaw clenched, struggling to maintain his composure. He took a deep breath and let it out shakily.

"There are so many things I wish I could say to him. I would tell him how much I've grown to hate him since he died. And how much I hate that I wasted my life trying to make him love me. I always thought *I* didn't deserve his love, but now I finally know that he didn't deserve *mine*."

Jonah's knuckles turned white as he gripped the steering wheel. Hannah put her hand on his shoulder to bring him back from his seething thoughts.

"Hey, hey." She spoke gently, running her fingers through his hair. "It's okay...How about we cool it on the deep talk for a while?"

He nodded, relaxing his tense muscles. "That sounds good."

"How about we listen to some music?" Hannah suggested, turning on the radio.

Jonah groaned. "Radio sucks. I have some CDs in my bag if you want to play something. I'm probably the last person on Earth who still makes mix CDs. That's the beauty of owning a car without an auxiliary jack...But not anymore, I guess."

"Yeah, it's endless playlists in the Mercedes for you now," Hannah said, smiling. She retrieved his large book of CDs and paged through them. "You've always been such a music buff. Always into all the obscure stuff no one's ever heard of. I could never forget that about you."

"So, I'm a music snob?" he joked.

"Well, kind of." Hannah chuckled.

"I just know what's good."

"Oh really. Then tell me which CD to play."

Jonah thought for a moment. "Find the one called '*H*.'"

She narrowed her eyebrows, wondering if *H* stood for the obvious. "What's on this one?"

"Exactly what you think," he said honestly. "It's all the songs that remind me of you. I listen to it whenever I miss you." Then Jonah looked at her for a brief moment. "I listen to it a lot, in case you were wondering."

Curiously, Hannah inserted the disc into the dash's CD player. Every song that played was either a love song or a song about missing someone. And every single one was beautiful. They didn't speak much for the duration of the mix. Hannah listened intently to the words as if Jonah was speaking them to her, sharing the emotions he'd been feeling while they were apart. She was grateful he'd shared it with her, allowing her to see another hidden piece of him.

Outside the auto body shop, Jonah rounded the truck to Hannah's side to help her climb down from the elevated cab. She followed him into the small office, where she excused herself to use the restroom while Jonah negotiated a deal with the shop owner.

Jonah smiled when he met Hannah out front a few moments later. "I got six hundred bucks for that thing," he said, carefully placing the check in his wallet.

"How'd you manage that?" she asked.

Jonah grinned facetiously. "I told him I was getting married soon."

Hannah looked at him sideways, her heart pounding. "Did you really say that?"

He shrugged. "Possibly."

She pointed her finger at him. "Hey, no secrets, remember?"

"All right, I didn't say that," he confessed, walking past her toward the truck. Then he stopped and turned to face her. "But I should have. Because it's true."

A smile formed on her lips as he reached for her hand.

NINE

The dark clouds rolled in, smothering what remained of the sunlight. When evening fell, a light drizzle rapidly became a relentless downpour. Jonah turned the windshield wipers as high as they would go, but it still wasn't enough. He slowed his speed considerably, struggling to see through the torrential rain.

"Wow, this is awful," Hannah said, anxiously biting her fingernail.

"The forecast said the storms would be coming during the night. I love how accurate they are," Jonah remarked sarcastically. He skimmed a large puddle that overflowed from the shoulder, skidding a little as water shot up.

"Do you think we should stop?" Hannah asked.

"Maybe…I was hoping to make it to my apartment tonight," Jonah said, trying to stay calm. "But we still have over three hours to go."

A large pickup truck raced by, its tires shooting a flood of water across their windshield, depleting visibility. Jonah instinctively hit the brakes, hydroplaning several feet before regaining control.

"Please, can we stop somewhere?" Hannah panicked, gripping the dashboard. "Just get off at the next exit and find a hotel or something, *please*?"

"Okay," Jonah agreed, his heart pounding.

Thankfully, the next exit wasn't much farther and Jonah pulled off, relieved to stop at the traffic light at the bottom of the ramp.

"Are you okay?" he asked, turning to look at her in the red glow. "I'm sorry if I scared you."

Hannah shook her head. "No, it's not you. I get nervous being on the road in rain like that. I think I was about to have an anxiety attack." She laughed at herself.

Jonah accelerated as the light turned green. "Well, we can't have that."

He drove along a Jacksonville street, passing up a few seedy-looking hotels before coming across one from a familiar chain. He pulled into the parking lot, stopping beneath the overhang outside of the lobby.

"Wait here. I shouldn't be long," he said, hopping out of the truck into the wet cold outside.

Hannah admired Jonah through the lobby window as he made his way to the front desk. The receptionist smiled as she spoke with him, obviously taken by his charm. Hannah felt butterflies in her stomach when Jonah turned to head back toward the truck.

"All right," he said when he'd gotten inside and closed the door. "I'm going to drop you off at our room, but then I have to park this in the back lot since it's so big."

Jonah drove around the side of the building and stopped in front of their ground-floor room. Opening the truck door, he motioned for Hannah to slide across the seat to him, and he helped her down. After retrieving their bags from the cab, Jonah used a key card to unlock the door and let Hannah in ahead of him. He set the bags down.

"I'll be right back, okay?" Jonah braced himself for the elements as he left her alone.

When the door closed behind him, Hannah turned to survey the room. There was only one bed, and she wondered if Jonah had chosen that or if they'd gotten it by default. She adjusted the heat on the unit beneath the window, then rummaged through her bag for her pajamas and her toothbrush.

After brushing her teeth and changing, Hannah was surprised Jonah still hadn't returned. Just as she was about to peer through the curtains, the door opened and he rushed in, thoroughly saturated.

"Oh, Jonah." Hannah hurried to grab some towels from the bathroom.

Jonah was shivering profusely, his wet hair trickling rivulets down his face, droplets falling from his chin and the tip of his nose. He swiftly unbuttoned his shirt, tugging it off and dropping it into a sopping heap on the carpet. His soaked white undershirt clung to his frame as he kicked off his soggy boots. Hannah boldly helped him peel off his T-shirt, exposing his goose-bump-covered flesh *and* a couple lines of script inked across the right side of his ribcage. She handed him a towel, trying not to gawk at him as he dried off.

"In case you were wondering, it's still raining," Jonah said, feeling self-conscious before her.

Hannah brushed his damp hair out of his eyes. "How far away was the back lot?"

He snickered. "Far enough."

Turning away, Jonah grabbed his bag and disappeared into the bathroom. A few moments later, he returned, wearing only a pair of black sweatpants. He crossed the room to set his bag down on the table, sifting through its contents for a shirt. Hannah stopped him, grabbing a hold of his shoulders and turning him to face her. Jonah looked at her, perplexed. Hannah ran her fingers delicately over his ribs, reading the words on his skin: *Darkness exists to make light truly count.*

Hannah gazed up at him, feeling as if she'd unraveled a new, intricate strand of him and who he was.

"It's from a song," Jonah said. "'Uneven Odds' by Sleeping At Last...and before you ask..." He turned to show her a fragment of sheet music, with a string of notes trailing off on his left shoulder blade.

"What song is that?" Hannah asked.

Jonah turned back to her. "'Amazing Grace.'"

She stared at him, her blue eyes wide, and let out a sharp breath. "Are you serious?"

He nodded. "Well, it's a beautiful, timeless classic...and I guess a little grace was what I've spent so much of my life looking for."

Hannah laughed off her embarrassment when tears filled her eyes. "Well, you found *our* little Grace."

Jonah fought the rise of emotions swelling in his chest and drew her in to him. She delighted in the feel of his bare skin against her.

"I have to say, that's the most amazing coincidence I've ever encountered," he said, kissing her on the head before releasing her.

Hannah wiped her eyes. "So, is that it then? Just the four?"

"Nope." Jonah bent to lift his pant leg and showed her an anchor with roses on his left calf. "I will have you know, I had the anchor *before* it was trendy."

"Doesn't it hurt to get a tattoo?" she asked, scrunching up her face.

"Well, yeah. But I guess I'm somewhat of a masochist."

"Do you still want to get more?"

"You know how they say it's addictive? They're not lying," Jonah said, walking over to the bed.

He reclined against the pillows, tucking his arm behind his head and crossing his ankles. He let out a relaxed sigh and reached for the television remote on the bedside table. Looking over at Hannah, Jonah patted the spot beside him. She eagerly obliged, lying down and snuggling into him.

"This is weird, isn't it?" Jonah commented suddenly, diverting his attention away from the TV.

"What do you mean?" she asked, though she was fairly certain she already knew what he was referring to.

"Okay. For the record, I didn't get to choose what kind of room we got. You were probably wondering, and I didn't want you to think I had any certain intentions," Jonah rambled nervously.

Hannah lifted her head to look at him. "Yeah, your striptease didn't help either."

He raised his eyebrows and dropped his jaw. "Hey. I was avoiding hypothermia."

"How convenient for me," Hannah said flirtatiously, leaning in to kiss him. She ran her hand over his toned stomach, and he pulled back.

"Keeping with the theme of honesty...I'd really like to take things slow, if that's okay," Jonah said gently.

"I feel the same way," Hannah agreed. "So now nothing has to be weird."

Jonah smiled. "Well, that was easy."

She shrugged, lightly running her fingertips in haphazard swirls on his chest. "We've spent a *long* time apart; I don't want to rush into anything. We have a child to think about now."

"So, do you think there's a chance we won't work out?" Jonah asked, holding his breath.

"If you asked me that question five years ago, I would've *sworn* there wasn't. I would've bet my life on it. So now? I can't bear to assume anything."

Jonah caressed her face, her trepidation paining him. "I wish I could tell you not to feel that way. But I'd be lying if I said I didn't worry too…Why does everything always feel so out of our control?"

Hannah grinned at him. "Well, if I get any say, you'll be stuck with me forever."

Jonah laughed. "And I would gladly accept my fate."

The following morning was sunny and clear, with not one cloud in the sky, as they continued their drive to Tampa.

"I want to hear that song," Hannah said, tickling Jonah's side where his tattoo was.

He smiled. "It's in my CD book. Toward the front."

"Which one?" she asked, leafing through the discs. "There are, like, fifty Sleeping At Last CDs here."

Jonah chuckled, quickly reaching over to flip the page. "That one." He pointed. "Track five."

"Big fan?" she asked, putting in the disc and skipping to the correct song.

He shrugged. "You could say that. It's hard to pick one favorite, but yeah, I'd say it's him."

Hannah restarted the track. "Okay, now hush, I want to hear it."

Jonah smiled. He loved how intrigued she was by the things that interested him. He'd forgotten what it was like to be so significant to someone. To matter. He had missed feeling worthy.

Jonah glanced at Hannah. Her eyes were closed, her expression tranquil, as she reveled in the captivating melody. Jonah still loved that song. Every time he heard it, he wanted to hear it again. He figured he was an odd person, the way he loved music, but he didn't mind. It was the biggest part of who he was.

"Oh, it's beautiful," Hannah breathed when the song ended. "I can see why you like it so much. Can we listen to more?"

Jonah grinned. "Of course we can. So what music are you into?"

"Well, I'm about to make your blood boil, because I never really have the time to listen to anything," she divulged.

"Oh, that's the saddest thing I've ever heard," Jonah remarked playfully. "How do you live?"

She laughed, loving the joy that flickered in his eyes. "I just don't know."

Jonah felt strange being back at his apartment building again. It had only been ten days, but it seemed like an entire lifetime had passed since he'd gotten into his car, in this very parking lot, to make the unexpected journey back home, so emotionally unprepared for all that would transpire.

Jonah led Hannah through the double glass doors into the building's small lobby. The wall to the left was covered in mailboxes, directly across from the manager's office on the right. Straight ahead stood a single elevator.

Jonah made his way to the end of the long rows of mailboxes before reaching his. He unlocked it and retrieved a large stack of mail. Tucking it beneath his arm, he approached the elevator and pressed the button.

"Which floor are you on?" Hannah wondered.

"Five," he answered as the doors opened.

They stepped on, and Hannah pressed the correct button. "This seems like a nice place so far."

"It's really not bad," Jonah replied.

"That's good. I've always hoped you were taking care of yourself."

The doors opened to a long carpeted hallway lined with black doors.

"I'm all the way down," Jonah said, motioning with his hand.

As they reached the end of the hall, the door across from Jonah's flung open, and a woman about their age breezed into the hallway.

"Jonah! Oh my gosh!" she exclaimed, failing to hide her smile. "Where have you been?" She twirled one of her dark curls around her finger.

"Zoe. Hey. I was...away for a funeral," Jonah answered.

"Oh, I'm sorry. I was wondering what happened to you. I was afraid you'd moved away or something." Zoe frowned, then gave Hannah a weird look. "Who's this?"

Hannah opened her mouth to introduce herself, but Jonah spoke first.

"This is my girlfriend, Hannah," he said casually, turning to unlock his door.

With a polite smile, Hannah extended her hand to shake Zoe's. "Nice to meet you, Zoe."

Zoe seemed to deflate as she chewed her lip. "Yeah, same. Well, I gotta get going. Glad you're home, Jonah. I'll see you around."

Without so much as glancing at Hannah, Zoe spun around and strutted off hastily toward the elevator. Jonah opened his apartment door, letting Hannah enter before him.

"She wants you," Hannah said once they were inside.

"What?"

"It's so obvious she has the hots for you."

Jonah made a face. "No. She doesn't."

"And you totally just broke her heart," Hannah teased, placing her hands on his waist.

Jonah rolled his eyes. "I feel bad now. I always thought she was just *really* nice... or maybe a little crazy."

Hannah giggled. "It's adorable how oblivious you are."

Jonah groaned in reply and turned away, scuffling into the kitchen.

Hannah took in her surroundings, excited to see where Jonah had been calling home. It was a humble space, but it was pleasant and well maintained. Hannah wandered into the living area, where several windows lent plenty of light to the room. A worn, brown leather couch sat on the far end across from a modest flat screen television affixed to the wall. The rest of the free spaces on the walls were covered in shelves lined with vinyl records, CDs, and books. An old record player sat on a table beneath the television, Ray Lamontagne on the turntable. The needle was still in place where the last song had ended. Hannah smiled as she looked around, seeing Jonah in every detail.

Jonah returned, offering Hannah a bottle of water. "I know, I'm kind of a hoarder, right?"

"No, it's nice. I like seeing where you live."

He pointed behind him to the rest of the place. "There's not much else to see, but do you want a tour?"

Jonah showed Hannah the simple kitchen and bathroom. Then came his bedroom, which was rather plain, with nothing but a double bed, a dresser, and a weathered acoustic guitar on a stand in the corner. Jonah gravitated toward the instrument and eagerly picked it up. He sat on the edge of his bed and began strumming and picking the strings.

Jonah was proud of his old, beaten-up Martin guitar. He'd bought it secondhand and had to fix it up a bit, replacing the bridge and tuning heads and repairing its bowed neck.

Hannah was mesmerized by Jonah's perfect, intricate melody. She had no idea his talent was so advanced.

Finally, Jonah came out of his daze and stopped playing. It was almost as if he'd gone somewhere else for a moment.

"That was really pretty. Who's it by?" Hannah asked.

He stood and returned the guitar to its stand. "Me."

She raised her eyebrows. "Seriously? It's awesome, Jonah. Does it have lyrics?" Jonah just nodded. "Wait, do you sing too? How could I not know this about you? Can you sing for me?"

He laughed at her enthusiasm but bashfully looked away. "Maybe another time."

Hannah sulked, taking his hands in hers. *"Jonah.* It's just me."

He sighed, his self-consciousness surprising him. "I know. It just makes me feel…nervous."

"Oh, fine." She gave in, giving him a quick kiss on the cheek.

"I will soon though, okay?" Jonah promised.

Jonah didn't have much beyond the main essentials, so it didn't take Hannah long to pack up the kitchen. While Jonah carefully boxed up his records, she made her way into his bedroom and opened the closet door.

Up on a high shelf was a box labeled "HANNAH." Curiously pulling it down, she set it on Jonah's bed and flipped the top open. Inside were letters she'd written him, including the ones she'd written for the three weeks she'd been in Texas. There were little gifts she'd given him, movie and concert ticket stubs, and countless photos of them together. Hannah felt as though she was in a time warp, easily recognizing all of these familiar pieces of their relationship. The time they had spent together suddenly didn't feel so distant, and she was touched that Jonah had held onto what remained of it.

All the years they'd been apart, Hannah had been convinced that Jonah could never be a part of her life again. It had consumed her every single day, her heart exhausted by a longing for him that never relented.

Hannah pushed the box aside as her emotions overwhelmed her. She crumbled onto Jonah's bed and cried into his pillow, realizing her incessant anguish had truly ceased. Despite everything, she couldn't fathom that Jonah had never given up on them. For that, and for infinite other reasons, Hannah loved him so deeply and unequivocally it made every fiber of her ache. It was all of these things that filled and mended her heart.

In the living room, Jonah sealed and labeled another box. It was surreal to be packing up his apartment and leaving it behind. He never dared to imagine that this was what would come of his trip back home.

Pausing for a moment, Jonah sat on the floor among the boxes of his music collection, reflecting on the new path his life was taking. Or maybe it was continuing on an old path he never should have strayed from. He was amazed how Hannah had come back to him, after all those years of believing she'd be missing from him forever. It was unbelievable that she was *here*, in his apartment, within the very walls in which he'd spent so much time pining for her. He couldn't express the joy that flooded him at the thought of another chance. They were tethered together, bonded by the child they'd brought into this world, and by the effortless love that time itself couldn't shake.

The movers arrived and hauled everything downstairs, loading it into the truck. With the job finished, Jonah paid a visit to the building manager to make his move official.

Hannah had just gotten off the phone with Gracie when Jonah returned to the empty apartment.

"Gracie says hi," Hannah said to him.

His eyes lit up. "How's she doing?"

"Good," Hannah replied. "She said she had a lot of fun with your mom. They made ice cream sundaes."

"Aw, I miss her," he gushed.

"I do too."

Jonah scanned the vacant space for a few silent moments, then placed his hands on his hips. "This is so weird..."

"Uh oh." Hannah smirked. "You're not getting cold feet about moving back, are you?"

"Not even for a second."

His answer brought a smile to her face. "Good."

"I want to take you on a date tonight," he said, reaching for her hand.

Hannah raised her eyebrows flirtatiously. "Now that I'm your girlfriend?"

Jonah let out a sheepish chuckle. "Oh, because of what I told Zoe? I just figured you already knew."

"Well, I had *hoped*," Hannah replied.

"Then you'll go out with me?"

She laughed. "Of course. Where are we going?"

"There's a place that's really special to me. It's this cool coffeehouse, but they also have great food. I worked there for, like, three years till I graduated from college. So, this may be my last chance to go there, and I think it would be fun."

"Sounds good to me," Hannah agreed.

The Venue was a popular local coffeehouse downtown. It attracted customers with its vast array of coffees and teas as well as its impressive menu of sandwiches and bakery goods. To make it an even more unique establishment, The Venue was also known for hosting live music and weekly open mic nights. Jonah had loved working there and would have stayed on if he could've lived off the meager pay.

Jonah held the door for Hannah as she stepped into the cozy ambience of the coffeehouse. The large space was filled with mismatched, trendy couches, tables, and chairs in bright colors and patterns. Their drinks were served in a plethora of differently shaped mugs, varying in print and hue. A small stage was off in the corner, set with a baby grand piano, microphone stands, and amps. Straight ahead was the counter with large chalkboard menus overhead, their offerings scrawled in ornate fonts. The pleasant fragrance of freshly brewed coffee hung in the air.

"Jonah! Hey, man! How's it going?" a barista greeted him when they approached the counter.

"Hey, Jeffrey. I'm good, you?"

"Staying busy. What can I get you two?" Jeffrey asked.

Jonah looked up at the menu even though he knew it by heart. They placed their order, and then Jonah led Hannah to his favorite table in the corner, directly across from the stage.

"This place is really neat," Hannah said.

"Oh, I love it here," he remarked as a girl approached them with a tray of drinks.

She set down an oversized mug of black Sumatra blend coffee. "Hey, Jonah."

"Hi, Rachel."

"I haven't seen much of you lately," Rachel said, serving Hannah her iced latte.

"Yeah, I've been away."

"Well, we missed you at open mic night last weekend. You're always the best one here." She grinned, patting him on the shoulder as she walked away.

Hannah narrowed her eyebrows as she tasted her latte. "Open mic night?"

Jonah sighed, carefully sipping his steaming coffee. "I may or may not perform once in a while."

"So, you'll sing in front of strangers but not in front of me?" She jokingly overplayed her disapproval.

"It's just different," Jonah explained. "It's so much easier to put yourself out there in front of people you don't know."

Hannah chuckled. "You seem to know *everyone* here."

He playfully squinted his eyes at her. "No. I don't know *everyone*."

"Well, then I guess they know *you*," she said, turning his coffee mug around to show him his name printed on it.

Jonah snickered. "Hey, I *earned* that. It's this cool thing they do here for regulars, okay?"

Hannah grinned. "I rest my case."

Yet another Venue employee came out and served them their food. "Hey, Jonah! You playing for us tonight?"

Hannah tried not to laugh as Jonah sheepishly pressed his lips together.

"Uh, I don't think so, Zac. I didn't bring my guitar."

"Oh, that's okay," Zac said. "I think Ryan has his. I'm sure he'd let you use it. Or there's always the piano."

Jonah shook his head. "Thanks, man, but it's all right. I'll sit this one out."

Zac seemed a little disappointed as he strode back to the kitchen. Jonah reached across the table, taking Hannah's hand.

"All right, you win."

The two of them enjoyed their dinner over pleasant conversation until that weekend's open mic night began. By this time, not a seat was empty at The Venue. Their functions always drew a large crowd, and this night was no different. The performances included a spoken word poet, a classic piece on piano, an a cappella group medley, and two covers on guitar.

When the stage was vacant, Ryan, the manager of The Venue, approached the microphone.

"Let's hear it for the great acts we've heard tonight," he said, evoking applause. "But the night is still young, do we have anyone else?"

After no one came forward, a voice in the back yelled Jonah's name. Several others cheered and clapped, egging him on.

"C'mon, Jonah," Ryan encouraged him.

Even if only to stop the embarrassing attention, Jonah stood up. Hannah could barely contain the excitement building within her. She couldn't wait to hear him.

With a quick glance at Hannah, Jonah made his way onto the stage and sat down at the piano, facing the audience. He adjusted the microphone and smiled, suddenly in his element.

"If you've been around for a while, you've probably figured out that all of my songs are about this one girl. But tonight is special because she's actually *here*. So, as always…this one's for Hannah," he said, his eyes finding hers.

Then Jonah slipped into another world as his fingers flitted along the keys. Hannah recognized it almost immediately. It was the same beautiful melody she had heard him play at his apartment. She found herself holding her breath as he began to open his mouth.

And so it was, the most glorious sound Hannah had ever heard. She watched him in awe, chills traveling swiftly through her body. Jonah's voice was soulful, with a raw, smoky tone to it. It was passionate and effortless, and Hannah hung on his every word:

I've struggled for some time now to spell you out in words
With intricate lines about elaborate designs
Inked into sonnets no one's ever heard

Because I just want the world to know that my heart beats to love you
And I'd rather take a breath underwater, or constantly falter
than ever know what life is without you

These clichéd phrases fail to depict
All the colors that dance in your eyes
Or the threads that you stitch through every inch
Of the fabrics that pattern my skies

I just need the world to know that my heart beats to love you
And I'd rather lose all my worth, or move Heaven and earth
than ever know what life is without you

And so I tried to compose the melody of your laugh and sketch the curves of your face
But God wrote it in pen, before we began, on these pages lined with grace
Your name has been etched in my margins, tethered to all of my strings

But I'm sorry I failed to find the right words to tell you all of these things.

After Jonah played the very last note, the entire audience erupted in applause. Hannah jumped out of her seat, tears streaming down her face. When Jonah rounded the piano, she was right there to throw her arms around him. The crowd only cheered louder as he embraced her and lifted her off of her feet.

TEN

Jonah was finishing off his third cup of coffee when Ryan sat down at their table.

"As always, man, that was awesome. Thanks for doing that. They just love you," Ryan said, grinning.

Jonah's eyes were still bright with euphoria. "I really enjoy it, so thank *you*."

Ryan turned to Hannah. "And it's an honor to finally meet you. Thank you for giving our biggest crowd pleaser all of his inspiration. I swear some people come here just to listen to him."

Hannah gazed proudly at Jonah, placing her hand over his. "I don't blame them."

"So, how've you been?" Ryan asked Jonah. "We haven't seen you for over a week. We were wondering about you."

Jonah sighed. "I went back home to Pennsylvania because my, uh…my dad died." He decided to keep his wording simple, preferring to avoid the details of the complicated situation.

"Oh, wow. I'm so sorry," Ryan said.

"It's really okay. But thanks."

Ryan smiled kindly. "It's good to have you back. I think you brought the cold weather with you, though."

136

"Cold? Ryan, it's, like, fifty degrees."

"Well, yesterday it was eighty."

Jonah chuckled. "Anyway. I'm only back in town to move out of my apartment. I'm going back to Pennsylvania for good…to be with Hannah."

Ryan's eyes widened. "Really? Well, I'm happy for you, Jonah. But that sucks for us. When do you leave?"

"Tomorrow," Jonah answered. "I'm going to take Hannah to Clearwater for the night."

"Awesome. Well, have a safe trip. And when you're shoveling snow in a few weeks, picture me on the beach, enjoying this bipolar Florida weather," Ryan said facetiously.

Jonah laughed as he stood to shake Ryan's hand. "Oh, I will. And thanks, man. For everything. You guys have done so much for me over the years."

"Hey, don't mention it. Just please, let me know when you get signed, okay? And take this with you." Ryan picked up Jonah's mug from the table and handed it to him.

Jonah grinned and hugged him, saying good-bye.

Once they were back in the truck, Hannah grabbed Jonah by the lapels of his coat and pulled him to her, kissing him intensely.

When she finally released him, he looked dazed, breathlessly staring at her.

"I love you," he whispered in the cold darkness, stroking her cheek.

"I love you too," Hannah said. "And I loved your song. Oh my gosh, Jonah. It was amazing. I can't believe you. You're…incredible." She wanted to cry again.

"I'm happy you liked it," Jonah said, starting the truck. "I still can't believe you finally heard it."

"When did you write it?" she asked.

"After you visited me at UT. I was dying when I got back to my dorm after I took you to the airport. I already missed you so badly. So I picked up my guitar to take my mind off it, and that's when it started coming together."

"Wow. So, how many songs have you written about me?" Hannah wondered.

"Too many to count, honestly."

"I can't wait to hear more," she said.

"Oh, I'm sure you will. You ready to go to the hotel?"

Hannah grinned mischievously. "Actually, no. There's something I really want to do first. And you can't talk me out of it."

Ten minutes later, per Hannah's insistence, Jonah parked outside his favorite tattoo shop.

"Are you sure about this?" he asked her. "You might want to think about it for a while."

"I'm aware of what I'm doing. I *have* been thinking about it, and I really want to. Right now. It just feels like the perfect night to do something crazy."

Jonah laughed, adoring her spunkiness. "Fine. If you do it, I'm doing it too."

"Fine."

When the couple walked into the shop, Andy, Jonah's usual artist, was perched behind the front counter, sketching intently. He looked up and smiled.

"Jonah! What can I do for ya, man?"

"Hey, Andy. Do you happen to have time for us tonight?"

Andy glanced around the empty shop. "I absolutely do. We've been so dead, I sent everyone home. What do you have in mind?"

"I just want something simple. My daughter's name on

my wrist," Jonah said.

Hannah looked up at him, her mouth hanging open. "That's what *I* wanted."

Andy seemed confused. "You have a daughter? Together?"

Jonah chuckled. "It's a long story, but yes."

"All right." Andy shrugged. "Let's get started."

Being very skilled in his art, it didn't take Andy long to finish both pieces, and soon, Jonah and Hannah were outside the shop, smiling down at their spontaneous new embellishments beneath the amber glow of the streetlight. They'd both gotten "Gracie" on their left wrists.

"Your mother's *really* gonna kill me this time," Jonah joked.

"Nah. There's no way she could object to *this*." Hannah smiled as her eyes teared up. "I don't know why, but this just makes me so happy."

He laughed. "See? I told you."

"This is already better than last night," Jonah said, the door falling closed behind him.

"Why, 'cause this room is beautiful?" Hannah asked, flopping onto the fluffy king bed.

"No, because I'm dry and fully clothed, that's why."

Hannah sat up. "Well, that doesn't sound better to me."

He squinted at her, trying not to smile. "Hey. Be good."

She laughed. "So, can you tell me what's in the bag now?"

Jonah picked up the bag he'd gone to great lengths to keep hidden from her since their trip began. He crossed the room to sit beside her and set it in her lap.

"Don't get too excited. It's silly," he warned her. "It's just some of your favorite things—well, according to your eighteen-year-old self anyway."

Intrigued, Hannah carefully emptied the bag's contents onto the bed. Jonah's collection consisted of a six-pack of Mountain Dew, a bag of mini Heath bars, a bag of kettle corn, and a copy of the movie *Forgetting Sarah Marshall*.

She threw her head back and laughed. "Jonah, this is perfect. How did you remember all this?"

He shrugged. "How could I forget?"

Hannah gazed at him, her expression soft. "You're amazing. Seriously. Thank you for everything."

"You're welcome," Jonah said. "Now, go ahead and get the movie started. I'll go get some ice."

It had been several hours since Jonah and Hannah had fallen asleep, neither making it to the end of the movie despite all the caffeine and sugar they'd indulged in. But now, Hannah lay awake, staring at the decorative ceiling tiles. Something nagged at her.

When Jonah rolled over, pulling his arm away from her, Hannah decided to carefully slip out of bed and into the bathroom. She sat on the floor and unzipped her bag, fishing an envelope out of the side pocket. She stared at her name and address across the front. Even Jonah's handwriting was artistic.

Hannah felt conflicted, just as she had upon finding the letter at Jonah's apartment. A part of her felt she had the right to read it, as she'd allowed Jonah to read the letters she'd never sent to him. But the other part of her felt deceitful and invasive, prying into Jonah's personal thoughts when he hadn't given her permission to do so.

Curiosity and suspense swaying her judgment, Hannah carefully tore into the envelope. She slid the letter out and quietly unfolded it, her heart racing with anticipation.

April 14, 2009

Hannah,

I miss you. I've sat here and stared at those last three words for the last twenty minutes because I don't know how to tell you how much this hurts. It's been an entire month since I've spoken to you. How is that possible? It's taken me a while to admit that we're falling apart, and I'm still trying to figure out how that happened. I know I've been so busy with classes this semester, and I'm sorry I haven't been there for you the way you deserve. I guess this is my last desperate attempt to make things right. If you still want me, I'd do anything. I would drop out of school and come home in a heartbeat. I don't care what it takes, because none of this matters without you. I love you. I always will.

Love,

Jonah

Hannah was weeping pitifully, her hand over her mouth to stifle any sound. Knowing how Jonah felt back then was one thing, but observing it firsthand was a completely different pain. Nevertheless, it confirmed once again that she had protected him from returning to the misery Jacob evoked. There was no way she would've been able to resist his plea if he'd sent the letter. She wondered why he hadn't.

After tucking the letter back into her bag and erasing the traces of tears, Hannah returned to the bed, entangling herself in Jonah's arms. She kissed him awake.

"What time is it?" he whispered.

"Almost six."

He sighed sleepily. "We should probably get going."

Jonah caressed her cheek before pushing the covers aside and getting up. He stretched as he made his way to the curtains and peered out into the predawn darkness.

"I have an idea," he said, turning back to Hannah. "Get dressed."

Jonah led Hannah across the beach until they reached the dry white sand before the shore. He sat down, motioning for her to join him. Wrapping a blanket around them in the cool gulf breeze, Jonah drew her close under the slowly brightening morning sky. Hannah snuggled against him, soothed by his closeness and the rhythmic ebb and flow of the crashing waves.

"It's so beautiful here," Hannah said, watching the sky come awake with the light that rose from the east behind them.

The soft colors spilled across the sky, tinting the wispy clouds that hung over the water.

"I never thought you'd ever be here with me," Jonah said, affectionately taking her hand into his. "I'm so happy you are."

Hannah gazed at the illuminated masterpiece above her, the fiery hues more vivid by the second as the sun rose higher. "Me too," she answered. "You have no idea."

After an endless day on the road, Jonah pulled onto their exit. He thought about the day he'd arrived home before Jacob's funeral and how different things were now. Glancing over at Hannah, asleep by his side, he smiled. For the first time in so long, Jonah was excited about life. Sure, he had no idea where his next paycheck would come from, but he couldn't think of a time he'd been happier.

Jonah parked in front of his mother's house and gently woke her.

"Hey, we're home," he said as she slowly opened her eyes.

"Oh no, I fell asleep. I'm sorry. Were you okay?" Hannah rubbed her eyes.

"I was fine," Jonah assured her. "I'm ready to collapse right now, but I managed. C'mon, let's go see our little girl."

Jonah and Hannah crept into the house and up the stairs to Nathan's old bedroom. They quietly climbed onto the bed on either side of their daughter.

"Gracie." Hannah spoke softly, stroking her dark curls.

Gracie opened her eyes, taking a moment to focus. "Mommy!" she exclaimed, throwing her arms around her mother's neck.

"Hi, baby." Hannah beamed, squeezing her tightly.

Jonah opened his arms wide. "Hey, what about me?"

Gracie turned to see him, and her face lit up. "Daddy!" She was quick to hug him as well, giggling as she did so.

"Did you have fun while we were away?" Hannah asked her.

Gracie nodded emphatically. "I did. I like my new grandma. And I still like my old one too." She looked down and noticed Jonah's wrist, the fresh ink visible. "What is *that*?"

Jonah chuckled, holding it out to her. "It's your name."

"Why?"

"Because I love you. And I want the whole world to know it."

She held onto his hand, staring at it. "Mommy says

we're not supposed to draw on ourselves." Then she licked her finger and tried to rub it off.

Jonah winced and pulled away. "No, Gracie, it's not like that. It's a tattoo. It's there forever."

"Look, honey, I have one too," Hannah chimed in, holding out her wrist.

"You want to tell the world you love me too, Mommy?" Gracie asked.

Hannah laughed. "Of course I do."

Gracie looked troubled. "How come yours get to stay forever, and *my* tattoos always come off in the bathtub?"

Jonah and Hannah exchanged amused glances. "Big people's tattoos are different, sweetie," Hannah replied.

"Well, when I get big," Gracie declared. "I'm going to show the world I love you too."

The next morning, Hannah and Scarlett helped Jonah unload the contents of his apartment into Scarlett's garage.

After returning the truck, Jonah, Hannah, and Gracie spent the mild autumn afternoon together as a family, having a picnic in the Morgans' backyard, drawing pictures in chalk on the patio, and playing tag. Hannah stood back at times, letting father and daughter bond, capturing moments they hadn't even begun to have enough of.

While Hannah and Gracie blew bubbles, Jonah received a text message from Nathan: *Hey Jonah. You home yet?*

Yeah, just got back last night. What's up? Jonah typed.

Then Jonah's phone rang. Jonah answered it, wandering out of earshot of his girls.

"Hello?"

"I didn't want to just call and bother you if you were still away," Nathan said.

144

"How would you be bothering me?" Jonah asked.

Nathan cleared his throat. "I wasn't sure what you'd be doing."

Jonah caught onto his brother's insinuation. "Ah, no. Not that."

Nathan laughed. "But all that time alone…"

Jonah sighed. "Why are we talking about this?"

"I'm your big brother. I'm *supposed* to harass you about girls. I never really got to when we were kids so I'm making up for lost time," Nathan teased.

"Lucky me," Jonah remarked sarcastically.

"Not yet."

"Nathan!"

"I'm sorry, you set it up so perfectly!"

"So, what are you calling for anyway?" Jonah changed the subject, switching the phone to his other ear.

"I just wanted to see when you'd be available to come with me to get our tux measurements. I get married less than six weeks from now," Nathan said, becoming serious.

"Well, I still have three more days with Hannah. She goes back to work on Friday."

"That's fine. Let's go Saturday," Nathan suggested. "I *hate* Black Friday."

Jonah snickered. "Sounds good to me."

"Oh, also," Nathan began. "Kendall and I are hosting Thanksgiving at our new place, and you guys are invited. I'll text you the address."

"Wow, I completely forgot that Thanksgiving is this week. Things have been so crazy," Jonah said.

"I know…oh, hey. How did everything go with selling your car?"

"Oh yeah. I meant to text you. I got six hundred dollars. I'll cash the check and bring it Thursday," Jonah offered.

Nathan chuckled into the phone. "No, man. Just keep it."

Jonah groaned. "Nathan. Don't do that. I feel guilty enough."

"You don't even have a job right now. I don't want to take money from you. Besides, you have a little girl to take care of, and an engagement ring to save up for."

"But that's not your problem."

Nathan became frustrated. "Jonah! Stop being so damn stubborn all the time."

"What the hell is your deal?" Jonah asked defensively.

"I'm just trying to help you! Dad didn't leave you anything in his will, okay? He left me almost fifty grand and not a single thing for you," Nathan blurted out before he could control himself. "I'm so sorry. I wasn't going to tell you."

"So, is it out of guilt that you've been so nice to me? Am I just a charity case to you?" Jonah asked dryly.

"Oh my God, no. Absolutely not. Jonah. You're my brother. Dad shouldn't have done that to you. I don't care if you weren't his son. He raised you like he was your father. You have his name. You don't deserve to get nothing."

Jonah sighed. "You don't have to correct his mistakes."

"I know I don't. But that doesn't mean I can't help you. I know you'd help me if I needed it. Just please, for the love of God, let me help you."

Jonah softened. "I'm sorry. I'm just not used to things like this."

"It's out of love, not pity. Just remember that," Nathan said.

"Thanks, Nate. Really."

"I know. I'll text you about Thursday, okay? Bring dessert."

Jonah found Hannah and Gracie inside cuddling on the couch beneath a warm blanket, watching a movie together.

"It just started, Dad!" Gracie informed him, patting the couch beside her. "You didn't miss anything yet."

Jonah sat down blankly. He stared at the TV but wasn't really looking at it.

Hannah watched him with concern. "You okay?"

He closed his eyes and shook his head, so infuriated that Jacob was *still* affecting him. "I don't really want to talk about it."

She stood up. "No, come here. Gracie, we'll be right back."

Hannah took his hand and led him into the kitchen.

"Tell me what's wrong," she insisted.

"I just found out that Jacob left me out of his will. I don't want anything from him. But I can't believe he did that to me. It just proves how little he thought of me as his son."

Hannah lovingly put her arms around him. "I'm so sorry. But he doesn't deserve all this space in your head."

Jonah nodded knowingly. "I want to meet Elliot. I'm ready now."

"Wait. Like, literally *now*?"

He grimaced. "Is that bad?"

She smiled. "I'll just let my mom know we're leaving."

Jonah sat behind the wheel of the Mercedes, staring ahead, lost in the thoughts that consumed him. His countenance easily depicted his inner turmoil.

"We don't have to go if you're not ready," Hannah finally said.

Jonah was startled by her voice as it brought him back. "I know. But I have to do this now before I change my mind."

He started the car and backed down the driveway.

"I can call Elliot for you. Or would you rather just surprise him?" she asked.

"Yeah, because if I see him and end up chickening out, it won't even matter. He'll never know."

"You'll be fine, Jonah. You won't change your mind."

"But you'll still come with me, right?"

Hannah smiled. "Of course."

When they'd gotten downtown, Hannah looked at the address Scarlett had given Jonah, trying to match the numbers with the storefronts they were passing.

"Do we even know what his store is?" Jonah asked.

"No, your mom only wrote down the address."

"Yeah, that helps," he muttered, slowing down a bit more so they wouldn't pass it.

"Wait, I think that's it," Hannah said, pointing to a small store.

Jonah parallel parked across the street and got out of the car.

"Tyler Music," he read aloud. "This can't be right…"

He took Hannah's hand, and they crossed the street together. According to the lettering on the window, the store sold a variety of musical instruments and offered music lessons. Jonah took a deep breath and tried peering inside without looking suspicious.

"Are you ready?" Hannah asked, loosening Jonah's grip on her hand.

He closed his eyes for a moment, willing himself to be calm. "Okay," he said, grabbing the handle and pulling the door open.

The modest space was covered wall to wall in a vast variety of guitars. A few keyboards were set up around the store, and a large display of instructional books and sheet music stood by the door. The glass counter that ran along the side wall encased pedals, tuners, guitar and bass strings, containers of picks, and other miscellaneous equipment. At the far end of the counter was the cash register, and there stood Elliot Tyler.

"Hi, there." His warm smile lit up his familiar blue eyes. "Can I help you find something?"

Elliot was tall and fit, his dark hair the same shade as Jonah's. His facial structure was similar as well. Hannah noticed the resemblance immediately.

"Umm..." Jonah struggled to form coherent words without his voice shaking. "Got any Gibsons?"

Elliot nodded. "Ah, good choice."

He motioned for them to follow him across the store to a display of guitars. "This one is my favorite. The Gibson Hummingbird." Elliot picked it up and strummed it.

"It's really nice," Jonah remarked.

"Yeah, I mean besides the obvious unique hummingbird pickguard, this thing is amazing. Mahogany back and sides, solid sikta spruce top, *and* it sounds beautiful. It's a bit pricey, but worth every penny." Elliot held it out to him. "You wanna try it out?"

Jonah took the guitar and fished a pick out of his pocket before sitting down.

"You must be a musician." Elliot chuckled, his grin also like Jonah's.

"He is," Hannah chimed in. "He's very talented. Writes his own music and everything."

Jonah began to play the guitar, instantly falling in love with it.

"Sounds good," Elliot said, visibly impressed.

Jonah couldn't take it any longer. He stopped playing and stood up, returning the guitar to its hook on the wall.

"So, what do you think?" Elliot asked. "Nice, right?"

"Yeah, it really is. But that's not why I'm here," Jonah said.

Elliot's eyebrows narrowed with confusion. "Is there something else I can help you find?"

Jonah sighed deeply. "I came to see *you*...You knew my mother."

It was all he needed to say. It was enough to make Elliot's eyes go wide and his mouth agape.

"Jonah," he said, just above a whisper.

"Yeah." Jonah nodded, his heart pounding.

Slowly, Elliot's lips formed a smile, tears pooling in his eyes. "My God," he said, putting a hand on Jonah's shoulder. "I can't believe you're here."

"Honestly, I wasn't sure I wanted to see you at first, but...I just had to."

"I'm so glad you did," Elliot said. "I haven't stopped thinking about you since I spoke to your mother the other day. I'm so sorry I didn't know about you."

Jonah's eyes welled up. "No. Don't apologize. It's not your fault."

Elliot nodded, Jonah's words evoking more emotion. "Thank you. I've been struggling with that."

"I know," Jonah replied. "I've been going through something very similar, actually."

Elliot stared at his son in disbelief. "Can we sit and chat? Do you have anywhere you need to be?"

Jonah smiled. "No, I'd love that."

Elliot closed the store and Hannah stepped out to browse the nearby shops, leaving Jonah to have some quality time with his father.

"I heard about your dad," Elliot started. "I read about his passing in the paper. I'm really sorry."

Jonah snickered. "Don't be. Let's just say, you're already a better father than he was."

Elliot raised his eyebrows. "Well, that doesn't sound good."

"I guess you could say he was abusive," Jonah said, casting his gaze to the floor. "He never laid a hand on me, but sometimes I wonder if that would've been easier."

Elliot frowned, studying the pain that marked his son's features. "What do you mean?"

"He was terrifying," Jonah continued bluntly. "Always looking for every possible opportunity to tear me apart. Apparently, I was being punished for my mom's affair even though I knew nothing about it until a week ago."

Elliot looked troubled. "I'm so sorry for that. I knew your mother was married, and that was very wrong on my part. I knew Jacob in high school. He was insane. I don't even know how your mother ended up with him. Why anyone would choose to be with him is beyond me."

Jonah grew quite curious. "So, you did know my mom in high school?"

Elliot nodded. "I did. We dated for six months during junior year. Things fizzled out over the summer, and when our senior year started, she was with Jacob. I think they broke up every other week, but she stuck by him. He was controlling and jealous, so she and I stopped talking until a couple months after we graduated. She'd broken up with Jacob again, supposedly for good, and I ran into her. We went on several dates and started getting serious again, but then Jacob came back around. Before I knew it, they were married and having a baby, and I didn't see her again for eleven years."

"And that's when I happened," Jonah added.

"Evidently." Elliot smiled. "I really believed she was finally going to be mine. I guess I was just a fool. Out of the

151

blue, she broke it off, and I never spoke to her again...until five days ago."

Jonah sighed. "Crazy, huh?"

"Yeah, that's for sure. That was one phone call I was *not* expecting. I won't bore you with the details, but my ex-wife and I were married for ten years. She couldn't have any children. And that was okay; I could live with it. But it caused a lot of insecurities for her, which in turn, caused a lot of problems for us. We divorced three years ago. So, I never had any children. I always wanted some of my own, and it's always been kind of tough watching my sisters have children. And with kids coming in and out of here, giving them lessons, I just felt like something was missing...but then that phone call..."

"So, it was good news, then?" Jonah asked.

Elliot grinned. "Of course it was. Hey, so tell me, who's the girl you came in with?"

"You mean Hannah?" Jonah asked, failing to suppress a smile.

"Ah, I see. I'm guessing she's pretty special?"

Jonah nodded. "Yes. I've been in love with her since I was thirteen. We have a daughter named Gracie."

Elliot's expression changed quickly. "Wait—what? You have a daughter? I have...a granddaughter?"

"You do. She's four. And this is crazy, just like everything else, but I found out about her the same day you found out about me."

Elliot paused in bewilderment. "Um...I don't even know what to say to that."

Jonah proceeded to tell Elliot the story of him and Hannah. As Jonah shared his journey, he couldn't believe how ridiculous it all sounded.

"Wow," Elliot said. "That's a lot to go through. But you

sure seem to be handling yourself well."

Jonah shrugged. "It's been a struggle, but I guess I've managed."

Elliot looked at him for a moment, mulling everything over. "You seem like a really great guy, and I'm so happy to see that. Knowing who raised you, I honestly wasn't sure what to expect. But oddly enough, I can't believe how much you remind me of myself. I don't know if that's weird, but...all of it's weird, right?"

Jonah laughed. "*Extremely* weird."

"I'm really glad you came here today. Thank you. I know that took a lot of guts," Elliot said.

"I was definitely nervous about it, but I figured you couldn't be worse than Jacob, so I had a pretty good chance of it going okay."

"Can I be honest with you?" Elliot asked. "It's taking a lot right now to just sit here calmly and not *freak out* about the fact that *my* son was raised by that man. Let me just say, if it were possible, I'd give him more than a piece of my mind."

Jonah didn't know how to respond. He hadn't expected such blatant honesty.

Elliot cleared his throat. "I'm sorry, Jonah. I shouldn't have said that. It was incredibly inappropriate."

"Trust me, I'm not offended," Jonah assured him. "It's nice to have a father that actually cares about me."

Elliot placed his hand on Jonah's shoulder. "Listen, I'm here and I am prepared to be in your life, if that's what you want. Or if you need time, that's okay too. I just want you to know that I *do* want to be your father."

Jonah struggled not to get choked up. "I'm definitely not opposed to that."

Elliot smiled, his eyes glistening again. He stood and crossed the room, retrieving the guitar he'd shown Jonah earlier.

"I'd like you to have this." He held it out to him.

"You can't be serious. That's much too generous," Jonah replied, wondering why he kept finding himself in these situations.

"Look, I've missed out on twenty-three years of taking care of you and buying you birthday and Christmas presents. Just please, let me do this," Elliot insisted.

Jonah took the flawless instrument. "Thank you. So much. This is incredible."

Without worrying whether he should or not, Jonah put his free arm around his father and hugged him. Elliot reciprocated, embracing him tightly.

"You're welcome, son."

ELEVEN

Hannah entered the kitchen and sat down at the table across from Jonah. He was staring intently at his laptop, his face illuminated by the screen.

"Gracie fell asleep on the couch. Do you want to tuck her in with me?" she asked him.

He looked up, having just realized she was there. "Oh. Yeah. Just a second."

"What are you doing anyway? You've been at this for a while now."

Jonah sighed. "I'm trying to find a job. I've been searching everywhere. I answered a couple ads, but I'm just getting frustrated."

"Well, it's only been a few hours. I'm sure it'll take some time," Hannah encouraged him.

"No, I mean, I'm frustrated because I don't even want to do this. I don't care about computers. I'm sick of digital design and web stuff," he confessed.

Hannah rested her chin in her hand, her elbow propped on the table. "Yeah, you don't strike me as the computer geek type."

He managed a half smile. "No, I'm serious. I don't even like it."

"So, why did you major in it then?"

"Well, I *wanted* to get my bachelors in music performance and try to get my music going," he admitted. "But Jacob freaked out and was going to stop paying my tuition if I didn't change my major. So I chose graphic design because, to Jacob, it was a 'normal' job, and I figured I could live with it."

"Okay, so if you could do *anything*, what would you do?" Hannah asked.

Jonah knew his answer immediately. "If I was brave enough, I'd record an album on my own and play shows. But I can't do that anyway, because I have a family to think about now. The term 'starving musician' exists for a reason."

Hannah frowned, reaching out to brush his hair out of his eyes. "I'm sorry. But we don't have to figure this out tonight, okay?"

She stood and rounded the table, taking Jonah's hand. He closed his laptop and followed her into the living room where Gracie was curled up on the couch. Jonah scooped her up and carried her into her room, placing her gently in her bed. He pulled the covers over her before giving her a soft kiss on the head.

Jonah entered Hannah's bedroom, looking somewhat troubled. "I'm actually going to sleep on the couch tonight…if you don't mind."

Hannah narrowed her eyebrows. "Is everything okay? Did I do something wrong?"

With a pained expression, he approached her, placing his hands on her shoulders. "No, you didn't do anything wrong. Why would you think that? I just feel like it's the more appropriate thing to do."

She nodded. "Yeah. I guess so."

Jonah bit his lower lip. "And actually…I was thinking I should stay at my mom's after tonight."

Hannah didn't hide her hurt. "Really?"

"I don't know, I guess I'm old-fashioned. I'm sorry if that upsets you, but I don't want to live like we're married...until we're *married*," he explained.

"But we have a *child* together. Isn't it a little late for the moral route?" she asked.

Jonah took her hands in his. "Hannah. I know. But we just got back together after *five* years apart. We're still dealing with so much, we don't need the distractions of the physical stuff right now."

"It's not like I'm trying to have sex with you. I just like having you here," Hannah said.

He sighed, brushing his hand across her cheek. "I just want to do things the right way. And I know if I stay here with you, I may not be strong enough to do that. I don't want our wedding to be a formality, where absolutely nothing changes because we've already been acting like we were married. I just need some things to stay sacred."

Hannah looked at him for a moment, both hating and loving everything he was saying. "That *is* how I always pictured it...the exciting way life would change after the wedding. Finally sharing day-to-day life together in a way we never had before."

"Otherwise, what's the point, right?" Jonah said, pulling her close.

A smile brightened her pretty face. "Just please don't make me wait too long."

Jonah chuckled and gave her a quick kiss. "I've wanted to marry you for ten years now. Trust me, it won't be any longer than it has to be."

Jonah carried Gracie on his shoulders, pausing at a large

window with an underwater view of the sea turtle tank. He and Hannah had taken Gracie to spend the day at the aquarium, something she'd always wanted to do. Gracie stared wide-eyed into the water before her, watching the turtles swim about.

She pointed excitedly. "Look at the baby one! Aww, I love him."

"Just wait until you see the penguins," Jonah said, securely gripping her little ankles over his chest.

Just as they were about to move on to the next exhibit, a voice stopped them.

"Jonah? Oh wow, it's you."

They turned to see two familiar faces.

"Oliver," Jonah said, accepting his handshake.

"And you remember Stella, of course." Oliver Grayson motioned to the woman beside him. "We got married about a year ago."

Hannah smiled. "Oh, congratulations."

"Thank you," Stella replied. "I'm not surprised to see you two still together. When did you get married?"

Jonah and Hannah exchanged uneasy glances.

"Umm...We're not, actually," Jonah said.

Stella frowned. "Oh. I'm sorry. I saw your daughter, and I just assumed. She *is* your daughter, right?"

Hannah nodded. "Yes. Her name is Gracie."

"I'm four!" Gracie supplied, proudly holding up four little fingers.

Everyone chuckled, the tension temporarily lifting.

"Four? Oops, right?" Oliver snidely commented.

"Oliver!" Stella hissed, elbowing his side.

Oliver snickered. "Hey, sorry. Now we know why they both disappeared off the face of the earth after high school."

Jonah handed Gracie off to Hannah, and she took her to look at more fish. Jonah turned back to Oliver. "All right, what's your problem?" he asked calmly.

"It should be obvious," Oliver said. "You were my best friend, Jonah. After everything we went through, you just left. And then something *this* big happens in your life, and you couldn't even tell me?"

Jonah sighed heavily. He certainly did not want to go into detail with Oliver about how he had just recently found out the news himself.

"I'm sorry. We didn't tell anyone. The last few years have been a little hectic. Hannah and I took some time apart. I *just* moved back here. So, I'm sorry I've been a bad friend, okay?"

Oliver looked away sheepishly. He was ashamed of his outburst after Jonah had reacted with such composure.

"No, I'm sorry. I shouldn't have said anything."

"It's fine. I'll see you around," Jonah said, turning away.

Oliver opened his mouth to further grovel, but decided to let it rest.

Jonah caught up with Hannah and Gracie, feeling a bit rattled but comforted by the sight of them.

"Hey. I'm so sorry about that." He spoke softly, touching Hannah's shoulder.

Hannah just nodded, refusing to look at him, but Jonah could tell she was upset. He placed his hand under her chin and gently lifted her face toward him.

"Are you crying?" he asked tenderly, his eyebrows knit together with worry. "Come here."

Jonah drew her into his embrace as she clutched Gracie's hand.

"How could he say that about our child?" Hannah

whispered to him. "Is that what everyone's going to say?"

Jonah pulled away to look at her. "No. No one is going to say that. Oliver's just upset about other things. And he apologized. Please don't worry, okay? I don't want you to worry."

"Mommy, don't cry," Gracie added, hugging Hannah's leg. "Today is a happy day, and me and Daddy love you."

Hannah smiled and ran her hand over Gracie's hair. "I love you too, baby."

Jonah quietly let himself into his mother's house. He thought about how long it had been since he'd unlocked that door with that same key he'd held onto all those years. It was strange to come through that door and feel no fear, to not have to worry what awaited him in those tainted rooms. Still, Jonah could remember every creaky floorboard.

As a teenager, he'd been sure to memorize the most silent route to his bedroom so as to avoid Jacob at all costs. Even when Jonah made it home by curfew, Jacob could still find an excuse to stir up conflict. And even now, as a board groaned beneath his foot, Jonah half expected to hear heavy footsteps overhead, coming to seal his doom. He quickly shook off the thought and let out the breath he hadn't realized he'd been holding. Jonah could finally feel at home here. It was an odd notion.

Scarlett appeared at the top of the stairs as Jonah hung up his coat.

"Oh, Mom, hey. I hope I didn't wake you up."

"No, I couldn't sleep. I heard you come in so I thought I'd see how you were doing."

Jonah smiled, grateful for her interest. "I'm good. We

went to the aquarium today. Ran into Oliver and Stella. That was interesting. Went out for pizza. It was a nice day."

"I'm glad," Scarlett remarked.

Jonah still hadn't told his mother about meeting Elliot. He hadn't been ready to share it with her. Just as he was contemplating bringing it up, his phone rang.

"I'll let you get that," Scarlett said. "Good night."

As she disappeared, Jonah answered Nathan's call.

"Hey," he said, walking into the kitchen.

"Hey, man, you weren't sleeping, were you?" Nathan asked.

"No, I just got home. What's up?"

"Kendall and I were talking tonight, and we thought it would be cool if the four of us went out for a drink. Maybe tomorrow? There's this nice lounge here. I think it could be a good time."

Jonah thought for a moment. "I have to double check with Hannah first, but sure. Sounds good."

"It'll be really fun," Jonah promised, pouring milk over Gracie's Cheerios the next morning. He set the bowl on the table in front of her.

"I don't know," Hannah replied, sipping her coffee. "I doubt I have anything in common with Kendall."

"Sure you do. You're both madly in love with Weston boys," he said with a facetious grin.

Hannah playfully rolled her eyes.

"Okay, you got me, I'm not really a Weston," Jonah said, filling a mug with coffee. "But what *is* true is that you're a lot more fun than you seem to think you are."

She grimaced. "I guess I feel like I'm just a boring mom who has no concept of what's even cool these days."

"You're a cool mom," Gracie said, shoveling a large spoonful of cereal into her mouth. "And you're fun and you're not boring. You should listen to Daddy."

Jonah flashed a wide grin. "See how smart our girl is? She knows what she's talking about."

Hannah chuckled. "Fine. I'll go. But I'm not so sure about the whole drinking part."

"Because of me that one night? When I was a *complete* idiot?" he asked sheepishly.

She shook her head. "Oh, no, not that. I've...never drank before."

Jonah raised his eyebrows. "Really? Never?"

"When would I have had the chance? I've had a child to take care of since I was nineteen."

"That makes sense," he remarked. "And that one time during sophomore year when we all tried to get drunk off of margarita mix at Oliver's dad's house certainly doesn't count."

Hannah laughed in reply at the memory.

"So you don't have to drink if you don't want to," Jonah said. "And I won't if you don't want me to. We'll just hang out for a bit, and we can leave whenever you want."

The Pompadour Lounge was a sophisticated, upscale establishment. The tables were intimately spread out along the perimeter of the dimly lit space, and the large bar sat in the center, serving the finest wine, liquor, and beer. A stage stood off to the side, always featuring low-key live entertainment ranging from acoustic sets to light jazz.

Following Hannah through the front door, Jonah immediately felt out of place. He was glad he'd overdressed for the occasion. Glancing at Hannah, he saw her nervously smoothing out her black dress and knew she was feeling the same. Jonah took her hand.

"Come on," he said. "Nathan said they'd be in the back."

Jonah led Hannah past tables of confident-looking men and women, who smiled as they chatted over their drinks. They didn't seem to have a care in the world. Jonah wondered what that felt like.

"Hey, you made it." Nathan grinned, standing to hug Hannah. "Thanks for coming all this way."

"Oh, it wasn't a bad ride. Thanks for inviting us," Hannah said, shaking Kendall's hand.

"This place is great. It's our favorite," Nathan said, waving down a server. He ordered Johnnie Walker Blue "with three ice cubes and a splash of water" for himself and Ciroc and Sprite for Kendall.

"And for you?" the server asked Jonah and Hannah. They exchanged glances, their knowledge of alcoholic drinks barely surpassing beer.

"Just get them what we're having," Nathan said to the server.

"You got it," he replied, hurrying off.

Hannah smiled apologetically. "Yeah, sorry. We're not experienced drinkers."

"That's why I invited you out with us tonight," Nathan remarked.

"To get us drunk?" Jonah joked.

Nathan snickered. "No, so you can loosen up and have some fun. You both need it."

Hannah nodded in agreement. "Yes. Things *have* been quite hectic lately."

The server returned with their drinks, and Nathan watched curiously as they tried his selections. He grinned proudly when they both approved.

"Maybe you're in the wrong field," Kendall teased. "You should've been a bartender instead."

Nathan laughed. "Dad would've *loved* that!"

"No, he really would have," Jonah said, motioning with his hand as if he was tilting back a drink.

"He did love to drink. Maybe that's where I get it from." Nathan took a swig from his glass.

Jonah grew quiet for a moment. "So, I met my dad the other day," he finally said.

Nathan's eyes widened. "Why didn't you tell me? How did it go?"

Jonah smiled. "It went very well, actually. He's a really nice guy."

"He's so much like Jonah," Hannah added. "And he owns a music store."

"That's awesome," Nathan remarked. "So...do you look like him?"

Jonah looked to Hannah for her input, and she nodded.

"He really does," she said.

Nathan paused. "This is still so weird to me...I still can't wrap my head around it."

"Me neither. You go your whole life thinking one thing, and then suddenly it changes. It's insane," Jonah expounded. He could feel his drink beginning to affect him.

"So, how are things going with you two?" Kendall chimed in. "I don't mean to pry, but your story just intrigues me."

"She's a journalist," Nathan said. "She lives for stuff like that."

"It's okay," Hannah replied. "We're doing well, actually. A bit rocky at first, but I think that was to be expected." She turned to look at Jonah. "But I'm pretty crazy about him."

The night progressed naturally as the two couples bonded. After a while, the women split off into their own conversation, leaving the brothers to themselves. Jonah excused himself for a moment to use the restroom. On his way, he spotted their server and approached him.

"Hey, could you do me a favor?" Jonah asked. "Could you put mine and my girlfriend's drinks on a separate check? I know my brother won't let me later, so I just wanted to let you know now."

"Yeah, sure thing." The server nodded with a smile.

"Thanks, I appreciate it," Jonah replied, continuing on to the restroom.

He was grateful for Nathan and everything he'd done for him, but he wanted to prove that he could stand on his own two feet. He needed Hannah to know he could too.

"So, you're going to marry him?" Kendall's tone was unapologetically incredulous as she leaned in close to Hannah for some one-on-one girl talk after Nathan went off to the bar.

Hannah maintained a cheerful disposition. "Yes. Well, after he asks me. We're taking things slow right now, so I'm not sure when that'll be."

"Are you sure you want to get married? I mean, Jonah is a nice guy. A little damaged...But don't you want to get out there and have some fun first? You've never had the chance to do that."

Hannah furrowed her brow. "Why would I want to do that if I've already found the one I want to be with?"

Kendall shrugged. "Well, what if you get married and then a few years down the road you wish you'd experienced more before you tied yourself down? You're only twenty-three. Why the hurry?"

"We have a daughter, remember? We're already tied *together*. And I love him. I could never love anyone else the way I love Jonah. I always have," Hannah said. She was frustrated, having to defend her feelings.

Kendall chuckled, sipping the last of her drink. "I just don't understand how you two can be so sure about each other, and *so* happy together, especially after everything that's happened."

"Why wouldn't we be sure about each other? I've known Jonah for nearly half my life," Hannah countered.

"Yeah, you knew him when you were in *high school*. There's no way he's the same guy you were dating five years ago. People grow up and change. He had all that time without you, on his own. And lots of other girls too, I'm sure."

Hannah shook her head. "No, he never dated anyone else. Just me."

Kendall laughed with pity and placed her hand on Hannah's shoulder. "Honey, if he told you that, then he's lying to you. There's no way a guy like him can resist all of his options. And I don't mean just *dating* other girls either."

"What *do* you mean?"

"Just *look* at him. He's an attractive guy, Hannah. He could probably get any girl he wants. So why wouldn't he?"

Hannah felt anxiety come over her like a weight on her chest. "Then why would he move *all* the way here if he didn't actually love me?"

Kendall smirked, toying with the corner of the beverage napkin beneath her empty glass. "Well, he has a kid with you. He kind of had no choice."

Hannah wasn't sure how to respond. Kendall had had quite a lot to drink, and Hannah knew she wasn't feeling very lucid herself, but still, their conversation upset her. She believed Jonah was genuine and had nothing to hide, but on the other hand, everything Kendall said had made sense.

Hannah suddenly feared it was unrealistic that things had fallen together so easily after five whole years apart. Could Kendall's warnings have any truth to them? Was Hannah naïve to think Jonah had been completely honest with her? And wasn't he himself under the influence when he'd shared that alleged honesty? Hannah couldn't shake the disturbing feeling that settled within her.

When Jonah returned from the restroom, he found his brother sitting at the bar.

"Where are Hannah and Kendall?" he asked.

Nathan pointed behind him. "They're having a little heart to heart. They seem to be getting along well."

"That's good." Jonah glanced over to steal a glimpse of Hannah.

"What can I get you?" the bartender asked Jonah.

"I'll just have a ginger ale," he said.

"Ginger ale?" Nathan questioned. "What are you, twelve?"

Jonah snickered. "Someone has to drive home tonight. And I don't think it's going to be Hannah."

"Yeah, she seems like she's having fun. Just watch her with Kendall, though. She knows how to throw 'em back," Nathan joked.

A few moments later, Hannah approached them, a little clumsy on her feet. She laughed at herself.

"Hey, where's Kendall?" Nathan asked her.

"Oh, she got a phone call. She went outside to answer it. I think she said it was the wedding coordinator." Hannah perched on the stool beside Jonah.

"Man, those two are always on the phone. She better

be worth all the money we're paying her," Nathan scoffed, downing the rest of his drink.

"Oh, Jonah, can you give your mom a call and check on Gracie?" Hannah requested, lightly tugging the lapels of his blazer.

He tucked a strand of hair behind her ear. "I'm sure she's fine."

"Please? It would just make me feel better," she said, flirtatiously toying with the top button of his shirt. She put on a pout for good measure.

"All right." He stood and gave Hannah a kiss on the head before he turned toward the door.

Jonah stepped outside into the crisp night breeze and made his way to the edge of the building to make his call. As he retrieved his phone from his front pocket, he heard someone just around the corner. He stopped, recognizing Kendall's voice.

"I told you not to call me tonight," she said into her phone. "He's going to figure it out...How many times can our *wedding coordinator* call before it looks suspicious? And what coordinator calls so late at night, Chris? Nathan's not stupid...Yes, I still want to marry *him*...I don't know, maybe because he's a *doctor*, and you're essentially the office coffee fetcher? I should go, Chris, I'm sorry."

Jonah had heard enough. Instantly nauseated, he spun around and hurried inside before Kendall ended her phone call. He tried to give her the benefit of the doubt, tried to imagine how it could be anything other than what it sounded like. But Jonah couldn't deny that he'd caught her. Whoever Chris was, Kendall was involved with him.

Mindlessly allowing his feet to carry him back to the bar, Jonah contemplated how he could tell his brother such an awful thing. But how could he *not* tell him?

When Jonah approached, Hannah was sitting next to a man he didn't recognize. They were talking and laughing, and Nathan was nowhere to be found.

"Hey." Jonah got Hannah's attention. He stepped between them, turning his back to the man.

"Oh, hey," she greeted him with a glazed grin. She took a swig from her glass.

"Hannah, I think you need to slow down a bit."

"Gabe bought me a sex on the beach." She giggled at the name.

Jonah turned to the man behind him. "You bought her that?"

"Hey, I didn't know she had a boyfriend. She didn't say anything," he defended himself.

"Sex on the beach? Really?" Jonah retorted, feeling on edge.

"I didn't mean anything by it. I saw a pretty girl, she wasn't wearing a ring, so I bought her a drink."

Hannah flashed her naked left hand in front of Jonah's face. "That's what happens when you take things too slow," she jabbed at him, her words slightly slurred.

Slowly, Jonah turned to look at her, pain in his eyes. "I think it's time to go." He spoke in a low voice, reaching for her hand.

Hannah dodged his touch, tipping her glass back to consume the rest of its contents. "I'm not ready yet. I was talking to Gabe about his job...because *he* has one."

Jonah swallowed the lump in his throat. "Fine," he managed, walking away.

He rounded the bar to the bartender. "Can I pay my bill?" he asked, pulling out his wallet.

The bartender swiftly tapped a few buttons on the touchscreen of his computer and printed out the check. He set it down in front of Jonah, who gawked in horror at the total: $122.56. There were several different drinks listed after the initial two that Nathan had ordered for them. Hannah had really gotten out of control. With his hands shaking, Jonah fished several bills from his wallet and handed them to the bartender.

"Keep the change," he muttered, turning toward the table to find his brother.

When Nathan wasn't there, Jonah trudged toward the stage and found him watching the band. Jonah put a hand on his brother's shoulder.

"I have to go," he said, leaning in so Nathan could hear him over the music.

"Oh, really?" Nathan seemed disappointed. "All right, man. Thanks for coming. I'll see you guys tomorrow, right?"

Jonah nodded, barely hearing what he said. Between Kendall's apparent cheating and Hannah's blatant aggression toward him, an overwhelming sense of anxiety was rapidly consuming him.

Jonah once again approached Hannah, who was still very much enthralled by Gabe's attention.

"Come on, Hannah," Jonah pleaded, praying she'd cooperate. "We should go."

She looked up at him, seeing the anguish laced in his features. "Okay." She turned back to Gabe. "Well, it was nice to meet you. Thanks for the drink."

He smiled with a friendly wave. "Good luck to you."

Hannah slid off the barstool, and Jonah reached out to steady her as she stumbled.

"I'm fine," she snapped, and he put his hands up as if to surrender.

Jonah followed Hannah to the door, his wounded heart aching. He was so confused, wondering why she was treating him this way. Sure, she was drunk, but there had to be some true emotions behind her outbursts. Jonah couldn't begin to imagine what had gotten into her.

As they exited the lounge, they ran into Kendall.

"Are you leaving?" she asked.

Hannah rolled her eyes. "Well, *I* wanted to stay, but *this* one isn't very much fun," she scoffed, pointing at Jonah.

"No, trust me, it's time to get home," he said.

Kendall gave a sympathetic smile. "Aw, well, we'll see you guys tomorrow, then."

Jonah could barely look her in the eye. "Yeah. See you then."

When they reached the car, Hannah froze, pressing her palms against the passenger door as if bracing herself.

"You okay?" Jonah asked.

"I don't feel so good," she mumbled, placing a hand on her stomach.

She abruptly turned toward the bushes and began to vomit. Immediately, Jonah was at her side, holding her hair away from her face as she heaved. He was surprised she didn't push him away.

When Hannah was certain the nausea had subsided, Jonah helped her into the car. After climbing in beside her, he sat there for a moment.

"Hannah…What is going on? Did I do something?" he asked in a quiet tone.

She sighed heavily, slouching in her seat. "Jonah, I don't want to talk right now. I just want to go to sleep."

"So, I get no explanation for why you treated me like shit in front of that guy."

"I don't know if I can trust you, okay?" Hannah finally said.

Jonah exhaled sharply, like he'd been punched in the

stomach. "Hannah. Of course you can trust me. What are you talking about?"

"We have grown up so much in five years. How do I know you're still the same guy? How do I even know I can trust you with my daughter?" The tears soaked her face.

Jonah slid his hands into his hair, clenching it in his fists. "How can you say that? I may not be a perfect father, but I'm learning…Listen, you *know* me. You're the only one who does."

Hannah gawked at him skeptically. "Is that what you tell *all* of your girls?"

His eyes went wide. "What girls? Hannah! There are no other girls. There never were. I *told* you that."

"How do I know you're telling the truth? You were gone for *years*. Half a *decade*. You thought you'd never see me again. So how could there have been no one else all that time?"

Jonah's heart pounded as he gripped the steering wheel. "Because I only wanted *you*. You know that, Hannah. I never stopped wanting you."

She crossed her arms over her chest. "Well, ever since we got back from Florida, it doesn't feel like you want me."

"What? What's changed since Florida?"

Hannah dropped her gaze to the floor. "Things were so perfect with us, and then you just pulled back. It's like you made things go backward with us."

Jonah stared at her. "Because I won't spend the night with you? That's all that's changed."

"But it makes me feel like you don't want me," Hannah confessed with a whimper.

He shook his head. "No. That is not it at all. I want you more than you can imagine."

"But it doesn't matter, does it, Jonah? Because you don't even have a job, so we can't get married for God knows how long. And what if we never get married? What if I lose you again before that happens?"

"Hannah, I am trying! You *know* I'm trying. And you are *not* going to lose me. Why would you think you could?" Jonah asked, agony brimming in his eyes.

Hannah looked at him, her eyelids heavy. "Because I already did once."

Twelve

Jonah hadn't gotten much more out of Hannah before she turned away from him and fell asleep, leaving him alone with his tormenting thoughts for the one-hour drive home.

With a heavy heart and a long sigh, Jonah pulled into his mother's driveway and turned off the engine. He looked at Hannah, who was still sleeping peacefully, and nearly crumbled. He imagined her waking up and smiling at him with her usual loving gaze, and it made him ache all the more. Maybe her inebriation had lent her an epiphany, making her realize she would never be happy with him. What if it had given her the clarity she needed to finally move on?

Brushing off the dreadful, gut-wrenching thought, Jonah got out and rounded the car to the passenger side. He opened the door and carefully unbuckled Hannah's seatbelt. She didn't stir when he gently slid his arms beneath her body to lift her out. Cradling her, Jonah pushed the door closed with his foot, then walked slowly toward the house. When Hannah nestled her head into his chest, he thought he might die right there on the pavement.

With a bit of a struggle, Jonah eased the front door open and stepped inside. Cautiously, he climbed the stairs, gripping Hannah tightly against him. He reached Nathan's old room, where he found Gracie asleep on the far side of the bed. Jonah wondered if it was safe for them to share a bed, but his tired arms decided for him, and he tenderly set Hannah down. He lingered in the doorway for a moment, incredibly distraught. He couldn't shake his worry as he turned off the light and closed the door.

Once in his own bedroom, Jonah undressed and eagerly collapsed onto his bed, staring up into the darkness. He needed a reprieve from his thoughts and prayed he could fall asleep quickly. Instead, he tossed and turned, felt hot and then cold, replayed conversations and ugly words in his head, worried about Nathan and what he would say to him, or if he should even say anything at all. The stream of thoughts wouldn't relent.

Somehow, after an hour of restlessness, Jonah drifted off. As he began to dream, a rustling beside him tugged him back toward consciousness. An arm slid around him from behind, a body drawing closely to his. His eyes shot open as he felt a trail of kisses travel along the back of his shoulder. When Hannah's hand began to wander too freely, Jonah abruptly turned from his side to his back and peered through the darkness to see her face.

"Hannah," he whispered, barely making out her silhouette beside him. "What are you doing?"

She loomed closer, kissing his jaw and his neck. "I want to be with you."

Jonah could still smell alcohol on her breath. "I think it would be better if we just went to sleep."

Hannah let out an agitated sigh and sat up, facing away from him. "Of course...God, Jonah, what is the big deal?"

He reached out to touch her shoulder, but she ducked away. "I don't understand you tonight, Hannah," he said, a slight tremble in his voice.

"I did a lot of thinking after I talked with Kendall," she remarked.

"Kendall? What did she say? You can't trust her. She's *cheating* on my brother."

Hannah snickered. "Oh, sure. You're perfect, and everyone else is a mess, right?"

"What? When have I ever implied *that*?"

She ignored his question. "Kendall said I should get out there and have some fun before I tie myself down. Maybe she's right, ya know? We're so young. I haven't done *anything*. You've done a lot of things. You're practically a celebrity in Tampa while I've been hiding out here in this hellhole. How do I know that I'll ever get to be anything?"

"How can you say you've done nothing? What about our daughter? Her world revolves around you. And you are a great mother. Even if you never did anything else with your life, being Gracie's mom is already the most beautiful thing you could ever do." With tears in his eyes, Jonah waited for her response.

"Forget I ever said anything. I just want to go home. Please take me home," she insisted, scooting off the bed.

Jonah sighed, deciding it was probably for the best. He got up and pulled his clothes back on.

"I'll keep Gracie here with me tonight," he said, buttoning his shirt.

"Why? You don't think I can take care of her? I thought I was such a good mother," Hannah retorted.

"No. Because she's already asleep, and I don't want to bother her." Jonah chose to ignore her rudeness, while Hannah said nothing in reply.

After Jonah woke his mother to let her know he was leaving Gracie in her care once again, he followed Hannah out to his car.

"I'm sorry you're so unhappy with everything," he said in a dull tone as he drove.

"I didn't say I was unhappy. I'm just...impatient."

"Things take time, Hannah. I'm doing the best I can."

"I'm tired of waiting. I hate it," she said sulkily.

"I know. I do too," Jonah agreed. "We want the same things, Hannah."

He pulled into her driveway and saw that her mother wasn't home. "Are you going to be okay by yourself tonight?"

Hannah groaned, opening the car door. "Yes. I'm fine. Why do you always worry about me?"

"That's what I'm supposed to do. 'Cause I love you," Jonah said, praying for a mutual response.

But Hannah said nothing. She ungracefully slid out of the car, shutting the door behind her. Jonah saw her wipe her eye and wondered if she was crying. He wanted so badly to run after her. To take her in his arms and beg her to stop whatever it was that was causing her to doubt. But he just sat there, watching her walk up the steps to the porch. He waited until she let herself into the house without turning back to look at him before he drove home.

Jonah slowly awoke from a deep sleep, his eyelids fluttering groggily. It didn't take him long to realize that Gracie was standing beside his bed, resting her chin in her hands as she watched him. He was startled and suddenly wide awake.

"You have pretty eyelashes, Daddy," she said, giggling.

Jonah smiled. "Thank you. I guess. When did you wake up?"

"Um, I don't know. I think the clock said seven-oh-oh," Gracie answered.

Lifting his heavy head, Jonah looked at the bedside alarm clock: 7:05. It was much too early for how terrible he felt. He had gotten only four hours of sleep after the night's bizarre antics.

"Where's Mommy?" Gracie asked.

Jonah hesitated. "She's at home. She felt sick, so she wanted to be there instead."

"Did she catch a fever?" Gracie wondered, her eyes wide with concern.

"No, sweetie. She had a tummy ache," he told her. Close enough.

"Are you sick too?" she questioned, her eyes inquisitive.

"No, why do you ask?"

"'Cause, Daddy. You don't look very good."

Jonah laughed. "Oh, Gracie. Come here."

He reached over and lifted her onto the bed, and she immediately cuddled against him. "Do you know what today is?" he asked his daughter.

"Nope."

"It's Thanksgiving. Do you know what that is?"

"When we eat turkey and pie?" Gracie guessed.

He smiled. "Yes, but it's also when we think about everything we're thankful for—all the things in our life that we're happy we have."

"Daddy?" she began.

"Yes, Gracie?"

She looked up at him, her big blue eyes serious. "I'm thankful for *you*."

When Jonah finally willed himself to get out of bed, he took a shower while his mother helped Gracie with breakfast. He spent way too much time choosing what to wear, as if he needed to impress Hannah. After deciding on a gray cable-knit cardigan over a navy henley with jeans, Jonah stood in the bathroom, staring at himself in the mirror. His focus flickered to the scar on his cheek, but he quickly darted his eyes away. He tousled his damp brown hair disapprovingly, then ran a hand over his stubble and wondered if he should've shaved. He couldn't help but feel inadequate.

Gracie knocked on the bathroom door, tearing him away from his self-deprecating thoughts. Jonah let her in.

"Ooh, Daddy, you look *handsome*."

Jonah glanced down at himself. "Thank you, baby."

"I'm ready to get ready too," she said.

Jonah helped her brush her teeth, get dressed, and tame her unruly curls.

Downstairs, Scarlett watched lovingly as Jonah knelt down to tie Gracie's shoes. He put her jacket on her and carefully zipped it up.

"You look beautiful, Gracie," he told her, standing up and taking her hand. "Say bye to Grandma."

"Bye, Gramma!"

"Thanks, Mom, for helping with Gracie. I'll see you later at Nathan's," Jonah said with a wave as they departed.

"Will Mommy be all better for Thanksgiving?" Gracie asked as they ascended the Morgans' porch steps.

"I hope so, baby." Jonah unlocked the front door with his recently acquired house key.

Gracie breezed into the house as Jonah closed the door behind them and set her bag on the foyer table. Caroline appeared in the kitchen doorway.

"Good morning, Jonah."

"Happy Thanksgiving, Mrs. Morgan." He forced a smile, wondering what Hannah's mother knew about the previous night. Even if she knew nothing, it would be equal to what Jonah knew.

"Hannah's in bed. She's hungover, as I'm sure you know," Caroline said with a snicker.

Jonah sighed. "I'm sorry about that."

"Don't apologize, Jonah. You're not responsible for her decisions. Some people have to learn the hard way."

He let out a chuckle, thinking of his own experiences. "Yes. That's definitely true."

Caroline nodded toward Hannah's room. "Go ahead and see her."

Jonah turned away and dragged his feet down the long hall, his stomach twisting with dread. He had absolutely no idea what to expect.

With a soft knock, Jonah eased the door open and slipped into her bedroom. "Hannah?"

He heard a groan as she rolled over and covered her head with her pillow. Jonah crossed the room and knelt beside her bed. He took a hold of the pillow and slowly pulled it away, revealing Hannah's weary, tear-stained face. She looked pale and exhausted.

"Don't look at me," she muttered, hiding behind her hands. "I look awful."

"Hannah, we need to talk," Jonah said tenderly, touching her shoulder.

She finally lowered her hands and looked at him, her eyes glistening with fresh tears. She forced herself to sit up, holding her pounding head.

"I know I said a lot of things last night."

Jonah nodded. "Yes. Yes, you did. Is that how you really feel?"

Hannah could see the flagrant anguish and fear in his blue eyes. She had to look away before she came undone.

"I'm not really sure how I feel," she confessed, toying with a loose thread on her bedspread.

"That's why I'm so confused," he said. "Everything was so perfect with us. I thought we were happy. Then all of a sudden, you just come at me with all of these crazy things, and I don't understand what I did."

Hannah bit her lower lip. "Jonah...I've spent the last four years with Gracie in the same routine. I never imagined you becoming a part of it, and I accepted that. Then, suddenly, here you are, and all of it has changed. Now, I have no idea what the future looks like. And every day, I'm scared to death that all of this is just going to go away. I barely survived the first time, and I know I could never do it again."

Jonah sat beside her and took her hand. "Why do you even think about me leaving you? I am never going to leave. I promise you that. I am *here* now. Always. Why do you question that?"

Hannah brushed her hand across her wet cheek. "I never thought I'd have this back, and now that I do, I'm afraid there's some sort of catch. What if you're only here because you feel obligated? What if you only *think* you still love me because you want to do the right thing for Gracie?"

He let go of her hand. "I can't believe you'd think that. I really hope that's just the bullshit Kendall filled your head with talking, because I know you know better. I love Gracie and I want to be here for her, but before I even knew about her, I wanted so badly to be us again. I'm here because I want to be—and I *have* to be here because I can't be without you anymore."

Hannah's voice trembled. "I'm sorry, Jonah."

"And why are you so worried about getting married?

181

Do you think I don't want to marry you just as badly?" he questioned.

She sighed. "Ever since we ran into Oliver and Stella, I feel like there's this urgency to correct our situation. Like if we get married, we won't be those teenagers that screwed up. We'll just be a family."

"We *are* a family," Jonah said. "Nothing changes that."

Hannah paused, collecting her thoughts. "I'm just...so scared of how much I *need* you."

He reached for her hand once more. "I am too. But I think we're safe now."

She looked at him with a fleck of hope in her pleading eyes. "I need you to tell me that everything isn't too good to be true. Because how could you possibly still be that perfect guy you always were?"

"Well, I wouldn't say 'perfect,' but I'm still me, right here in front of you. But your doubt is going to create exactly what you're afraid of," Jonah emphasized. "I need you to trust me. I've never given you a reason not to. You were *killing* me last night, Hannah. I can't take that."

"I'm so embarrassed," she said, unable to meet his gaze.

"About what?"

"About everything. How drunk I got. All the horrific things I said to you...I remember *all* of it. And it's not me at all. I am *so* sorry, Jonah."

Jonah didn't know what to say. He couldn't forget how badly she'd made him hurt.

"Do you forgive me?" Hannah whispered, her blue eyes wide with fear.

He sighed, fighting his emotions. "To be honest, I still can't shake the way you made me feel."

"Please, Jonah," she begged, grasping his hand.

"Let me finish," he said. "Last night hurt like hell. But I forgive you. Because losing *us* would hurt so much more."

Hannah seemed to deflate with relief. She collapsed against Jonah, sobbing into his chest. He wrapped his arms around her, rubbing her back to console her.

"Never second-guess who I am and how much you mean to me, okay?" he said. "And promise me you won't listen to another word Kendall says. She's toxic."

Hannah pulled away and placed her hand on his cheek. "I promise. I love you, Jonah. I really do. I'm so sorry I made you think otherwise."

He pressed his lips against her forehead. "I love you too."

Jonah, Hannah, and Gracie arrived at Nathan's new house, marveling their way up the brick-paved driveway to the Mediterranean-style home. They approached the tall, arched front doors, and Gracie excitedly rang the doorbell.

Within seconds, Nathan's smile greeted them, welcoming them inside. The interior was even more impressive, impeccably decorated and simply gorgeous. The scent of the cooking turkey wafted from the kitchen, and soft music played on Nathan's stereo system.

Kendall emerged, wiping her hands on a dishtowel. "Hey, guys. I'm so glad you could make it."

"Do you need help with anything?" Hannah asked, handing her the two pumpkin pies Caroline had insisted on baking before going to work.

Kendall smiled. "Everything is just about ready, but thank you. Please make yourselves at home."

The doorbell rang, and Nathan let Scarlett in.

The group made themselves comfortable on the

leather couches in the living room, in front of the flickering fireplace. The doorbell chimed once more, and Nathan looked puzzled, not expecting anyone else.

As Nathan stood to answer the door, Jonah decided to give warning.

"I may have forgotten to mention that I invited Elliot tonight."

"What?" Scarlett's face went pale.

"I know, I'm sorry. I should've told you I went to see him." Jonah caught his mother smoothing her hair, and he smiled.

"This should be interesting," Nathan commented, exiting the room.

He wasn't quite sure he was prepared to meet the man that Scarlett had preferred over his father. With apprehension, Nathan opened the door and laid eyes on a tall, pleasant-looking man who was unquestionably Jonah's father. Nathan found it odd to see a stranger who looked so familiar to him.

"Oh, wow," Elliot said with a warm smile. "You must be Nathan."

Perplexed, Nathan shook his hand. "Yes."

"Sorry, I'm Elliot. Your mom talked about you all the time, showed me lots of pictures...You haven't changed an awful lot."

"I may be a little taller," Nathan joked, stepping aside to welcome Elliot into his home.

Elliot laughed, flashing his Jonah-like grin. "Thank you so much for having me tonight. I know it's a bit of an awkward situation, and I apologize for imposing on your family gathering. I just can't pass up an opportunity to get to know my son."

"No, it's all right," Nathan insisted, appreciating his honesty. "It's important to Jonah, so it's important to us."

Scarlett waited anxiously as she listened to the voices looming in the foyer. When Elliot came into view, her breath nearly caught in her throat. His same sparkling blue eyes met hers for the first time in over two decades, and she nearly lost herself.

Jonah stood to greet Elliot with a handshake. "I'm so glad you could make it."

"Of course. I wouldn't miss it." Elliot eagerly turned his attention to Scarlett.

She approached him slowly, fighting to keep her composure. Elliot was still just as handsome, if not more so. It was inexplicably surreal to be in his presence once again without feeling guilty for it.

He grinned, reaching out to her. "Scarlett."

"Hello, Elliot." She smiled back, shaking his hand. "Good to see you."

"Good to see you as well. I'm so sorry about your husband. How are you doing?" he asked tenderly.

"I'm doing just fine," Scarlett declared with a nod.

"I'm happy to hear that," Elliot said, fondly noticing that she still blushed when she was nervous.

Jonah interrupted them. "Elliot, I'd like you to meet my daughter, Gracie," he said proudly, picking her up. "Gracie, this is your Grandpa...He's my dad."

"Oh," Gracie marveled, giving Elliot a big smile. "I just got a new Gramma, and now I have a new Grampa too!"

Elliot chuckled. "It's very lovely to meet you, Gracie." He was in awe of his son's child. His *grandchild*. His heart was full.

"Dinner is ready," Kendall announced, motioning everyone to the large dining room table. It was flawlessly set with china and cloth napkins over an elegant tablecloth.

"This looks amazing," Elliot commented on the

spread.

They took their seats and began filling their plates as they passed around the platters.

"So, Elliot, what do you do?" Kendall asked.

"I own and run a music store. I mostly sell guitars—acoustic and electric—and bass guitars, some pianos and keyboards. And I also teach music lessons, for both guitar and piano. It keeps me very busy. Sometimes too busy, but I love it," Elliot answered.

"How did you get into that?" Nathan asked.

"Well, my dad and I ran a small company for several years that ended up being very successful. About ten years ago, we sold it. I invested my half and did rather well. It might sound silly, but it was always a dream of mine to have a music store, and a few years ago, I finally had the means to do so." Elliot's eyes lit up the same way Jonah's did when he spoke of the things he loved.

"That's really great, Elliot. I'm so happy things have turned out so well for you," Scarlett said.

He smiled. "I've been very blessed."

Jonah couldn't help but notice how polished his father was, how he spoke with such confidence. Jonah wondered if he would be bolder, more refined, had Elliot been the one who raised him.

"Mommy," Gracie said suddenly. "What are you thankful for? Daddy said today means we think about what we're thankful for."

Hannah exchanged glances with Jonah and chuckled. "I'm thankful for you. And I'm thankful for your daddy, and that he's here with us."

Jonah smiled sheepishly, dropping his gaze.

"Hey, *I'm* thankful for Daddy too. You copied, Mom." Gracie giggled, turning to Scarlett. "Gramma, how about you?"

"I'm thankful that my sons are happy," Scarlett answered, smiling at both of them.

"Uncle Nathan?" Gracie said, pointing her fork at him.

Naturally, Nathan looked at Kendall, a loving expression on his face as he grasped her hand on the table between them.

"I am thankful for the most amazing fiancée I could have ever hoped for."

Kendall grinned back at him. "And *I* am thankful for this wonderful, hard-working guy, who has so easily become the love of my life."

Her statement caused Jonah to choke a little, and he coughed to clear his throat. Everyone turned their attention to him.

"Are you okay?" Hannah asked.

"All clear," Jonah said after the fit subsided. "*Crys*tal clear." He locked eyes with Kendall, staring blankly at her for just a moment before looking away.

Thirteen

Jonah was exiting the restroom when Kendall blindsided him. She sternly placed her hands on his chest and backed him into the bathroom, closing the door behind them. She turned on the faucet to drown out their forthcoming conversation.

"How the hell do you know about Chris?"

Jonah sighed and leaned against the counter, crossing his arms over his chest. "I heard you on the phone last night."

"What, were you spying on me or something?"

"No. I went outside to make a phone call, and there you were."

Kendall rubbed her lips together, worry laced in her features. "Jonah, please. You *cannot* tell Nathan."

He straightened his posture, dropping his arms to his sides with a chuckle. "Why would I just let you do this to him?"

Kendall stared at the tile floor. "I never meant for anything to happen with Chris. It was a mistake, and it's over."

"If you really loved my brother, you would've been able to control yourself. How long have you been hiding this?"

She hesitated. "Three months."

Jonah gawked at her. "Three *months*? That's a bit long to keep making the same supposed mistake, isn't it?"

"Shh! Please, keep it down!" Kendall pleaded in a harsh whisper. "I know I screwed up. It's been killing me that I've been caught up in this."

Jonah snickered. "Am I supposed to feel sorry for you?"

Before Kendall could respond, her phone went off. She slid it out of her pocket and looked at the screen, chewing her bottom lip.

"It's him, isn't it?" Jonah smirked. "If it's over, why's he still calling you?"

She gave in. "You have no idea what I have been dealing with. You don't even know me; you barely know Nathan for that matter. He works *all* the time, so it's easy to feel lonely. Chris works with me, and he's always there, every day."

Jonah put up his hand to stop her. "I don't want to hear it. You say I don't know what you're *dealing* with, as if you're engaged to some kind of monster who treats you like shit. But no, my brother spent nearly a decade in school so he could work his ass off to *help* people for a living. A damn good living, if you ask me. And look at this house! He built this for *you* with that job he's always at. He is so good to you, and he *loves* you! So you feel lonely? Yeah? You don't know what lonely is."

Kendall stood there, speechless for a moment. She thought of all the ugly things she could say in retaliation, but the truth was, Jonah was absolutely right.

"What do I have to do to keep you from telling Nathan?" she finally asked in a defeated tone.

"Tell him yourself," Jonah replied without hesitation.

Kendall rolled her eyes. "I am *not* going to tell him."

Jonah shrugged, walking past her to the door. "If you're not going to tell my brother the truth, then I will."

Scarlett cut the pumpkin pies, serving the slices on dessert plates. Elliot had Gracie sitting on the granite countertop, teaching her how to squirt whipped cream out of the can onto each slice. She giggled as some of her attempts went out of control, and Elliot would have to intervene. Gracie accidentally squirted it in his face, and he erupted into joyful laughter.

Hannah smiled, approaching them. "Looks like someone is having fun."

"Look what Grampa taught me!" Gracie bragged, handing Hannah a plate. The pie to whipped cream ratio was a bit off.

Elliot chuckled. "It's a work in progress. Hope you don't mind."

Hannah shook her head. "No, of course not. I'm glad you're spending time with her."

A grateful smile brightened Elliot's face. "Thank you, Hannah. She is an amazing little girl."

"Aww, Grampa," Gracie cooed. "I know we just met, but I think you're amazing too."

"So, when's the big day?" Elliot asked as he sat down on the couch across from Nathan and Kendall.

"Five weeks and two days," Nathan answered without thinking.

"Someone's excited," Scarlett remarked.

Nathan grinned, unable to contain it. "Yeah, too bad

it's not *this* weekend."

Jonah couldn't take it any longer. He got up from the couch and let himself out the French doors to the lanai to get some air. It was noticeably colder than it had been lately, rendering his cardigan insufficient. Just as Jonah was about to head back in, Elliot appeared, rubbing his hands together.

"It's cooling down, huh?" he commented.

Jonah slipped his cold hands into his pockets. "Sure is."

"Forgive me for prying but I thought I sensed a tense vibe in there," Elliot said, pointing behind him to the house.

Jonah sighed, his breath forming clouds in the air. "I'm sorry. I couldn't help it. Did everyone else notice too?"

Elliot shook his head. "I don't think so. Your mother started asking them more questions about the wedding. Maybe it's some sort of father-son intuition or something. Do you want to talk about it?"

Jonah was delighted that his father cared. It wasn't something he was used to.

"Well…Kendall has been cheating on Nathan, and she knows that I know."

Elliot winced. "That's terrible. And now you're caught in the middle, right?"

Jonah shrugged. "She refuses to tell him, so I told her I will."

"That's a tough situation," Elliot said sympathetically. "Because how do you let your brother just go along with something like that? That's not fair."

"Exactly. What if she doesn't stop? I don't want him to marry someone who would do that to him."

Elliot put a hand on his son's shoulder. "Nathan is lucky to have a brother who cares about him so much. I know it's difficult to do the right thing, but it always works out in the end."

Jonah smiled, feeling a strong sense of gratitude for his guidance. "I wish I had grown up with you."

Elliot was taken aback by his sudden statement and stared at him. "I wish that too."

"I'm sorry if this is weird, but I feel like we're the same person sometimes," Jonah said timidly. "You say exactly what I'm thinking. You pick up on my thoughts while other people who have known me my whole life don't even notice. It's just crazy."

"I keep marveling over how similar we are as well," Elliot agreed. "It's amazing how that works. You go all those years without *any* of my influence and still, I see so much of myself in you. I guess that's why we've been able to talk to each other so easily."

Jonah nodded. "Now, if only everything else could so easily fall into place, right?"

"That reminds me, there's something I wanted to talk to you about," Elliot began. "Earlier at dinner, when I mentioned that my store keeps me busy, it was a bit of an understatement. Some days, I am extremely overwhelmed and wish I had some help. But I've been afraid to trust anyone, and I have never once called back any of the people I've interviewed. So...what do you think, Jonah? Would you be interested in working with me at the store?"

"Yes. Absolutely," Jonah answered immediately, a sense of relief flooding him.

Elliot smiled. "I could really use your help with the lessons. I have twenty-four students now, and I'm only open six days a week. I have more students on a waiting list because I just don't have enough time. I'd also love if you could help on the floor, answer customers' questions, work the register, that sort of thing."

Jonah was wide-eyed and enthusiastic, unable to keep the grin from his face. "Yes. I can definitely do that. I would love that."

Elliot laughed. "Well, you sure seem excited to get to work."

"Oh, you have no idea how much this helps my family. It's a *huge* burden lifted off my shoulders."

"Good. We're helping each other then. And I understand that Hannah works a lot as well, mostly evenings and nights, right? We're open from nine to seven, so I was thinking you could open and I could close," Elliot suggested.

"This is too perfect. What's the catch?" Jonah asked.

Elliot snickered. "I'm only paying you four dollars an hour." They both laughed. "No, actually, I'll start you at ten dollars an hour, plus commission. Then, we'll see how it goes with my budget and everything. I can accept several more students, so this will be very good for business. We should both do pretty well. So, yeah, no catch."

Jonah couldn't believe his predicament had been resolved. He was thrilled he didn't have to return to the kind of work he had no interest in. He would finally be doing something he loved.

As the evening wound down, both Elliot and Scarlett decided they were ready to head home. The two couples walked them to the door, and hugs, handshakes, and friendly words were exchanged.

"I will see you at nine on Monday morning," Elliot said to Jonah, exaggerating a stern expression.

"Monday? Won't you need some help for tomorrow?" Jonah asked.

Elliot shook his head. "Nah. Training the new guy on Black Friday will just make me even busier. Take the weekend to spend some time with your family."

With a wave, Elliot followed Scarlett outside as Nathan closed the door behind them.

"Well, that went better than I imagined." Elliot smiled, accompanying Scarlett down the brick-paved driveway to their cars.

"When Jonah told us you were coming, *as* you were knocking on the door, I honestly wasn't sure what to expect. But, in a weird way, it kind of feels...the same," Scarlett bravely confessed.

"I know what you mean. I think it was always easy with us, wasn't it? Maybe that was the problem." He chuckled, his hands in his pockets, as he strolled nonchalantly beside her.

Scarlett unlocked her car door. "I guess so."

Elliot hesitated for a moment, studying her face. "Do you ever think about how things would be if you had chosen differently back then?"

Scarlett nodded, dropping her gaze to the ground. "All the time. I see you every time I look at Jonah. And every time he endured another one of Jacob's outbursts, I wished I'd made a different choice." She pursed her lips, having shared more than she'd intended.

Elliot ruminated on her words, imagining Jacob raising his son. "I *hate* that Jonah grew up with all of that. Honestly, it breaks my heart, Scarlett."

She sighed. "Mine too...You really care about Jonah, don't you?"

"I *love* Jonah," Elliot easily admitted. "He's an amazing kid."

Scarlett snickered. "Good, so I did *something* right."

Elliot touched her shoulder, his countenance tender. "Listen, you are a good mother. You're not responsible for the kind of person Jacob was. Do not carry that with you. Both of your boys have grown into great men. You should be proud of that."

"Thank you," Scarlett said quietly, her eyes welling up. "I should've let you be there. I'm sorry."

"Let's not do this now, okay?" Elliot said, sliding his arm around her. She leaned into him, trying to compose herself.

"You're right," Scarlett agreed, pulling away to open her car door.

Elliot took a few steps backward toward his truck and smiled. "It was great seeing you, Scarlett. I'd like to see you again soon."

"So, what was Elliot talking about when he was leaving?" Hannah asked Jonah as they sat on the couch in Nathan's living room. Gracie had fallen asleep between them.

"He offered me a job."

"Oh, that's great!" Hannah rejoiced, her smile wide.

Jonah nodded excitedly. "I get to sell instruments and give guitar lessons for a living."

"Jonah, that is perfect. Congratulations, man," Nathan said, jumping to his feet. "Ya know what? We should celebrate."

He made his way to the refrigerator. "Honey, where's the wine?" he asked when he couldn't find any.

"Um, you finished it off last night, remember?" Kendall informed him.

He laughed. "No, I don't. Oh well. Rain check on the celebrating."

Jonah stood up, quickly glancing at Kendall. "No, let's go get some. I could really use a glass."

Kendall knew what Jonah was doing. "It's

Thanksgiving. All the stores are closed."

"That convenience store a couple miles down the road is open today. I saw it on their sign on the way here," Jonah countered.

"Ah, good eye," Nathan replied, completely oblivious. "C'mon, Jonah, let's go."

"Can I come?" Kendall asked eagerly.

Nathan gave her a funny look. "No, stay here with Hannah. We'll be right back."

Kendall shot Jonah a furious glance before he turned away and followed Nathan outside to his car.

The brothers strolled across the parking lot to Nathan's Lexus after purchasing the wine. Once inside, Nathan started the car, but Jonah stopped him before he put it in reverse.

"Nathan...I really need to talk to you about something."

Nathan eyed his brother's troubled demeanor. "What? What's wrong?"

Jonah let out a long breath, still unsure if he should divulge the news that would derail his brother's life. "I don't even know how to tell you this, Nate. But I have to...When Kendall says she's on the phone with the wedding coordinator, she's actually talking to a coworker she's been seeing."

Nathan looked at him blankly. "Wait. What?"

"She's cheating on you, Nathan. I'm so sorry."

Nathan stared at the steering wheel with a confused expression. "That can't be right," he muttered quietly. "You must be mistaken."

Jonah shook his head. "No, Nate. I'm not. I overheard her on the phone outside the lounge last night, and then today,

I actually *spoke* to her about it."

"No. She wouldn't do that to me. You're wrong, Jonah."

"She *admitted* it to me."

Nathan's eyes were wide. "Stop. Just stop. I can't hear this. You've got to be lying to me."

"Why the hell would I lie to you about *this*?"

Nathan threw the car in reverse and jerked it out of the parking spot. He peeled out of the lot and into the street.

Jonah nervously gripped the dashboard. "Nathan, please slow down."

Turning the wheel, Nathan abruptly pulled off the road, coming to a screeching halt. He faced Jonah, breathing rapidly as his emotions escalated.

"If this is true, what's his name?"

"Chris," Jonah answered simply.

Nathan snickered. "I have never heard of anyone she works with named Chris."

"That doesn't mean he doesn't exist. I doubt she would mention him to you."

"But why would she do this to me? It doesn't make sense," Nathan said, staring off.

"I'm really sorry," Jonah repeated himself. "I was afraid to tell you because I didn't want to hurt you, but you don't deserve this."

Nathan sighed deeply, dropping his head back against the seat. "Ugh, this sucks. I don't believe it. Please just tell me you're lying. I'd rather my brother be a liar than my fiancée a cheater."

"I told you, Nathan. I'm not lying."

Nathan put the car into drive and pulled back onto the road, driving home in silence. Jonah was nervous to go inside the house, unsure of how Nathan would handle things.

Thankfully, all he did was look at Kendall with a blank stare and suggest they call it a night.

"Thanks for having us," Jonah said with a thin smile as he scooped Gracie up off the couch.

"We had a nice time, thank you," Hannah added, feeling the tension.

Nathan walked them to the foyer, briefly saying good-bye. When they got to the car, Jonah buckled Gracie into her seat and Hannah got in the passenger side. As Jonah was about to climb in, Kendall stormed out the front door and stalked toward him. Cautiously, he took several steps away from the car to approach her.

"What the hell did you say to him?" Kendall asked bitterly.

"The truth."

"I told you not to say anything. I thought I made myself clear."

Jonah shrugged. "And *I* told you I was going to tell him. If you didn't want him to find out, you shouldn't have done it."

Hannah curiously watched the two of them, wishing she could hear what they were saying. She could tell Kendall was livid, but Jonah appeared calm. After what seemed like one last furious statement, Hannah saw Kendall lash out and smack Jonah across the face before she spun around and hurried back into the house. Stunned, Jonah stood still, staring at the ground.

Hannah was shocked by what she'd just witnessed. As she vengefully fantasized about dragging Kendall out of the house by her hair, Jonah slowly walked back to the car.

"What just happened? Are you okay?" Hannah asked, touching his face.

Jonah turned to her, his cheek throbbing and inflamed.

"I'm fine. Kendall is just upset that I told Nathan her little secret."

"So, she *is* cheating on him? I thought I remembered you saying that last night."

"Yup. Unfortunately."

"Well, you didn't do anything wrong," Hannah replied.

"I know." Jonah started the car and backed out of the driveway. "Sure seems like they're both blaming *me* though."

"So, is it true?" Nathan questioned when Kendall returned from outside.

"Is what true?" she asked, massaging her stinging hand. She hadn't meant to hit Jonah so hard. She hadn't intended to hit him at all, but she'd gotten so angry, she hadn't been able to control herself.

"My brother had some pretty awful news for me. You know nothing about that?" Nathan asked.

Kendall rolled her eyes. "No, Nathan. I don't."

"He said you're seeing someone behind my back."

"And you believe him?" She brushed past him to the kitchen for a bottle of water.

"Well, why would he tell me that if it wasn't true, Kendall?"

She took a long sip of her water, realizing she could not live with Nathan believing the truth. "He told me earlier that I'm not right for you and he would do whatever he had to do to break us up," she lied.

Nathan narrowed his eyebrows. "That doesn't sound like him. Why would he say that?"

Kendall shrugged. "I don't know. Maybe he's jealous."

Nathan made a face. "Jealous? Of what? Kendall, you

need to be honest with me."

"You don't trust me, Nathan?"

He sighed. "I feel like you're trying to turn me against my own brother. He wouldn't make up something like that."

"I didn't want to tell you this," she began, feeling desperate. "But I felt like Jonah was hitting on me last night. That's gotta be it. That's why he wants us to break up. That's why he's jealous."

Nathan stared at her incredulously. "Wow. That is complete bullshit. Are you serious with that right now? Did you really think I would fall for *that*?"

Kendall looked away. "I'm sorry."

"You're sorry. For what? Lying? Making up shit about my brother? Or cheating on me? Which one is it, Kendall? Because right now, I don't feel like I even know you," Nathan exploded.

She began to cry. "Nathan, I *am* sorry. I didn't want Jonah to tell you about Chris because I'm breaking things off with him. I just want to be with you."

"I think it's a little late for that, Kendall. There shouldn't be anything to break off. We're supposed to get *married* in five weeks! A woman about to get married should be so in love that her fiancé is all she can think about. She shouldn't have another guy on the side. How can you love me if that's what you're doing?"

"You and your brother are such hopeless romantics, it's disgusting. Seriously, you both need to get in touch with reality," Kendall retorted, evading his question.

"No, it's not about being a hopeless romantic, it's what's right. Loyalty in a relationship is how it *should* be. There's nothing dated or odd about that. No one wants a cheater," Nathan said, opening the wine and taking a swig straight out of the bottle.

Kendall bit her lip, at a loss. "I'm sorry," she repeated. "I love you, Nathan. You might not think so, but I do. I only started seeing Chris after you started working those extra shifts."

"That was three months ago!" Nathan exclaimed. "You've been seeing him for *three* months?"

"I was lonely, Nathan! I couldn't help it. He was there every day. When you were too tired to stay up and talk to me, he was there. When I was stressed out about planning the wedding, he was the one who was available to help me."

"Are you kidding me? You had *him* help you with *our* wedding? Wow. That is just inappropriate on so many levels. This guy must be a moron." Nathan laughed, throwing the bottle back and downing more wine. "Oh, and sorry I was too tired to chit-chat with you after working twenty-four hours straight. I'm such a sucky boyfriend."

"Can we start over?" she asked in a small voice. "I still want you, Nathan."

He gawked at her, setting the bottle down loudly on the counter. His heart was shattering, the shards piercing him to the core. It pained him so deeply, he couldn't bear it.

"No," he answered dryly. "I don't want *you* anymore."

"Please, Nathan. Don't do this," Kendall pleaded, taking his hands.

He pulled away from her. "*You* did this. You need to go. Now." He pointed to the door with one hand and grabbed the wine with the other. "And you can leave my ring on the table on your way out."

Glaring at him, Kendall yanked the three-carat diamond ring from her finger and chucked it at his chest. It fell to the tile floor with a clinking sound.

"That's not the table, but it'll do," Nathan commented without bothering to pick it up.

Kendall stomped out of the room, grabbing her purse and coat before she threw open the front door and slammed it behind her. The clamor was deafening as it echoed throughout the house, puncturing Nathan's already broken heart.

FOURTEEN

Hannah awoke the next morning on the couch, surprised to still be wrapped in Jonah's arms. Neither of them had planned on falling asleep. Quickly, Hannah's grogginess was replaced by an alarming thought.

"Oh no, what time is it?" She yanked herself away from Jonah, startling him.

He sat up, his heart racing. "What? What's happening?"

"I'm so sorry. I have to be at work in thirty-five minutes," Hannah said.

Jonah let out a sigh as he turned to the window. The sun had barely begun to color the sky. "But it's so early."

"I know. I'm pretty sure I'm being punished with an early shift for taking a week off," Hannah speculated, reluctantly leaving him to get herself ready.

She returned fifteen minutes later to see that Jonah had fallen back to sleep. She took his hands and tugged.

As he stirred, she said, "You don't look very comfortable. C'mon, you can sleep in my bed."

He got up and allowed her to lead him to her room, where he gladly climbed into her soft and cozy bed. When Hannah leaned over to kiss him good-bye, Jonah grabbed her and pulled her to him, holding her tightly.

She laughed. "Jonah! I *really* have to go."

He nestled his face into her neck, planting a soft kiss on her collarbone. "No, don't leave," he muttered. "Stay with me."

Hannah groaned. "Jonah, you are not making this any easier. I have to go."

"Okay," he said in a defeated tone, releasing her.

She got up and bent to kiss his cheek. "I'll see you at three."

"I love you *so* much," Jonah said, closing his eyes. "Please be careful."

"I will," Hannah promised, smiling, as she slipped out the door.

Jonah's phone went off in his pocket, the vibration instantly forcing him awake. He clumsily retrieved it and answered without reading the screen.

"Hello?" His voice was groggy.

"Jonah…"

Jonah sat up in Hannah's bed, shaking away his drowsiness. "Nathan. Hey."

"I'm sorry it's so early. I just couldn't wait anymore."

"No, it's fine," Jonah assured him. "Are you okay?"

Nathan sighed heavily into the phone. "No, man, I'm not okay. We broke up last night."

"I'm so sorry, Nate. I keep wondering if I did the right thing…"

"No, I'm glad you told me. I can't marry someone who would do that," Nathan replied. "I still can't believe she did that to me."

Jonah struggled to muster a comforting word but had nothing. "I'm sorry," he repeated.

"What are you doing later? Wanna go to Gatsby's and grab a beer?" Nathan asked.

"Umm…"

Nathan snickered. "Right…I just need to get out of this house."

"Hannah's working all day so I've got Gracie. But how about you come by later, and we'll do something?" Jonah suggested.

"Okay. Sounds good. See you then."

Then Nathan hung up without another word.

It was only 10:30, but already, Hannah swore time was standing still. A week away from the diner had made her realize how much she truly despised it. How had she managed to work there so long? She wasn't even halfway into her shift, and she was about to go insane.

Hannah heard the bell ring as the door opened. She took a deep breath, preparing to greet yet another customer, but her phony smile was quickly replaced by a genuine, joyful one.

"Mommy!" Gracie threw her arms around Hannah's legs.

"Hi, baby! What are you doing here?" Hannah asked, gazing up at Jonah.

Seeing his face erased all the frustrations of the morning. And then he smiled, and she nearly lost her head.

"I hope this is okay," Jonah said. "I wanted to take Gracie out for breakfast, and I missed you, so I thought Murphy's was the best solution."

Hannah grabbed a menu, realizing her hands were shaking. "Of course it's okay. It's nice to see you."

Jonah grinned, taking Gracie's hand and following

Hannah to a table.

"Mommy, sit with us," Gracie said.

Hannah frowned, tousling her daughter's brown curls. "Aw, Gracie, I can't. I'm working right now. I wish I could though, baby."

"Remember how we talked in the car about visiting Mommy at work? This is where Mommy works," Jonah said to her. "Do you still want French toast, or do you want to look at the menu together?"

Gracie opened the menu. "Let's see what else they have, just in case." She looked at the pictures, swinging her dangling feet.

"I'll be back in a few minutes, okay?" Hannah said, seeing that she had an order up.

After she served one of her other tables, Hannah rounded the counter to return her tray. She ran into her coworker, Lily Quinn.

"Oh my God, Hannah. Look at *him*. He is gorgeous."

Hannah glanced up, following Lily's gaze to Jonah.

"Seriously. He's, like, Chace Crawford's doppelgänger," Lily added.

Hannah tried to keep a straight face. "Yeah, he's pretty hot."

"It looks like he has a kid. But I don't see a ring. Do you think he could be single?" Lily asked, smoothing her dark hair.

Hannah shrugged. "I'd say it's unlikely." She knew she should just tell Lily the truth, but this was much more fun.

Jonah turned his head and smiled at Hannah when their eyes met.

"He just smiled at you!" Lily squealed with playful envy. "I wonder what his name is." She continued to watch him dreamily.

"It's Jonah," Hannah said.

Lily narrowed her eyebrows. "How do you know?"

"Because he's my boyfriend," Hannah confessed, breaking into a grin.

Lily gasped, grabbing her arm. "Shut up! Are you serious? Oh, I hate you!"

"I'm sorry," Hannah said, laughing. "I couldn't resist."

Lily mentally put the pieces together. "Wait, so *that's* your daughter? And with *him*?"

Hannah nodded. "Yes and yes."

"Wow," Lily remarked. "You are a lucky girl."

Hannah thanked her with a grateful smile. She liked Lily. Lily was always bubbly and kind, and she was the closest thing Hannah had to a best friend.

With a content heart, Hannah returned to Jonah and Gracie's table.

"Are you ready?" she asked, notepad in hand.

"Coffee for me, please, and orange juice for Gracie. And she can't decide between pancakes and French toast, so we'll order both and we'll share," Jonah said.

Gracie giggled. "Daddy, you're so smart."

Hannah jotted down the order. "And he's gorgeous too."

Jonah made a face and snickered. "What?"

"My friend was checking you out," she divulged.

Jonah blushed. "Nuh uh."

"Yes. But don't worry, I let her know you were taken." Hannah flashed him a sly smile as she turned away.

After they'd finished and received the check, Hannah cleared away their plates. She returned, placing a small plastic tray with Jonah's debit card and receipt in front of him.

"You don't have to leave me a tip," she said as he picked up the pen.

He gave her a funny look. "I'll do what I want," he jokingly replied.

"You're good at your job, Mom," Gracie chimed in, shifting her attention away from the creamer tower she'd been working on.

Hannah melted. "Aw, thank you, baby."

Jonah smiled affectionately. "I agree."

It was Hannah's turn to blush.

"Oh, hey, before I forget, I talked to Nathan this morning. He and Kendall broke up last night, and he's kind of a mess. I told him I'd hang out with him later. Not sure what that entails, but I need to be there for him," Jonah said.

"Of course. Poor Nathan. I still can't believe that."

"Me neither," Jonah said, shaking his head. He scrawled his signature on the slip.

"I'm so glad you stopped in," Hannah said. "I was having a rough morning, and it really helped to see you."

"I could say the same." Jonah stood up and helped Gracie out of the booth.

"So, I'll see you at home later?" Hannah asked, liking the sound of it.

"Yes, you will." Jonah briefly took her hand and then slowly pulled away.

Hannah watched lovingly as her entire world walked out the door, taking her joy with them.

After Jonah had buckled Gracie's harness, he received a text message. He climbed into the front seat and closed the door, taking out his phone.

It was from Hannah. *You still give me butterflies.*

A smile spread across Jonah's face as he typed back: *Would you believe I already miss you?*

The sun dipped low in the April sky, its golden reflection glimmering across the ripples of the lake. Their favorite tree in the entire park lent a lush canopy as Jonah leaned against its trunk. Hannah sat between his legs, lounging against him. He wrapped her in the comfort of his arms, a warm breeze gracing them.

"What are you thinking about?" he asked.

Hannah chuckled. "Actually, I was thinking about prom."

"What about it?"

"I think it's kinda funny that you got voted onto prom court," she said, amused.

Jonah rolled his eyes. "Ugh, I know. What is wrong with people?"

"Oh, stop it, Jonah. If anyone deserves senior prom king, it's you."

"That stuff is silly though," he reasoned. "It's just a stupid popularity contest that makes everyone else feel bad."

"So you're saying you're popular," Hannah teased.

Jonah snickered. "No...I don't know, am I? I don't try to be."

"You're so cute." She giggled, snuggling against him. "I know you don't even want to go, and you're only going for me, so thank you."

"Well, no, I'm going because I have to. Since I'm on court and everything."

"Hey, you're mean!" Hannah laughed, playfully pinching his leg.

"I'm just kidding." Jonah grinned widely, pressing his lips to the top of her head. "I'm happy to go with you."

"It'll be fun, I promise. And hopefully my dress won't clash with your scepter." She laughed again.

Jonah smirked. "You just love this, don't you?"

"I might." Hannah twisted around to kiss him.

They savored each other's company, watching the painted

sky change by the minute as the sun slipped through the horizon. Jonah broke their silence.

"So, I was going to wait, but...I have something for you," he said hesitantly, retrieving a small black box from his pocket.

Hannah turned to face him, her heart racing with excitement. Jonah grew nervous as she took the box, and he reached out, cupping his hands over hers.

"Okay, wait. I just wanted to tell you...I love you. And I promise I'd do anything for you. I'll always protect you and take care of you...no matter what." His blue eyes stared fiercely into hers.

She smiled, her heart melting. "Can I open it now?"

Jonah released her hands. "Yes, sorry. Go ahead."

Hannah eagerly eased the box open. Inside was a ring with a shiny oval moonstone set into an ornate silver band.

"Do you like it?" Jonah asked timidly.

"I love it." Hannah grinned through happy tears.

He removed it from the box and took her hand, carefully sliding the ring onto her finger.

Hannah threw her arms around him. "Thank you, Jonah. I love you so much."

Jonah held her tightly. "I love you too...You know it's a promise ring, right?"

She nodded, appreciating how important it was to him.

"I am going to marry you someday, Hannah," he vowed longingly. "I promise you I will."

Jonah took out his pocketknife, flipping the blade open. He turned and began carving their initials into the tree, making their love as permanent as he knew how until he could carry out his promise.

Nathan sat alone at the bar with a newly drawn mug of beer, watching the bubbles rise. All he wanted was to slip into oblivion and engorge himself with apathy. But nothing helped. He hadn't even been able to sleep to get a reprieve from his own mind.

Nathan picked up the mug and guzzled half of its contents. He hoped alcohol would numb the pain a little. Any bit would do. He'd never felt this empty. Never this hopeless. He couldn't believe how much it hurt.

The vibration in his pocket temporarily deterred him from his plaguing thoughts. Nathan pulled out his phone and saw his brother's name on the screen. *Oops*, he thought, as he answered it.

"Hey."

"Nathan, where are you? I've been trying to get a hold of you." Jonah sounded upset.

"Calm down, I'm at Gatsby's. Where you should be," Nathan said, downing the other half of his beer.

"I thought we planned for you to come *here*," Jonah replied.

"We did. I just didn't feel like it. I needed a drink...or ten."

"Nathan, I have been here waiting for you. You could've told me you weren't coming."

Nathan snickered. "Oh. Yeah. Let me remember *your* feelings while my life is falling apart. *Okay*."

Jonah sighed. "That is not what I meant. I was worried about you. I'm trying to help you."

"All right. Then come to Gatsby's, Jonah. Drown my pain with me."

"Nathan, you know that's not really my thing."

"Oh, right. I forgot. You're too good for that...or maybe it's because you *and* your girlfriend just can't handle some fun without losing your shit."

Jonah hesitated, holding back a snide remark. "I know

you're hurting, but you don't have to be a dick, Nathan."

"Ah, well, I am my father's son."

"Why did you even call this morning?" Jonah questioned. "You really don't seem like you want my help."

"And *you* really don't seem like you want to help me, Jonah. If you did, you'd be here."

Jonah let out an agitated breath. "I'm still not sure how it even escalated to this, but I don't want to fight with you. You win, okay? I'll be there in half an hour."

Jonah pulled the door open and stepped inside, scanning the loud, crowded space for his brother. He caught sight of Nathan at the far end of the bar and weaved his way through the array of people and tables to get to him. Jonah patted Nathan's shoulder when he approached, then sat down on the empty stool beside him.

"I'm sorry I was a jerk," Nathan finally spoke.

"I'm sorry I was being selfish," Jonah said.

Nathan turned to him. "Thank you for coming. I know you didn't want to. And that's okay. But I'm glad you're here."

Jonah smiled. "Me too."

"So, are you going to order a Shirley Temple?" Nathan teased.

"Actually, I was thinking chocolate milk," Jonah replied.

Nathan laughed, the knot in his stomach loosening a bit.

"So, are you okay?" Jonah asked.

Nathan hung his head. "I'm really not. What would I have done if I had found this out *after* the wedding?"

Jonah grimaced. "Yeah, that would've been a lot

worse."

"Instead, I'm stuck with a wedding I've already paid for," Nathan said with a groan.

"That's rough, Nate. If I can help at all, you know, canceling vendors or whatever, let me know," Jonah offered, trying to choose sensitive wording.

Nathan chuckled to himself. "What *would* help, is if all that money wasn't being wasted. You and Hannah should just get married."

Jonah couldn't tell if his brother was joking or not. Either way, the idea was absurd.

"There is no way Hannah and I could get married in five weeks."

Nathan smirked. "You're right, it's ridiculous. You've only been in love with each other for ten years, and you're raising a four-year-old together. Five weeks is moving *much* too quickly."

"You're not serious," Jonah said. "You don't really think we should take your wedding."

Nathan shrugged. "Honestly, yeah, I was kidding. But all jokes aside, I actually think you should consider it. You know you're going to marry her anyway. I mean, why not?"

Jonah chewed his lip as he contemplated for a moment. "Sure, it's tempting, but it just seems wrong. It's *your* wedding that you and Kendall planned."

"That Kendall and *Chris* planned," Nathan interjected under his breath.

Jonah continued on. "I don't want to rush it, I guess. I want it to be natural. Save up for her ring. Plan a decent proposal...I don't want to come at her with a proposition, ya know?"

Nathan nodded. "No, you're right. It's a silly idea. I guess I'm just trying to look out for my baby brother."

"And I appreciate that, Nate. I really do."

"I know," Nathan said with a wry smile. "Let me know if you change your mind."

FIFTEEN

When Jonah walked into the Morgans' kitchen later that night, he found Caroline packing her bag for work.

"Oh, hey, Jonah," she greeted him.

"Hi, Mrs. Morgan."

"I told you, you can call me Caroline."

Jonah nodded. "I know."

Caroline mentally noted her approval of his manners. "So Hannah told me you got a job."

"Yes, I did. My dad—um, *Elliot*—gave me a job at his music store," he stammered.

"Jonah. You can call him your dad. It's okay," Caroline said tenderly.

He dropped his gaze to the floor and ran a hand through his hair. "I'm never sure how to refer to him in front of other people. It's...complicated."

"Don't worry about other people. They'll catch on." She smiled at him and gave his shoulder a caring pat.

"Oh, before you go," Jonah began. "Are you available tomorrow afternoon to watch Gracie? I have something special planned for Hannah before she goes to work."

Caroline nodded, pulling her bag onto her shoulder. "I can do that."

He grinned. "Thank you so much, Mrs. Morgan. Have a good night at work."

"Thanks, Jonah." Caroline smiled as she watched him eagerly disappear down the hall toward her daughter's room.

After peeking in at Gracie, Jonah knocked softly on Hannah's door.

"Come in."

He stepped in and closed the door behind him. "What are you doing?" he asked, eyeing the mess of photographs and paper scattered around her on the bed.

Hannah reached down to the floor and picked up the large plastic lid of a storage container to show him "JONAH" written across it.

"Oh." He crossed the room to sit at the foot of her bed.

"Your 'Hannah' box inspired me to dig it out. It's so weird to go through these things and not cry," she said, flipping through a small stack of photos.

Jonah frowned. "That makes me really sad."

Hannah looked up at him. "Aw, no, I'm sorry. I meant it in a good way. Like, 'look how perfect everything is *now*.'"

"I know. I just don't like to think of you crying at the sight of my face." His full lips formed a lighthearted smile.

Hannah laughed. "You're *very* hard to look at."

"Ouch." Jonah played along, putting his hand on his chest. He shifted his attention to her collection of memories. "Hey, do you have pictures from spring break, senior year, when we all went to Wildwood for the weekend?"

"Of course I do." She reached across the heap for a small album.

Jonah carefully cleared the spot beside Hannah and settled in close to look at the photos along with her.

"Oh, that was so much fun," Hannah reminisced. "And look at you, all pre-ink."

Jonah snickered. "Yeah, weird...I still can't believe our parents let us go to Jersey together."

"My parents fought about it for a *week*. I was so sure they were going to say no."

"I guess it helped that a bunch of us went," Jonah added.

Hannah squinted her eyes, willing herself to recall the details. "Wasn't Oliver annoyed because you spent the whole weekend with me?"

He smirked. "He was just mad because he and Stella were fighting."

"Oh, right. And how about Paige?"

Jonah tilted his head back with a light-hearted groan. "Oh, my gosh. Paige. Do you remember how crazy she was? Your dad told her to keep an eye on us, and she took her task *way* too seriously."

"Yes! She would follow me to the *bathroom* to make sure I wasn't trying to sneak to your room at night."

"Good times," Jonah said, turning to the next page in the album. Most of the photos were self-taken shots of the two of them together, so young and blissful.

"Aw, look!" Hannah pointed, frowning. "That was right before I lost my ring."

In the photo, they were facing each other, Hannah's left hand on Jonah's chest, the moonstone promise ring he'd given her fully visible.

"You were so upset," Jonah said.

She sighed, staring at the picture. "I'm still mad at myself for forgetting to take it off before I went swimming."

"You had us looking for it for hours and I felt so bad because you kept telling me you were sorry," Jonah recounted glumly.

"Wow, that's depressing!" Hannah let out a chuckle.

"But seriously, I actually think about that ring a lot...I only had it for a week. I still hate that I lost it."

"I know."

Hannah decided to lighten the mood, lifting a photo from the pile. "Hey! Do you remember when you were prom king?"

He rolled his eyes. "Oh no. Burn that one."

She laughed. "Nope. I think Gracie would *love* to see her dad wearing a crown."

"That makes it so much worse!" Jonah said, snatching it from her and burying it at the bottom of the pile.

"This is fun." Hannah leaned her head against his shoulder. "I still can't believe it though."

Jonah rested his head against hers. "Believe what?"

"That all of these memories lead to you and me sitting right here. For so long, I believed our story was over. But it's like it's beginning all over again." Her words were alive with joy.

"It is incredible," he agreed, caressing her arm with his fingertips. "I loved you *infinitely* back then...but I love you infinitely more than that *now*. How is that even possible, right?"

Hannah had tears in her eyes as she filled the spaces between his fingers with her own. "I feel that too," she said softly, gazing up at him.

Before she could speak another word, Jonah kissed her.

"Thank you so much for lunch, Jonah," Scarlett said as they crossed the parking lot toward his car.

"Oh, you're welcome, Mom."

Her warm expression transformed. "It's such a shame

that it's taken us this long to spend quality time together."

"It's okay. Things are good *now*, and that's all that matters," he assured her.

She gave a slight nod. "Good point. How did my son get to be so wise?"

"Good genetics."

Scarlett laughed. "Well, Elliot has always been a smart man. Can't really say the same about *my* intellect."

Jonah opened the passenger side door for his mother. "You're going to have to learn to stop that."

"Stop what?" she asked, situating herself in the leather seat.

"Seeing yourself through Jacob's eyes. You're far better than that, Mom. Just saying."

Jonah closed the door and rounded the car, sliding in behind the wheel. When he turned to his mother, he saw that she was crying. He touched her shoulder, his eyebrows knit together with concern.

"You're right, Jonah," she said quietly, wiping her eyes. "I still hear him. I still let him control me."

Jonah's heart broke. All this while, his own mother had felt the exact way he had, torn down and oppressed by the same man. He felt guilty for not realizing that she had suffered a similar torment.

"It gets better, Mom, I promise," Jonah said. "It's taken me a while, but I'm finally learning how to live without his voice in the back of my head."

Scarlett smiled through her tears and reached over to give his hand a squeeze. "Thank you, Jonah."

Jonah started the car and made his way out of the parking lot toward home. They remained in a comfortable silence, ruminating on each other's words. Scarlett couldn't help but let her mind wander.

Scarlett nervously chewed her fingernail, her heart racing. She'd been sick to her stomach for days, so bothered by the dishonesty she'd submersed herself in.

"Elliot, can you please pull over?" she finally requested, unable to bear another moment.

Elliot pulled his truck onto the side of the road. "What's wrong?"

Scarlett covered her face with her hands, struggling to will the threat of tears away. She was unsuccessful.

"Can you please tell me what's going on?" Elliot pleaded, worry creasing his forehead.

Scarlett lowered her hands, exposing her sad eyes. "I'm sorry, Elliot," she whispered.

His stomach tightened. "Scarlett..."

Her voice came out in a whimper. "I can't do this anymore. I'm so sorry."

Elliot turned his gaze to the windshield, staring blindly as his breathing quickened. He'd been so naïve, completely unaware that it could all come crashing down at any moment. But there he was, with the shattered pieces scattered around him.

"I don't understand. Everything has been so perfect. I thought you wanted to be with me," he said in a hushed tone.

Scarlett slid across the bench seat and placed a hand on his shoulder. "I do, Elliot."

"Then what's the problem? Why can't you do this?" he asked, pain laced in his features.

Scarlett buried her face in his shoulder. "I don't know if I can leave him."

Elliot huffed incredulously. "Scarlett, he's horrible to you! You told me yourself how unhappy he makes you. And you don't know if you can leave that? Sounds like a no-brainer to me."

Scarlett sighed heavily. "I know. But I'm scared. And I'm scared for Nathan. What if Jacob takes him away from me?"

"I won't let that happen, I promise. Please, Scarlett, don't do this," Elliot begged, taking her hands in his.

Scarlett began to sob, overwhelmed by her predicament. She collapsed against Elliot, gripping him desperately. He wrapped her tightly in his embrace, praying she would change her mind.

"I love you so much, Scarlett." His voice was shaking.

Scarlett straightened and grabbed Elliot's face, drawing him in for a passionate kiss. When they parted, she wiped her tear-stained cheeks with the backs of her hands.

"Can you please take me home?" she asked dryly.

Elliot took a moment to collect himself before he started his truck and headed back the way they came. Neither of them spoke for the duration of the drive.

Elliot pulled over in front of the empty lot at the end of Scarlett's street where they'd always met. It had been the most careful plan they could come up with, since Scarlett didn't have her own vehicle.

"I can take care of you, Scarlett. And Nathan too," Elliot tried once more. "You would be happy with me."

Again, Scarlett failed to refrain from crying as she flung the door open. "Please don't try to call me...and don't come here anymore." Avoiding his eyes, she slid out of the truck and slammed the door.

Elliot wanted to call out to her. He wanted to jump out and chase after her. But instead, he sat there and fell apart as he watched Scarlett walk away for the last time.

A soft, cool breeze graced Jonah and Hannah as they strolled hand in hand through Oak Lake Park. It was a sublime afternoon, the sky a resplendent blue.

"You're taking me to our tree, aren't you?" Hannah smiled at him.

"I'm so predictable," Jonah said with a grin.

"Ya know, I haven't been there since you left. I just couldn't."

He slipped his arm around her shoulders, drawing her close. "Well, we've shared a lot of big moments there."

Their spot came into view, the tree towering much larger than either of them remembered. Or maybe enough time really had passed to allow it to grow that considerably. It still held the majority of its gloriously colored leaves. Hannah reached out to trace the lines of their initials, delighted that Jonah's carving was still perfectly etched into its trunk.

"That feels like yesterday and a thousand years ago all at the same time," Hannah reflected, turning to Jonah.

He nodded. "That was a good day."

She put her hands on his waist and smiled fondly. "All of our days were good days."

"Yes. They were." He lovingly brushed a strand of hair away from her face, then let the backs of his fingers trail softly down her cheek.

Hannah closed her eyes, nuzzling his hand. His touch still had the power to render her helpless. When she lifted her gaze to meet his, his blue eyes stared intensely back at her, glinting in the patches of sunlight that streamed through the leafy covering above them.

"What are you thinking about?" Hannah whispered.

"The reason I brought you here."

She raised an eyebrow inquisitively. "Oh?"

He sighed. "But I have to tell you, it's not the reason you're probably hoping for. I just don't want you to be disappointed."

"Jonah, it's okay."

"But I do have something for you," he said, reaching into his pocket. "Because I need to make sure you know that I still promise all of the things I promised you here five and a half years ago." He took her hand and slid a ring onto her finger.

Hannah looked down, gasping at the sight of a familiar-looking silver moonstone ring. "Oh, my gosh, Jonah! This can't be—how did you...?"

Jonah adored her reaction. "It looks just like it, doesn't it? I couldn't believe it when I saw it."

Hannah admired it closely. "Where did you find it?"

"I found it at this little jewelry store when I took Gracie downtown after breakfast yesterday."

Hannah couldn't stop smiling, joyful tears filling her eyes. She threw her arms around Jonah, squeezing him tightly.

"*That's* why you brought up Wildwood last night...Thank you so much, Jonah. It's like I have my ring back. You have no idea how happy that makes me."

He savored her embrace. "Oh, I think I might."

Elliot stood at Scarlett's doorstep, wondering how he had allowed himself to get this far. Ignoring the protesting voice of reason in his head, he knocked, but immediately regretted it when a pestering nervousness twisted his stomach. He should have known better than to act on a whim.

Just as Elliot turned away, he heard the door ease open behind him.

"Elliot?" came Scarlett's soft voice.

He spun around awkwardly and approached her. He had never before been this close to Scarlett's house. An odd notion fell upon him, of having no one to fear and nothing to be ashamed of.

"I'm sorry to just drop by like this," Elliot said, shakily.

Scarlett smiled warmly, failing to hide her approval. "No, it's okay. Would you like to come in?"

Elliot nodded, stepping past her into the house. He was disappointed in himself for becoming so easily unhinged, but he never thought he'd find himself in Scarlett's presence ever again.

Scarlett led Elliot to the living room, and he sat down across from her. His nearness made her heart pound, but she couldn't let him know it.

"You have a very nice home," Elliot said, his eyes taking a panoramic glance around him.

Scarlett looked around as well, struggling to find whatever pleasantness he had noticed. "Thank you, but I don't see it."

He tilted his head quizzically. "What do you mean?"

She shrugged. "I don't know. I guess there's just been so much ugliness in this house for the past thirty-six years, it's hard to see it as anything but ugly."

"That's awful, Scarlett," Elliot said, his voice tender.

"I was thinking about selling it eventually. I guess I'll figure it out." She painted on a smile and changed the subject. "So, how are things with you?"

Before Elliot could answer, the phone rang on the end table beside Scarlett. The caller ID flashed the name of Nathan's hospital.

"Hello?" she answered it, casting Elliot an apologetic glance.

"Hi, this is Debbie O'Dell over at Chestnut Hill Hospital. Am I speaking with Scarlett Weston?"

"Yes, this is she."

"Mrs. Weston, I'm calling because you're the emergency contact in Nathan's file. This is the second day in a row that he's been scheduled and hasn't shown up. We

224

haven't been able to get a hold of him. Would you happen to know anything?"

A dreadful worry gripped Scarlett. "No, I haven't seen him in a couple days."

"All right. Well, if you hear from him, just have him give us a call, okay?"

"Sure," Scarlett said before hanging up.

She swiftly dialed Nathan's number, and it went straight to voicemail. He didn't answer his house phone either.

"Scarlett, what's wrong?" Elliot asked, watching her grow considerably upset.

"Nathan hasn't been showing up for work, and no one can get a hold of him. I have to call Jonah. Maybe he knows something."

She dialed with trembling fingers, easily fearing the worst. When Jonah answered, she emotionally explained the situation to him.

"Mom, please calm down. I'm sure he's fine. He's just going through a lot right now. He and Kendall broke up," Jonah told her.

"What? That doesn't make me feel any better," Scarlett replied. "How come no one told me?"

"I'm sorry, Mom. It wasn't my news to tell," Jonah answered. "Listen, I'll drive over to his house and check on him. Would that make you feel better?"

"Yes, it would. Thank you so much."

"I'm going to leave Gracie with Caroline, and I'll be on the road in ten minutes. I'll call you as soon as I know anything, okay?"

Scarlett thanked her son once more and hung up the phone. Elliot moved from his seat to sit beside her and placed a comforting hand on her shoulder.

"Jonah's going to check on him," she said.

"That's good."

Scarlett looked up at him, her eyes begging for solace. "Nathan's fine, right?"

Elliot offered a thin smile. "I'm sure there's a good explanation."

Jonah sped through Nathan's neighborhood, having made it there in only forty-five minutes. He hastily got out of the car and sprinted to Nathan's front door, shaking away horrific thoughts. He knocked loudly and repeatedly rang the doorbell. When Nathan didn't answer, Jonah tried the handle, and the door opened.

He nervously went inside, the sick feeling in his stomach worsening. "Nathan?"

In the kitchen, Jonah found bits of shattered glass and the smashed remains of presumably Nathan's cell phone.

"Nathan!" Jonah tried again.

Silence.

He made his way through the living room, noticing a few empty bottles of wine and several crushed beer cans strewn on the coffee table. Jonah entered the master bedroom, fearfully holding his breath as he crept through the dim room.

"Nathan?" he whispered, his eyes adjusting to the darkness.

"What the hell do you want?" came a muffled groan from the bed.

With agitation replacing his panic, Jonah threw the curtains open, allowing the evening sunlight to pour in.

"Jonah!" Nathan scolded. He sat up and glared at his younger brother. "Just get out. I don't need you."

Jonah snickered, shaking his head. "Do you have any

idea what your mother is doing right now?" He pulled his phone from his back pocket to call her, and when she eagerly answered, he simply said, "Nathan is here and he's fine, he's just an asshole."

"Seriously, Jonah?" Nathan suddenly had the energy to get out of bed and approach him. "My entire life is shit right now, and you're going to barge into my house and treat me like that?"

Jonah stood his ground. "You know, for the last hour, Mom and I have been worried sick trying to get a hold of you. You've blown off work for *two* days. They can't get a hold of you either. First thought? You either killed yourself or you drank yourself to death."

Nathan's eyes went wide. "Oh, c'mon. That's a little dramatic, don't you think?"

"I don't know, Nathan, is it? You make it pretty damn easy to worry about you these days. It'd be nice if you could have the decency to call into work or maybe answer your phone when your mother calls you."

"I broke my phone," Nathan stated dryly.

Jonah nodded. "Yeah. I saw that."

"I'd been drinking, and I called Kendall. We got into a fight...and I got angry," Nathan confessed sheepishly.

"Okay, and how about your landline?" Jonah asked.

"Yeah, I just ignore that one."

Jonah rolled his eyes. "Nathan! You can't just do that. You have responsibilities. You have people who care about you. You should've heard how *worried* Mom was. She doesn't deserve that."

"I don't need a new dad, Jonah." Nathan turned away from him to arrange the pillows on his bed. All he wanted was to go back to sleep.

"That is *not* what I'm trying to do," Jonah said.

Nathan turned back to him. "Then what *are* you trying to do? Because I didn't realize I had to be sensitive to everyone else's feelings while *I'm* having a nervous breakdown."

Jonah put his hands on his hips, choosing his words carefully. "Nathan. You are allowed to hurt right now. You can be angry. You can be upset. But when I have to drive all the way here to make sure you're not *dead*, you don't even *care?* How is that okay?"

Nathan shrugged. "I don't know, Jonah. If I tell you I'm sorry, will you leave me alone? I just want to go to bed."

"Fine." Jonah surrendered, clenching his jaw. "Just *please* take care of yourself?"

"I'll call Mom later, okay?" Nathan offered. "And I'll get a new phone."

Jonah half smiled with a nod and left the room. His interaction with his brother hadn't gone how he would have preferred, but he was thankful Nathan was safe.

After he took the generous liberty of straightening up Nathan's mess in the living room, Jonah stepped out the front door, pulling it closed behind him. As he turned to head down the driveway, his breath caught in his throat. Kendall was coming straight toward him.

Sixteen

"Go home, Kendall."

"For once, mind your own business, Jonah," Kendall retorted, rolling her eyes.

Jonah stepped in front of the door to block her, crossing his arms over his chest. "If it has to do with *my* brother, then yeah, it's my business."

"*Half*-brother," she snidely corrected.

Jonah grinned. "Was that supposed to offend me?"

With her frustration getting the best of her, Kendall tried to shove Jonah out of the way, but his tall frame didn't budge. He just laughed at her.

"Ya know, I'd be willing to bet that you're the last person Nathan wants to see right now."

She put her hands on her hips, slightly out of breath from her pathetic antics. "Oh yeah? How would you know that?"

"He didn't even want to see *me*," Jonah replied.

Kendall snickered. "Well, *that's* not surprising. I don't blame him."

He shook his head, grinding his teeth. "Why are you even here? What do you want?"

"I just need to talk to Nathan. He won't take my calls."

"Well, apparently, the *last* time you talked to him, you

made him pretty angry, so…no."

Kendall finally lost her patience. "You know what, Jonah? If it wasn't for you, Nathan would still be happy. And I'd be getting married in five weeks. You ruined *everything*, and I hate you."

Jonah stood frozen, staring blankly at Kendall. Her harsh words cut through him.

"You're really selfish, you know that?" he said, his voice low.

"Excuse me?"

"You heard what I said, you're selfish," Jonah replied calmly. "You don't love my brother. If you did, you wouldn't have hurt him like that."

"People make mistakes, Jonah. No one's perfect."

"You're right. But someone who truly made a mistake would show some remorse. You're not upset that you hurt Nathan. You're mad 'cause you got caught."

Kendall sighed, looking away. "You don't even know what you're talking about."

Jonah ignored her comment and continued. "And then you're attacking *me* because I protected my brother? All I did was tell the truth. If you want to hate me for *that*, and blame me for *your* mistakes, then that just shows what kind of person you are."

She glared at him. "And what kind of person is that?"

"Someone who never deserved my brother in the first place."

As Kendall was scrambling for a witty reply, the front door opened, and Nathan appeared with a downcast demeanor.

"I heard everything," he said. "Kendall, I told you I *never* wanted to see you again."

Kendall seemed embarrassed. "I thought you were just

drunk. I didn't think you meant it."

"What makes you think I still want you after everything you've done? And after the way you've treated my brother, I am getting a much clearer picture of who you really are." Nathan turned to Jonah. "So again, Jonah, thank you for helping me dodge a bullet."

Kendall fidgeted, refusing defeat. "I guess forgiveness is beneath you, then."

"Chris dumped you, didn't he?" Nathan asked.

She diverted her eyes, refusing to answer.

Nathan snickered. "That's it. *That's* why you're here. You don't want me, you just don't want to be alone."

"Nathan, please. I'll be better."

He shook his head. "Just go home, Kendall."

With one last exasperated huff, Kendall spun around and stomped off to her car. Within seconds, she peeled out of the driveway, narrowly avoiding Jonah's car, and disappeared.

Nathan plopped down on the front step with a long sigh.

"You all right?" Jonah asked, sitting beside him.

"We were supposed to get fitted for our tuxes today," Nathan said, looking out over the front yard.

Jonah frowned. "I know. I thought about that this morning."

Nathan turned to him, placing a hand on his shoulder. "Dodged a bullet," he repeated, a smile slowly lighting up his face.

Jonah chuckled as Nathan jumped to his feet and opened the front door. They both went inside.

"Hey, thanks for cleaning up. You didn't have to do that." Nathan motioned to the living room.

Jonah shrugged. "Eh, it wasn't a big deal."

Nathan hesitated for a moment. "So, listen...I came out to call Mom, and I really did hear you two arguing. I was getting so pissed off at how she was talking to you, and then I realized...I wasn't much better. So, I'm really sorry for being so horrible to you."

"Nathan, it's okay."

"No, you came all this way just to make sure I was all right, and I treated you like shit. You're a good brother, Jonah."

Jonah smiled. It meant more to him than Nathan could ever imagine.

"Well, I don't endure verbal abuse for just anyone," he joked.

Nathan grimaced. "Yeah, sorry about that too. Who knew she was so crazy? I swear she wasn't like that when I met her."

"Everyone is always on their best behavior in the beginning," Jonah said.

Nathan sighed. "You're lucky you found your girl when you were twelve—so many years to really *know* each other. No sudden surprises just weeks before the wedding."

Jonah chuckled. "Oh, there are still surprises."

Nathan nodded with a laugh. "Right, 'Surprise, you're a dad!' But that's different. Hannah's not crazy. Her secrets started with good intentions. So even at her supposed worst, she's the best thing I could ever want for you."

"Wow, thanks, Nate."

Nathan dropped his gaze, his mind wandering. "Am I doomed to become Dad? *My* dad, I mean...You pretty much became yours."

"What? What are you talking about?"

"You know, the whole 'apple doesn't fall far from the tree' bit. I feel like it's already happening," Nathan fretted.

Jonah's brow furrowed. "Why would you say that?"

"Well, it's no secret that I probably drink too much. But, also like him, I couldn't keep my woman from wanting someone else."

Jonah shook his head. "Nathan, no. You are *nothing* like him. He was hostile and controlling. *That's* what made Mom cheat. Not that I condone cheating, but he had it coming. *You* didn't."

"But there must be something," Nathan insisted. "Some ugly part of him that's been passed down to me. 'Cause you and I are nothing alike...Jonah, you're everything I wish I was, and you've got everything I wish I had."

Jonah was speechless. His brother, who stood before him in his gorgeous mansion, who was a wealthy and successful doctor, who had the means to do any of the things Jonah could only dream of, envied *him*. Jonah, the computer-savvy musician who'd fathered a child at nineteen and barely had two nickels to rub together.

It was then that Jonah had an epiphany, finally seeing beyond the mind-sets that Jacob had instilled in him. Jonah had been blindly basing his worth on what he *did* rather than who he was. Nathan possessed all the tangible things that indicated success, and Jonah had held himself to that standard, pressuring himself to measure up to his brother. And all this time, they'd both envied the other.

"I didn't know you felt that way," Jonah said.

"Money might make some things easier, but it's not everything," Nathan replied. "I'm grateful to have such a great job, but I'd love to come home to my wife and kids every evening and be happy."

"You can still have that, Nate. Just because it didn't happen with Kendall doesn't mean it can't happen for you."

It had been a while since Nathan had been uncertain

of the future. He had to admit there was a bit of excitement in that. Maybe his seemingly devastating situation would turn out to be the blessing he never expected.

Jonah relaxed on Hannah's porch swing as it swayed in the cool breeze. It was a beautiful night, and he had decided to take advantage of it after tucking Gracie into bed. Lounging comfortably, Jonah worked on a new song, penning the lyrics as they came to him. He always had words and melodies playing in his head. Music came as naturally to him as breathing.

As Jonah closed his eyes to piece it together in his mind, his cell phone went off. He snapped out of his creative daze and smiled when he saw Hannah's name on the screen.

"Hey you," he answered.

"Um, Jonah?" It wasn't Hannah.

"Yeah. Who's this?" he asked, sitting up straight. There was something in the stranger's voice he didn't like.

"Hi, this is Lily. I work with Hannah. She asked me to call you because she's talking to the police right now—"

"The police?" Jonah interrupted. "Why is she talking to the police? Is she okay?"

"Someone attacked her in the parking lot," Lily answered vaguely. "She needs you to come to Murphy's."

Jonah didn't hesitate. He hung up and jumped to his feet, bolting inside for his keys. And then he realized that Caroline was at work.

With a heavy sigh, Jonah rushed down the hall into Gracie's room. Without waking her, he pulled her jacket on and scooped her up into his arms. Carefully and quickly, Jonah carried her out to the car, buckling her in with shaking hands.

When he was finally en route, he began to worry. Lily hadn't been incredibly informative, leaving most of the details to Jonah's imagination. He kept reminding himself that Hannah was okay enough to speak to police officers instead of being rushed to the hospital. It made him feel a little better, but he was angry at the thought of someone causing her harm.

Jonah saw the flashing red and blue lights as he pulled into the diner's parking lot. He parked close to the scene and jumped out, leaving the car running.

An officer immediately approached him. "Sir, you can't come through here."

Before Jonah could object, he heard Hannah call his name. Looking up, he saw her coming toward him. He blew past the officer, gathering Hannah up in his arms the second they made contact.

Hannah was trembling as she clung to him, her tears flowing.

"Are you okay?" Jonah asked tenderly.

She wouldn't let go of him, calmed by the safety of his arms. She pressed her cheek into his chest, letting his rapid heartbeat console her.

"Hannah, please talk to me." He placed his hands on her shoulders, gently pulling her away to see her face.

"I'm okay," she said quietly.

"What happened?" He tucked a stray lock of hair behind her ear.

Hannah took a deep breath, her anxiety creeping back in. "I was walking to my car and getting my keys out, and someone came out of nowhere and grabbed my purse. They shoved me on the ground and just took off."

Jonah eyed her with concern. "Are you hurt?"

Hannah held out her scraped hands, palms up, then showed Jonah her skinned knee through the tear in her jeans.

"I think I might live," she joked, despite the situation.

Jonah smiled, drawing her close once again, and kissed her on the head. "I'm so glad you're all right."

Lily approached as they parted. "Hey, Hannah, I'm going to head home. You doing okay?"

Hannah nodded. "Yes, much better. Thank you, Lily. And thanks for calling Jonah for me."

Lily smiled bashfully at Jonah. "Yeah, that was me. Hi, Jonah." She reached for his hand and shook it.

He grinned. "Nice to finally meet you."

"Well, I'll see you Monday then," Lily said to Hannah, giving her a hug. "Glad you're okay."

"Monday?" Jonah asked once Lily had walked away.

"Yeah, this got me a day off. That's *one* good thing, I guess."

He glanced back at his car, concerned about Gracie. "Are you free to go yet?"

Hannah nodded. "They have all my information. That's all they can do right now."

Jonah took Hannah by the hand, careful not to hurt her. "Just come with me so you don't have to drive. We'll get your car tomorrow."

Hannah sighed. "Well, my keys were in my purse, so...I'd be coming with you anyway."

After Gracie had been returned to her room, Hannah and Jonah sat together at the foot of their daughter's bed, watching her sleep.

"She has no idea she went anywhere tonight," Jonah said, amused.

Hannah chuckled. "She has always slept like a rock."

"I guess that's good. There's really no need for her to

know what happened tonight."

Hannah nodded. "Yeah. She's too young to live in fear of people, right?"

Jonah looked at Hannah, sensing her distress. "You okay?"

Her eyes welled up. "I just keep thinking about how that person has my wallet and they know where I live, they have pictures of Gracie...Jonah, they have a key to my *house*."

"Hey, hey." He hushed her, pulling her close to him. "They got what they wanted from you. They're not going to come after you."

Hannah clung to him, tightly gripping handfuls of his shirt. "What if they're mad that I told the cops? They might be mad that they're going to get caught."

Jonah pulled away and took her face in his hands. "I am not going to let anything happen to you."

She stared back at him with pleading eyes. "Please don't leave me tonight."

Jonah stood and walked to the door, reaching for her. "C'mon."

Hannah slipped her hand into his, and he led her to her room, stopping outside the door.

"Meet me in the bathroom after you change," Jonah instructed, easing the door closed.

Hannah pulled off her torn jeans and dirty T-shirt and tossed them into the hamper. She grabbed an oversized shirt and a pair of plaid pajama shorts and put them on.

Curious what Jonah was up to, she made her way to the bathroom. When Hannah saw her reflection in the mirror behind him, her disheveled appearance shocked her. Jonah came toward her, wiping her mascara-stained cheeks with a washcloth. She was touched by his sweetness, trying so hard not to start crying again. After helping her clean up, Jonah rinsed her hands and her knee with peroxide, placing bandages where necessary.

When he turned away from the medicine cabinet, Hannah grabbed his face and yanked him to her for a kiss. Jonah reciprocated and kissed her intensely, forcing his hands not to stray from her waist. Hannah began unbuttoning his shirt, but he didn't stop her until she started tugging it off of his shoulders, her kisses trailing down his neck.

"Hannah," he whispered breathlessly, gently grabbing her wrists.

She sighed reluctantly and folded against him, feeling his bare chest against her cheek. "I know."

With a sigh of his own, Jonah lifted her face to look at him. "Let's get some sleep."

Hannah nodded, turning from him. Jonah buttoned his shirt as he followed her into her room.

With the euphoria wearing off, Hannah flopped onto her bed. "Why did that have to happen tonight?" she asked, burying her face in her pillow.

Jonah kicked off his shoes and lay down beside her, running his hand through her hair. "I don't know, Hannah. Bad things happen sometimes."

She lifted her head to face him. "I just don't like the way I feel right now."

"How do you feel?"

"Scared. Violated. Angry...like I've lost my faith in humanity."

Jonah pressed his lips together, watching the stress mark Hannah's delicate features. "I don't want you working there anymore."

"What?"

"I want you to quit your job," he reiterated.

Hannah looked confused. "Why?"

"I've never liked the hours they make you work. Especially when they schedule you to get off in the middle of the night. It's just not safe. Obviously."

"I really hate it there," she admitted. "I'll start looking for something else."

"No, just quit," Jonah said. "I know giving notice is the right thing to do, but in this case, I'm sure they wouldn't blame you for leaving."

"But we can't afford that," Hannah reasoned. "We don't need to take a step backward right now."

Jonah stroked her cheek. "Listen, I'll get another job if I have to. I'll work *three* jobs. Whatever it takes. I just want to know you're safe, and I *don't* want you in a place where they're taking advantage of you. You deserve so much better."

A slight smile curved Hannah's pretty lips. "I love how you protect me," she said, brushing his hair away from his eyes.

His expression softened. "Well, I love you. I'll *always* protect you. That's how we met, right?"

Hannah traced Jonah's jawline with her fingertips and smiled. "Right. The bully on the bus. You beat him up for me."

He grinned. "So you like guys that punch people in the face..."

She laughed. "Oh yeah, that's exactly what I meant."

"I know, I know...It's weird to think, though, that if he never bothered you, maybe you and I never would've happened."

"Yeah, weird," Hannah replied. "*Maybe* we would've still met, but it would've just been different."

He smiled. "So, what I'm trying to say is...Bad things happen, but sometimes they set greater things in motion."

"Ah, I see what you did there," Hannah said, playfully shaking a finger at him. "But you're right. I have to remember that. Good things can come from this."

"And they *will*," Jonah said, kissing her forehead.

Hannah awoke as the early morning sunlight began to spill through the part in her curtains. She could feel Jonah's arms around her, cradling her in the contour of his body. Closing her eyes, Hannah savored the stillness and warmth.

As she began to drift back to sleep, Jonah tightened his grasp and brushed his lips softly against the nape of her neck. Hannah affectionately ran her fingers over his arm.

"Hey," he whispered into her hair. "How are you feeling?"

"All right, I guess." She unfolded his embrace so she could turn to face him.

"Well, you were tossing and turning all night. You didn't stop until I held you," Jonah told her.

"Wow, really? I don't remember doing that."

"No crazy dreams?" he asked.

Hannah shook her head. "Not that I recall."

"Hmm. Weird."

She touched Jonah's cheek, her fingers brushing over his scar. "Thank you for staying with me. I know it's against the rules and everything."

He took her hand from his face and kissed it. "I wasn't going to just leave you here alone. And for the record, I dislike those rules just as much as you do."

Hannah smiled, snuggling into his chest. "I know."

Hannah was sitting at the kitchen table, having just finished breakfast with Gracie, when her mother came through the front door.

"Hi, girls." Caroline barely got a kiss out of Gracie before she ran off. "So, Jonah couldn't stay long? I passed him down the street."

Hannah sat cross-legged in her chair and sipped her coffee as her mother sat across from her. "Actually, he was here all night. He went home to change."

Caroline wrinkled her forehead. "Thought you guys weren't doing the whole sleepover thing anymore."

"Oh my gosh, I didn't tell you!" Hannah blurted out, startling her mother. "Someone jumped me after work last night and stole my purse."

"What?" Caroline's eyes were wide.

"The cops came and everything. It was pretty scary. That's why Jonah stayed. I didn't want to be alone, just me and Gracie."

Caroline shook her head. "I don't blame you. I'm so glad you're okay and Jonah was here to help you. But you can always call me at work if there's ever anything you need, ya know."

Caroline was reluctantly aware that her daughter was needing her less and less. She was no longer the one Hannah ran to for comfort, and it wasn't easy to accept.

"Oh, and just so you know, I'm quitting my job," Hannah added.

"Quitting your job? Wait, Hannah, you can't do that."

Hannah straightened in her chair, putting her feet on the floor. "Why not? I hate it there, and it's obviously not the safest. Jonah wants me to quit."

Caroline sighed. "Jonah wants you to…of course. You would do *anything* when it comes to Jonah."

Hannah scowled. "What is *that* supposed to mean?"

"I just don't think quitting your job is the right thing to do. You know we can't make things work on one income. And you know how much I hate asking your father for help."

"So I'm supposed to help support you for the rest of my life? I can't stay here forever, Mom. Or is that what you were counting on?"

Caroline let out another sigh. "No, Hannah! I knew one day you would find someone and want a life of your own, but I figured I would cross that bridge when we got there."

"Well, here's the bridge, Mom. I'm sorry Dad left you four years ago, but I'm done suffering for it," Hannah said, her voice shaking.

Caroline stared at her daughter. "I never wanted it to be like that. I didn't want you to have to grow up so fast and have so much responsibility so young. But when Gracie came along and your father left, we didn't really have a choice."

"So, what would you have done if I hadn't gotten pregnant and had gone off to college? No, wait—what if I *had* told Jonah the truth from the beginning and we had gotten married? What would you have done without my help?" Hannah asked.

Caroline bit her lip and shrugged. "I don't know...I probably would've had to sell this house."

Hannah slumped in her seat. "I don't want to fight with you. But this is something we need to figure out. I don't know when, but soon Jonah will ask me to marry him. And when he does, I'm leaving. I've waited so long to start a life with him."

Caroline nodded. "I know. And that's how it should be. I want you to be happy, and I never wanted to hold you back. I just thought we were helping each other."

Hannah reached across the table and placed a hand over her mother's. "No, you never held me back. I think I've always held *myself* back. I'm sure if I really tried, I could've bettered my life, but I just didn't have the drive. That job has had me in a rut all these years. I'm miserable there, Mom. I need to move on."

"Okay, Hannah. I'll talk to your father and see what he says about the house. We'll figure this out."

Jonah stood at Stephen Morgan's front door, his heart drumming. Regardless of how uncomfortable he felt, he knew it was the right thing to do. With a newfound sense of boldness, Jonah rang the doorbell.

Stephen curiously cocked his head to the side when he opened the door and saw Jonah standing there. "Jonah. What a surprise."

With his hands in his pockets, Jonah forced a casual smile. "I hope I'm not bothering you. I just wanted to talk to you for a moment if you have the time."

Stephen stepped aside. "Sure. Come in."

When they were seated in the living room, Jonah took a deep breath, unsure of where to start. His nervousness returned.

"So, what can I do for you? Is everything all right?" Stephen asked.

Jonah nodded. "Yes, I just...I wanted to talk to you about Hannah and me."

"Okay."

"I know I was gone for a while and I'm not exactly sure what you think of me now, but I need you to know that I truly love Hannah. And I will do anything necessary to take care of her and be everything she deserves," Jonah said earnestly.

Stephen held up his hand. "Listen, Jonah. I need to apologize for how I treated you a couple weeks back. It was unfair and it was inappropriate of me, and I'm sorry. You shouldn't have to come here and convince me that you're capable. I know you love my daughter. You always have."

Jonah let out a relieved breath, his rigid posture relaxing. "I'm glad you know that, but to be honest, that's not exactly why I'm here."

Stephen narrowed his eyebrows, a deep crease forming across his forehead. "Then what is it?"

Jonah pressed his lips together, collecting his courage. "I want to ask your daughter to marry me, but I'd like to have your permission first."

Stephen's features softened, and he smiled. "Jonah...I'd be very pleased to see my daughter marry you."

Jonah shook Stephen's outstretched hand. "Thank you, sir."

"Ya know, I'm an old-fashioned guy myself, and I appreciate you coming to me."

Jonah shrugged. "Well, I hope Gracie's boyfriend will respect me enough to come to me someday."

Stephen chuckled. "You're a good guy, Jonah. And I have to say, I'm glad you've come back for my Hannah. I kinda hoped it would turn out that way."

Seventeen

Jonah arrived at Tyler Music twenty minutes early. He was leaning against the wall outside the store, his cold hands jammed into his pockets, when Elliot rounded the corner, a lidded paper cup in each hand.

"I hope you like coffee." He smiled, handing one to Jonah.

"Yes, absolutely." Jonah inhaled the robust aroma as it escaped through the lid.

Elliot unlocked the door, motioning his son in ahead of him. He turned on the lights and flipped the sign on the door, ready to begin training his new associate.

Jonah caught on quickly to every facet of the store's operation. It didn't take long for Elliot to step back and allow Jonah to work on his own.

Before they knew it, it was time for Jonah to clock out for the day. As the steady flow of customers slowed down, the two of them took a seat behind the counter.

"Man, Jonah." Elliot shook his head. "You did great today. And you already made your first sale. I am impressed."

Jonah smiled, feeling accomplished. "Thanks. I still can't believe this is my *job*."

"Good. I'm happy you like it because it was definitely nice having help. What a difference another person makes,"

Elliot said.

"Thank you again for this opportunity. I need it now more than ever. Hannah quit her job yesterday." Jonah explained the scary situation that had taken place with Hannah that night at the diner.

"Oh, wow," Elliot replied. "I'm so glad she's okay. Does this delay the whole marriage plan?"

Jonah sighed. "I really hope not. Right now, I'm helping Hannah out with her bills, so I can't just save like I'd planned. I want to be able to get her the perfect ring...and I want to give her a home she can be proud of and feel safe in."

Elliot chuckled. "Such a hopeless romantic. You're definitely my son."

"I know it's silly, but I just want everything to be perfect. She deserves that," Jonah said.

Elliot paused, looking at his son for a moment. He felt an undeniable tugging at his heart.

"Come here. There's something I want to show you."

Jonah followed him to his office in the back of the store. Jonah stood in the doorway as Elliot opened a small closet and bent to spin the combination on his safe. With a quick motion, Elliot jerked it open and carefully sorted through its contents until he found what he'd been looking for.

He motioned for Jonah to sit down across from him at his desk. Setting a small tattered box between them, Elliot took a deep breath and let it out slowly.

"I was extremely close to my mother," he began, lightly tracing the corners of the box with his fingers. "I was the second born, but the only boy of four children, so my mother and I had a special bond. Well, ten years ago, she passed away and left me something very precious to her."

Opening the box, Elliot retrieved a small object and held it out in the palm of his hand.

"This was my mom's ring. My dad gave it to her when they were nineteen. It had been his grandmother's."

"Wow" was all Jonah could say, as he marveled at the vintage ring's intricate design.

Elliot smiled. "I want you to have this...so you can ask Hannah to marry you."

Jonah's jaw dropped. "What? Are you sure?"

"Of course. She was your grandmother, whether she got the chance to meet you or not. I really want you to have it, Jonah. You are the next one in line, after all."

Slowly, Jonah reached out and took the ring from his father's hand. He turned it, noting its perfection, as the large diamond sparkled wildly under the florescent lights. Jonah stared at the heirloom, in disbelief of what it meant. He could finally propose to Hannah. Jonah wanted to cry.

"Elliot..." He stood to hug his father, the threat of tears stinging his eyes. "You don't know how much this means to me."

A joyful grin lit Elliot's face as he embraced his son. "I think I have an idea."

"Seriously. Thank you so much," Jonah said, wiping his eyes.

Elliot placed a hand on Jonah's shoulder. "You're welcome, son. I'm happy to have someone like you to pass it on to."

Jonah collected himself, unable to keep from smiling.

"Here, I'll walk you out," Elliot offered.

Jonah grabbed his coat, and the two of them made their way outside into the December chill.

"So, I'll see you tomorrow, then," Jonah said, gripping the ring box tightly in one hand while he fished his keys out of his pocket with the other.

"Yes, you will." Elliot contemplated for a moment

before he continued. "Listen, there's something I'd like to speak with you about."

"Sure."

Elliot nervously cleared his throat. "I went to see your mother Saturday night. She was pretty worked up about everything with Nathan, so I stayed with her awhile. We ended up having dinner together, and, to be honest, we had a really nice time. I'd love to take her out again, but I wanted to make sure it's okay with you."

Jonah raised his eyebrows with an amused smile. "You're asking *my* permission to date my mom?"

"Well, yeah, I guess I am."

"Then yes. You have my definite approval."

"Good to know. Thanks, Jonah."

Jonah chuckled. "You sure *you* don't need this ring?"

Elliot laughed. "No, it's yours. I still have to get her to agree to a second date."

The next two weeks passed quickly. Jonah easily grew comfortable and quite efficient at his new job. Elliot gave him a raise and allowed him to work overtime. Jonah enjoyed going to work and loved giving guitar lessons the most. He spent his extra time during the day recording his music with the equipment Elliot had in the store. It wasn't the most professional quality, but it was definitely enough to satisfy his creative itch.

Jonah got out of his car one evening, a bouquet of flowers in his hand. He had barely taken two steps toward Hannah's house when Gracie came running out the front door and down the porch steps.

"Daddy!" she shrieked, jumping into his arms and nearly knocking him over.

Jonah's face was bright with an elated grin. "How's my girl?"

She wrapped her little arms around his neck. "Good! I'm happy you're home, Dad."

Jonah clutched her tightly. "Me too, baby."

Switching Gracie to his left arm, Jonah trudged up the driveway to the porch and let himself into the house. He set Gracie down and entered the kitchen, where he found Hannah washing the dinner dishes.

"Hey," he said tenderly, coming up behind her to plant a kiss on her cheek.

Hannah grabbed a dish towel to dry her hands as she turned to him. Her gaze traveled down to the bouquet he was holding, and her face lit up.

"Aw, you got me flowers?"

Jonah smiled, fond of her easily pleased nature. "Gracie attacked me in the driveway so they're a little beat up, but yes."

She took the flowers, admiring their vivid color. "No, they're beautiful. Tulips are my favorite."

"I remember."

"Why are you so good to me?" she asked.

"Because I love you" came Jonah's simple reply. "And I like making you smile."

"You are perfect, you know that?"

He snickered. "Your belief in that is your only flaw. Which reminds me...I'm so sorry I'm late. My last lesson ran longer than I thought it would."

Hannah reached into the cabinet behind him to retrieve a vase for her flowers. "It's okay. I saved you a plate," she said, filling the vase with water and arranging the colorful blooms.

Jonah opened the refrigerator but Hannah stopped him.

"Just sit. I'll get it," she insisted, briefly touching his face with her hand.

Hannah heated up his dinner and brought it to him at the table. She sat across from him, a smile on her face.

"Guess what?" she said, her eyes sparkling with excitement.

Jonah chuckled, finding her adorable. "What?"

"My mom has been talking to my dad, and today he told her that he wants the house. I guess his lease is up at his place so he's going to move in whenever we're all out of here. And my mom has been checking out apartments. She said she found one she really likes."

"Wow, that's kind of perfect," Jonah remarked.

"I know, it's exciting."

Gracie came into the kitchen just then, carrying her favorite doll with her. "What's exciting? That Santa is coming soon? He's coming in *nine* days. I know 'cause Gramma told me."

Jonah lifted Gracie onto his knee. "Is that right?"

"Yes," she replied emphatically. "I want him to bring me a puppy."

"Hmm, we'll have to see about that," Hannah said.

Jonah kissed his daughter on the head. "How about you get your pajamas on and brush your teeth, and I'll come tuck you in?"

"Okay, Daddy!" Gracie hopped down from her father's lap and ran out of the kitchen, the sound of her tiny feet fading as she disappeared down the hall.

Hannah and Jonah exchanged amused glances.

"It'll be so great to have you here for Christmas this

year," Hannah said wistfully.

"And *every* year forever and ever," Jonah added with a playful smile.

When Jonah stepped into his daughter's room, she was sitting in the middle of the floor, scribbling intently in her sketch pad.

"Hey, you," he said, fondly noticing her mismatched pajamas. "You ready for bed?"

Gracie jumped up, handing her masterpiece to her father. "Look, Daddy! I made this for you and Mommy."

"Oh, very nice, Gracie. Tell me about this picture."

Gracie took Jonah by the hand and guided him to sit on her bed beside her. "This is you, all dressed up. And this is Mommy, wearing a princess dress. And that's me, and we're all happy."

"Why are we dressed up?" Jonah asked.

"Because you're getting married."

He grinned. "What do you know about getting married?"

"That's what people do when they're in love," she answered without missing a beat.

"You're right. How did you get to be so smart?"

Gracie shrugged. "I don't know. Maybe God gave me a good brain."

Jonah laughed, sliding his arm around her. "Well, I love your drawing. I think it's beautiful."

"Hey, Dad?"

"Yeah?"

"Why did you take so long to find me?" Gracie asked.

Jonah froze, her question catching him off guard. "I don't know, sweetheart. But I wish I could have found you sooner."

She sighed and took Jonah's hand, tracing over her name on his wrist with her little finger. "Well...I'm happy you're here *now*."

"Me too, Gracie."

Nathan arrived at his mother's small birthday gathering an hour late, delayed by a hectic day at the hospital. No one realized he was there at first, as they sat around the living room, listening intently to an amusing story Elliot was telling. Nathan couldn't help but notice how close to Elliot his mother was sitting, or the way her eyes lit up as she watched him. Nathan unexpectedly found himself feeling left out.

"Uncle Nathan!" Gracie called, sliding off of Elliot's lap to rush to him.

"Oh, hi, Nathan. I didn't hear you come in," Scarlett said.

Nathan set Gracie down and painted on a thin smile as he crossed the room. "Happy birthday, Mom." He leaned down to hug her.

"Hey, Nathan. Good to see you again." Elliot grinned, extending his hand.

Nathan hesitated at first and then shook it, still shocked by all the ways Elliot resembled his little brother.

Jonah immediately caught onto the awkward tension and stood. "Hey, Nathan, let me get you some coffee," he suggested, motioning him into the kitchen.

"Is everything okay?" Jonah asked him once they were out of earshot.

Nathan sighed. "I don't know. I guess I wasn't prepared to walk in on the happy new family."

Jonah narrowed his eyebrows. "What are you talking about?"

"It's just weird. Mom and Elliot...I see the way she looks at him. I'm not stupid; I know what's going on."

Jonah opened the cabinet and retrieved two mugs. "She's really happy for once. What's wrong with that?"

Nathan shrugged. "I *do* want Mom to be happy, but then it'll make you three the family you probably should've been...and then I'm just the outcast, the black sheep who doesn't fit in."

"Like I used to be?" Jonah asked.

Nathan bit his bottom lip. "Well, when you put it that way, I just sound like a jerk."

"Everything will be fine if it works out between them," Jonah began, pouring their coffee. "Because the differences between my father and your father are infinite. I spent my entire life feeling like I didn't belong. I felt like an intruder in my own home on a constant basis. I can promise you that you'll never feel that way."

Nathan looked away. "I'm sorry, Jonah. I know you had it rough. I'm probably too old to care so much, but I'm just not used to this. My father *died*, and no one cares. And then my brother gets this new perfect father that everyone loves. I'm the only one who's lost something."

Jonah slowly sipped his coffee, watching his brother begin to unravel. "Nathan...You're not alone in any of this, okay? You've been going through so much lately, and it's a bit overwhelming, I know. But we are *all* a family. *Finally*."

Nathan nodded, wondering how he and Jonah had exchanged roles. Lately, his little brother was so full of support and guidance, always there for him when he became unsure of his next step. When Nathan was graduating from high school, Jonah was just finishing kindergarten, but despite the distance in their years, Jonah still possessed so much wisdom. He proved it time and time again.

As he saw the confident assurance in his brother's eyes, Nathan felt the peace wash over him. He realized, as he heard his mother laughing from the other room, how seemingly out of place the sound of laughter was within these tainted walls. And he knew Jonah was right. Elliot would be the saving grace that would make them a family for the very first time.

EIGHTEEN

Jonah awoke to his alarm reverberating painfully through his throbbing temples. Groaning, he silenced it and dropped his heavy head back onto his pillow. The pressure in his sinuses was almost unbearable.

For the past couple of days, Jonah hadn't been feeling well. He'd been in denial, insisting it was allergies or exhaustion. But noting the way he could hardly breathe, accompanied by the relentless stabbing headache, among other things, he finally gave in to defeat.

Scarlett was in the kitchen when her son staggered in, devoid of his usual light. Jonah went straight for his Chemex to brew some coffee, hoping a little caffeine would help. Despite his efforts to pull himself together, Scarlett could immediately see he wasn't well.

"Jonah, you're not going to work today, are you?" She got up from the table to approach him, a concerned frown wrinkling her features. She gently placed her hands on his flushed cheek and forehead. "You're burning up. Go back to bed."

"Mom—"

"I'll call Elliot. Just go to bed," Scarlett insisted, picking up her phone.

Feeling like a child again, but this time with a much more attentive mother, Jonah dragged himself up the stairs to his room.

After undressing and shrouding himself in the welcoming warmth of the covers, Jonah eagerly went back to sleep.

Hannah slipped quietly into Jonah's room, illuminated by the afternoon sunlight streaming through the missing slats of the old blinds. It still felt strange to be in his room again, the one place frozen in time since he'd gone away.

Kneeling beside the bed, Hannah let out a soft sigh and gently ran her fingers through Jonah's dark hair. He lay curled on his side, the plaid comforter cocooned tightly around him up to his neck. He was breathing loudly through his mouth, congestion rattling in his chest. Even in his sleep, his eyebrows were furrowed.

Hannah could feel the heat radiating off of him and began loosening the blanket. Jonah stirred, torn from his fever dream, his heavy eyelids fluttering open. Through his drowsiness, he saw Hannah's face, and one corner of his mouth turned in a groggy smile.

"Hi, babe," Hannah said tenderly, touching his hot cheek. It had been so long since she'd called him that, but it came out so naturally. "How are you feeling?"

Jonah arched his back to stretch and then winced when the motion made his head throb. "Not too good," he answered hoarsely, reaching down to pull the covers back over him.

Hannah grabbed his hand to stop him. "You need to keep your temperature down. That's not going to help."

He returned to his curled position, crossing his arms tightly over his midsection. "I'm so cold though," he mumbled nasally, shivering as he fought to stay awake.

"I know, I'm sorry," Hannah said, brushing his hair out of his eyes. Even in his misery, he was beautiful. "Your mom said you've been in bed all day. Have you had anything to eat or drink?"

Jonah barely shook his head and muttered in a quiet voice, "I'm not hungry."

"You at least need to drink some water. Please?" She offered him a lidded plastic cup with a straw.

Jonah lifted his head and took the cup, the ice tinkering inside, and sucked down half of it. He hadn't realized how thirsty he was until the wetness doused the fire in his dry, aching throat. He felt the cold liquid pass through his chest into his empty stomach, and he shuddered. "Thanks," he said, nearly out of breath.

"I also brought you some cold medicine." Hannah offered her open hand to him, two green gel capsules in her palm.

With another swig of water, Jonah downed both pills in one gulp. He sank back into his pillow, trying to ward off the threatening sensation to sneeze. He was almost certain if he couldn't hold it back, his head would explode. Thankfully, it dissipated, and he willed himself to relax as best as he could.

"I'm sorry you're sick," Hannah said, her pretty face sympathetic. It pained her to see him so weak.

"Well, I'm usually sick for Christmas, remember? I guess this year is no exception." Jonah forced a smile.

"We still have five days. Hopefully you'll feel a lot better by then."

He reached for her hand, threading his fingers through hers. "Don't get me anything for Christmas," he said, his expression serious.

Hannah chuckled. "Why not?"

"Because..." He paused to sniffle. "I'd rather spend money on Gracie instead."

"Fair enough," Hannah agreed, standing up. "But let's not worry about that right now, okay? You need to rest."

"Okay," Jonah breathed, closing his tired blue eyes.

Hannah bent down to kiss his forehead, his skin blazing against her lips. "I love you," she whispered, but he was already asleep.

Jonah waited in Hannah's foyer as she finished getting ready. He kept glancing nervously in the large mirror hanging on the wall beside him, scrutinizing his new appearance. He sighed, brushing the lint off of his navy blue sweater. It was Christmas Eve, and he would finally be meeting Elliot's family. *His* family.

Jonah's anxious thoughts were interrupted when Gracie came running toward him.

"Daddy!" She gasped dramatically, nearly knocking him backward. "You look handsome...like a prince!"

He smiled and stroked her soft cheek. "Well, thank you."

Gracie pouted. "Are you all better yet? I missed you."

"I missed you too, sweetheart. I'm trying to get better."

Hannah appeared, slinging her bag over her shoulder. She stopped dead in her tracks when she saw Jonah.

His shoulders slumped. "You hate it."

A grin formed on her lips as she shook her head. "No, I don't. Not at all." She reached up to run her fingers over the side of Jonah's much shorter hair. The top was neatly combed back, pompadour style. His amazing eyes stood out better than ever.

"Doesn't he look like a prince, Mommy?" Gracie said.

Hannah chuckled. "He does. Gosh, Jonah…" She stood on her tippy-toes to kiss him.

"I thought it was time for a change, ya know? Start taking care of myself a bit better," Jonah said.

Hannah looked at him incredulously.

"Okay, fine, and I'm nervous about tonight. And I just really want them to like me," he added honestly. "But forget the haircut, I still look like I've been in bed for three days, don't I?"

Hannah laughed melodically. "No. Stop worrying. They're going to love you."

Jonah was in awe over his father's gorgeous property. White Christmas lights were strung along the roof on both levels of the large colonial, casting a warm glow on the front porch. Gracie excitedly rang the doorbell, and Jonah took a deep breath.

Hannah gave his hand a squeeze. "Just remember, they're *your* family. I bet they cannot wait to meet you."

Jonah nodded, sniffling in the chilling breeze, and pulled his pea coat tighter around his body.

When the wreath-clad door opened and Elliot's kind smile greeted them, Jonah felt much calmer. Elliot welcomed them inside, and Gracie gave him a hug.

"Merry Christmas Eve, Grampa!" she said.

As they removed their coats, a tall, slender woman approached them. She had the same kind eyes as Elliot, and her friendly smile was wide and excited.

"Oh my goodness," she began, placing her hands on Jonah's shoulders to study him. "You *do* look like your father…only *much* better-looking."

"Gloria," Elliot scolded playfully.

Gloria laughed. "I'm your favorite aunt, Gloria, Elliot's older and *also* much better-looking sister."

"*And* the family comedian," Elliot added.

Jonah smiled, accepting her hug. "It's nice to meet you." Then he motioned behind him. "This is Hannah, and our daughter, Gracie."

"Ooh, pretty things, both of you. Goodness." Gloria shook Hannah's hand, then tousled Gracie's curls.

"Anyway, why don't you guys come on in and make yourselves at home? Everyone is looking forward to meeting you," Elliot said, placing his arm around Jonah. He led him past the staircase into the living room.

Jonah observed the familiar-looking strangers scattered about the living room and adjoining kitchen area. Small groups here and there were chatting and laughing together as the fireplace crackled and Bing Crosby played softly on the record player beside the large, illuminated Christmas tree. A couple small children ran by, chasing each other, and were immediately scolded by a woman across the room.

"Everyone..." Elliot began with a proud grin. "This is my son, Jonah."

Every face was smiling, thrilled to finally lay eyes on the nephew, cousin, and grandson they never knew they had. Thankfully, they took their time approaching Jonah throughout the night, allowing him to get comfortable in his new environment without bombarding him all at once.

After Elliot led a prayer to bless the food, the family gathered in the kitchen. They filled their plates from large platters set out buffet style on the center island counter. Everyone once again dispersed to wherever they could find a place to sit and eat their dinner, but three spots were saved at the dining room table for the guests of honor, Jonah and his family.

While he picked at some lasagna he couldn't taste and fought through a worsening headache, Jonah met Elliot's younger sister, Sara, and her husband, Ron. They had three kids: Addison, Matty, and Olivia. Oddly enough, Jonah recognized Matty from high school. They hadn't been friends, barely even acquaintances, but they both remembered sharing a class or two. Addison was married to Shaun, and they had two boys, Declan and Chase, who were younger than Gracie.

Gloria was married to a reserved man named Scott. Jonah guessed their opposite personalities balanced each other out. They had flown in for Christmas from New York, where they lived close to their son, Michael. He was a single, successful Wall Street type and hadn't been able to make the trip. The way Gloria described him, he sounded a lot like Nathan.

The last to approach Jonah after dinner was Elliot's youngest sister, Annie. She was ten years younger than Elliot and married to Sam. Their three children—Luke, Sage, and Brynn—were all in high school.

It was a lot of information to take in, and Jonah wished his sickness wasn't distracting him from better retaining it. He hoped no one could tell how awful he felt. Hannah, however, could.

Cornering Jonah in the hallway on his way back from a coughing fit in the bathroom, Hannah gently held his face in her hands.

"You okay?" she asked attentively.

Jonah sighed. "Probably not."

"I guess it was too much too soon, huh?"

He folded against her, burying his face in the crook of her neck. "Hold me, I'm dizzy."

Hannah chuckled, rubbing his back. "Aw, we should

get you home."

He straightened up and frowned. "I haven't had a chance to spend any time with my grandfather yet."

As if on cue, Elliot came around the corner. "Ah, Jonah, there you are. Now that my sisters are finished smothering you, I'd really love for you to meet my father."

Hannah and Jonah exchanged glances.

"I'd love to," Jonah replied, kissing Hannah on the cheek before he followed Elliot back into the living room.

Henry Tyler was seated in a large, fluffy armchair in the corner of the room, contentedly watching his family exchange and open gifts. It had been ten years since his wife, Elaine, had passed away. The holidays without her were unbearable at first, but as the years flew by, it had somehow gotten easier. He never missed her less; he just learned to live with her absence. It helped to have such a wonderful family by his side, the family he'd built with Elaine. And beautiful surprises, like his grandson, Jonah, were enough to fill his heart's empty spaces as well.

"Hey, Dad, I finally rescued him from the girls," Elliot said, leading Jonah to Henry. Henry was fit for his age with a full head of white hair, combed neatly and parted on the side.

Jonah shook his grandfather's hand. "Nice to meet you, sir."

"Eh, call me Grandpa. If that's what you like. That's what your cousins call me," Henry said with a slight New York accent. "Have a seat, son."

Jonah sat on the couch beside Henry's chair.

Henry smirked. "Overwhelmed yet?"

Jonah let out a nervous chuckle. "I guess you could say that. It's a lot to get used to…an entire side of a family you never knew existed."

"Oh, absolutely. But I have to tell ya, Jonah, when your

father told me about you…Nothing has made me that happy in a *long* time. And I'm a pretty happy guy, ya know."

Jonah smiled. "Well, good. I'm glad."

"Having no brothers and only one son of my own, I was afraid the Tyler name would end with Elliot. But here you are…"

Jonah bit his lower lip. "Actually…"

"Oh, forgive me for being presumptuous. You don't want to change your name?" Henry asked.

Jonah snickered. "Oh, no, I would *love* to, trust me. It's just that my mom kinda made that difficult. She decided to be sneaky and make Tyler my *middle* name, so…"

"Jonah Tyler Tyler!" Henry cracked up, thoroughly amused.

Jonah laughed. "Yeah, it's pretty funny. But Weston is also my daughter's last name…But it's not impossible, I guess."

"Either way, you *will* be changing Hannah's name, though, won't you?" Henry asked facetiously, adjusting his wire-framed glasses.

A smile slowly spread across Jonah's lips. "Absolutely."

"That's good," Henry said approvingly. "Ya know, your Gracie is my first great-grandchild. That's pretty special."

Jonah thought for a moment, recalling his cousin's two little boys he'd met earlier. "Wow, you're right. She is."

"She's a sweet little girl, that Gracie. And a stunning little thing. She was sitting with me earlier, and all she wanted to talk about was her daddy. You are her hero, ya know."

Jonah glanced fondly across the room at his daughter, who was playing with Declan. "That's nice to hear."

"Your father has told me a lot about you. You've sure

been through a lot," Henry said. Jonah shrugged as Henry continued. "But look at you, you're a pretty stand-up guy. Your father sure is proud of ya. He also told me he gave you his mother's ring."

Jonah pressed his lips together. "Yes...Is that okay?"

Henry chuckled. "Of course it is. It was very important to Elliot to give it to you. Ya know, in a way, he mourned the children he never had—no one to raise and pour his heart and soul into. That ring was kind of a reminder to him of that missing piece, having no one to pass it on to as my wife had wished. But again, here you are, Jonah, making everything right."

Jonah shifted his eyes to the floor, not exactly sure how to process such serious compliments. His chest nearly ached with emotion, and all he could manage was, "Thank you."

"Ah, well it's what's true, son. When ya get old like me, you learn to speak your mind. There's nothing more important than the people around you...which reminds me..." Henry leaned down to a small Christmas-printed gift bag on the floor beside his chair and lifted it to his lap. After rummaging through it for a moment, he pulled out an envelope and handed it to Jonah. "Just a little Christmas gift."

Jonah raised his eyebrows as he looked down at his name scrawled across the red envelope. He had never expected anything. He lifted the unsealed flap and slipped the card out.

Henry reached over and placed his wrinkled hand over Jonah's before he could open the card. "Listen," he started, looking intently into Jonah's eyes. "You must know, I give each of my grandkids one hundred dollars for Christmas every year. You should've always been here with us, Jonah. When I realized I missed *twenty-three* Christmases with my grandson, it broke my heart. So I wanted to do something special, the only thing I *can* do to make it as if you were here all those years…"

Henry released Jonah's hand, letting him open the card. Nestled in the bend of the cardboard was a check for $2,400. Jonah's eyes went wide, and he shook his head.

"You barely even know me. I can't—"

Henry stopped him. "Yes, you can. How well do you think I know my grandson Michael? I've probably seen him three times in the past ten years, but I still send him a gift…because I love him. What makes him any more my grandson than you are? Listen, I'm a very blessed man, and I am more than able to give you this gift, and anything else if you should ever need it. So please, let me do this for you. Go buy some music equipment or put it toward your wedding. Whatever you want. Just enjoy it."

Jonah's eyes stung as his emotions escalated. He was deeply touched by his grandfather's generous gesture and couldn't help but throw his arms around him in a grateful hug. "Thank you."

"You're welcome, Jonah. I'm so glad you're here with us."

"So do you think tonight went well?" Jonah asked as they rocked slowly on Hannah's front porch swing. They had just tucked Gracie into bed and were in the midst of their usual long good night.

"I think it did." Hannah snuggled against him to keep warm. "They really loved you."

Jonah shielded his mouth to cough, then sighed deeply, his breath a wispy fog in the air. "I just want to feel better."

"I know," she said sympathetically, placing her hand

on his leg. "You will soon."

Jonah closed his heavy eyelids and laid his head back. "I should go. I can't wait to take some NyQuil and pass out."

Hannah slid off of the swing and took Jonah's hands in hers. Feeling so achy and weak, he let her help him to his feet. Hand in hand, they made their way to Jonah's SUV, the stars dotting the dark canvas overhead. It felt cold enough to snow.

"So, what happens tomorrow?" Hannah wondered, smoothing the lapels of Jonah's coat.

"We find out if Santa brought us coal or presents," he answered without missing a beat.

Hannah laughed, sliding her arms into his coat and around his torso. "No, I mean, will I be able to see you?" she asked, nestling her head against his chest.

"Of course you will." He gently ran his fingers through her hair. "I've spent the last four Christmases without you. It would take a hell of a lot more than the flu to keep me from you *this* year."

Hannah smiled against the softness of his sweater, lulled by his heartbeat beneath her ear. "I can't believe it's really been *five* years since that Christmas together." She squeezed Jonah tighter.

"Yeah," he breathed. "It's so strange to think about that night…knowing what I know now."

Hannah lifted her head to gaze up at him. "You mean when Gracie happened?"

Jonah swallowed, taken aback by her candidness. "Yeah, I do."

"Can I ask you something?"

Jonah didn't hesitate. "Anything."

"What do you think made us wait so long to be together?" Hannah asked bravely.

He stared at her for a moment. They'd never talked about it before. Not like this. "I guess we weren't typical teenagers," he said with a shrug.

His vague answer wasn't acceptable. "No, Jonah. We should be able to talk about this…about anything."

Jonah sighed heavily, tilting his head upward as he contemplated. "I always wanted to; it wasn't about that…But honestly, sometimes I was afraid of how much I loved you. I knew sharing that with you would just push me over the edge, and I didn't know if I could allow myself to be that vulnerable to someone."

Hannah squinted her eyes, analyzing his words. "I guess you have always seemed a bit guarded. But why were you afraid to be vulnerable to *me*? You knew I would never hurt you…Not then, not now."

"When you're forsaken by your own father, you grow up believing everyone is capable of anything," Jonah said, dropping his gaze to the ground. He struggled to find a wording he felt comfortable with saying. "Also…I guess I wasn't sure I deserved to be the one you gave yourself to."

Hannah had always been pained by his distorted self-image. "I'm limited by a vocabulary that doesn't contain the words to convey how truly incredible you are, but you have always been worthy, Jonah."

His eyes were deep pools of bright blue as he looked intently at her. "You were the only one who ever made me feel like I mattered."

She caressed his cheek with her hand. "But the thing is…you've mattered *so* much more than you ever realized. People have always adored you, Jonah. I guess if you could really grasp that, it would take away all the sweet, timid, and humble parts of you that make you so perfectly 'Jonah.'"

His lip began to quiver, and he laughed to keep his

emotions at bay. "What happened to that limited vocabulary that prevented you from all this nonsense?"

"Well, a lack of communication nearly ruined us before, so I never want to hold back with you ever again," she said.

Jonah stroked her hair, tucking it behind her ears. "Okay, so what about you then? Why do you think we waited?"

Hannah rested her hands on Jonah's waist as she thought to herself for a brief moment. "This probably sounds dumb, but I really liked being different from everyone else. In a weird way, I felt like we were rebelling against what society expected." She paused, shrugging. "I don't know...I loved everything about us. I loved our naivety and our innocence. Just being together was enough. And taking it to the next level was always just something to look forward to."

"Also, our parents made it pretty impossible, so there's that," Jonah added for comic relief.

Hannah laughed. "That is true. But I don't regret at all the way things played out."

Jonah looked at her, tracing the details of her face with his eyes. "I love you, Hannah," he said wholeheartedly.

He leaned in to kiss her, but just as his lips covered hers, she reluctantly pulled away.

"We really shouldn't. I'm sorry."

Jonah groaned. "I forgot I have cooties."

Laughing, Hannah wrapped her arms around him, returning her cheek to the warmth of his chest. "Oh, you make me so happy, you know that?" she whispered.

He grinned and kissed her on the head before they finally said good night.

Christmas morning brought flurries and a festive crispness to the northern air. Hannah was in the kitchen putting tea on for her mother when she heard the loud creak of the opening front door.

Hannah turned to see Jonah's sleepy grin as he entered the kitchen. His messenger bag was slung across his chest, and he was holding a box of doughnuts and a carrier of steaming coffees.

"I come bearing morning goodness." He smiled, setting everything down on the kitchen table.

"Aw, you're so sweet."

"Merry Christmas, Hannah," Jonah said, gathering her in his arms.

"I'm surprised you're here so early," she said when they parted. "Shouldn't you be resting?"

He shrugged. "I didn't want to miss the look on Gracie's face when she sees her presents."

Hannah's heart swelled. "Well, she's still asleep. Why don't you go wake her?"

"I have to give you your present first."

She looked at him sideways. "I thought you said no presents."

A sly smile brightened Jonah's eyes. "I said no presents for *me*."

"All right then."

He reached into his bag and proudly presented her with an impeccably wrapped box.

Hannah eagerly tore into the red-and-green paper, and her jaw dropped. "A *camera*?" She gawked at the Nikon DSLR in her hands. "I love it, Jonah, but how can you afford this?"

Jonah grinned at her child-like surprise. "Well, it's not one of the more expensive, top-of-the-line models. But it's still a good one, and it'll take nice pictures. We need that. Like right now, when Gracie sees what Santa brought her."

Hannah grinned. "You're right. This is perfect. Thank you so much, Jonah."

"You are so welcome. Oh, and I already charged the battery, so you're good to go."

"Wait, how do you use this thing?" Hannah asked, lifting it out of the box.

Jonah chuckled. "Just put it on 'auto' for now. I'll help you figure it out later."

He kissed her forehead, then sauntered down the hall into Gracie's dim room. Kneeling beside her bed, he stroked her curls. Her cherub face was peaceful with sleep, and Jonah couldn't help but admire her.

"Gracie," he whispered.

Her eyes opened and met his. "Hi, Daddy," her soft voice chimed. "Did Santa come yet?"

"Why don't you come and see?"

Gracie's face lit up as she bolted out of bed, suddenly full of energy. She took Jonah by the hand, leading him down the hall and into the living room.

Hannah was snapping photos as Gracie approached the tree, mouth agape and blue eyes wide. Jonah and Hannah looked at one another, touched by their daughter's joy and immensely grateful to be sharing in the moment together.

NINETEEN

Jonah was sitting cross-legged on the floor, carefully placing stickers in their correct places on Gracie's new dollhouse, when Hannah came up behind him.

"Are you ready for your present?" she asked.

He looked up at her, surprised. "I thought I said no presents."

Hannah snickered. "Too bad."

Jonah set the several sheets of stickers aside and stood with a sly grin. "I love when you get rebellious."

"*Actually*, I technically didn't break any rules because I didn't spend anything on you," Hannah said.

Jonah was intrigued. "All right, well, let's see this present then."

She led him to sit beside her on the couch and handed him a manila envelope. He opened it, sliding its contents onto the coffee table before him.

There were two tickets, an "all access" wristband, a CD, and a flyer spread across the walnut table. Jonah went for the flyer first, his eyebrows narrowed quizzically. It was an advertisement for the seventh annual *'Twas the Night After Christmas*, an indie music showcase in New York City. Jonah's name was listed as one of the three featured artists. His eyes went wide.

"*I'm* playing this tomorrow?"

Hannah nodded. "If you're up to it."

Jonah was still in shock. "We went to this the first year they put it on, remember? It's a pretty big deal. How did you do this?"

"They do an online contest. I was on your laptop one day, and I stumbled across the music you recorded at work. I uploaded a song, and they chose yours as one of the ten finalists for people to vote for."

"Wait…people voted for my song?" Jonah questioned.

"Yup! So you and the other two winners get to perform up to three original songs in an awesome venue in front of hundreds of people. Oh and look—your song is on here, along with the other nine finalists. They'll be selling it at the show." Hannah picked up the CD and pointed out track one: "Write You Down" by Jonah Weston.

Jonah stared at his name and song title, finding it surreal to see them in the track listing on the back of a CD. It was the same song he'd sang for Hannah at the coffeehouse. A smile formed on his lips as he looked back at her.

"This is so cool," he said, hugging her. "Thank you so much."

"I really think you should be pursuing your music," Hannah said, pulling back to look at him. "You need to put yourself out there, just like you did in Tampa. You are so talented, and you could really be something, I know it."

Jonah grinned, the excitement rising inside him. "You don't know how much it means to me to hear you say that."

"I'm just sorry you're still feeling bad," she said with a frown. "I entered your song *before* you got sick. But I called and explained the situation, and they said you can give up your spot if you need to. They just have to know by this afternoon."

He shook his head. "No, I want to go. I'll just suck it up. I can't pass up something like this."

Hannah smiled. "All right. Then you should probably rest as much as you can today."

Jonah's sly smile returned. "Hey, Hannah...What would you have done if I hadn't made the top three?"

She shrugged. "You'd have no present, and I would've followed the rules. But I wasn't worried about it. I knew you'd get in."

After Jonah attempted to nap away a headache all afternoon, the evening was spent at Scarlett's for Christmas dinner. Elliot, Nathan, and Caroline were also in attendance and were thrilled to hear of Jonah's wonderful opportunity.

"So," Nathan began, coming up beside Jonah and placing a stack of dirty dishes in the sink. "Do you know who's taking your extra ticket tomorrow night?"

Jonah rinsed the plates and handed them one by one to Nathan to load into the dishwasher. "I actually hadn't thought that far."

"If you want to invite Elliot, that's cool," Nathan said, closing the dishwasher door. He grabbed a sponge to wipe the counters.

Jonah smiled. "Hey, Nathan...Would you like to come to the show with us?"

Nathan stopped, wiping his damp hands on his jeans. "Well, yeah. Are you just asking me if I *want* to, or...?"

"I am inviting you," Jonah said, chuckling. "I would love for you to come."

A wide grin spread across Nathan's face. "Really?"

"Yes, really. Geez, Nate, why wouldn't I?"

Nathan shrugged. "I guess it just seemed like

something you'd rather have Elliot come to, since you both share the whole music thing."

"Yeah, but you're my brother," Jonah said.

Nathan nodded with a smile. "Yes. And hey, if it'll help, I can drive. I mean, no thanks to Kendall, I could drive to New York in my sleep. Not that I would…and that way, you can rest up for the show." The doctor side of him probably would've suggested to skip the function altogether, but he knew it was too important to Jonah.

"That's actually pretty perfect," Jonah agreed. "Thanks, man."

"And I'll even take care of your girl while you're up on stage being famous."

Jonah laughed, rolling his eyes. "Well, I wouldn't say *famous*."

Nathan patted his little brother on the shoulder. "It's definitely a good start."

"I hope Jonah's up for this," Nathan said as he let Hannah into his mother's house.

Hannah carried a snoozing Gracie into the living room and set her bag down on the coffee table. Jonah was sitting on the far end of the couch, sound asleep, his head propped up in his hand. Hannah carefully placed Gracie down at the opposite end.

"How is he today?" she quietly asked Nathan.

Nathan grimaced. "Worse than yesterday. He came downstairs after he got ready, and he was pretty out of it. I went to the kitchen to get him some coffee, and when I got back, he had fallen asleep."

Hannah bent closer to Jonah, gently running the backs of her fingers down his cheek. His eyes opened, somehow more vivid than ever, and he smiled at the sight of her, despite himself.

"Hey, Jonah. Are you ready to go?" Hannah asked softly.

He clumsily stood, rubbing his eye. "Yeah, I'm ready." He gave Gracie a quick kiss on the cheek before bending to pick up his guitar case.

Scarlett came out from the kitchen to see them off.

"Good luck, Jonah. I'm so proud of you," she said as she hugged her younger son. Then, hugging Nathan, she said, "Please take care of your brother. And drive safe."

"I will, Mom."

"So if it starts at seven, why do we have to get there so early?" Nathan asked once they were on the road.

"Jonah has some interviews with local radio stations and stuff, a photo shoot for the showcase website, and then sound check," Hannah replied as she programmed the venue address into the GPS on her phone. It would take them about two hours.

"Wow, this is kinda huge then," Nathan remarked.

"Yeah, they make a big deal out of the performers. It's pretty neat." Hannah glanced at the backseat of the Mercedes where Jonah was curled up, sleeping. Her motherly instincts cringed at his lack of seatbelt use, but she forced away the worries and returned her attention to Nathan.

"So, how have you been?" she asked, plugging Jonah's iPod into the auxiliary jack. She selected Anberlin, playing them quietly on shuffle.

"I'm doing much better. At least I think I am, anyway," Nathan said, keeping his eyes on the road.

She frowned. "I know your wedding date is coming

up next weekend. That must be hard."

He sighed. "Yeah, it's a little tough, but, ya know, the person I thought I loved never really existed. So I can't miss someone who would hurt me like that. In the end, that's all she was."

"Well, I'm glad it's getting better for you."

Nathan snickered. "Next weekend could've still been awesome, but Jonah shot that one down."

Hannah narrowed her eyebrows. "What are you talking about?"

"Oh. He didn't tell you?"

"Tell me what?"

"I *half* seriously offered him my wedding a few weeks ago, because I paid large non-refundable deposits for the ridiculously huge wedding Kendall wanted. So the deposits would've covered a nice, normal wedding...but he didn't go for it," Nathan explained.

Hannah's eyes went wide. "Really...What did he say?"

"Don't get me wrong, he was tempted. But he said you deserved your own wedding, one that you planned together. And he didn't want to rush you into it and offer you a proposition instead of a proper marriage proposal."

Hannah looked back at Jonah once again and smiled. "He said that?"

Nathan nodded. "He really loves you, Hannah."

"Don't worry, I know."

Nathan parked his Jeep in Hannah's driveway and looked over at his little brother. "You nervous?" he asked him.

Jonah shrugged off the question, though it was apparent on his face. Taking a deep breath, he opened the door.

Nathan stopped him. "Hey, Jonah...Don't worry. It's just Hannah."

Jonah nodded, climbing out and shutting the door behind him. He made his way up the driveway toward the walk, feeling silly that his big brother had to chauffeur him on his first date with Hannah. But with both of them being just fourteen, they had no choice. It was better than getting a ride from their parents, after all.

Jonah timidly knocked on the front door of the Morgans' home, and her father, Stephen, answered.

"Hey, Jonah," he greeted him.

They shook hands. "Hi, Mr. Morgan."

"Hannah will be out in just a minute," Stephen said, peering at the Jeep in the driveway. "Who's driving you?"

"Oh, that's my brother, Nathan."

"He's a careful driver, right? Has he had his license long?" Stephen questioned.

"Well, he's twenty-six, so..."

Stephen's eyes widened. "Oh."

Thankfully, Hannah appeared beside her father, a giddy smile on her face. She was wearing a pale pink sundress and a white cardigan. Jonah's heart nearly stopped at the sight of her.

"Hi, Jonah." She stepped out onto the porch and slipped her hand into his.

Stephen tightened his jaw. He wasn't ready for his daughter's first date.

"Hannah, I want you home by eleven. Please be careful. Wear your seatbelt. And Jonah, please be good to my little girl."

Jonah opened his mouth to reply, but Hannah spoke instead. "Dad, stop worrying. We will be fine."

She kissed her father on the cheek and bounded down the porch steps, Jonah following behind her. He watched the sunlight catch her flowing blond hair.

"Sorry about my dad," she said. "He's a little

overprotective."

Jonah shoved his hands into his pockets. "It's okay. It's good that he cares about you."

When they reached the car, he opened the door for Hannah, then slid into the backseat beside her.

"Hey, Nathan." Hannah smiled, clicking her seatbelt into place. "Thanks so much for agreeing to drive us kids around tonight."

Nathan chuckled. "Not a problem...skating rink or Chuck E. Cheese?"

"Ha ha, funny. We're young, I get it," Jonah said with a playful sarcasm.

Nathan turned to his little brother when they arrived at the restaurant ten minutes later. "You have Mom's phone, right? Call me when the movie's over later...and have fun."

"I will. Thanks, Nathan."

After Nathan pulled away, Jonah looked at Hannah. "Yeah, I know, the cliché dinner and a movie," he said sheepishly.

She smiled. "I've never been to dinner and a movie, so it's not cliché to me."

Inside the bustling restaurant, they were seated at a small table close to the loud kitchen, making conversation difficult. Despite the busyness, the service was quick, and they found themselves back outside on the sidewalk just forty-five minutes later.

"Well, that wasn't what I expected." Jonah laughed nervously, certain their date was headed for failure.

"No, it was nice," Hannah assured him. "Thank you."

He led her across the parking lot to the theater next door. They were a bit early for their movie, but they stepped up to the end of the long ticket line anyway. The sun was beginning to set, the evening air growing cooler. Jonah noticed Hannah shivering, so he took off his jacket and placed it around her.

"Thanks," she said, sliding her arms through the sleeves.

Jonah's scent engulfed her.

When they were next in line, Jonah sighed and turned to Hannah. "Do you really want to see a movie?"

She didn't hesitate. "I'd rather just be with you."

"Yes. Exactly." Jonah took her by the hand, and they stepped out of line, heading down the sidewalk.

"Where are we going?" Hannah asked.

"Just for a walk. Is that okay?"

She nodded. "I'm with you. That's all that matters."

"Do you think we're too young?" Jonah asked after a few silent moments.

"What, to be together?" Hannah wondered.

He shrugged. "It might seem silly, but I'm serious about us."

"I am too," she admitted without missing a beat.

"I really don't care what anyone thinks. I think we have something here. And I'm willing to take the chance...if you are," he said.

"You don't have to convince me." Hannah tightened her grip on his hand. "I'm in."

Jonah smiled. "Glad we're on the same page."

"I think we always have been."

He gazed at her longingly, her golden hair framing her beautiful face. "I hope I marry you someday," he confessed, his boldness accelerating his heartbeat.

Hannah blushed and looked down at her feet. "I think you just might."

Cars raced by on the street as the pair strolled down the sidewalk, the sun hanging lower in the sky. They shared in unhindered conversation like never before in the two years they'd known each other, until they reached the entrance of Oak Lake Park.

"Should we watch the sun set on the lake? If we hurry, we might be able to make it," Hannah eagerly suggested.

With a grin, Jonah grabbed her hand once again and whisked her into the park. They ran and laughed until they reached the lake, breathless and alive. They looked at each other, their eyes bright with excitement. In the dissipating orange-pink light, beneath the autumn hues of the prettiest tree in the park, Jonah took Hannah's face in his hands and kissed her for the first time.

They arrived at the venue with time to spare. After washing down two pain relievers with half a can of energy drink, Jonah popped in a cough drop and kissed Hannah on the cheek.

"Gotta go pretend to be important," he joked, the scent of cherry and menthol on his breath.

"Hey, you *are*. That's why you're here." Hannah smiled, helping him secure the all-access band around his wrist.

"Have fun," Nathan chimed in. "We'll be around."

With a slight wave, Jonah disappeared backstage to check in. A woman with a headset and a clipboard took his guitar case and led him to a room with craft service tables along the back. Jonah wasn't hungry so he grabbed a bottle of water.

Before he could sit down and speculate who the other people in the room were, a different headset-clad person whisked him away to another room for interviews. Jonah tried his best to be personable despite his condition. They mainly asked predictable questions, but the third interview, with a woman from a local magazine, was the most interesting.

"Hi Jonah. I'm Bree Harris," she said, smiling cordially. She shook his hand as she sat down across from him. "You know there's a rumor that the third performer is the one who actually had the most votes, right?"

Jonah narrowed his eyebrows. "No, I haven't heard

that."

"Track one on the compilation, yes?"

He nodded.

"Yup. You won the whole thing then. I don't know why they never come out and share that information. *I* think it matters." Bree tapped a button on her phone to begin recording their conversation, then she glanced through her notes, mumbling to herself. "Let's see...Jonah Weston. Date of birth, May 17, 1990. Age twenty-three...okay." Bree looked up at him through her black, plastic-framed glasses. "Let's get the standard questions over with. When did you start getting into music?"

Jonah had answered this one before. "I asked for a guitar for my twelfth birthday, but I was fourteen when I finally taught myself how to play it. I started writing my own stuff around fifteen."

"And what was your writing inspiration then?" Bree asked.

"Same as it is now."

"Is 'Write You Down' also a product of this same inspiration?"

Jonah nodded. "I wrote it in college when I was eighteen."

Bree's mouth curved. "So, what's her name?"

"Hannah." He couldn't keep from grinning.

"I *was* going to ask if you're single, but I guess that answers it." Bree looked over her notes again. "Things are serious?"

"Absolutely."

"Ya know...If I'm being honest, you have teen-mag centerfold potential. Your face could easily be plastered all over girls' bedroom walls. You sure you don't want to appear more available?"

"You're joking, right?" Jonah chuckled bashfully. "Well, regardless of...anything, I have no interest in appearing available. Because I'm not."

She smiled. "She's a lucky girl. Tell me more about yourself apart from your music."

"Well...I have a daughter."

Bree was surprised. "Oh really. How old is she?"

"Four."

"What's her name?"

"Grace. We call her Gracie." Jonah exuded pride at the mere mention of her.

"*That* would explain why you're so unavailable," Bree remarked. "Tell me about your family. Brothers, sisters. What your parents do."

"My family? Isn't that irrelevant?" Jonah asked uneasily.

"Jonah, have you *seen* the message boards on the showcase website? I'd say three quarters of the posts are about you. There's a definite demand for you and any and all information they can get their hands on."

Jonah cleared his sore throat. "Fine. I'm guessing you'd prefer the dramatic version...My accountant stepfather was verbally and emotionally abusive, until he passed away last month. But I have a lovely stay-at-home mom and an incredible older brother who's a doctor. Oh, and I *just* recently found out about *and* met my biological father, a retired businessman turned musician, who owns a music store. How's that?"

Bree stared at Jonah for a moment. "Oh...So, I guess you get your musical talents from your father then?"

He snickered, leaning back from the table. "That's what you got from that? Okay."

She sighed. "No, I'm sorry. I guess I wasn't expecting

that response."

"Because you assume everyone's lives are typical? And that you can just ask a stranger any question you want without any concern that it may be a sensitive subject?"

Bree looked away. "I guess journalism can be brutal. But if you're going to put yourself out there, you can't be so sensitive."

Jonah shook his head. "I can't control the upbringing I had, but I should be able to control if it follows me around and defines who I am publicly. I have every right to enjoy making music without exposing my every pitiful detail."

Bree pursed her lips. "Well, I suppose you have a point, and I apologize. I won't pry any further into your story, but it sounds like you've had a lot to overcome."

Jonah shrugged. "Everyone does sooner or later."

"But not all rise back up so gracefully."

He pondered her compliment, wondering how he'd given her that impression.

"One more question," Bree said, straightening her glasses. "How's that cold working for you?"

Jonah was relieved by the change of topic. "I guess I'm not fooling anyone, am I?"

She laughed. "No, you look *and* sound like you need a good nap."

"Oh, thanks," he sarcastically replied.

"Don't worry, I think they're shipping you off to makeup next, so that might help."

"Yeah, let's hope."

"Well, Jonah, it was a pleasure to meet you. I know, sick or not, you're going to be great tonight and beyond that. I see big things coming for you, and I wish you the very best." Bree extended her hand to him once again.

Jonah smiled. "Thank you. I really appreciate that."

With a pleased countenance, Bree pressed the button on her phone to stop recording before standing up to leave.

Back in the first room, after the surreal and somewhat awkward photo shoot, Jonah was allowed to have his guests visit him. An additional headset-wearing person magically located Hannah and Nathan and brought them to Jonah. His weary face lit up when he saw Hannah.

"Hey!" She threw her arms around him. "How's it going?"

"I'm already exhausted," Jonah admitted. "But it's been really good."

"There are already people lining up at the door," Nathan said. "I can't believe how big this is. It's pretty cool."

Jonah frowned. "I wish I felt better so I could enjoy it more."

Hannah took his hand and led him to a couch to sit down. She guided his head to her shoulder, and he snuggled into her, closing his eyes.

"When's sound check?" Hannah asked, softly running her hand over his arm.

"Thirty minutes," Jonah muttered.

"I'm so proud of you…You know that, right, Jonah?"

He lifted his head to look at her, his blue eyes level with hers. With a nod, Jonah leaned in and planted a soft kiss on her lips.

TWENTY

Jonah sat backstage, tuning his guitar while he waited to go on.

"Are you still sure you want to do this?" Hannah asked, feeling Jonah's warm forehead with the back of her hand. "I feel so bad I got you into this."

"I absolutely want to. Seriously, it's the coolest thing anyone has ever done for me. You have nothing to feel bad about."

"Can I get you anything?"

Jonah shook his throbbing head. "I've already consumed as many drugs as is safely possible."

Hannah patted his shoulder. "Well, I hope it helps...Picture?" She lifted her new camera to her eye and took a photo of him. "Nathan said he'll take pictures for me so I can just enjoy your set. He's so great. I'm happy he came."

Jonah smiled. "Good. I'm glad you're having a nice time together." He gave Hannah a kiss on the cheek.

"Good luck, Jonah." She hugged him tightly. "You're going to be great."

Hannah left him to go find Nathan in the crowd.

Jonah took a deep breath, praying the congestion would miraculously subside, even if only for a few moments. He forced away the nerves that crept in as he heard himself

285

being introduced on stage. Then came his cue to go on.

Gripping the neck of his guitar in his clammy hand, Jonah made his way out into the shining lights and thunderous applause. He slipped the guitar strap over his head and stepped in front of the microphone, amazed by the multitude of people before him.

"Wow, thank you." He grinned, adjusting the height of the mic stand. "As you just heard, I'm Jonah Weston. And tonight, I have a surprise for you...I'm sick." He began strumming his guitar as he chuckled. "I decided to be stubborn though and do this anyway. But the deal is, if I sound bad or mess up, you can't laugh."

The crowd cheered, already taken by his charm.

"This first song is very special to me. It's also the one that got me here. It's called 'Write You Down' and it's about the most amazing girl in the entire world. I won't point her out and embarrass her in front of *all* these people, though." Jonah paused to wink at Hannah. "All right, here goes..."

Jonah's fingers danced flawlessly on the strings of the Hummingbird. Out in the middle of the crowd, Hannah held her breath, hoping Jonah's voice wouldn't be too affected by his sickness. She felt so nervous for him as he drew in a breath.

Jonah's vocals carried across the hushed audience, possessing a more raw and raspy element. But it was still beautiful. His words were passionate and effective, leaving the crowd mesmerized.

Three quarters of the way through the song, Jonah's scratchy throat began to fail him, his voice growing increasingly hoarse. He stopped abruptly and turned away from the microphone, coughing forcefully.

The audience clapped and cheered for him anyway, raising his spirits.

Jonah took a long swig from a bottle of water on the

stool behind him, then smiled. "Thank you for not laughing."

He picked quietly on the guitar as the crowd continued to cheer for him.

"I guess this whole singing thing isn't going to happen for me tonight...So, I thought I would tell you a story. Entertain you in a different way, if you don't mind." Jonah flashed a cheeky grin, the applause urging him on.

"So, there's this girl. We were together all through high school, and I had loved her since I was thirteen. I know that's a bit young to be in love, but if you knew this girl, you'd understand how easy it was to fall for her...Well, today, *five* years ago, I said good-bye to that girl, praying it wouldn't be long before I could see her again. But life happened, and time and distance came between us like we promised it wouldn't. And I didn't see that girl again...until six weeks ago. I know I said I wouldn't embarrass her, but—"

Jonah stopped talking when he dropped his pick into the soundhole of his guitar. He laughed apologetically and gently shook the guitar to try easing the pick out. But it only rattled inside the body, and he quickly gave up.

He set the guitar down, leaning it against the stool, and reached into the pocket of his jeans for another pick. Locking eyes with Hannah in the crowd, Jonah pulled his hand out, holding up a ring between his thumb and forefinger. The diamond glinted fiercely beneath the stage lights as he smiled sweetly at her.

The audience rooted Jonah on as he hopped off the stage. He made his way to her, the crowd eagerly parting for him. When he reached Hannah, she was already crying. He got down on one knee, and the crowd fell silent, straining to listen. Jonah gazed up at Hannah, his blue eyes glistening.

"Hannah," he began, his voice shaking with emotion. "After all this while, you're still the song in my head, and it's like I knew it by heart before I even heard it…It's always been you, and it'll always be you. I would be glad to fall in love with you over and over for the rest of my life. Will you marry me, Hannah?"

Hannah nodded emphatically, unable to form words through her tears. Grinning, Jonah stood and took her left hand, sliding the ring onto her finger. He drew her into his embrace as the crowd erupted around them.

"Jonah, I love you," Hannah said into his ear.

He pulled back and kissed her passionately, their surroundings disappearing. For a moment, it was just the two of them, setting their greatest dream into motion.

It was past 10:00 when the trio was back on the road heading toward home. Nathan was once again driving, with Jonah and Hannah cuddling in the backseat.

"Oh my gosh, I'm having déjà vu," Nathan complained. "It's like driving you home from your first date all over again, with you two being all giggly and stupid in the backseat."

Jonah laughed. "Then turn on the music."

"Fine," Nathan retorted playfully, reaching over to press play on Jonah's iPod.

The upbeat melodies of The 1975 filled the car as Jonah settled back into the space beside Hannah. She folded against him, laying her head on his chest.

"Thank you again for today. It was incredible," he said quietly, resting his cheek in her hair as he held her.

She lifted her hand to peer at her ring through the darkness, sighing contentedly. "Yes, it was quite the night."

Jonah took her hand in his, running his thumb over the ring. "You know, this was my grandmother's, and my great-

great-grandmother's before that. Elliot gave it to me...our first family heirloom."

"Oh, wow," Hannah marveled.

"I have been dying to give it to you," he confessed. "But I was trying to find the perfect moment. For the past week, I've actually been carrying it on me, hoping the right opportunity would present itself."

She laughed. "Was tonight planned, or spur of the moment?"

"I can't tell you that," Jonah replied sheepishly.

"C'mon, I have to know."

He sighed. "I decided to go for it after I couldn't sing anymore."

"So the whole clumsy pick drop was on purpose?"

"I can't reveal *all* my tricks."

"Jonah."

He chuckled bashfully. "Okay, it was."

"And everything you said?"

Jonah shrugged. "That stuff is easy when it comes to you."

Hannah tilted her head upward to look at him, her eyes wide and alive. "I want to take Nathan's wedding."

"What? How do you know about that?"

She straightened up in her seat. "Nathan told me. He said you turned it down because I deserved my own wedding. But Jonah, I don't care."

He stared at her in the dimness, his heart racing. "Are you sure?"

Hannah placed her hand on his face. "I just want to marry you. It doesn't matter how or where. As long as I get to marry you, *that's* all that matters to me."

"But it's only nine days away," Jonah reasoned. "I'm

sure Nathan has cancelled everything by now."

"Um, actually I haven't," Nathan chimed in. "Sorry, I'm listening."

"No, it's fine. How come you never cancelled it?" Jonah asked.

"I don't know, procrastination? Because it was easier to ignore it? Because maybe I hoped *this* would happen?" Nathan replied honestly.

"Jonah, tell me what you're thinking," Hannah said, taking his hand.

"It just seems too perfect."

Nathan laughed. "Well, it is. But that doesn't mean it's not good. I'm sure you can still make some changes. Not the location, but the cake, the menu, the flowers, things like that. The changes would just have to stay within the budget of what I've already paid to each vendor."

"So, what do ya say, Jonah?" Hannah asked eagerly, trying to contain her giddiness.

A grin slowly spread across Jonah's face. "We're getting married in nine days."

Scarlett and Gracie were both asleep on the couch when Jonah quietly entered the living room, Hannah and Nathan behind him. The menu of Gracie's favorite DVD was looping on the television, and a half-eaten bowl of popcorn sat on the coffee table.

Jonah softly nudged his mother awake.

"Oh, what time is it?" she asked, sitting up.

"It's a little after one," Jonah answered.

Scarlett yawned. "How was your show?"

Knowing he couldn't wait any longer, Jonah took Hannah's hand and held it out toward his mother. "It was pretty great."

Scarlett stared in bewilderment at Hannah's ring, suddenly wide awake. She jumped up and threw her arms around Jonah when it sank in. "Oh, honey, I'm so happy for you. I always knew you'd come back to her." Then she moved to Hannah, squeezing her tightly. "I've always wanted a daughter, and I'm so glad it's you."

"It gets better," Jonah said. "We're getting married January fourth."

Scarlett looked at him, her eyebrows raised. "Like in nine days? Or like a *year* and nine days?"

Nathan appeared at his mother's side, putting his arm around her shoulders. "Mom, they're going to take my wedding."

Scarlett pondered for a moment. "Ya know, that's a pretty good idea."

Jonah sighed with relief. "I'm glad you agree. We're going to need your help."

"Whatever you need, let me know," she offered. "Now, why don't you all go upstairs and get some sleep?"

After their good nights, Jonah lifted Gracie up from the couch and cautiously carried her up the stairs to his bedroom, Hannah in step behind him. He carefully laid Gracie at the far left side of his bed, pulling the covers over her. She curled up and snuggled into the pillows.

Nathan stood in the doorway. "I just wanted to say good night...and today was awesome. Thanks for letting me tag along."

"We are so glad you came," Hannah said. "Thank you for driving and for keeping me company. It was fun."

Nathan smiled. "Yeah, it was. Listen, I'm so happy for you guys, and it makes me even happier to help you out. I just hope you know that."

"Thanks, Nate," Jonah replied. "You have no idea how much this means to us."

"I'll see you in the morning," Nathan said, turning away to his old room next door.

Jonah rummaged through his dresser drawer for something to change into and then turned to Hannah.

"You can grab whatever you want and change here. I'll be right back," he said before disappearing to the bathroom.

When he returned, clad in an A-shirt and sweatpants, he smiled at the sight of Hannah in his clothes. She was wearing a waffle-knit henley and a pair of plaid boxer shorts, the waistband rolled several times at her hips. She self-consciously pulled the long sleeves over her hands as Jonah slid quietly to the center of his bed beside Gracie. Lying on his back, he patted the vacant spot at his side.

"Special occasion?" she joked, turning off the light and eagerly filling the space beside him.

"Yeah, I guess so," he said, sliding his arm around her.

Hannah sighed, nestling her cheek into his chest. "This feels like a dream."

Jonah delicately ran his fingers through her hair. "I can't believe it's finally happening."

"This might sound stupid, but every December twenty-sixth since the last time we saw each other, I have felt so sad thinking about how it was yet another year apart," she confessed.

"That's not stupid. I always thought about it too."

"But now, this year, it's the best day of my life," Hannah added, her smile evident in her tone.

"Wow, the *best*?" Jonah remarked.

"Well, I *would* say the day Gracie was born if I hadn't been cheated out of a normal full-term birth...and if her dad

292

could've been there."

He kissed her head. "Well, next time will be different. And I will definitely be there."

"As long as you're not on tour," Hannah said playfully.

Jonah grew serious. "No. Even then. No matter what happens, music or otherwise, you and our children will always be first."

"I know," she said, then paused for a moment. "I can't wait to share 'next time' with you."

"Oh, Mommy!"

Hannah awoke to her daughter's gasp and a tugging on her hand. Gracie was sitting cross-legged between Hannah and Jonah, her small fingers grasping her mother's newly ringed finger.

"Mommy...Are you getting married?"

Jonah rolled over, making groggy eye contact with Hannah. Gracie put her hands on Jonah's face and turned his head to look at her.

"Daddy. Is Mommy your fiancée now?"

He pulled Gracie down, tickling her with kisses on her neck. She shrieked with laughter.

"Someone tell me the truth," Gracie requested, catching her breath once Jonah released her.

"Yes, baby," Hannah said, smoothing Gracie's curls with her hand. "Daddy and I are getting married."

"When? Today?"

Jonah grinned. "Close...next weekend."

Her delicate face lit up, and she threw her arms around him. "Thank you, Daddy. Now you really can stay forever."

While Hannah showered, Jonah made pancakes for Gracie.

"Ooh, got enough for me?" Nathan asked, entering the kitchen.

"Of course," Jonah answered from the stove.

Nathan leaned against the counter behind his brother. "So, I just talked to Kelly, the *actual* wedding coordinator. She's going to contact all the vendors and see how much leeway you have for making changes."

"Oh, that's great. Thanks, Nate."

Nathan shrugged. "No problem. Also, Kelly will probably want to meet with you and Hannah this afternoon to go over everything. Are you available?"

Jonah nodded. "I *was* hoping to go back to work today since I'm feeling a lot better, but I talked to Elliot and he said to just wait till Monday. So yeah. I'm free."

"Good. So what did Elliot say when you told him you're getting married?" Nathan asked.

Jonah flipped the pancakes with a spatula. "Oh, he was thrilled. He said I was blessed to have you for a brother."

Nathan chuckled sheepishly and turned away to pour himself a cup of coffee. "I guess it goes both ways," he said casually, sitting down at the kitchen table across from his niece. She was intently playing a game on Jonah's cell phone.

"Good morning, Gracie," Nathan said, but she barely looked at him.

"All right, Gracie, you've had enough. Turn off the game and say hello to your uncle," Jonah instructed, filling a few plates with pancakes.

Gracie immediately set her father's phone aside and smiled at Nathan. "Sorry, Uncle Nathan. I was beating the level."

Nathan laughed. "That's okay."

Jonah served Gracie and Nathan, then went back for

the maple syrup and his own plate. When he was seated, he looked to his brother, his expression serious.

"Hey, Nathan...I wanted to ask you something."

"Sure. What is it?"

"Would you mind being my best man?"

Nathan smiled. "Of course I wouldn't mind. I'd love to."

Jonah returned a smile of his own. "Okay, awesome. I just wasn't sure if it would be too much for you *that* day."

"Thank you for considering my feelings, but honestly, I'm good. I'm looking forward to Saturday, I promise," Nathan assured him, taking a huge bite of his breakfast.

"I'm glad."

"Seriously, Jonah. You and Hannah are *finally* happening. How could that ever be a bad day?"

"How did the meeting with Kelly go yesterday?" Nathan asked from the passenger seat of the Mercedes.

Jonah had been lost in thought, mentally penning his wedding vows, as he drove across town to go suit shopping with his brother. Nathan's voice had nearly startled him.

"Oh, um...It went very well, actually. She spoke with the vendors, as you said, and they all seemed very gracious. Your deposits will definitely cover our *much* smaller wedding. We just have a lot to do now, like picking out the song for our first dance, and our colors. Things like that."

Nathan snickered. "As long as Hannah doesn't want pink, you're good."

"No, I think we're leaning toward gray and aqua," Jonah said.

Nathan made a face. "Aqua? What is that, blue?"

"Yeah, it's like a...light...I don't know, it's...light

295

bluish."

Nathan laughed. "Sounds nice. Do you have any songs in mind for the first dance?"

"Yeah, there's this Foy Vance song—"

Nathan's ringing phone interrupted Jonah's reply.

"Hold on, I have to take this," Nathan said, grimacing.

The conversation was brief and solemn, and Nathan sighed heavily as he hung up.

"Everything okay?" Jonah asked, stealing a glance at his brother.

"It was the cemetery. They wanted to let me know that...Dad's headstone was placed this morning." Nathan turned his head to stare out the window.

Jonah swallowed. "Oh. Have you...visited since the funeral?"

Nathan shook his head. "I wanted to. I haven't really been in this part of town. And I didn't want to go alone."

Jonah contemplated for a moment. "Do you want me to go with you? We'll be passing by there in a few minutes."

"I can't ask you to do that, Jonah."

"You have done *so* much for me. I can do this for you."

Nathan sighed again. "If you're sure it's all right, then it would really mean a lot to me."

Moments later, Jonah pulled onto the long road that wound through the cemetery. He reached over to switch off the music, feeling that silence was more appropriate in such a place. Flashbacks of Jacob's funeral flooded in as Jonah stopped the car in front of the proper section.

"You ready?" he asked, placing his hand on Nathan's shoulder.

Nathan merely nodded and eased the door open to step out. The air was eerily still, but frigid. Crossing his arms tightly over his chest, Jonah silently followed his brother through the rows of granite and marble, spread out beneath towering old trees and a cloudless sky.

Jonah felt his stomach drop when Nathan stopped in front of Jacob's grave. It was much closer to the road than Jonah remembered. The outline of recently laid sod formed a large rectangle at the foot of the stone, not yet grown into the rest of the landscape. Jonah forced himself not to think of the depths beneath his feet and lifted his eyes to the polished stone.

Jacob Nathaniel Weston
September 14, 1959 - November 10, 2013
Loving husband and father

Jonah read the inscription over and over, his breath quickening as anger consumed him. Nathan turned to his younger brother, noticing his visible distress.

"Jonah…"

"*Loving*?" Jonah questioned, barely above a whisper. He gritted his teeth as bitter tears stung his eyes.

"Jonah, I'm sorry. Mom and I didn't know what else to put."

"How about nothing? It's better than a lie," Jonah scoffed.

Nathan pressed his lips together. "I didn't know this would upset you so much. I'm sorry."

Jonah ran his numb hands over his hair and let out a long breath. "I didn't know it would either."

"Do you want to talk about it?" Nathan asked.

Jonah shook his head, jamming his hands into his pockets. "I can't. He's your father."

"And for your entire life, up until a month ago, he was supposed to be *your* father too, Jonah. Yeah, he's my dad and

I love him, but I could never deny how rough things were. I have no problem admitting that he failed you."

Jonah stared at the granite without actually looking at it, taking in his brother's words. "I guess this bothers me because it makes a mockery of everything he put me through. I spent twenty-three terrifying years under his depraved authority, and he gets a monument that applauds his parenting skills for the rest of time." Jonah paused for a few moments, clenching his jaw. "It's not fair...He ruined me and he got away with it. No one stopped him."

"*You* stopped him," Nathan said. "He lost when you left."

Jonah let out a rancorous snicker. "No. *I* lost when I left. I lost everything."

"Maybe...but everything is as it should be *now*." Nathan placed his hand on his brother's shoulder. "Listen, this is supposed to be a good day. I'm ready to go if you are."

Jonah sighed, still staring at the gravestone. "I just need a few minutes, if you don't mind."

Nathan gave Jonah's shoulder a consoling squeeze before backing away. "Take your time. I'll be in the car."

After Nathan disappeared, Jonah carefully sat down cross-legged on the browning, weather-beaten grass in front of Jacob's grave. He hunched over in the cold with his hands clenched deep in his coat pockets. His eyes scanned the rolling landscape of the cemetery beyond him, sprinkled with pops of color from the flowers placed at various plots. Jacob's grave had no flowers. Jonah wondered if it ever would.

"When *I* die, I know people will bring *me* flowers," Jonah muttered aloud, freeing one hand to pick at the grass in front of him. "Because I'm nothing like you."

Jonah chuckled sheepishly for talking to himself, although it felt oddly liberating. It sent an undeniable urge through him. There were so many things he wished he could say to Jacob, and in a way, this was the only chance he would ever get.

"Do you have any idea what you did?" he began calmly. "That's what I keep wishing I could ask you…I just want to know *why*. I know I wasn't your son, but I didn't ask for that. All I *ever* wanted was what I watched you give my brother. You so easily loved him, and you went out of your way to hate me…Why couldn't you just pretend? I grew up believing I wasn't worthy of my own father's love. And I didn't know why, so I just blamed myself. Do you know what that does to a kid? I lived in constant fear because I couldn't figure out how to please you. I had panic attacks at twelve, ulcers at fifteen…How did you not care? It's not because you were incapable of love, because I know you loved Nathan. He is the *only* good thing you *ever* did your entire life, and I'm not even sure you deserve any credit for him."

Jonah paused for a moment, trying to organize his rampant thoughts. For so long, he'd let the darkness fester within him. But he'd finally cracked, allowing the light to pour in, forcing open the floodgates.

"So, I have a daughter. She is beautiful and smart and full of life…But I lost the first four years of her life because of you. Hannah had to hide her to protect us from you. And you know what? I'm glad she did, because I know exactly what you would've done. You would've done everything you could to make me feel ashamed of her. And she would've grown up in fear of you like I did. She would've felt unwanted and profoundly disappointing…*just* like I did. The only thing I can thank you for is showing me exactly what kind of father *not* to be. I will never let my little girl question her worth. She will *never* wonder if she is loved. I will teach her to hold her head high and be proud of who she is, whether she fails or succeeds.

You *never* did *anything* for me. You never showed an interest in what I cared about. You didn't go to any of my games in high school. You never cared about my music. You didn't even care when I got in my accident. *That's* when I knew I had to leave. I could've *died*, and you still just wanted to tear me down...You were probably wishing I hadn't been so lucky."

Jonah looked down at the ground and shook his head. "I don't know why I wanted you to love me so badly. You were overwhelming and despicable...I wish I hadn't made so many decisions based on your opinions. I wish I hadn't let you bully me and dictate the way I saw myself. I always wonder who I would be now if I'd been stronger and stood up for myself...but I'm done. I don't want to think about you anymore, or all the horrible ways you made me feel. I want to forget all the rotten things you said and all the things you ruined. Because you're gone and you don't *get* to hurt me anymore. I refuse to carry this with me any longer."

Jonah stood to his feet, brushing the grass from his jeans as he looked down at Jacob's grave.

"I forgive you," he whispered, tears staining his cheeks.

Then he turned away, passing through the rows of stone as the heaviness he'd been holding onto began to dissipate.

"Hey...Dad?"

Jacob Weston breathed an agitated sigh and looked up from his newspaper, peering at Jonah over his reading glasses. He did not bother to hide his irritation.

"What, Jonah?"

Jonah nervously shifted his weight from one foot to the other. "I, um...wanted to remind you about my game tonight. It's the last game of the season, so —"

"Did you wash my car? Did you take the trash out?" Jacob interrupted, returning to his paper.

"Well, no. I just finished mowing the lawn so I was going to shower and get ready for my game," Jonah replied, glancing at the clock on the mantel.

Snickering, Jacob removed his glasses and tossed the paper aside before standing up. Jonah cowered instinctively as his father stepped toward him.

"I suggest you do what I told you before I make you miss that game."

Without a word of protest, Jonah spun around and hurried to complete his chores in time.

Jonah was a senior on the varsity soccer team at his high school. He played center forward and did rather well. It wasn't that Jonah loved soccer; sometimes he wasn't sure he even liked it. But he had played in hopes of making his father proud. Nevertheless, his father hadn't come to one game that fall season, and this day would prove to be no different.

"You were amazing!" Hannah shrieked, jumping into Jonah's arms after his team's victory. She didn't care that he was covered in sweat.

"Thanks." He grinned, still out of breath.

The rest of the team cheered in celebration as the excited crowd descended the bleachers. Jonah leaned over and planted a quick kiss on Hannah's cheek before following his teammates to the locker room.

After he'd changed, Jonah returned to Hannah, his duffel bag slung over his shoulder.

"So the guys want to go grab something to eat to celebrate. You wanna come?" he asked, taking her hands into his.

"No, I'm going to head home. I think you should just go have fun with the team," Hannah replied.

"Are you sure?"

She nodded with a smile. "Yeah. Plus I have a ton of homework."

"Do you need some help?" Jonah asked playfully, placing his hands on the small of her back to pull her closer.

She laughed. "No. Go hang out with your friends."

He kissed her on the forehead. "Homework with you sounds better."

"You're silly." Hannah giggled, kissing his lips.

"Jonah! Geez, let's go!" It was Oliver.

Jonah hesitantly released Hannah from his affectionate hold. "I have to go. I love you." He kissed her once more.

"Jonah!" More grumbling came from his impatient teammates.

"I love you too." Hannah reluctantly let his hand slip away from hers. The lovesick feeling that always gripped her in his absence instantly returned as she watched him go.

The last thing Jonah saw was the blinding headlights barreling toward him before the sickening crunch of impact made everything go black.

When Jonah awoke some time later, every fiber of his body was fraught with pain. It took him a moment to realize where he was and what had happened, but what bothered him most was that he was alone.

His eyes traveled to the IV in his left arm, accompanied by dark bruising. He grimaced when he realized his right arm was in a cast, held against his midsection by a sling. Alarmed, Jonah quickly looked down and was relieved to see the movement of both legs beneath the blanket. He could feel aching and stinging in his face, *and after careful probing with the fingertips of his free hand, he found a row of stitches both above his right eyebrow and across his inflamed right cheek-bone. His bottom lip was cut and swollen, and he noted the faint metallic taste of blood lingering in his mouth. He wondered what he looked like.*

Just as Jonah reached for the call button, the door opened, and the exact face he needed to see appeared before him. Hannah's somber countenance was replaced by relief when her tired eyes met Jonah's. She set her coffee down, nearly spilling it, and rushed to his side, her tears flowing again. She'd cried so much in the past several hours, waiting and praying for Jonah to wake up and forcing images of a life without him out of her mind.

"Jonah," she whispered, gently caressing his cheek. "I'm so happy you're okay."

"Where are my parents?" Jonah winced as he tried to adjust his position.

Hannah bit her lip. "Um...A nurse spoke to your dad about an hour ago. They're not here yet." She hated the look of grief that tinged his features as her unfortunate news sank in.

Jonah studied Hannah's face. "Why are you crying?" he asked, his deep voice concerned and groggy.

His question made Hannah come undone, and she crumbled against him, sobbing into his chest. "I could've lost you."

Pain seared through him under the weight of her contact, but he didn't dare pull away. He needed her closeness.

"But you didn't," Jonah finally said, running his free hand through her long hair.

She lifted her head to look at him. "Oliver said it was awful. He said a drunk driver ran a red light and T-boned your side of the car. Oliver thought you were..." She couldn't say the word. The mere thought nearly paralyzed her.

"Oliver," Jonah remembered. "He's okay?"

Hannah nodded. *"His parents took him home a little while ago."*

"Is that when he called you?" Jonah wondered.

She shook her head, her lip quivering. *"He called me from the accident...right after he called 911."*

"No wonder you're so upset," Jonah said, reaching for her hand.

Hannah shrugged, recalling Oliver's panic and fear over the phone. *"There's so much blood,"* he had told her, tremors in his voice. *"I don't know if he's breathing..."*

Hannah wiped at her tears, shaking away the images. She pressed her lips against Jonah's temple and nestled her cheek in his disheveled hair. *"I love you, Jonah. You know that, right?"*

He barely chuckled. *"Of course I know that. I love you too."*

Their tender moment was interrupted by the doctor entering the room.

"Oh, good, you're awake. How are you feeling, Jonah?"

Jonah slowly processed the question. *"My head hurts really bad."*

"Well, you have a concussion, so a headache is normal. Do you remember what happened?" the doctor asked.

Jonah sighed, struggling through the haziness. *"I don't remember anything. I only know what Hannah told me."*

"It's all right," the doctor said. *"Would you like to see your parents? They've just arrived."*

Jonah hesitated. *"Okay."*

A few moments later, his mother barreled into the room, immediately at his side.

"Oh my God," she cried, her eyes surveying the damage. *"I'm so glad you're all right."*

Jonah's stomach dropped when he saw his father appear in the doorway. Jacob didn't step into the small room, he just leaned against the doorframe, his arms crossed tightly over his chest. His *face was stern with furrowed eyebrows, devoid of any concern. Jonah waited with bated breath for his father to speak.*

"Just so you know," Jacob began dryly, "you're no longer allowed to accept rides from friends."

"Dad. It wasn't Oliver's fault."

Jacob glared at Jonah. "Are you talking back to me?"

"No, sir."

"Oh, and your curfew is ten o'clock from now on," Jacob added.

"What? That's so early."

"Do you want to make it nine? Watch it, Jonah— you're already grounded this weekend."

Jonah was confused. "Grounded?"

"Do you not recall my asking you to take the trash out before you left for your little game tonight?" Jacob said snidely.

Jonah took a deep breath, his ribs aching. "I'm sorry. I was running late."

Jacob shook his head with a disapproving sigh. "I don't know why you waste your time with such pointless things. Your brother never did."

Jonah swallowed the lump in his throat, utterly astounded by his father's relentlessness despite the dire situation at hand. Even in the face of near-death, his father did not value him. Jonah was faced with the cruel realization that there was absolutely nothing he could do to vanquish his father's disdain. Never before had Jonah felt so worthless and broken, both inside and out. And in that disheartening moment, he vowed to himself that he'd run like hell the first chance he got.

TWENTY-ONE

Jonah stood before the full-length mirrors, critiquing the gray fitted suit he'd chosen. It flawlessly complimented his tall, thin frame. He smiled at his reflection and straightened his skinny black tie, a newfound sense of confidence washing over him. It was something he'd never quite experienced before.

Nathan emerged from the fitting room, a pleased expression on his face. His suit was identical to his brother's, but with an aqua tie at Hannah's request. "Good choice, Jonah. I like it."

Jonah grinned. "Well, that was easy."

"Well, it *would* be easy, 'cause you're not a woman. They have to try on, like, a thousand dresses at a thousand stores before they can decide," Nathan said, chuckling.

Jonah laughed, shaking his head. "Oh yeah? Is that how it is?"

Nathan shrugged. "Just going by experience…which, I guess, doesn't actually count for much since she was crazy."

"Yeah, she definitely doesn't speak for the entire female population," Jonah said, glancing at his phone. "Oh, hey…question. Would you mind if I invited Elliot to have lunch with us?"

"No, of course not."

"You would tell me, right?"

Nathan nodded. "Jonah. It's fine."

"I just want to make sure." Jonah quickly thumbed a text to Elliot before heading back to the fitting room to change.

"I can't believe you want *me* to be in your wedding," Lily said, browsing through a rack of dresses at the bridal shop.

Hannah glanced up from the price tag she'd been frowning at. "Lily, we've worked together for years. And I know we don't hang out much, but we should."

Lily smiled. "I agree. And we will."

Caroline approached them with several flower girl dresses draped over her arm, Gracie trailing behind her. "How's the search going?"

Hannah shrugged. "Apparently, I have expensive taste. Everything I like is out of my price range."

"And what's that?" Caroline asked.

"Jonah gave me twelve hundred dollars," Hannah divulged. Before they had parted ways that morning, Jonah had insisted Hannah take some of the money his grandfather had given him. She had tried to turn it down, but to no avail.

Caroline gravitated toward another rack. "Keep it. Your father gave me his credit card."

Hannah's eyes went wide. "Are you serious?"

Caroline chuckled at her daughter's shock. "You deserve it, honey."

Hannah's eyes flooded. "Thank you, Mom."

Caroline smiled. "And I guess Dad has taken a liking to Jonah again. Apparently, Jonah stopped by your dad's several weeks back to ask for permission to marry you."

"What? I didn't know that," Hannah replied, her heart melting.

Lily sighed heavily. "Seriously, how is he even real?"

Caroline laughed. "He's something else, that's for sure. Now use that money to buy Jonah a wedding band. He deserves a nice one."

"What's next on your list of things to do?" Elliot asked. He sat across from Jonah and Nathan, sipping his sweet tea. "Anything I can help you with?"

Jonah smiled kindly at the waitress as she refilled his water glass. "Everything is coming along, wedding-wise. I just have the big stuff to worry about now, like where we're going to live…and if a honeymoon is possible."

"I wouldn't worry about a house right now," Nathan said. "Between all of us, you've always got a place to stay until you find something."

"Jonah, if you're okay with it, I'd really love to help you with your honeymoon," Elliot offered. "My wedding gift to you and Hannah."

Jonah was speechless, trying to articulate his gratitude. "That would be…incredible. Wow, thank you."

Elliot smiled. "Of course. And don't worry about Gracie. Your mother and I already discussed it, and we'd love to watch her while you're away for the week."

"Wow, a *week*?" Jonah sighed. "Okay, just one thing though…I am *so* grateful for all you have done for me lately, both of you. I seriously can't thank you enough. But after the wedding and everything, I really want to take care of things myself. I just need to be able to provide for my family on my own."

Nathan grinned at his little brother, his pride radiating. "I can respect that. Good for you, man."

"I completely understand. But if you ever do need anything, please don't be afraid to ask," Elliot reminded him.

Jonah nodded. "Thank you."

When they reached a lull in the conversation, Nathan nervously cleared his throat. "Hey, Elliot?"

"Yeah, Nate?"

Nathan rubbed at the droplets of condensation on his beer bottle. "I know I was kind of distant for a while, but I wanted you to know that I'm glad you're here."

Elliot's face lit up. "I'm sure this has been difficult for you, and I apologize if I've added to that in any way."

"At first, it bothered me, to be honest. But I see how happy you make my mother. I didn't fully realize how negatively my father affected everyone until he was gone and you stepped in. The way you father my brother and how you take care of my mother...There's no comparison." Nathan dropped his gaze, fearing he'd said too much.

When he looked back up, Elliot's eyes were brimming with tears.

"Nathan, thank you. You don't know what that means to me."

Jonah sat back, taking in the moment. Nathan's acceptance of his father meant a great deal to him as well.

Hannah burst into her bedroom and practically pounced on Jonah, who had been lying on his stomach across her bed.

"Whoa, hey." He quickly locked the screen on his phone.

"Sorry, I really missed you today." Hannah smiled, lounging beside him. "So, what were you doing?"

Jonah glanced back at his phone. "I was working on my vows."

She propped up her elbow and rested her head against her hand. "I still have to finish mine too."

He flashed a sly grin. "I know. There are *way* too many

nice things to say about me, aren't there?"

Hannah laughed. "No, seriously, trying to write down how I feel about you and all of my promises for the rest of our lives together...There are no words for that."

Jonah gazed at her fondly, his mouth slowly curving into a smile. "Trust me, I know. That's why I've written so many songs about you. And I still think every word falls short."

"Is that so?" She leaned her head affectionately against his shoulder.

"Yes," Jonah answered matter-of-factly. "When it comes to you, everything else pales in comparison."

Hannah's eyes gleamed with fervor as she sat up to look at him. His countenance was tender and vulnerable while his blue eyes spoke multitudes in the silence. With an impassioned urgency, she took his face into her hands and leaned in to kiss him. Jonah matched her eagerness, turning onto his back and pulling her down onto him. He entangled his fingers in her long blond hair, getting lost in their blissful haze.

Hannah was astounded by the rush of emotions that consumed her. The love she felt for Jonah was so immense, it hurt. His touch, the feel of his skin, the softness of his lips—it was never enough. But for now, it would have to be.

Breathless and euphoric, Hannah pulled away, her face still hovering over Jonah's. He sighed with reluctance as she gave him one last little kiss on the tip of his nose before settling her head on his chest. They basked in the quiet of each other's presence, Hannah soothed by the cadence of Jonah's fluttering heart.

Jonah's voice perforated the stillness. "If you could go anywhere, where would you go?"

Hannah softly strummed her fingertips over the dark

fabric of his chambray shirt, pondering his question. "Would I be with you?"

"Of course."

She shrugged against him. "Then the place is irrelevant."

Jonah smiled. "Okay, but for now, just humor me and let's say it *is* relevant. Where would you want to go?"

"Are we talking hypothetical or realistic?" Hannah asked.

"Somewhere in between, I guess."

"All right...London. Or maybe Hawaii. Then again, I've never been to Disney World."

Jonah laughed. "How did you go from London to Disney?"

She pouted playfully. "Hey, be quiet. I guess London is more hypothetical. Plus, I really have never been to Disney."

"I've never been to Disney either," he admitted.

"Five years in Florida, and you never went?"

"It's not really something you do with your college buddies," he said with a smirk.

Hannah laughed. "Growing up, I always thought I was the only kid who never got to go."

Jonah snickered. "Nope. Can you picture Jacob packing up the family for a trip to Disney World?"

Hannah squeezed him tightly. "No. I bet Elliot would've taken you."

Jonah thought for a moment. "Well, he can, actually."

She lifted her head to look at him. "What?"

"Elliot wants to pay for our honeymoon as our wedding gift. He and my mom offered to take Gracie for us, for a *week*," Jonah replied.

"Seriously? And you're not joking..."

"No. I promise." He traced an X over his heart with his

index finger.

"And you'd really go to *Disney* for me?" Hannah asked with a giddy smile.

Jonah grinned. "I'd go anywhere you asked me to. It's irrelevant, remember?"

Jonah rang Elliot's doorbell the following afternoon, Gracie in his arms and Hannah by his side. Elliot had invited them over for an after-church family brunch. The door opened, and Elliot's friendly smile met them.

"Hey guys. So glad you could make it." He stepped aside to welcome them in.

As soon as they rounded the corner of the foyer into the living room, they were greeted by an enthusiastic "Surprise!"

The room was filled with a plethora of wrapped gifts, arranged among members of Elliot's family, Scarlett, Nathan, Hannah's parents, and Lily.

Elliot came up behind Jonah, placing his hands on his son's shoulders. "It's sort of a wedding shower. I hope that's okay."

Jonah's perplexed expression transformed into excitement. "It's great. Wow, thank you so much, all of you." He glanced at Hannah, who had tears of gratitude in her eyes.

"Whose birthday is it?" Gracie whispered loudly into Jonah's ear.

He chuckled, giving her a little squeeze. "It's not anyone's birthday, baby. Our family is throwing us a party to celebrate our new life together."

"Oh," Gracie said. "Our family is so nice."

Lunch was served then, catered by a local deli. As Jonah chatted with his cousin, Matty, Elliot answered a knock at the door. Jonah looked up when Elliot led the new guest into the living room.

Oliver stood at the edge of the room, nervously fidgeting with his hands. His dark eyes met Jonah's, and he took a deep breath, stepping toward him. Jonah stood to greet him.

"Hey, man. I hope it's okay that I'm here. Your mom invited me," Oliver said sheepishly.

Jonah glanced at his mother across the room, and she gave him an encouraging nod. "No, it's cool."

"Listen, can we talk?" Oliver asked.

The old friends slipped away from the party and stepped outside onto the front porch. Jonah hoisted himself up to sit on the railing, Oliver following suit a few feet away from him. They endured a moment of awkward silence before Oliver finally spoke.

"Jonah, I'm really sorry about that day at the aquarium. Especially on top of you finding out about your real dad. Your mom told me, and...I just feel really bad about giving you a hard time."

Jonah shook his head. "You know, I was kinda mad at first but I've been thinking about it a lot since I ran into you. I have not been a good friend to you, and I'm sorry."

Oliver sighed. "It's just...After the accident, I had a really rough time with anxiety and stuff, and you were the only one I had because you were *with me* when it happened."

"I remember," Jonah said quietly. "They made us go to counseling together at school."

Oliver forced himself to open up. It had never been easy for him. "We were *best friends* when that happened, and I thought going through that made us tighter. When you left, you just disappeared, and I lost my best friend. That was hard for me."

Jonah stared down at the painted slats of the wooden porch floor. In all his agonizing awareness of Jacob's blatant disdain, Jonah had failed to realize the magnitude of his worth to both Hannah *and* Oliver.

"You're right," Jonah said. "I was trying to run from the issues with my dad, but all I did was ruin everything else."

Oliver felt guilty. "Well, no, not everything. You still had Hannah. And your daughter."

Jonah chuckled ruefully. "You don't even *know* the truth about that. Hannah was one of the biggest casualties in my selfish quest for freedom."

"What do you mean?" Oliver asked.

"Hannah and I were apart for almost five years. Until I came back for Jacob's funeral last month, we hadn't seen each other since Christmas break of my first semester away. I didn't even *know* about Gracie…"

Dumbfounded, Oliver ran a hand through his dark hair. "Shit, now I *really* feel bad about the other day. I am so sorry. I had no idea."

"That's why it's okay. You didn't know, because *I* never told you," Jonah assured him.

"And it was probably selfish of me to bring up all that other stuff after everything you've been dealing with. I guess I just wish I could've been there for you like you were for me, ya know?" Oliver said.

Jonah nodded. "When Hannah and I fell apart, I cut myself off into my own little world. Maybe I was depressed. I don't know. But I shouldn't have done that. It really would've been nice to have a friend through all of it. Instead, I pushed everyone away. And I missed your wedding, man. That sucks."

Oliver chuckled. "It was really small. And my best man got drunk *before* the ceremony and pretty much ruined the whole thing, so...You really didn't miss much."

"I still wish I could've been there. You're coming next weekend, right?" Jonah asked.

Oliver looked at him. "Absolutely, man. As long as it's cool with Hannah."

"Yeah, of course. Besides, she and Stella probably have a lot of catching up to do."

"They definitely do," Oliver said, grinning. "Stella's pregnant."

Jonah smiled, but on the inside, he felt a stabbing pang of envy. "Wow, Oliver, congratulations! That's awesome."

Oliver nodded, the happiness apparent in his eyes. "Thanks, man. I was going to wait till after the wedding to tell you 'cause this is your time and everything, but...She's ten weeks along and just starting to show. It's incredible."

Jonah pressed his lips together, imagining the joy. "That must be really amazing. I'm happy for you."

The front door opened, and Hannah appeared. The mere sight of her brought Jonah out of the dark, his face lighting up.

"Time for presents," she announced excitedly, grabbing his hands.

The two reconciled friends followed Hannah back inside to the party.

Jonah and Hannah opened dozens of gifts, with Gracie's help, of course. When the last of the presents had been unwrapped, Jonah stood and cleared his throat.

"I don't even know where to begin to thank all of you for today. Most of you don't even *know* me, and you have welcomed me without question. And now with this, you have gone beyond anything I could've ever imagined. To be honest, Hannah and I barely have a thing, and now..." He paused to glance over the gifts before him. "I don't have to worry anymore. I hope you all know how much we appreciate what you've done for us."

"We love you, Jonah," Henry said plainly. "You're the greatest thing that could ever happen to this family."

Jonah couldn't fight the tears that stung his eyes. The acceptance and esteem made his chest ache. For the first time in his entire life, he felt a sense of belonging. There were no words for that.

It was New Year's Eve, and Jonah sat on the back porch steps of his childhood home, looking out over the moonlit yard. There had never been a swing set in that yard, nor had there ever been a swimming pool. Just a small shed and Jacob's hammock attached between two tall trees. Jonah hadn't done much playing there. Even those old, vague memories of playing catch were fading more and more, leaving room for the new memories he could make there with Gracie. He smiled to himself. Life really had a funny way of turning around.

"There you are."

Jonah looked up to see Hannah's friendly face. She sat down beside him, sharing in his silent reminiscing for a moment.

"That night on these steps—the night of Jacob's funeral—it all feels like a lifetime ago, doesn't it?" she said.

He nodded. "And how about that night before I left for college? *Ten* lifetimes ago."

"These steps have seen a lot of tears." Hannah threaded her fingers through his, so easily recalling the ache of all their good-byes.

"I'll never have to miss you again," Jonah said wistfully.

Hannah grinned at the thought. "No more good-byes. Just good nights. That's all I've ever wanted for as long as I can remember…I've loved you half my life, Jonah."

His expression was soft. "And I get to love you for the rest of mine."

Jonah gently cradled Hannah's face in his hands and kissed her fervently until an eruption of cheering sounded from inside the house. The couple turned to the windows to see Nathan whirling around with Gracie in his arms, her face beaming with excitement. Nathan put Gracie down and settled onto the couch beside Lily, giving her a timid peck on the cheek. Across the room, Elliot and Scarlett looked tenderly at each other before Elliot leaned in for a simple but loving kiss.

"It must be midnight," Hannah said, her gaze meeting Jonah's.

"Happy New Year." Jonah smiled, his eyes bright and alive with all he felt for her.

He put his arm around Hannah, drawing her close to his side. She rested her head in the warmth of his chest, her joyful heart content.

"I love you," Jonah whispered, meaning it more than ever.

Then he planted a soft kiss on her head. Just like he always did.

Epilogue

Jonah absent-mindedly pressed a button on the soda machine in the small, empty waiting room. With a tired sigh, he bent to retrieve his selection and twisted off the cap. He was in desperate need of caffeine, and the cold carbonation satisfied his dry throat.

"Jonah Tyler?"

He spun around, the sudden voice like a shout in the deserted quiet.

"Oh, my gosh. It *is* you." The young girl grinned widely at him, trying to contain her excitement. "I'm sorry, I'm Emily. You're, like, my favorite singer. I went to your show in Philly a few months ago...and the one in Baltimore after that. I bought your album the day it came out, and it's incredible. It's, like, all I listen to."

Jonah smiled. "Well, thank you, Emily. I really appreciate that. It's nice to meet you." He extended his hand, and she eagerly shook it.

"So, is your wife having her baby now?" Emily asked.

He nodded. "Yeah, he'll be here real soon."

"I'm here visiting my sister. She just had a baby girl," Emily said.

"Congratulations to your sister then." Jonah took a few steps toward the doorway. "I better get back now.

Thanks again, Emily."

Jonah stepped out into the long hall of the labor and delivery ward, making his way to their birthing suite. It was nearly 5:00 a.m., and Hannah had been in labor for close to seventeen hours. Thankfully, this pregnancy had been without any issues and Hannah had carried to term.

The past nine months had felt endless to Jonah, between the worries of another premature birth and the longing to meet his son. But the day had finally arrived and soon, he would hold his baby boy in his arms.

Jonah sat on the small couch while Hannah slept, the tiniest bundle in his careful hands. He stared at his sweet baby, tears escaping silently. Jonah could see Gracie in that little face and undeniable flecks of Hannah and himself. He ran his thumb over his son's velvety soft temple, caressing his dark hair.

"Ezra Jude Tyler," Jonah whispered with a smile, delighted to put a face to the name they'd chosen so many months ago.

He gently kissed Ezra's downy cheek, pride and love welling in his chest. This was that moment he'd dreamt about, the moment he'd missed and ached for. It was more than he'd ever imagined. And it was glorious.

A soft knock sounded on the door as it slowly eased open. Scarlett popped her head in, excitement illuminating her face.

"Come in, Mom," Jonah said with a wave of his hand.

Scarlett opened the door wider and stepped in. Elliot was behind her, carrying a vase of tulips with a few congratulatory balloons attached.

"These are for you, Hannah." Elliot smiled, setting

them on the table across the room before he approached Hannah and kissed her on the cheek.

Scarlett was already lathering her hands up with hand sanitizer as she sat down beside Jonah. "I've been dying to hold him," she squealed.

Cautiously, Jonah placed his son into his mother's eager arms. She teared up as she gazed at his small face. "Oh, he's so beautiful, you guys."

Elliot stood over Scarlett, looking fondly at his new grandson. "I am so proud of you two," he said.

"Thanks, Dad." Jonah gave a teary smile. "Do you want to hold him?"

Scarlett playfully sulked as Elliot scooped Ezra out of her arms and placed him gently against his chest. He closed his eyes, imagining what it would've been like to hold his newborn son this way. He pictured being by Scarlett's side and knowing Jonah since the moment of his first breath. But it hadn't been that way, and in the end it didn't matter. Because he was here now, cuddling Jonah's baby boy, who was just seven hours old.

"So, how was the honeymoon? I haven't had a chance to catch up with you guys since you got back," Hannah said apologetically.

Scarlett sighed. "Hawaii is lovely. We had a wonderful time. It's nice to be home though; I'm loving Elliot's magnificent kitchen."

"Hey, it's *our* kitchen," Elliot corrected her with a loving smile.

Another knock at the door brought Hannah's parents into the room.

"Where's that sweet boy? I've missed him all day," Caroline gushed.

"Wow, Caroline. I didn't know you were so fond of

me," Jonah said with a facetious grin.

She rolled her eyes and laughed, swatting at him as she approached Elliot. "Maybe Ezra will grow up to be a comedian like his father."

Elliot passed the baby off to Caroline. "I don't know. With those long fingers, I'm thinking he might be a guitar player."

"Or maybe he'll take pictures like his mommy," Hannah interjected.

Stephen looked at his grandson for the first time and smiled. "It doesn't matter what he does, he's already perfect."

Nathan entered the room, accompanied by Lily, who was holding Gracie's hand. Gracie's face lit up when she saw her little brother in her Stephen's arms.

"Ezra!" she rejoiced, skipping across the room. "Daddy, can I hold him?"

"After you wash your hands and sit down," Jonah said, tousling her curls.

"Don't I even get a hello?" Hannah asked.

"Hi, Mom!" Gracie called over her shoulder as she hurried to the sink.

Jonah approached Nathan. "Thanks for picking Gracie up from school."

"Hey, no problem. Congratulations, man," Nathan replied, giving his brother a hug.

Lily gave Jonah a quick squeeze before making her way to Hannah. "Hey, girl," she greeted her joyfully, bending to hug her. "How are you feeling?"

"Tired but good. I'm just glad he's here and he's healthy…and that I didn't have to have another C-section."

Lily grinned. "Well, you look pretty hot for someone

who just had a baby."

Hannah threw her head back and laughed. "Oh, yeah right. You're too sweet, Lil."

Nathan smiled, watching Lily across the room. He turned to Jonah.

"So...I bought Lily a ring."

Jonah raised his eyebrows. "Really? That's awesome, Nate. When are you going to ask her?"

Nathan shrugged. "I'm not sure. I just hope she's not expecting some huge romantic scene like the one her best friend got."

Jonah let out a chuckle. "Ah, yes, my infamous Nyquil-drunk proposal. Listen, Lily will be thrilled no matter how you ask her. To her, it *will* be a 'huge romantic scene' because it's with you."

Nathan nodded. "Yeah, you're right. She's a good one, huh?"

"She is. Those Murphy's girls, ya know?" Jonah joked.

"Yeah," Nathan reflected. "I'm so glad we got them out of there."

Jonah patted his brother on the shoulder. "Who would've thought when you started your practice that you'd fall in love with your receptionist?"

"Right?" Nathan played along. "I hire her as a favor to *your* wife, and then look what happens."

Jonah laughed. "Life is rough, isn't it?"

Nathan smiled, growing serious. "Not anymore."

Gracie sat calmly on the couch, her feet dangling over the front of the cushion. She waited patiently for her father to bring her baby brother to her. She positioned her arms as her dad lowered Ezra into them. Ezra grunted and squirmed as he grew accustomed to his new spot. Gracie smiled down at him, filled with excitement and happiness. She'd been so impatient all day at school. She couldn't wait for Uncle Nathan to pick her up and take her to see her new brother.

As she gently cradled Ezra, Gracie knew he'd had been worth the wait. She was eager to help take care of him, and she figured, being six years old, she had a lot to teach him as well. She knew one day they would be friends, just like her dad and Uncle Nathan were friends. Gracie decided this day was her second favorite, meeting her new brother. The day her dad found her would always come in first.

"I love you, baby Ezra," Gracie said, leaning down to give him a little kiss.

After Elliot had returned to take Gracie for the night, Jonah tiredly climbed into the small bed beside Hannah. Ezra was asleep in the plastic bassinet beside them.

"Can you believe he's here?" Jonah asked quietly, sliding his arm around his wife.

Hannah sighed. "I know...and I'm so glad *you're* here."

Jonah looked at her, his eyes depicting his adoration. "I told you I would be. You were amazing, Hannah. I am so proud of you." His eyes filled with tears, prompting hers to do the same.

Jonah reached into his pocket and took out a small box. "I got you something," he said, handing it to her.

Hannah lifted the top off, and inside lay a white-gold toggle bracelet. Across the bracelet spanned a series of hand-stamped charms. The first circular charm was stamped "J & H 10.2.04" and Jonah and Hannah's May and August birthstones dangled above it.

Hannah smiled. "Aw, that was our first date."

"Our official beginning," Jonah said.

The next charm was stamped with "Grace" accompanied by July's ruby. The last charm read "Ezra" beneath March's aquamarine.

"It's beautiful, Jonah. Thank you, I love it."

He helped her put it on. "It's the least I could do to thank you for how supportive you've been this past year with my music and the tour. It's really happening now."

Hannah kissed him briefly. "And no one deserves it more than you do."

Their attention shifted to Ezra when he began to fuss.

"I'll get him," Jonah offered, getting up and rounding the bed to the bassinet. He changed Ezra's diaper and swaddled him tightly in his blanket before returning to Hannah's side.

Ezra continued sleeping in Jonah's arms and they gazed at him, marveling over his sweet, delicate features together. It was late, and they were undoubtedly in need of sleep, but they stayed awake to bask in the joy of each other, and in the precious new blessing nestled between them.

Acknowledgments

God, for blessing me with a passion for writing. It has healed my heart in more ways than I knew possible.

My parents, Ron and Debbie Fee, for your guidance in my youth, your friendship in my adulthood, and your love always. I'm proud to be yours.
Thank you for all the times you watched Jude so I could get this finished, and for the immense generosity that brought this dream to life.

My brothers: Ron, for all our late-night talks, and for letting me blab about my ideas (when you're trying to go to bed). Shaun, for helping me with details in your areas of expertise, and for sharing in the excitement of this journey with me. Sam, for answering all my random, late-night texts when I was up writing or editing and needed some help. I enjoy sharing our love of books together. (Now, finish writing yours!)

Rachel, for all the times you sat with me and read my new chapters. I believe you and I are the first members of the Jonah fan club. ("I made them!")

Aunt Eileen, Grace, and Regan (and you too, Mom), for being some of my first readers. Your input on this book meant more to me than you know.

Ryan O'Neal, thank you for making the most beautiful music this world has ever heard. It was the perfect soundtrack to a

lot of late-night writing and it inspired me more than I can express. Your talent never fails to astound me. I am truly honored to honor you in my story.
Kim O'Neal, for all your kindness and help! You were an absolute joy to work with.

Jill, for editing! Your pointers have taught me so much. Thank you for helping me polish the rough edges to make my novel something I can be proud of.

Marion Hunt, my first-grade teacher, for the spark that began my love for writing. You always said, "If you can say it, you can spell it."

Family and friends (you too, Instagram fam), for supporting me by expressing your interest and excitement along the way. It's meant so much.

Jude, thank you for sleeping in every day since Mommy always stayed up too late writing! When you're old enough to read this book, you'll see that you've inspired special parts of it.

Last but not least, Daniel, my sweet husband, for supporting me through this entire journey and being my biggest fan. Thank you for staying up to hear my latest work and always giving me the best feedback. You have believed in me since the beginning, and it's because of you that I believed I could do this. I hope I can make you as proud as you make me. I love you. ("Lemonade, please!")

About The Author

Nicole Feller acquired a love for reading at an early age, which quickly progressed into a love for writing. Always a hopeless romantic, she grew up dreaming of love stories and writing letters to her future husband. She is now a proud mother of two: a daughter who makes Heaven sweeter, and a preemie son who is her life's greatest miracle. Nicole is prone to sentimentality, music obsession, and taking too many photos. *Still the Song* is her first book.

Nicole lives her own love story in Florida with her husband, Daniel, and their son, Jude.

Visit Nicole online: www.nicolefeller.com
Follow Nicole on Twitter: @cole_feller

30154267R00203

Made in the USA
Charleston, SC
03 June 2014